"I AM FALCON, YOUR LEADER."

"You are the forerunners, the nucleus, of the great Palestinian Army that will rule a vast Arab nation, an empire, which will be born when we have destroyed the illegitimate state that calls itself Israel."

"Hear me! Your mission has the favor and blessing of Allah. You will succeed and survive! Do you believe that?"

Twenty emotional voices shouted as one, "We believe! We believe!"

"You will succeed!"

"We will succeed!"

"You will return!"

"We will return!"

17
Ben
Gurion

Jack Hoffenberg

A BERKLEY BOOK
published by
BERKLEY PUBLISHING CORPORATION

With deepest admiration, this book is dedicated to the Israeli commandos who participated in the raid on the Entebbe Airport, Uganda, on July 3, 1976, and rescued 104 hostages . . . and to the memory of Lieutenant Colonel Yonatan Netanyahu, who led it . . . and to those who did not survive.

17
Ben
Gurion

1

Geneva, January 4

In his room at the Hotel Etoile, Viktor Yurevitch Sokolnikov arose in predawn darkness. Without turning on a light, he quickly dressed in the clothes he had laid out carefully on the small sofa the night before, each piece in proper order, so that it would be unnecessary to turn on a light. Quietly, he felt his way to the bathroom, emptied his bladder in the toilet but did not flush it for fear the noise of rushing water might awaken his associates in the rooms on either side of number 326. He now felt for the water glass, filled it from the tap, rinsed his mouth and sipped some of the icy water.

He returned to the bedroom and walked softly to the window and drew the heavy curtain aside a few inches. Outside, the empty street lay in snow-blanketed silence, cold and cheerless. For a few moments he stared out upon the scene, then returned to the sofa and shrugged into his heavy black overcoat, made certain the 9-mm automatic was in the righthand pocket. He wrapped a woolen scarf around his neck, slipped on a pair of fur-lined gloves, leaving the rest of his clothing, toilet articles and luggage with a sense of regret as he went to the door, picked up a heavy briefcase and stepped into the hallway.

The corridor was dimly lit and empty. He walked to the end of the hall toward the rear of the hotel. There, he unlocked the window catch, raised the lower section slowly and looked out. Below, the snow lay deep and soft on the automobiles and ground of the rear car park. Perfect. He picked up the briefcase, held it outside as far as he could reach, then let it drop. He looked out, trying to follow the leather case with his eyes; and heard, rather than saw, it drop into the snowbank with a soft thud.

He now closed the window, relatched it and walked to the

1

stairway in favor of the bank of elevators. Walking down three flights, Sokolnikov felt his first apprehension. The lobby. If the night KGB man stationed there was on his toes and became suspicious, all his preparations would come to naught; but he was hopeful that at this early hour, he might completely avoid the security guard; or bluff him out of position.

Sokolnikov's confidence faltered somewhat as he stepped through the door into the lobby. On a sofa against the wall, positioned so that both the front entrance and the door leading to the stairway, as well as the rear exit, were within his sight, sat Andrei Igor Katarian, who had the four A.M. to eight A.M. watch on the delegates who slept on the third floor, reserved exclusively for the Russian delegation.

Katarian stirred, then came alert as Sokolnikov entered the lobby. The clerk at the desk was busy riffling through his accounts and a uniformed lobby attendant sat on a chair beside the one elevator whose door was open. Sokolnikov walked directly to Katarian, a large man with a brutish-looking, much lined face, and now, narrowed eyes under heavy hoods. It occurred to Sokolnikov at this moment that he had perhaps made a mistake in not having rung for the elevator.

"Good morning, Comrade," Katarian greeted unsmilingly. "You are up early."

"Yes. I awoke and was unable to fall asleep again. I decided I would take a walk and get some fresh air. These rooms are so overheated it is hard to breathe."

"Comrade," Katarian replied, shaking his massive head from side to side, "you know the orders. It is forbidden to leave the hotel alone."

The friendliness faded from Sokolnikov's face as he said sharply, "I know the orders, Comrade. I gave them myself."

"Yes, but the Chief of Mission—"

"The Chief of Mission is my concern, Comrade. Yours is to keep a close watch to see that no one disturbs him or the other delegates, no?"

The stony look on Katarian's face remained one of questioning doubt. "The Chief of Mission *issued* those orders, Comrade Sokolnikov. You only repeated them to us."

"Comrade Katarian," Sokolnikov said with measured patience, "I am head of the security detail. Do you believe I am not competent enough to understand orders, those of the Chief of Mission or my own?"

Katarian's thick lips formed a tight line. "As you say, Comrade. The responsibility rests with you."

"Very well, then. I will be no longer than twenty or thirty minutes." Having won his point, he now said in a softer tone, "Talk to the attendant there. Ask him if we can have some coffee when I return, eh?"

Katarian's dour expression did not change. "I will ask him, but it is not even five o'clock. I don't think the kitchen staff is on duty yet."

"Then ask him if he will brew some for us." Without waiting for a reply, Sokolnikov walked briskly toward the front door. At this hour, there was no doorman. He pushed the double-paned glass panel open and walked down four cleared steps and across the driveway to the pavement on Avenue Wendt.

Momentarily, Sokolnikov enjoyed the cold, clean air, relishing its crisp bite; and the sense that he was free of Katarian. He strolled to the end of the block, made a right turn and accelerated his pace until he reached the narrow street that opened into the rear parking area behind the hotel. He turned right again and made his way between a row of snow-topped cars to the spot beneath the window through which he had dropped his briefcase. Ankle deep in snow, he bent to retrieve it and, as he stood up and began brushing the snow from the leather case, in the act of turning toward the alley driveway, the rear door of the hotel opened suddenly.

Katarian.

The huge, granite-faced guard had no doubt watched him, and then, either suspicious or restless, properly guessed his destination. Detected with the briefcase clutched in his hands, Sokolnikov knew there was no way he could explain his curious presence here. He turned and began to run.

Slender, more athletic than Katarian, he moved with agility, out of the snowbank and onto the narrow sidewalk, hearing the big man's footsteps crunching snow behind him, then the roar of his guttural voice, "Halt, Comrade, or I will shoot!"

Sololnikov was at the end of the narrow street when Katarian fired a single shot. He heard the bullet whistle past his head and instinctively crouched lower, turned the corner and stopped abruptly. The briefcase dropped to the ground as Sokolnikov removed the glove from his right hand, whipped out his 9-mm automatic and, as Katarian lumbered around the corner, fired once. The bullet struck the larger man in his upper chest. Katarian staggered awkwardly, slipped and fell to the pavement, one hand clutching his chest. His gun slithered across the ground and well out of his reach.

Sokolnikov wasted no time. He pocketed his automatic, picked up the briefcase and ran hurriedly toward Avenue Wendt, noting that lights in the upper stories of two or three nearby houses had come on. From somewhere behind him, a considerable distance away, he heard the faint sound of a police whistle. He ran down Wendt to the next side street and turned into it. The street was lined with private homes, snow-covered cars parked and sleeping at the curbs on both sides. Desperately, he moved up the street, following the ruts left by several cars that had passed earlier, rather than make new tracks in the undisturbed snow on the pavement.

As he walked along swiftly, he tried the handles of each car and, in mid-block, found one whose rear door was unlocked; a large Mercedes sedan. He got into the rear compartment and lay on the carpeted floor, breathing heavily from the exertion, then reached up and locked the door from the inside. On both the front and rear seats lay heavy, fur-lined lap robes. He pulled the one from the rear seat over him and, at that moment, heard a police car turn into the street and race by, its siren sounding the alarm.

Moments later, he heard footsteps along the pavement, but lay still beneath the robe, hoping no one would be flashing lights into the parked cars, and expecting that the entire KGB security unit would now be out in force, determined to find the defector and kill him if he offered the least resistance. Thus, he remained covered and motionless except for breathing. Waiting.

It seemed hours later when he risked peering out from under the thick robe. It was daylight now, a January day without sunlight. Menacing clouds glowered overhead as he drew back beneath the tenuous protection of the robe, realizing that he had actually slept through several hours. He lay quietly in safety and warmth, thinking of the events that had led to his decision to make this move to escape to the freedom of the Western world and what future it offered.

It was now nine o'clock and he wondered how much longer he could lie here undisturbed, and what dangers lay waiting for him outside, certain that members of the security unit would still be moving around the area, searching for him. Then he was overcome with warmth and began to doze again, lulled by the sounds of passing cars.

He came fully awake sometime later when he heard the door on the driver's side open, the crunch of a body as it settled into the upholstery of the driver's seat, the slam of the door as it closed again. Then the growl of a cold motor as it turned over sluggishly, and caught. The driver allowed it to run for a while and Sokolnikov caught the aroma of a cigar. Good. He preferred it to be a man rather than a woman, whose reaction to the sudden appearance of an armed stowaway could be far less predictable.

Then the Mercedes moved out, made several turns, finally entered what was obviously a main, well-trafficked thoroughfare. A few minutes passed and Sokolnikov decided it was time to make his move. He managed to reach into the pocket of his overcoat and withdraw the automatic. Cautiously, he raised one corner of the robe. The time was ten twenty by his wristwatch. Slowly, he lifted the robe and moved it to one side. Behind the wheel sat a thickset man who wore a dark felt hat over a fur-lined collar that was turned up to the brim of his hat. Cigar smoke layered in clouds over his large head.

Crouched low on his knees, Sokolnikov decided to try the man in German first. He said softly, "Do not be alarmed, *mein Herr,* I am holding a gun on you, but I mean no harm to you."

The man's head jerked to the right in a half turn. In German he replied, "My *God*! Who are you? What are you doing in my car? What do you want, money?"

"I don't want your—*watch where you are driving*!" The car swerved back into its proper lane. Sokolnikov said, "That's better. Listen to me. I don't want your money and I will not harm you. Only do as I order. Relax and keep driving."

When the man finally was restored to some sense of calm, he said, "What do you want from me? Who are you?"

"Who I am is of no importance. What I want is for you to drive me to twenty-one Rue du Rhone. It is the address of the United States Consulate General. I want you to be very careful. There may be one or two men, even more, who will try to prevent me from entering the consulate building. They may be on foot or in a car, parked or moving. I—"

"You must be crazy!" the man expostulated. "I am a banker. I cannot become involved in a thing like this—" And accusingly, "You are Russian. A defector?"

"Look to your right again." The man's head turned and he saw the automatic pistol in Sokolnikov's ungloved hand. "You are already involved, *mein Herr,* so do as I say if you wish to see your family again."

The man merely nodded his agreement, unable to speak.

"When we reach our destination, I want you to continue to drive at a normal speed. When I give you the word, you will brake to a hard stop. Give me time to jump out, then get away as quickly as you wish. Agreed?"

"Y . . . yes. What if there is shooting?"

"Any shooting will be directed at me, not you."

The man's nervousness showed in the stiffness of his head and

shoulders as he drove along, robotlike. "Relax," Sokolnikov said
with a calm he did not feel. "Two streets ahead is the Rue du Rhone.
Make a right turn into it. The consulate building is four streets
down, on the right side."

"I live in Geneva. I know where it is," the man replied as if in
pain.

"Good. Then there should be no problems."

There were cars parked on both sides of the street when the
Mercedes approached number 21. A quick visual assessment gave
Sokolnikov no indication that he was either safe or in danger. The
decision, nevertheless, must be made quickly. "Ready," he said to
the car's owner. "Do not slow down or speed up. Maintain this pace
until we reach the gateway entrance. A hard stop. Give me two
seconds, then move out fast. You understand?"

The man nodded, gripped the wheel hard in anticipation of the
jolting stop. Briefcase in left hand, Sokolnikov braced himself
between the rear seat and upholstered back of the front seat. His
right hand, clutching the automatic, was on the curb side door
handle. Within six feet of his goal, he shouted, "*Now!*"

The Mercedes screeched to a stop, skidding slightly toward the
curb. The right rear door was flung open and Sokolnikov, to the
alarm of several passing pedestrians, rocketed out of the car in a
crouch. He fell to his knees, pushed himself up and ran across the
pavement to the open gateway.

At that moment, caught by surprise, two men leaped from a black
sedan across the street and began running toward the consulate
gates, slowed by passing vehicles in the street and aghast pedestrians on the near pavement. As they reached the swept pavement,
both men began firing at the figure who was then rounding the
driveway, heading toward the main entrance, zigzagging as he ran
in a crouch.

Sokolnikov heard neither the shouts nor shots, but was keenly
aware of the bullets that flew over his head and past him. He looked
up at the white doorway which had been suddenly thrown open,
then decided against it as a perfect frame to target him for the two
KGB assailants who were firing from beyond the gateway. Instead,
he continued on, weaving toward the end of the driveway, where it
turned toward the right. He tore around it, out of target range, and
found a side entrance. Before he could pound his raised gun butt on
the wooden panel, it was thrown open and a pair of hands pulled him
inside to safety.

On the Rue du Rhone he heard police sirens, but they, and the
KGB were now well behind him.

*   *   *

George Arthur, the senior American official delegated to take charge of the matter, had questioned the Russian defector briefly. He made a number of notes, then left the room to place a call to the Bern embassy. A secretary brought coffee and cigarettes to Sokolnikov, still shaken by his narrow escape, trying to control his trembling hands. He had removed his hat and overcoat but kept the briefcase on his lap as though it was his passport to freedom.

In Arthur's private office there were urgent messages waiting for him; from the Russian embassy and from the head of the Russian mission to the conference, demanding that Sololnikov be released to their representatives. Arthur ignored these and placed his call to the American ambassador in Bern.

When he finally returned to the smaller office, the Russian had regained his composure and seemed more relaxed, although grim-faced and unsmiling. Arthur sat behind the desk and spoke a few quiet, reassuring words while an aide placed a tape recorder on the desk and inserted a 120-minute cassette into the machine. A secretary entered and seated herself at a smaller desk, prepared to take notes.

Arthur said, indicating the machine, "You understand the necessity for this?"

"Yes," Sokolnikov said in thickly accented English. "I have no objections."

"What I record here will be simultaneously transcribed by this young lady. You will be required to authenticate it with your signature before two witnesses."

The Russian nodded. "I understand the procedure."

Arthur activated the recorder and spoke into the self-contained microphone, stating his name, official position, the place, date, time of day, then a brief account of the circumstances of Sokolnikov's arrival. After a pause, he directed his first words to the Russian. "Your name, please."

"Viktor Yurevitch Sokolnikov."

"You have told me earlier that you are the chief security officer of the Russian mission to the International Disarmament Conference now meeting in Geneva. Is that correct?"

"Yes."

"Will you now please tell me in your own words your reasons for . . . ah . . . contacting the American consulate this morning."

"Yes." Sokolnikov took a deep breath, then spoke for almost thirty minutes without interruption. He gave his rank and explained his offical duties in detail, his decision to defect and the manner in which he had eluded his KGB associates earlier that morning. He then disclosed the fact that the briefcase he had brought with him— pointing to it—contained documents of extreme value to the United States State Department, particularly in matters concerning the disarmament discussions in progress, and whose disclosure would cause serious embarrassment for the Russian mission.

George Arthur did not seem impressed. He smiled and said, "Suppose we let that rest for the moment, Mr. Sokolnikov—" The Russian looked up in surprise. "Tell me," Arthur continued blandly, "why you believe your life is in danger from the KGB, the agency in which you are employed."

Sokolnikov took a deep breath and expelled it slowly. "There have been . . . things . . . some I cannot describe . . . unpleasant occurrences . . . rumors—"

"Can you please be more specific?" Arthur suggested.

"I will try. In the past year or two, new officials have replaced old ones. Agents have been called in for severe interrogation and some have not been seen nor heard from again. Those who were cleared, old friends with whom I have worked, refuse to discuss the matter. Questions have been asked of outside, personal friends of mine, of my neighbors, and told to say nothing about being questioned.

"I became aware that I was being watched, followed. My apartment was searched several times. Soon it became necessary to cut myself off from my oldest and closest associates in the Bureau, just as many cut themselves off from me. Four months ago my wife of fourteen years became so unnerved by this that she left me and received a divorce.

"Suddenly, the crazy behavior stopped, the spying, the questioning. I assumed they had found nothing to incriminate me in whatever they thought they were looking for, but I had already begun to plan to . . . to escape . . . defect. I could not go through with the same thing again later and felt I had nothing more to lose. I then began to gather these documents, microfilms and other information that would be useful. Lists of agents operating in the United States, Europe, Africa—" again tapping the briefcase.

An aide entered the office, went directly to Arthur and whispered a message. Arthur shut off the recorder and turned to Sokolnikov. "Sorry for the interruption. Will you please wait here while I take a call from Bern?"

When he returned an hour later, George Arthur was accompanied by a man he introduced as Lee Collier. Smiling, Arthur added, "I have spoken with our ambassador and received final instructions from Washington. We will continue with your statement after lunch. Arrangements are being made to fly you out under escort later this evening. Mr. Collier will accompany you. By tomorrow you will be in the United States.''

Sokolnikov's response was a sigh of relief.

2

Now that they were this close to enemy territory, Mousa Awad was keenly aware that the high mood of adventure and confidence with which they had left their camp three days earlier had evaporated. Not that he had not expected this. They had experienced no difficulties getting through the PLO lines in the south, since it was a PLO mission they were on, but had been warned to be on the alert for invading Syrians who were reportedly making a three-pronged drive toward Beirut in strength.

This close to the border, they felt safe since the Syrian tanks and troops would not wish to invite a secondary action with the Israelis. But now, Awad's concerns were two: his own group at the moment, Israeli patrols later.

Of the other five with him on this mission, Mousa Awad felt that only Zayim Samdat, with whom he had trained in the PLO, could be relied upon in the face of danger. Zayim was twenty-three, one year younger than Mousa, but had shown courage on other missions. On second thought, Mousa reflected, Tahsin Aflek, who was nineteen and a recent trainee graduate, might give a good account of himself.

But of the other three, Hassan Magd, who was seventeen, and the two cousins, Aziz and Samar Bashir, both eighteen, none was with field experience. With the shortage of manpower created by the battle now raging to control Beirut, their PLO camp commander had insisted on the latter three for the mission "to improve their training." Sons of camels, Mousa mused with contempt. Whining children who should have remained at home with their mothers.

The night was moonless and black, a perfect cover; but they had not expected the bitterly cold winds that swept westward from the snow-blanketed heights of Mount Hermon toward the Mediterranean. Zayim stirred beside Mousa, seeking to relieve the stiffness in

11

his arms and shoulders. Behind them some fifteen yards lay the other four, huddled together, guarding the two large suitcases they had been carrying since early afternoon, when the driver of the pickup truck had dropped them off six kilometers to the north. The weight of the suitcases had slowed them down considerably, but Mousa had driven them relentlessly and brought them to their jumping off spot in surprisingly good time; this despite the adolescent resentment and rebellious mutterings of Magd and the Bashirs; yet moving quite satisfactorily toward the border under his threats and curses.

"What time is it?" Zayim asked in a whisper.

Mousa used a thin penlight to check his wristwatch with a quick glance, shielding the light with his right hand. "It is nearly eight o'clock."

"We should cross over soon. The patrol is due in half an hour."

"I'll give them another five minutes to rest."

"Yes. That will be good."

Half an hour earlier, when they had reached this point, Mousa and Zayim had crept up to the wire fence and cut an upward slit into it with a pair of heavy wire cutters, then twisted the bottom ends together and piled some loose brush and sand against it to keep the ends from flapping in the wind. Once through the slit, they would have to move quickly across the dirt road and continue southward to a point just north of Adamit, due there no later than ten thirty, to meet the truck.

Mousa shivered and clamped his jaws tightly together to keep his teeth from chattering. If only he could smoke one of the four cigarettes in his shirt pocket—but he, himself, had laid down a firm order against lighting a match or smoking this close to the border and must now abide by his own rule. He heard a rustling in the sand behind them and turned quickly, instinctively reaching for the revolver tucked into his waistbelt.

"Who is it?" he challenged in an angry whisper, unable to distinguish the face in the darkness.

"Bashir. Samar Bashir."

"What do you want? I told you to lie quietly until I give the order to move up."

"We are freezing. In Allah's name, let us move on."

Mousa began a biting retort, but checked it. At this point, the last thing he wanted was an argument or disturbance. "All right," he said in a sharp whisper. "Bring up the suitcases and we will cross over now. Quietly. No talking."

He stood up, the revolver in his hand. Zayim rose to his feet beside him. Without speaking, Mousa walked quickly to the fence,

where he knelt and untangled the wires, then pulled the ends back
and upward. When the others reached the fence, he and Zayim held
up the separate ends to permit them to slip through, dragging the
heavy suitcases after them. While they made their way across the
dirt road, Mousa and Zayim drew the two ends together and twisted
them so that they would remain intact. Now they gathered up some
loose brush and stones to hide the cut at the bottom. Hopefully, the
patrol jeep would pass by without noticing.

Crossing the road behind the other four, Mousa and Zayim
looked both ways for any sign of the border patrol jeep's headlights,
listening for the sound of its motor. Hearing nothing, seeing nothing, both breathed easier as they crossed into Israeli territory. Arab
homeland, now in the hands of the enemy.

Quickly, they moved across sand and stubbled growth, heading
southward in the direction of the agricultural community of Adamit,
which lay, according to their roughly penciled map, approximately
two kilometers south. Only half that distance lay their destination, a
dirt road used by local farmers to haul their fruits and produce out to
the main road.

After a penetration of two hundred yards, they halted to rest,
check their map and the time. This modest success heightened
Mousa's feeling of confidence momentarily.

"Eat and drink now," he ordered. "Once we start moving again,
there will be no stopping until we reach the farm road where we will
meet the truck."

From their shoulder-slung rucksacks, each man withdrew some
cold meat and *pita* and wolfed it down, drinking water from his
canteen. Mousa moved to one side to eat his meal with Zayim, who
was seldom far from his side.

"Eh," Mousa said, "this damned, cursed wind. I would give my
next three meals for a warm robe."

"Yes," Zayim agreed. "It is past nine. I wonder where the patrol
is."

Mousa shrugged. "We can't depend on the Jews to keep a
timetable set for us by our commander. It makes little difference
now. We are across the border and well out of their sight. All we
need do is reach our rendezvous and get the truck."

"If he is on time," Zayim said.

"That, too, is in the hands of Allah."

"What if he fails to meet us?"

"Let us not look ahead too far. If he is there, we will be on our
way to Nazareth and get rid of this cargo. It will be good to see my
birthplace again. It has been seven long years now."

"How soon before we must return to Lebanon?"

"At once, the commander said, but we will find reasons to delay for a few days, Zayim. I still have some family and a few friends I want to visit with." Mousa shook himself to drive out the chill within. "Let us get them on their feet and moving. We still have more than a kilometer to cover."

There was no argument from the other four now, eager to be moving again if only to keep warm. Of the six, only Mousa and Zayim had been born and raised in the Palestine that was now Israel. The other four had been born in refugee camps in Jordan and Lebanon, and this was their first time on what they still considered to be foreign soil, despite what they had been told in their camps. To them, Israel was alien land, their lives in jeopardy if discovered. By necessity, they must now rely on Mousa Awad to bring them through this, their first mission, and return to the familiar comfort of their camp.

* * *

The Israeli border patrol jeep that, according to the intelligence given Mousa Awad, was due at eight thirty, had been delayed at Irbin, to the east, where a civilian settlement guard had flagged them down to report suspicious movement across the road to the north. The two patrolmen had investigated and found no sign of infiltrators, then checked through the village to make doubly sure that all was well.

Satisfied finally, the settlement guard invited them to share a cup of coffee from his thermos jug, which they accepted and, in the chilled night air, enjoyed. The entire incident had taken no more than forty-five minutes.

Back in the jeep, Yossi Stern reported the incident to his base camp by radio, then said to his driver, Ehud Mishkon, "Let's move, make up for lost time."

Mishkon pulled his wool scarf tighter around his throat and raised the collar of his padded field jacket higher on his neck. He nodded and said, "Keep a close watch, *chaver*. This wind is blowing up a lot of sand. It could cover up some activity by our friends."

* * *

At exactly ten thirty the fedayeen group had been at their rendez-vous point for twelve minutes. Mousa had left them to go southward through some cultivated fields to make certain that the village of Adamit lay there below them. He had gone quickly and soon returned to announce that they were in the correct spot; he had been able to see a few pinpoint lights and some physical characteristics that matched those given to him by their camp commander. Yet, Mousa was unhappy and showed his irritation. The man who was to meet them here with the truck had not shown up on time.

Only two things were in their favor; the darkness and the fact that the village of Adamit was fast asleep. There was, probably, at least one settlement guard awake there, but this was of little concern; Mousa had no intention of moving his group any closer than they were now, and a full kilometer separated them from the village.

Magd and the two Bashirs, however, were also unhappy with the waiting and voiced their anxieties in whining tones. "What if he doesn't come at all?" Aziz Bashir said. "What then?"

"He will come," Mousa stated firmly.

"How can you be so sure, Mousa?" Samar Bashir demanded. "If he doesn't come, what will we do with these heavy suitcases, carry them on our backs to Nazareth?"

"Keep your voice down and your childish questions to yourself, you ass," Mousa growled, "or you will waken every Jew in Israel."

Tahsin Aflek and Hassan Magd said nothing, although showing interest in the exchange. Aziz Bashir moved in closer to Mousa Awad, his voice lowered, but nevertheless challenging. "This is crazy. The suitcases are too heavy, we have eaten the last of our food and drunk all our water. We have been freezing for two nights and now there is no truck."

What little patience remained in Mousa came to an abrupt end. "You—you *children*!" he snapped angrily. "I thought you were soldiers, men of action, eager to do your duty. Now I find you are acting like *women*!" He paused to take a deep breath. "The man is late. These things happen. A bad tire, something to repair. He will be here."

"Ah all-knowing one," Samar Bashir sneered, "then tell us when."

"When he gets here. Now sit down and keep quiet. I warn you for the last time—" He broke off abruptly and moved away from the group lest he be forced to take physical action. Zayim Samdat moved away with him, neither speaking. Twenty yards away, Mousa stopped.

"On a mission like this," he grumbled, "I am saddled with infants who should still be sucking at their mothers' breasts. What idiot decided they were to be trusted as soldiers, I don't know." He noticed then that Zayim, not entirely certain that a more serious confrontation might not be too far off, had withdrawn his revolver and was holding it at his side. "Put it away, Zayim," he said with

contempt tingeing his voice. "It will not come to that." Yet he was
sufficiently agitated to reach into his shirt pocket and take out one of
his cigarettes. He placed it between his lips and sucked on it,
unlighted.

Zayim heard the motor first, a faint sound coming from the east
along the narrow dirt road. Then the others heard it and rose to their
feet, silent in anticipation, eager to load up and move out. They
peered into the darkness for some sign of headlights, but there were
none.

Then Hassan Magd, the youngest of the group, said, "There it is!
I see it!"

The truck came on toward them, a large dark shadow, showing no
lights. The six fedayeen moved closer to the edge of the road,
watching as the vehicle slowed. From the cab, a thin beam of light
flashed on, off, on, and off again; the recognition signal.

Elated, Mousa pulled out his penlight and responded similarly.
The truck rolled up and braked to a stop. The driver, a middle-aged
man wearing farm clothes under a heavy wool-lined coat, got out
and came toward them. "Khodr Hamshari," he said softly.

It was the name the camp commander had given to Mousa. He
stepped out into the road and replied, "Habib Mafouz," which was
the name of the camp commander.

"I am late," Hamshari said in semiapology. "This was the best
truck I could get. Earlier, it broke down and I had to stop to repair it.
Nothing serious. The fan belt. I mended it."

The truck, close up, was smaller than it had first appeared to be
from a distance; stake body, covered with a worn, patched canvas
tarpaulin that was tied down on both sides and at the rear. Its fenders
were dented, paint flaked from its hood and body, the tires worn
smooth. Mousa walked around it, the others following him in his
inspection. Mousa was not happy.

"In this," he said caustically to Hamshari, "we are supposed to
reach Nazareth? It will fall apart before we can find a smooth road."

Hamshari took it all in stride. "Listen to me, young soldier," he
said softly. "The motor is good, which is more important than how
it looks. How long do you think you could travel in a shiny new
Mercedes before you would be stopped and examined by police,
eh?" He reached into a pocket and withdrew some documents.
"Here are your papers. Two sets. Identification. License and legal
registration for the truck. You are farm workers, delivering produce
to Nazareth. Two will ride in the cab. Beneath the produce is room
for four to ride flat, lying on their bellies. Also for the goods you
brought with you."

"What about checkpoints?" Zayim asked.

Hamshari drew out another sheet of paper from an inside pocket and used his flashlight, which Zayim shielded with the edges of his jacket. "This is the route you will take. West from here to Hanita, then backtrack east, using only the secondary roads used by farmers, which are marked out for you. In this way you will avoid places where checkpoints are likely. At Eilon, drop down to Montfort by the dirt road, into Ma'alot or Rama Eilabun, here, here, here, by the markings. It is a long way to Nazareth, but safe if you are careful."

While Mousa and Zayim studied the route plan, not without some misgivings, Hamshari continued. "You will deliver the suitcases and truck to the man in Nazareth whose name and telephone number are at the bottom of this paper. The other names below his are not important to you. Hide it with care. It must not be found if you are questioned by the police. You have a safe place to hide it?"

"Yes." Mousa folded the sheet and tore away the bottom portion with the names on it. He bent over and removed his left shoe. Its upper edge showed a small slit, about an inch deep. Mousa folded the small strip of paper, inserted it into the slit. From behind his jacket lapel, he removed a small, strong needle that was threaded with waxed cotton. Under the light held by Zayim, he laced the thread through the original holes and sewed the slit closed, then returned the needle to his lapel.

The bottom row of produce crates was now removed from the rear of the truck, revealing a cavern beneath the wooden platform that reached back toward the cab, but not fully.

"What is in those boxes back there?" Mousa asked Hamshari.

"Canned foods and bottled drinks that were requested by the man in Nazareth," Hamshari replied glibly.

"They can't get those things in Nazareth?"

"Not these kinds. Hurry, Mafouz. We are wasting time. It can be dangerous to linger like this."

Mousa opened one of the large suitcases and removed six of the dozen Russian machine pistols and several boxes of ammunition, six hand grenades. The guns were loaded and handed out to the other fedayeen, along with one grenade each. The suitcases with the remaining weapons were then pushed deep into the cavern. Tahsin, Hassan, Aziz and Samar were then ordered into the cavern, the six crates replaced to conceal them, the tarpaulin laced back into place.

"They will not be comfortable," Hamshari remarked, "but they will be safe."

"Their comfort or discomfort is of little concern," Mousa replied coldly. "Only the mission is important."

"Yes. Well . . . I must leave you now. Be careful in your manner toward the Jews if you are stopped. Good fortune go with you.''

"*In sha'Allah,*" Zayim replied. "It is in the hands of Allah."
And, as Hamshari turned and began walking eastward, "Is your
name truly Khodr Hamshari?"

The older man turned back and grinned broadly, showing two
rows of yellowing teeth. "No more than his," indicating Awad, "is
Habib Mafouz. Names are of little importance, my young friend,
only deeds. *Salaam.*" He began walking along the rutted dirt road
in the direction from which he had come. Within seconds, he was no
longer visible.

Mousa, now showing impatience, handed the keys to Zayim.
"You drive. I will try to get some sleep. Later, I will relieve you.
Get in now and let's move out."

They got into the cab. Mousa wedged his machine pistol in the
space between the seat and the door. Zayim reached down and
rested his weapon on the floor. The motor started at once and before
they had traveled a full kilometer, Mousa was fast asleep.

But not for long. They had passed through the outskirts of Hanita
and begun doubling back when the motor broke into a fit of coughing. The break in its rhythm brought Mousa fully awake, clutching
for his machine pistol. "What is it, Zayim?"

At that moment, the motor gave a final gasp and died. "I don't
know," Zayim replied. He turned the key in the ignition. The motor
stuttered and died almost at once. Mousa flung himself out of the
cab, raised the hood over the motor and stared at it in disgust, as
though it were a corpse, muttering obscenities under his breath.
Zayim, standing beside him, leaned in with his flashlight, less
disturbed than his colleague. "This wire—" he said.

"Which wire?" Mousa demanded.

"Here, this one, dangling there. It has been torn away from this
piece near the top."

"Do you think you can fix it?"

"If there is some tape and a tool in the metal box. Pliers to tighten
the connection. Get the toolbox from under the seat."

From inside, they heard a pounding of pistol butts against the
wooden bed of the truck. Mousa barked, "Quiet! Quiet in there,
you asses!"

But the pounding and muffled cries continued and Mousa, after
handing the toolbox over to Zayim, went to the rear, untied the
tarpaulin straps and removed a single crate. "What is it with you
fools? Do you want the whole world to know you are in there?"

Aziz Bashir's head poked out through the opening. "In Allah's
name, we are suffocating in this place. Let us get some fresh air or

we will be dead long before we reach Nazareth.'' Behind Aziz, the clamor of complaints was louder now.

Mousa removed three more crates and the confined fedayeen slid forward singly and gained the road. Bitingly, Mousa admonished them. ''Get over to the side of the road. Lie down and keep quiet. We will soon be on our way again. Be ready when I call you.''

Standing his ground firmly, Samar Bashir said, ''We have talked it over among ourselves, Mousa. We are not going on. This mission is cursed and it will fail. We have agreed to return to our camp before the Jews find us and arrest us.''

Mousa turned on him, eyes glittering with fury. ''You bastard son of a camel! I knew you were sniveling cowards when we started out. You have the courage of a vulture who never kills, but feeds off the foul flesh of the dead. I should kill you here and now. All of you!''

Even as he spoke, he became aware that Samar, Aziz and Hassan were holding their revolvers aimed at him. Tahsin Aflek's hands were empty. And now, Zayim Samdat, at the front of the truck, flashlight in one hand, pliers in the other, overheard only a part of the dispute and came toward Mousa. Aziz Bashir's revolver moved to cover him.

''What is this foolishness?'' Zayim demanded heatedly.

''We have decided,'' Samar said, ''to return to camp. When you and Mousa are rotting in prison here, remember us.'' To Aziz, ''Get behind them and take their revolvers. Empty them. We don't want to be shot in the back when we leave.''

Aziz reached behind Mousa and Zayim and collected their revolvers. Samar said, ''You will find these about a hundred yards from here, where it will be too late and too dangerous to use them to kill us.''

''One day,'' Mousa said bitterly, ''we will return to camp and find you. It will be a day of regret for all of you.''

''If,'' Samar replied, ''you live to see that day.'' To the others, ''Let us go and be done with it. Quickly.''

Aziz and Hassan fell in behind Samar, but Tahsin Aflek stood his ground. ''Come, Tahsin,'' Samar called to him, ''or do you want to die or rot in prison with these two fools?''

Tahsin said calmly, ''I will stay with Mousa and Zayim as I was ordered to do. Here, take my gun, too.''

''Aziz, take it and let us go.''

When the three defectors were gone, Mousa assumed command again. ''Let them go, the bastards,'' he said. ''They would only bring trouble to us. At least, they left their machine pistols in the truck. Zayim, go back and finish with the wire. Tahsin, follow them and bring back our revolvers. Hurry. We have wasted too much time already."

With Mousa holding the flashlight, Zayim stripped away an inch or two of insulation from each end of the severed wires. Fortunately, the wire was long enough so that both ends would still meet. He meshed and twisted the ends together, bound the raw copper with black tape, then tightened the connections at both posts. By now, Tahsin had returned with the three revolvers, empty of their shells.

Zayim closed the hood. "If Allah wills it," he said, "the motor will start."

"*In sha'Allah*," Mousa replied, hoping against hope, regarding the black beast with grim distaste. "We will all ride in the cab. There is room enough."

The crates were replaced, the tarpaulin lashed down again. Zayim reached for the ignition key and, with a soft prayer, turned it, The motor caught, coughed and died. It caught on the second attempt and held. Mousa said, "Good, Zayim, good. Drive on."

He now reloaded the three revolvers and passed one to Zayim, the other to Tahsin.

* * *

Yossi Stern and Ehud Mishkon moved along the road toward Adamit through a haze of sand that the continuing wind, somewhat stronger now, raised in swirls that cut visibility to a matter of several yards. At a greater distance, the hood-mounted spotlight, operated from inside the vehicle by Stern, was almost totally ineffective; but this was of small concern to the two Israelis. What was more important was that the light was strong enough to pick up the border fence on their right and show any break that may have been made by guerrilla infiltrators. Occasionally, Stern swung the light to the left to inspect that fringe of roadside for any sign of tracks or unusual movement. On such a night as this, that effort was useless and Stern turned the light back toward his right.

The cold, if anything, was more intense now. Mishkon had thrown a blanket over his shoulders and pulled his knitted cap down over his forehead and ears. "In Adamit," he said to Stern, "let us see if there is someone awake to give us coffee or tea."

"In Adamit," Stern replied, "anyone with any sense will be in bed under every blanket he can pile on top of himself. Only idiots like ourselves would be awake and freezing."

They purred along for another three kilometers and Mishkon said, "We'll be coming to the turnoff in another—"

"Hold it," Stern called out suddenly, peering out toward his right.

"What is it?"

"You passed it. Back up a bit. There, there. Stop."

"What do you see, Yossi?"

"Something. Maybe nothing." Leaving the spotlight on, holding his shoulder-slung Uzi at the ready, Stern got out of the jeep, looked around cautiously, then walked to the fence. Mishkon got out on the other side, Uzi gripped in both hands, trying to scan the left side through the near pitch-blackness.

"Ehud! Here!" Stern called.

Mishkon skirted the rear end of the jeep and, walking backwards, joined Stern, "What is it?"

"Look." Stern had kicked away some loose brush and a few rocks and was holding up two ends of the cut fence for his partner to see. "Some tracks, too, made recently, but the wind has washed most of them out."

"Can you see how many?"

"I can't tell, but they lead across the road . . . here . . ."

Mishkon returned to the jeep and picked up his radio mike. Within seconds he was reporting their find to his base camp. "The tracks are weak, but they lead toward Adamit, across the fields. We will take the cutoff into the village and search it. If you have a standby team there, send them along."

The base camp watch commander acknowledged. Mishkon cut out and got behind the wheel, racing his motor. Yossi Stern came running. "The tracks are more firm in the dirt on the other side of the road. Four, maybe five. Go ahead to the cutoff road, quickly."

"That will take too long," Mishkon said, activating his four-wheel drive. "We'll cut across right here and take the same route they did."

The jeep turned left over the roadside hump and continued in a southwesterly direction, over brush and sand, finally through one of the village farms. Two hundred and fifty yards later they came to the single-laned dirt farm track, used principally for local traffic. Here, the dirt, protected from the night wind by trees, was more firm. "Let's follow the tracks," Mishkon said. "I only hope they didn't get into Adamit."

They moved along the track slowly, using the spotlight and later came to where there was a jumble of fresh tracks. Stern saw the indentations first—deep enough to have been made by strongly shod feet, then the imprint of tire treads; tires that were worn, but had borne the weight of a heavy vehicle. They reentered the jeep and cut southward through an orchard, then across several more cultivated fields, into the sleeping village. Driving through it, they saw nothing to give them cause for alarm. They drove into its center, parked, got out and began an inspection on foot. There was no sign of the settlement guard who was supposed to be on duty and Stern made a mental note to report his absence to his base camp commander.

The search concluded, Mishkon radioed in and was informed that a standby team was en route to assist them in their search. Mishkon was inclined to order the assistance team recalled, then decided against it. It was still possible they might turn up something. Stern agreed.

They returned to the farm road and checked the tire tracks again. The vehicle had apparently come from the east, parked here for a while, then continued westward toward Hanita. They decided to do likewise. Where the farm road joined the main border road to the north, they discovered that the truck had turned south; and later, picked up a secondary road that swung eastward again.

This was the two-lane road that led toward Eilon and Goren, the produce distribution center for the area. Making better time now, Stern radioed their position to the base camp, advising them they would proceed from there in the direction of Ma'alot. Base camp advised that they would so inform the assistance team.

At Goren, Mishkon and Stern stopped to check with the two settlement guards there. Inside the small guard station they warmed themselves at the wood-burning stove and gratefully accepted large mugs of steaming coffee. All was quiet and, yes, a medium-sized farm truck had passed through about twenty or thirty minutes earlier, headed southeast toward Montfort. No, it had not stopped, nor had they seen any reason to stop it and talk to the three men in the cab.

"At this hour of morning, you were not suspicious?" Mishkon asked.

"Why should we be?" the older guard asked. "They were probably trying to reach the marketplace in Ma'alot for the early morning opening."

"Or," Stern suggested, "maybe it was too cold to leave your warm stove and hot coffee." He put his unfinished coffee down and said to Mishkon, "Let's go, Ehud."

*   *   *

Halfway to Ma'alot, moving at a highly accelerated speed along the dirt road, they caught their first glint of red taillights up ahead. Mishkon threw the switch to activate his siren and twirling warning light. For a few hundred feet the truck continued on, then the brake lights flashed, the vehicle still moving, but at a slightly reduced speed. The jeep was within thirty yards when the truck pulled to the side and came to a full stop. Two men exited on the right side, the driver on the left, all standing close to the sides of the truck.

Yossi Stern had a firm grip on his Uzi as the jeep rolled up just behind and to the left of the truck, about twelve feet separating the two vehicles. Ehud Mishkon had lifted his left leg to get out of the jeep when flashes from three machine pistols came alive. Bullets smashed into the windshield, into the radiator, into the jeep's headlights.

Stern reacted swiftly. In a single move, he dropped to the ground and brought his Uzi into play, returning the fire of the two men on the right. Mishkon slid down below the windshield level and opened the door on the left side. He leaped out and fell flat on the ground, opening fire from the prone position, cursing as he saw water running from the jeep's radiator.

Stern, on the right side, crawled to the edge of the road and rolled over into a depression, giving him some small cover. From that position, he fired burst after burst, then replaced the spent ammo clip with a fresh one. There was a lull for a moment and, hearing nothing from Mishkon's position, called out, "Ehud! Ehud! Are you all right?"

There was no reply. Assuming the worst, hoping it was no more than a minor wound, Stern probed with a single burst and received two in return. Now he tried a burst at the rear of the truck, trying for its petrol tank; then a second and a third.

The third burst achieved the result he had hoped for. The rear end erupted in flames, reaching upward to the tarpaulin, setting it afire. He heard a scream, then saw a figure roll out from beneath the truck into the road, where, in the flash of flame, it lay still. The man on the right side, stunned by the sudden change from darkness to brilliant light, dropped his machine pistol and raised his hands above his head.

Stern rose in a crouch. "Don't move!" he shouted in Arabic. "Don't move or I'll cut you down!" When the man obeyed, Stern motioned him forward. Hands upraised, the man complied. "Down," Stern ordered. "On the ground. Face down. Hands behind your back."

The Uzi in his right hand, Stern reached into his belt and removed a pair of handcuffs, linked the man's wrists behind him. On the right side of the truck, one man lay dead. On the left side lay Mishkon's victim, weapon out of reach, legs thrashing, then still. Stern ran to the left side of the jeep where Ehud Mishkon lay motionless.

Quickly, he felt for a pulse beat in Ehud's neck. There was none. He could not see the wounds, nor did he take the time to locate the reason for his partner's death, knowing only that his life had come to its destined end.

He stood up now and walked toward the burning truck, the stench of petrol and frying vegetables fouling the air. For a moment he felt the weakness of shock, then he kneeled beside the wounded man and turned him face up. He felt for a pulse beat and found it; the man was alive, seemingly unconscious. No wounds or bleeding showed, but there was a large, raised lump on his upper forehead. It was possible, when the petrol tank burst into flames, that he had raised himself up suddenly to escape and, in doing so, had cracked his head on the understructure. At that moment, the man whimpered. His eyes opened, filled with fright at the sight of the Israeli.

"Don't kill me. Please," he said.

"Shut up!" Stern ran back to where Ehud lay and removed the handcuffs from his belt, then returned and handcuffed the second man's wrists behind him. Then he remembered.

He went to the jeep and tried the radio. It was dead. He tried the walkie-talkie unit but could raise no one. He opened the toolbox and removed his flare pistol and a large cartridge. Aiming it skyward, he pulled the trigger. A few sparks flew as the projectile arced upward with a *thuck*, then exploded about three hundred feet overhead, turning the night momentarily into daylight, then began to float slowly downward; the emergency signal that would, hopefully, direct the assistance team to his position if they were anywhere within sight.

He returned to where Ehud Mishkon lay, found his weapon and placed it on the seat of the jeep beside his own. Then he moved Ehud's body from its awkward position, straightened it out and removed the blanket from the driver's seat and covered his friend, weeping softly. With his Uzi cradled in his lap, Yossi Stern sat down beside his friend's body and waited.

3

Rome, March 21

The man in the public phone booth in the airport building was suffering from the frustrations of having to deal with an apparently overworked or indifferent overseas operator and the sudden rainstorm that had drenched him thoroughly during the brief moments between exiting his plane and crossing the tarmac to reach protective cover. Outside the booth, two men and a woman glowered at him while he waited impatiently for some sign that the operator was still alive and in contact.

After two annoying disconnects, she came on for the third time. *"Mi dispiacente.* I am trying, *signore,"* she apologized, and he found himself on "hold" once more. The waiting trio, hardly less patient, now turned away and ran to a booth down the line that had just been vacated and he found little comfort in the steaming glass-and-aluminum coffin.

Fully five minutes passed before the operator finally came through with, "On your call to Tel Aviv, *signore,* your party is ready now."

"Grazie, signorina." The line cleared, screeched with static, then cleared again as the voice announced, "Rosental here."

"Judah, this is Lee Collier. *Shalom."*

"Lee—*Collier?* Ah, *Lee!* Shalom, shalom! How good to hear your voice after so long." A pause, then, "So we are still friends, at least unofficially?"

Collier grimaced at Rosental's unsubtle reference to the recent change in attitudes among certain officials in the Executive as well as Capitol Hill families in Washington toward what they were calling "Israel's intransigence" in the matter of the unresolved Golan Heights situation. More recently, talk of providing Egypt with nuclear capability and approval of the sale of U.S. arms to Sadat, had further strained diplomatic tensions.

"Of course we are, Judah," Collier said firmly. "I never allow politics to intrude on personal feelings, nor do a good number of your other friends back home."

"That is good to hear, Lee. Very reassuring." Rosental's mellow voice came across warmly but in somewhat accented English, creating a need on Collier's part to pay close attention. "So, Lee, I take it this is not a social call, eh?"

"Not entirely, Judah. Listen carefully. I am between planes en route to my station in Geneva, but I have something of a confidential nature that could be of considerable importance to you. However, I can't give it to you over the telephone. You understand?"

"I understand. Are you suggesting I fly to Rome to meet with you? You know that with the recent upsurge of demonstrations on our West Bank, I am heavily involved and it would be difficult—"

"No, no," Collier said. "I am aware of your situation and I'm not suggesting you come here, only that I can spare a day to come to Israel on tomorrow's early morning flight, if we can meet somewhere. Alone. Not in Tel Aviv or Jerusalem—"

"Lee, this is something you can't present formally, officially?"

"Affirmative. If it were official, it would be handled through normal channels. This requires a one-to-one meeting and with the very firm understanding that once it is in your hands, we are out of it and under no circumstances can we be brought into it. Therefore, unofficial channels. Understood?"

There was a moment of hesitation, then Rosental sighed and said, "Let me think—"

"Make it fast, Judah. If the answer is negative, my connection to Geneva takes off in about thirty minutes. Yes or no?"

"Then yes, of course. I will work it out some way. I will meet you on arrival at Ben Gurion Airport and have my helicopter waiting to take us somewhere so we can talk privately."

"And safely. I don't want to be seen—"

"I will arrange it, Lee."

"Good. Have me cleared here and there so I won't have to go through Customs and Immigration. I don't want this side trip to show on my passport. It's important."

"Very well. I will call El Al in Rome and make the arrangements there, also here."

"Do that. I've got to move fast if I expect to find decent accommodations in Rome for the night. See you on the other end. *Shalom*, Judah."

"*Shalom*, Lee. I am looking forward to meeting you again."

Rosental hung up, stared vacantly at the phone for a moment or two, then asked his secretary to put through the necessary call to El Al's security chief in Rome. He pondered over Collier's message for a while, then sent for Saul Lahav's secretary. When she entered his office a minute later, he said, "Leah, did Major Lahav leave word where he would be on his holiday?"

With a painful *Not again*! expression, Leah Barak replied, "I believe Sharm el Sheikh, General."

"Which hotel?"

"He didn't say."

Rosental smiled wanly. "Your major is a suspicious, apprehensive man, Leah."

She returned his smile, but only as a courtesy. "From past experience, General, I think he has reason to be. Shall I start telephoning the hotels there to try to locate him?"

"No. No need for a lot of nosy hotel clerks to get curious. Instead, telephone Colonel Aaronson at the army base there and ask him to have someone quietly check and locate him."

"The message?"

"The major's leave of absence has been canceled. Arrange with Aaronson for a car and driver. He is to meet me at the military commander's office in Bashra as early tomorrow afternoon as possible."

"If I may suggest, General, a helicopter or plane would be much faster."

"No, Leah. I will need the extra time to discuss a matter of importance with someone while the major is en route."

"Yes, sir."

Sharm el Sheikh, March 22

Luxuriating in the warmth of the brilliant morning sun, it occurred to Saul Lahav that there had been few days such as this one, and the day before, in his life. Peace and calm. It was the second day of a seven-day leave of absence, a rarity in itself. He raised his left wrist and noted the time. Twenty minutes to ten. On the hour, a news broadcast would be coming through.

Lying on a long beach towel, his head resting comfortably against a small air pillow, he surveyed the wide beach through amber-tinted sunglasses. Except for about a dozen young couples, mostly European and American vacationers by their various languages as they called to one another, the noises of the bustling northern cities were well behind him. He reached for a cigarette, lit it, then raised up on one elbow and turned up the volume on his transistor radio slightly to catch the musical program.

He stared across the sweep of beach and out over the strait to Tiran, Sanafir beyond it, with the southern tip of Saudi Arabia, from this low-level angle, almost within touching distance. He looked around and tried to find Shana's head among the few bobbing around in the sea but the glare of sun on the water's surface prevented him from distinguishing hers from the others. He rolled over on his stomach to expose his back to the hot sun and cradled his head on his arms, one hand still toying with the enameled cigarette lighter he had brought back from Amsterdam for Shana the year before. Fully relaxed now, he began to doze.

"Saul, you lazy man! You don't know what you're missing!"

He turned on his right side and saw her standing at the bottom of her beach towel, bending over to pick up a smaller towel to wipe away the droplets of water that still clung to her glowing sun-tinged skin. Tall, elegant and golden, shining black hair cut short to resemble a helmet, he viewed Shana Altman with total pleasure. Now, as when he had first become aware of her, the sight of her in uniform, in civilian dress or, as now, near naked in a bikini, never failed to stir him.

A native-born Israeli, a Sabra like himself, her figure had the lissome grace of a dancer; slender-waisted, firm-bosomed without heaviness in her upper body, long, perfectly sculptured legs. Her face was remarkably striking with dark, luminous eyes that were slightly almond-shaped, patrician nose and full generous lips that were parted in a smile to reveal glistening white teeth.

"I'm not missing anything, Shana. As soon as the next news broadcast is over, I intend to swim all the way to Tiran," he replied with a smile.

"Ha!" she exclaimed with a short laugh. "In only thirty meters I'll have to jump in and rescue you."

"So what more can a man ask?"

She had toweled herself dry and lay down beside him, reaching across him for a cigarette, taking the light he offered; an innocent act in itself, yet intimate, even sensual in its closeness. The moment passed. She withdrew, lying so that their bodies barely touched, her right hand clasped in his left.

"This is truly a lovely day, isn't it?" Shana said.

"Yes, even though once in a while I can still hear my telephone ringing all the way from Tel Aviv."

"You are incurable. Can't you forget Tel Aviv and telephones for a few days? You're on leave, remember? Are we going to visit St. Catherine's Monastery tomorrow?"

"Yes, of course. I've been looking forward to it for a long time. I flew over it after the sixty-seven war, but I've never seen it from the ground.''

"And I've never seen it from above *or* below.''

"So we'll remedy that together. What about tonight?''

"All planned. Dinner, a special movie at the hotel that has been flown down, a long night of restful sleep, then up early tomorrow for St. Catherine's.''

"Good. By then, I'll ready for an outing.''

"And the day after—''

The musical program had come to its end and they heard the familiar pinging signal that indicated an upcoming news broadcast. Suddenly, physical activity on the beach seemed to come to an end as bathers and loungers gathered around what radios were available, eager for the latest news from the capitals of the world through Radio Israel. The first item of the broadcast was of local importance.

"Early this morning, terrorist infiltrators crossed the border from Lebanon north of Adamit, carrying with them a quantity of machine pistols, AK-47 paratroop rifles, ammunition, hand grenades and explosives intended to manufacture bombs.

"Later, on the road leading to Ma'alot, the terrorists were intercepted by a two-man border patrol unit. In the ensuing engagement, one Israeli patrolman was killed, one terrorist killed, another slightly wounded. The third member of the invading group was unhurt. The truck they were using was partially damaged by fire. The two survivors were taken into custody for questioning. The name of the Israeli victim is being withheld until his next of kin have been notified.

"From Beirut comes word that the latest truce between Christian and Moslem forces has broken down and the struggle for control of the city renewed with greater intensity. It is reported that Syrian troops are moving toward Lebanon in strength to attempt to hasten a political settlement. However—''

"Adamit," Shana said. "I thought the border there was well patroled.''

"Until recently, yes," Saul replied, "but with the Syrians moving closer to our borders to the east and south, we were forced to pull most of our people out of that area temporarily. Just spot patrols at night, helicopter overflights by day.''

They continued to listen as the Radio Israel commentator quoted a statement from the prime minister's morning press conference, a warning that Israel "cannot remain indifferent should Lebanon lose its independence and fall under domination of terrorist organizations, or should it be trampled under Syrian rule.''

When the news turned to the more pressing internal problems of soaring inflation, rising costs and another likely increase in taxes, Shana turned away and burrowed her head into her air pillow. Saul continued to listen until the broadcast was concluded, then turned the radio off.

Softly, he said, "Shana?"

There was no response. Shana was asleep.

He lay fully awake, envying Shana's ability to fall into relaxed sleep so effortlessly. How happy life would be, Saul mused, if all undertakings retained to the end the joys and enthusiasms of their beginnings; if the dregs of a glass of wine were as sweet as the first taste.

Even here, so distant from the pressures of his work, there was no escape from the terrors and threats of terror from the hostile world that surrounded them.

Saul had been born in 1930, the only child of German-born Aaron and Rachel Lahav, who had emigrated from their native Berlin two years before. Aaron, a physician, and Rachel, a professional violinist, had married in their middle thirties; both from Orthodox Jewish backgrounds, in good financial circumstances, their careers firmly established.

Their decision to leave Germany, then hardly recovered from post-World War I upheaval, had not been an easy one to make; but Aaron had correctly read certain events that must one day come to an inevitable and frightening conclusion. The rantings and ravings of the man most people regarded as a deranged rabblerouser were gaining audiences of increasingly mounting proportions. Thus they decided to leave, opting for the challenge of Palestine.

In Haifa, the Lahavs were promptly embraced by the intellectual community, such as it was. Aaron was soon well-established in practice and, after the birth of Saul, Rachel joined a group of musicians who were anxious to found a symphony orchestra. Here, both became deeply immersed in their work and began building a new life, free from the continuing rumblings that came to them in letters from family and friends who had remained in Berlin. The self-proclaimed Messiah, Adolf Hitler, was shouting openly from pulpits throughout Germany that the only way to cleanse, purify and save his adopted country was to destroy its Jews, whom he blamed for all its ills.

Saul was five when Rachel fell ill for the first time in her active, robust life. Hospitalized, examined by specialists, she lost weight at so alarming a rate that Aaron was finally forced to accept the desperate conclusion that Rachel had fallen victim to that most dreaded of diseases, cancer. Within two months, she was dead.

On a raw December day, Arron and Saul stood sorrowfully as Rachel was lowered into her grave. Dark clouds, swollen with rain, hung overhead until the rabbi's final words were spoken, then began to empty themselves upon the gathered mourners. His hand clasped in Aaron's firm grip, Saul looked up at his father and heard his solemn voice through tears. "Today, my son, even God and His angels weep with us."

Distraught and despondent, Aaron Lahav began to neglect his practice, devoting most of his time and attention to the single living memory of his wife, their son. Daily, he walked with Saul, carried him when he tired, played simple tunes for him on Rachel's violin, read to him, almost resenting those times when Saul chose to play with other children in the nearby park. Friends and colleagues tried to persuade Aaron to return to his practice; doctors were in dire need, they persisted, and his refusal to take up his profession again was an act of pure selfishness. Aaron refused to be persuaded.

Not until Saul was six and began attending school, when those hours of his absence were emptiest, did Aaron again become active in medicine; and then not in private practice but in a hospital where he could benefit a greater number of people in need, using the hospital's library and facilities to broaden his knowledge in the field of cancer. Home became a place where Saul was; a place where, once Saul had been fed, bathed and put to bed by their Arab housekeeper, Aaron could continue his research studies.

Then it was 1940. Hitler's armies were rampaging across Europe, aimed at conquering England; later the world. The Middle East was in a state of frenzy, Jews siding with Great Britain, Arabs aligning with Nazi Germany. Aaron Lahav, caught up in the desperation of the times, with anxiety over family and friends caught in Hitler's trap, volunteered for service. He was accepted and ordered to serve in a London military hospital despite his repeated requests for duty at a front line. However, his age was against his serving in a combat situation and he was persuaded to perform where he could do the most good.

Saul, now ten, was permitted to accompany Aaron and was placed in a school just outside London, close enough to witness the violence and cold terror unleashed on that city and its environs by *Luftwaffe* bombers and later, pilotless V-1 and V-2 rockets.

In 1945 it was over and Saul was fifteen; mature and an excellent student. Aaron seemed to have aged by twenty years rather than five. His hair had turned totally white, skin translucent, body shrunken, once-erect shoulders stooped. They returned to Haifa later that year to resume a life-style that no longer existed.

It came as a keen disappointment to Aaron that Saul had neither his mother's great love for the violin nor his father's passion for medicine. His fondest interest was in languages, having learned German from his parents, studied Hebrew and Arabic in Haifa, English, French and Russian in London. It was his intention, he told Aaron, to become a teacher—even professor—of languages, with emphasis on modernizing biblical Hebrew into modern *Ivrit*. Aaron seemed pleased.

The world was now fully aware of the horrible details of Hitler's concentration camps; and the determination of the Arab world, supported by the British, to prevent Jewish refugees from emigrating to Palestine freely. Jewish soldiers, freed from military duty with the British, began swelling the ranks of Haganah, the secret army organization developed to protect Jewish lives and property from marauding Arab terrorists, and dedicated to force the British to live up to the Balfour Declaration, which would provide Jews with a homeland of their own.

Aaron bought a house in suburban Tel Aviv. In the secrecy of night, floors were removed and a basement dug, equipment brought in to establish an emergency hospital for wounded members of Haganah. Once in operation, it was reasonable to expect that Saul would volunteer to serve Haganah in any way a fifteen-year-old could. Through one of the young officers assigned to assist Aaron, Lieutenant Judah Rosental, the son of a doctor colleague, Saul was inducted into Haganah's Youth Group.

Assigned to a small unit under an older instructor, Saul was sent to a secret training camp in the interior, where he underwent strenuous physical exercises, learned to handle and fire many makes of weapons and explosives. Later, he was moved to the Tel Aviv-Jaffa area, where he became familiar with its geography, learned its streets, alleys, passageways, safe houses, cellars and rooftops—all important in evading British patrols, to be used as escape routes. Meanwhile, he became experienced in espionage and operated in Haifa and Jerusalem as needed. In what spare time fell to him, he studied various complicated codes and transmission methods.

Growing older, taller, stronger, he was sent into danger areas, acting as interpreter to his commander, Judah Rosental, now a Palmach captain.

In 1947, Aaron Lahav died in his bed in Tel Aviv of a not too mysterious, yet incurable, ailment; he had given up his will to live in a hostile world.

Alone now, Saul mourned his loss deeply, but was soon caught up with the need to return to duty. As a member of Judah Rosental's unit, he engaged more directly in espionage against the British and, on one occasion, played an active role in attacking a small detention camp where seven arrested Haganah members were awaiting removal to Acre for trial. On that night, three British soldiers were killed, two wounded, with one of their own dead and one wounded. The seven prisoners were successfully liberated.

Thus, Saul moved through 1947 into 1948 with the state of Israel a realistic possibility, yet fraught with dangers. When statehood was proclaimed by Ben Gurion on May fourteenth, and was at once recognized by President Harry Truman, Haganah emerged as Israel's principal defense force.

With the aid of the Rosental family lawyer, the Lahav house in Haifa was sold, leaving the one in Tel Aviv to be rented, and for Saul's future use. He was surprised to learn that Aaron had possessed an estate of over forty thousand British pounds, apart from personal jewelry and other effects, including a massive library and his mother's treasured Cremona violin. The money, by direction of Aaron's will, was placed under guardianship of Judah's father, Benyamin Rosental, until Saul would reach his twenty-fifth birthday, the income from rent and investments to be paid to him until then. It was Saul's own decision to remain in the military service.

In the historic war that ensued against an overwhelming array of Arabs, Saul performed with remarkable coolness and professionalism that earned for him the rank of sergeant. He did not, however, escape unscathed.

On the outskirts of Gaza, under heavy artillery attack, Saul received a serious head wound that threatened the loss of his eyesight. After receiving emergency first aid at a field station, he was removed to a hospital in Tel Aviv, where he lay in a darkened room, eyes bandaged, frantic with fear and wracked with anxieties. Emotionally immersed in self-pity, with only evasive answers from the doctors who examined him daily, he lived from day to day in desperation.

Weeks passed before he received his first glimmer of hope. An eminent American ophthalmologist who, with his wife, had been visiting their daughter, a student at Hebrew University, had become trapped by the war and stayed on to offer his services to Israel's war wounded. Hearing of Saul's case, he became interested. After a series of thorough examinations, Dr. Robert Hirsch recommended an intricate operation, in which he specialized. With Saul's all-or-nothing consent, the operation was performed. Another three weeks of darkness passed, then Saul was overjoyed to learn from Dr. Hirsch that his eyesight would be fully restored.

Saul gained two new friends, Robert Hirsch and his wife, Ruth. Then a third. On a subsequent visit, Ruth Hirsch brought their student daughter, Miriam; and now, with a warming relationship forming, it was almost like having a family again: father, mother, and something he had never known before, a sister.

For the next few weeks, Miriam Hirsch became a constant visitor. Unable to put his eyes to full use, she read the daily papers to him, benefiting by his corrections of her halting Hebrew. She aided Saul on short walks, talked of her life in Los Angeles, of other cities in America, her interest in Israel, about her father, who was chief of ophthalmology at UCLA Medical Center. And Saul talked of Aaron and Rachel, his wartime travel to England. More binding, it appeared, was the fact that both came from families with medical backgrounds, though neither was inclined in that direction.

A month later, the Hirsches returned to Los Angeles. Miriam, on her own insistence, remained behind to continue her studies, although there would be two months before the fall term would begin. One week later, Saul was discharged from the hospital and went on convalescent leave.

In Miriam's small car, they drove to safe interior areas, to the coastal beaches, to Haifa to explore the city of Saul's birth and youth. On the way back to Tel Aviv, they decided to stay overnight in the resort town of Netanya and there, as though it had been prearranged, they went to bed together for the first time. It was an exhilarating experience for both and they stayed for several days, totally immersed in their new adventure, excited by each new discovery in each other.

When they returned to Tel Aviv in a more settled state, Saul proposed marriage and was dismayed when Miriam showed a lack of interest.

"Why, Miriam? I don't understand. Is it me? I thought—"

"It isn't you, Saul. Of course not."

"Then what is it?"

"This—this country. Israel."

"Then why are you here? You could have gone home with your parents. Why did you stay on?"

She smiled enigmatically. "If you haven't figured that out by now, I can't explain it to you."

Frowning, "I need to hear it from you. Your own lips."

"All right. I'll try." She paused, then continued. "Israel is a hard, rough country with so much to be done. I've been here almost two years now and still feel like an outsider, not really a part of it. As an American, I'm not really accepted. Acceptable, maybe, but not accepted, if you can understand that.''

"I understand what you are saying, but not what you mean by it. There is a word for it, I think. Rhetoric.''

"Let me say it this way. I feel—excluded. The Sabras here regard me with curiosity, knowing that I can run home to the safety of America whenever I please, while they are forced to remain here.''

Saul let her words sink in for a few moments, then said, ''I think you are wrong on two counts, Miri. One, in order to be what you call 'accepted' in another country, you must first accept what is there without making critical comparisons of that country and its people with your own.''

Miriam accepted his statement without comment, perhaps with the feeling that he was correct in his assessment. ''And the other count?''

"You are a Jew. You have every right to be here. It is where you belong if you want to stay.''

"I don't honestly feel that, Saul. To your Israeli Sabras, I am a rich American, spoiled by material possessions. They resent the money my parents send me, the clothes, my car, all with a feeling so superior that I feel guilty for having wealthy parents.''

"Yet you cannot say you have been unhappy here.''

She laughed and said, ''No, I can't say that.''

"Then marry me. Stay with me here. It will all change. If I can love you, so can others, but only if you will permit them.''

"Saul, I am tired now and I can't say—I don't want to say yes, then later say no. Let it wait. We'll see.''

Meanwhile, they saw each other every day, slept together every night. Then Saul received new orders to report to headquarters in Tel Aviv for reassignment. On that same evening, he met Miriam for supper and later, she drove them to the beach.

"I have to report to headquarters in the morning for reassignment, Miri,'' he said quietly when they were parked.

"Oh, no! Where will they send you?''

"That depends.''

"On what?''

He took her into his arms and said, ''Miri, if you marry me, I am sure I can arrange an assignment so that we can be together.''

He felt her body stiffen, then relax again. ''I have a better idea,'' she said. ''Come back to America with me, Saul. Dad can arrange it, I'm sure—'' Her voice heightened as the idea took hold, as though it had only now occurred to her. ''Saul, listen—''

He shook his head negatively. ''I have told you, Miri. Israel needs me. America doesn't.''

"Saul, please. We can both enroll at UCLA, live together, study together. Your father was a doctor. Mine is a doctor. There's no reason why we couldn't—"

"I can't, Miri. I have told you before, I have no great love for medicine. I am already a soldier and Israel needs every trained soldier she can find. I am necessary here."

"Please, Saul. You're all alone here, no parents, no family. With me, us, you will have all that and so much more."

"No, Miri. I am a man and a man takes care of his own wife and family. In Israel, with what I have, what more I will have when I am twenty-five, I can do that. In America, it would be impossible."

When she remained silent, he said, "If we are married, Miri, I can go to Judah Rosental and he will help arrange an assignment in Tel Aviv, where I have a house. I know he will do that for me, but only if I am married."

On the following day, Miriam phoned her parents and spoke to both at great length; explained, discussed, argued, wept. And won. Exactly ten days later, in the presence of Robert and Ruth Hirsch, Judah and Toba Rosental, a few close university and army friends, Saul Lahav and Miriam Hirsch were married in Jerusalem.

They moved into Saul's house in Tel Aviv and with Miriam's tax-exempt status still in effect, the Hirsches bought new furniture and linens, dishes and appliances, with promises of more to be shipped from Los Angeles. To this they would add a new car, a stereo unit, Miri's own familiar furniture and the balance of her clothes. Robert and Ruth's parting gift was a draft for ten thousand dollars which, both argued, "is far less than half of what a wedding would cost us in Los Angeles."

After a brief honeymoon in the Galilee, Saul received new orders, restoring him to full duty at Lod, a mere twenty-two kilometers from Tel Aviv, enabling him to spend his off-duty nights and weekends at home with Miri. This was the happiest time of their lives, made happier later when Miri announced that she was pregnant.

In the sixth month of her pregnancy, her University career was temporarily terminated and, three months later, in September of 1950, Robert and Ruth Hirsch returned to be present at the birth of their grandchild, a healthy eight-pound, three-ounce boy whom Saul and Miri named Dov.

                        *   *   *

An Egged tour bus roared by on the paved road upbeach from where Saul and Shana lay and the noise woke Shana. She sat up, put on her sunglasses and said, "An invasion?"

"Yes. Tourists to crowd our beach and inflate our economy. How was your nap?"

"Wonderful. Delicious. If only all of life could be so sane and uncomplicated."

"What a dull thing to contemplate. Shall we try that swim now?"

"In a few minutes. Let me wake up completely first."

They turned over on their stomachs and looked up toward where the tourists were getting out of the bus, waiting for the driver to get their baggage out before crossing the road to their hotel. As they watched, an army jeep pulled up behind the bus and parked. A sergeant got out and began crossing the sand, heading in their direction. He paused after a few steps and looked around at the inert bodies lying or sitting on the sand, then started walking with more certainty, directly toward them. With a sense of misgiving, Shana said, "Saul—"

"I see him."

They waited silently as the man in faded fatigue uniform, cap or beret inserted beneath his left shoulder epaulet, stopped when he reached their towels. "Major Lahav?"

Looking up, "Yes. What is it, Sergeant?"

With his eyes on Shana's body, "We received a message for you, Major, from Major General Rosental. Your leave of absence is canceled and you are ordered to report to him at once. There will be a car waiting at your hotel in an hour to take you to him."

Saul muttered an under-the-breath imprecation and said to Shana, "Three leaves of absence in five years and every damned one canceled after a day or two."

"Could it be the Adamit thing?" she asked.

"A border incident? I doubt it very much."

"One hour, Major," the sergeant said.

"I heard you," Saul snapped. "You have delivered your message. What are you waiting for?"

Shana had risen to her feet and the sergeant was eyeing her appreciatively. At Saul's petulant rebuke, he turned slowly, grinning, and headed back toward his jeep. Saul stood up and began gathering their belongings.

Like his father before him, Saul was tall, with a lean, slender frame that had been conditioned by an active military life from his fifteenth year into a well-coordinated and athletic body. Smooth muscles rippled along his strong legs and arms, across his chest, shoulders and back, his belly flat, weight problems unknown to him. His hair, once dark brown, was now, in his forty-sixth year, sandy colored. His face, like his body, was lean, clean-shaven, with even features and dark brown inquisitive eyes. His overall appearance was one of youthful eagerness, seldom at rest, a man in constant motion.

He was considerably and understandably angered by the order that so abruptly terminated his rare leave, but did not voice his annoyance at greater length than this first outburst. General Rosental, perhaps his closest friend from his earliest days in Haganah, was not an insensitive man. Both he and his wife, Toba, knew of, understood and accepted his relationship with Shana Altman and had often entertained them in their home, and Judah would not have issued such an order unless he felt it was necessary.

As he and Shana walked toward their beachfront hotel, he said, "Will you stay on, Shana? It may only be a conference, a day. Then I would fly back."

"I don't think so, Saul. If it was a minor matter, it could have been easily handled by telephone. I think I'll take the four o'clock Arkia back to Jerusalem. Let's get you packed."

Her docile acceptance and decision added to Saul's feelings of guilt. It was hardly less difficult for Shana to leave her job for an entire week and now, after less than two full days, her vacation was over. In their room, packing their clothes in separate suitcases, Saul said, "Will you take the rest of your leave or go back to your office?"

"The office, I think. I'll save the other five days for sometime later."

"I'm sorry, Shana. With you in Jerusalem and me headquartered in Tel Aviv, moving around so much, I'd hoped we could have this time together, to talk about many things—"

"So did I, Saul, but let's not give up hope." She laughed lightly and added, "Hopefully, there will be another time."

"I keep telling myself that, but damn it, something always comes up. We live on top of a volcano that never stops bubbling."

"I know, but what choice do we have? Do you think we could have some time for lunch before you leave?"

"We'll take the time."

They left Shana's suitcase in the room and took Saul's to the lobby and left it with the bell captain. He checked them out at the desk and told the clerk where they would be if his car came for him. It was then ten minutes to noon and as he and Shana headed away from the desk, he saw the army sedan draw up at the entrance. Ignoring it, they went into the dining room and spent a full hour over their meal. Shortly after one o'clock, Saul kissed Shana and went out to the car.

The same sergeant sat slumped behind the wheel and scarcely moved or took notice as Saul dropped his suitcase in the rear compartment, then climbed into the front seat. Without the exchange of a single word, the sergeant started the car, made a U-turn and headed toward the main road that led northward to Eilat.

They passed through Ras Nusrani and Nabak, making excellent time on a good road that was almost entirely free of traffic at this hour. In the intense heat, Saul fell into a half doze, nodding, squirming in discomfort, waking, tempted to take the wheel from the driver in order to be doing something. But the sergeant was obviously expert behind the wheel and Saul fell back into a half sleep wondering again, why the car? If this were a matter important enough to bring him back to Tel Aviv, why hadn't Judah ordered him flown back?

At Dahab, a considerable distance north of Eilat, he came fully awake, rudely jolted when the driver turned off the main highway onto a narrow two-laned road. Aroused, Saul exclaimed, ''What the hell! This isn't the road to Tel Aviv, Sergeant.''

''Tel Aviv? Who said we were going to Tel Aviv?'' the driver, eyes on the road ahead, replied with a sly grin. ''If we were going to Tel Aviv, we would be flying.''

''So unless it is a secret you are afraid will fall into the hands of the enemy, maybe you will be generous enough to share it with me?''

''No secret, Major. You didn't ask before. We are going to Bashra to meet the general.''

''Bashra?'' Saul said in surprise.

''Bashra.'' The sergeant, still grinning at Saul's confusion and loss of cool, bit the name off sharply, then added, ''Relax, Major. We'll be there in three hours.''

What, Saul wondered, had happened to require his, and Judah Rosental's, presence at the Bashra oil field? A security matter?

When, two years earlier, Israeli geologists first reported their belief that there was oil present in the Bashra area, there had been tremendous excitement generated among a few top officials in Jerusalem and Tel Aviv. Long before the news was made public, additional experts were immediately dispatched to check out this extraordinary discovery and spent several months in preliminary exploration; seeking outcroppings that would indicate alternating layers of porous and impermeable sedimentary rock that would be uplifted into domes, or anticlines.

Using modern geophysical techniques, magnetic, seismic and gravitational theories, they found supportable evidence of source beds, reservoir beds and traps, all suggesting the possibility that a wealth of oil lay beneath the surface. It was entirely logical, probable, in this arid stretch of desert valley, that the area had once centuries ago, been a seabed and, posing as archaeologists, teams of geologists and geophysicists began uncovering traces of age-old fossils, sea organisms, and shells. Digging, boring deeper, they came upon signs of alternate layers of mud, their ooze which, in time, had compacted and solidified into sandstones, shales and limestones.

Together with oil engineers and more sophisticated electronic devices brought in from the United States, where interest in a major oil field during a crucial energy crisis was enormous, exploration continued at an accelerated pace. Further testing confirmed the initial reports. All that remained was to open the field and commence drilling operations.

It was hardly possible, with the arrival of tons upon tons of steel, rigging lumber, tools, equipment and heavy machinery, to keep an operation of such magnitude a secret. As buildings to house oil engineers, construction and supply crews were built, additional warehouses, tents and barracks began to spread out over a wide area. Bashra took on the appearance of an overnight boomtown, roads were constructed eastward to link up with a major inland highway and, eventually, would connect up with the Eilat-Ashdod pipeline.

Russian satellite overflights made early discovery of the activity. Photographs taken with ultrasophisticated cameras from well over seven hundred kilometers above the Sinai, and with an absence of cloud cover or atmospheric turbulence, caught the scene with amazing clarity. At once, Cosmos began relaying that intelligence back to its home station computers, which translated the ultrahigh frequency transmissions into hundreds of high-resolution photographs.

Space intelligence evaluators immediately and correctly defined these photographs in their minutest details, down to the very trademarks on some of the American equipment and, within hours, complete reports were humming across land lines to Moscow. Shortly thereafter, a meeting was held, a decision arrived at, and the information was passed on to every Arab oil-producing nation. Almost at once, the collective Arab voice joined in a clamorous demand in the United Nations for the immediate return of all Sinai territory captured by the Israelis during the 1967 War. In this, the Arabs were joined by the Third World nations, China, India and, naturally, Russia.

Cool to this massive pressure, the United States and other Western nations stood firmly behind Israel's stiffened rejection of these latest demands despite the fact that no one had mentioned oil as the reason behind the accelerated movement. Thus, while heated debates continued, the now not-so-secret secret Bashra oil field was being developed and growing into a considerable oil industrial complex, although at that point, the amount of crude recovered had not come up to earlier extravagant predictions.

Gradually, however, storage tanks began filling while others were being constructed at a stepped-up pace. A pipeline had begun to stretch across the vast desert toward the foothills of a huge rock formation and would one day creep over its spine and link up with the existing line that ran from Eilat to Ashdod. More recently, as production rates increased, the foundation for a new refinery was laid in Bashra, its structural steel skeleton rising well above the height of all other buildings in that barren area. Primitive roads were being hacked out so that tank trucks, moving over steel mesh mats, were able to transport the crude to Haifa, slowed only by the need for more labor and equipment.

Israeli immigrants and Israeli Arabs made up the principal work force, laboring under the direction of engineers imported from the United States, South America and northern Europe; yet the field had by no means shown its full potential, which was expected to make Israel totally independent of previous outside sources, plus generate great export possibilities.

Saul was fully awake as they arrived at the posted warning signs which marked the two-kilometer restricted zone that ringed the entire operational field. There were no wire fences; none were necessary because of the four watchtowers in which sentries could see for miles in every direction—across barren stretches of sand, dunes, rock formations and wadis. Military guards on foot and in jeeps patrolled the inside limits of the installation throughout the day and night.

"We're here, Major," the sergeant announced wearily.

"I know," Saul retorted with a tinge of exasperation, brushing sand from his open-throated shirt front; then, in contrition, "You handle a car very well, Sergeant."

"I should. I know this desert like you know Tel Aviv. I've driven across it in cars, jeeps, armored personnel carriers and tanks."

The reference to Tel Aviv nettled Saul into replying crisply, "So have I, Sergeant. So have I."

The car drew up to the entrance gate where an Uzi-bearing sentry asked for their identification. The sergeant flipped down his sunshade, to which his plastic ID was clipped. Saul removed his card from his wallet. The sentry examined the photograph, recorded names, license of the car and the time of entry on a sheet attached to a clipboard, then opened the gate. As they entered, a jeep raced up and swerved to a stop, partially blocking the progress of the sedan. A young lieutenant, wearing side arms, leaped out and approached. Saul grunted and got out of the car and waited, cataloging the junior officer as a Dizengoff commando with a look of mild disdain.

"Major Lahav?"

"Yes." As he replied, Saul turned to one side, surveying the desert toward the north.

"General Rosental is waiting at headquarters, Major. If you will have your driver follow me—"

Without looking at the young officer, Saul said, "I think the sergeant can manage to find the headquarters without any trouble, don't you, Lieutenant?"

Taken aback by the question, the lieutenant said, "Why . . . ah . . . yes, Major, but—"

"Lieutenant," Saul said, turning back to face him, "just what is that Bedouin encampment doing out there, inside the restricted zone?"

"Ah—where, Major?"

"There—" pointing northward, "*inside the restricted zone*," he repeated with emphasis.

"I—" peering intently, then, "I see them."

"Good. Very good. What are they doing there?"

"Why, resting, or stopping for a meal, I suppose. They're only Bedouin nomads, Major, just passing through. It happens frequently and we seldom bother them—"

"Lieutenant, we make security rules for the purpose of being carried out, not ignored. That is your job and the job of every security man on duty here. Get your watch officer to move them outside the two-kilometer line, then climb every watchtower and wake up the sentries who are asleep there. At once, Lieutenant—"

"Yes, Major!"

"—or you will find yourself back in Tel Aviv explaining to your friends on Dizengoff why you are no longer a lieutenant."

The chastened officer backed off, climbed into his jeep and roared away, raising clouds of sand dust. As Saul got back into the sedan, he said to the grinning sergeant, "You do know the way to headquarters, don't you?"

"I'm sure I can find it, Major."

As the car drove up to the wooden structure that served as a military and engineering headquarters, Judah Rosental came out to greet Saul with a handshake. "*Shalom,* Saul. I hated to do this to you—"

"You always hate it, Judah, always. But you *do* it."

"This time, Saul, it was unavoidable."

"I know. Last time, it was essential. The time before, a desperate situation, the time before that—"

Rosental laughed pleasantly. "Saul, Saul, what more can I say to apologize, eh? Come inside. I want you to meet someone. A friend."

"This is a social thing?"

"A friend of Israel." Somber tone and meaning were explicit.

With a light grip on Saul's arm, Rosental led him down a hallway past the vacant office of the camp's military commander, Major Yuval Wolf, into the one next to it. Inside the dusty, austere room, seated in a chair beside a desk that showed the scars of much hard wear, sat a tall, blond, hazel-eyed man of about thirty-six, who wore an elegantly tailored lightweight plaid suit, white shirt, blue-and-white striped tie and black loafer-type shoes. The man stood up and smiled, extended a hand as Rosental introduced him.

"Saul, this is Mr. Lee Collier, here on a quick stopover from Washington on his way back to his station in Geneva. Lee, Saul Lahav. Major Lahav, my executive officer for operations."

"A pleasure, Major," Collier said with a broadening smile. "I've heard many things about you today. All good, I might add."

"Thank you," Saul replied, his hand in Collier's unusually hard grip that spoke of underlying strength. In a half turn, he directed his next blunt question to Rosental. "This has to do with oil, Judah?"

"No, Saul. Something much move important at the moment."

"Then why here in Bashra?"

"Because it seemed a safer place to talk without Lee being seen in Tel Aviv, Jerusalem or Haifa. His visit here is for no one but us to know about. I didn't want to order out a plane or helicopter to bring you here because I didn't want any official questions raised in case anyone took notice."

Rosental seated himself behind the desk, Saul and Collier in hard chairs on either side of him. Cigarettes were lighted and the general waved a hand toward the American. "Lee?"

Collier turned in his chair to face Saul. "Major," he began, "are you familiar with the name Viktor Sokolnikov?"

Saul reacted immediately, interest heightened. "Yes, of course. The KGB agent. According to the last report I saw, he was in Geneva with the World Disarmament Conference."

"Same man, yes, but the location has changed. Three months ago, as chief security officer to the Russian delegation there, Sokolnikov defected to our consulate. We flew him to the United States the same evening. While the Russians were demanding his return, we moved him out of Washington to where security could be fully and better maintained. Debriefing sessions began as soon as he was comfortably settled. They are, in fact, still being continued.''

"And," Saul said, "Israel is somehow involved?"

"Yes, but in a way that came about accidentally, or, I should say, incidentally." When this elicited no further comment from either Rosental or Lahav, Collier continued, his voice flowing smoothly.

"Debriefing sessions, as you are aware, are long, tiring, tedious and often boring to both the questioned and interrogators. Even with the most willing defectors, despite their resolution to cooperate, there is often a reluctance to go beyond certain limits. After each of those sessions, sometimes three or four a day, there would be a rest period for both sides; food, drinks, a little relaxation to prevent overtiredness.''

Saul squirmed in his hard chair and opened another button of his sweat-stained shirt in the oppressive heat, wondering at Collier's ability to ignore it all and remain fresh-looking and unrumpled, an enviable accomplishment. Thinking, *Get on with it, please*.

"During one such period of relaxation," Collier continued, "at which I was present at lunch, Sokolnikov fell into a purely conversational mood. The papers that morning carried a headline about an infiltration by fedayeen across one of your borders, which resulted in the deaths of two Israelis and four guerrillas. Sokolnikov remarked on it. Someone else added to his remark and the Russian made an oblique, yet interesting, ovservation; something to the effect, if I am quoting him correctly, that 'soon this whole thing will be in Arab hands and the Jewish problem will no longer exist.'

"All of us at the table with Sokolnikov seemed to deliberately avoid showing undue interest in that remark, then Ancil Gordon quietly and indirectly said something that encouraged Sokolnikov to go on. Which brings us to the reason for my presence here.''

Collier removed an envelope from his inner jacket pocket and without opening it said, "Of course, all our conversations, wherever possible, were taped, even at mealtimes. In this case, the tape recorder was concealed in the floral centerpiece on the table. This—" tapping one corner of the envelope on the desk, "is a transcript of that particular taped conversation.'' He withdrew several sheets of paper from the envelope and displayed them. There were six sheets in all, letter-size, with double-spaced typed material. The sheets were on plain white paper and bore neither heading nor signature for identification of its source. Leaning across the desk, Saul could make out the two-word heading, in capital letters and underlined:

SOKOLNIKOV MEMORANDUM

Collier now refolded the sheets, replaced them in the envelope which he held in one hand. "In essence, gentlemen, this is the meat of that single, singular conversation. First, however, I must tell you that Viktor Sokolnikov has no particular love for Israel, and even less respect or admiration for the Arabs. Although he was not officially involved in this particular matter, we feel he was using it to impress us with his knowledge of matters outside the sphere of his own particular activities.

"To get to the point, we learned that there is an entirely new movement being created, with indirect Russian support, a completely different organization from those presently existing in the Middle East, dedicated to solving the so-called Jewish problem.

"The name of that organization is UPFP, for United Palestinian Freedom Party. Sokolnikov states that it is unaligned with any other Palestinian political or fedayeen group, which it holds in contempt, along with their leaders, particularly Arafat and Habash, for their ineffective guerrilla actions and failures to bring Israel to its knees after so many years of misdirected effort. His words, gentlemen, not ours."

"Who," Saul interjected, "is behind this?"

"Good question, but only a partial answer. Our Russian canary had seen its leader-organizer only one time, in Dresden, where Sokolnikov, on KGB orders, was keeping an eye on the East German firm, EismanOptiks, which was then supplying Russia with ultrasophisticated optical lenses for night aerial observation and photography, also for night use by Red Army tanks, navy submarines, etc. The EismanOptiks plant is also noted for its advanced experiments with electronic weaponry, high-powered explosives in concentrated form, also—"

Rosental smiled. "We are fairly well acquainted with Herr Eugen Eisman and EismanOptiks, Lee."

"Of course," Collier acknowledged. A pause, then, "Sokolnikov did give us some other information on this UPFP leader, from personal eyeball observation and from questioning a colleague who had pointed out the man to him. It is included in this memorandum.

"The man is an Egyptian, six feet tall, about a hundred eighty-five pounds, dark to medium complexion, strongly built, black hair, brown eyes, full lips, prominent nose, clean-shaven at the time, and in Sokolnikov's words, extremely handsome in an Oriental way. He is reputedly well-educated, intelligent, of good family background, but for some reason, went into exile after Nasser's death in 1970.

"That the Egyptian is well-known in high Russian circles was made evident when Sokolnikov made an incidental report of his presence in Dresden to his KGB superiors and was told to drop it and concentrate on his own assignment; that the Egyptian was, quote, 'assisting Russia in matters concerning Israel,' unquote, with Moscow's full approval, and technical support from EismanOptiks. Also, there is the strong suspicion that the UPFP is receiving financial assistance from one or more oil-rich Arab countries, not identified, and in all likelihood, has set up sympathetic members inside Israel, 'sleepers' or 'future assets' sent in some time ago to await instructions they would receive at some time in the future when their services are needed."

Collier stopped then and lit a fresh cigarette. "That's it, gentlemen," he said quietly.

"And we are to take seriously the word of a Russian defector to the United States about a mysterious Egyptian who heads a vague organization in an unknown Arab country?" Saul asked.

Collier now showed his first trace of surface irritation. He looked directly at Saul with a slight frown. "Take it or leave it, Major. That's your prerogative."

"Now, wait," Rosental interjected hurriedly, trying to stem a possible confrontation in the making.

Collier turned back to face his stocky host with the barest glimmer of a smile. "General," he said, "if you can accept the judgment of our most skilled evaluators, men thoroughly experienced in their science who were present at these debriefing sessions, Sokolnikov was speaking the truth as he knows it. What I have here may seem inadequate to support positive fact that the UPFP actually exists, but it is the best we could get. For what it is worth, it is yours. The rest is up to you."

"And for which, Lee, we are very grateful," Rosental said.

"Of course," Saul added with a scant show of warmth. "We appreciate this very much, Mr. Collier. I am sure it will be helpful in any further investigation."

Collier handed the envelope containing the memorandum to Rosental. "I am certain you understand the need for secrecy in this matter at a time of utter confusion in the Middle East. While Moslems and Christians are trying to destroy each other in Beirut, with Syria threatening to invade Lebanon, if she hasn't already, with Egypt and Libya rattling swords, our position would become diplomatically untenable if it were known, even hinted at, that we were in any way involved in what the Arabs may well regard as a purely internal matter. Therefore it is imperative that this be kept under wraps as far as we are concerned."

"Naturally," Rosental said ressuringly. He checked his watch and said, "Come, Lee, I will fly you to the airport to catch your plane to Rome." As the three men stood, the general handed the envelope to Saul. "Stay here tonight, Saul. Study this very carefully. In the morning I will send my helicopter back to bring you to Tel Aviv. We will discuss this there, in private."

Saul's first act, once in the barracks cubicle assigned to him, was to strip down, wrap a towel around his waist and head for the outdoor shower area. Scrubbed clean, he returned to his cell-like quarters and was soundly asleep within minutes and before the intense heat could envelop him.

After supper with the camp's military commander, Major Yuval Wolf, Saul became engaged in a prolonged discussion relative to Wolf's previous requests for an electrified fence to surround the entire installation, a project that had been rejected for lack of funds. After an hour of this and other of the major's security problems, Saul managed to escape to his cubicle, where he removed the Sokolnikov memorandum from his locked suitcase and settled down for a first reading.

He skimmed through the narrative and certain pointed sections of dialogue, then concentrated on the last page, singlespaced, which contained the collective opinions and analyses of several evaluators and psychologists, identified only by their initials. Saul's attention was riveted to the name of Eugen Eisman, managing director of EismanOptiks.

Nothing in the memorandum supplied enough information to conjure up even the vaguest identification of the mystery figure who allegedly headed the equally mysterious UPFP organization. Who was he? Who was supplying the financial backing for such a broad movement?

It was common knowledge that the Soviets had done their utmost to prevent the United States from achieving a major diplomatic stroke in the matter of the Israeli-Egyptian Sinai accord and had been trying desperately ever since to sabotage any further gains by supplying arms and other credits to Egypt's most outspoken critic, Muammar Qaddafi, of Libya, as well as to Iraq and Syria. However, it was inconceivable that Moscow would deal with a single Arab on an individual basis where important funds were concerned unless it came under tightest control of the KGB. Saul's curiosity was also triggered by the mention of the Egyptian's exile from Egypt after Nasser's death. Here could be a possible means for discovering his identity, perhaps even a lead to his whereabouts.

More questions occurred to him, none that were at once answerable in his tired condition. Sokolnikov, admittedly, had no love for Israel. Collier (and the American evaluators) had made that point expressly clear. Therefore, could this be a sly plot to draw Israel's attention away from some other, more insidious and far more important plot in the making? Had, in fact, the Americans been taken in by Viktor Sokolnikov? Was he an actual defector or a KGB plant?

There were reasons for his suspicions. In the past, the KGB had sent agents into Israel masqueraded as emigrants. A few were caught, some disappeared, perhaps recalled to Russia on orders. Later, it was assumed that KGB had discontinued this practice, relying on Arabs already inside the country, eager and willing to do the Russians' work for them. Correct or not in that assumption, the Israelis had never relaxed their vigilance.

At ten o'clock, Saul went to the administration building office. Outside, under dark velvet skies liberally sprinkled with stars that seemed to be within reach, the work went steadily on. Generators hummed, artificial lighting illuminated active drilling rigs and other round-the-clock operations. Rig operators, tool pushers, shooters, acidizers, drilling and production crews were all busily occupied in their work. Construction gangs toiled under the direction of shouting foremen and supervisors. Engineers moved from unit to unit, checking, checking, checking. Water tankers continued to arrive from the north to add to the camp's supply, a constant operation. Off-duty engineers, crewmen and laborers lounged in their separate recreation areas or quarters, sleeping, reading, playing cards and chess, writing letters, listening to their radios or record players. The mess hall remained open for anyone who wanted coffee or a between-meal snack, no matter the hour.

Security guards, increased in number for night duty, patrolled the interior area. Searchlights mounted on high posts swept across the restricted zone under the eyes of sentries in their watchtowers. Saul entered the main building, showed his ID to the guard at the desk, and signed in. He went directly to the office where he and Rosental had earlier held their discussion with Lee Collier. At the desk, he picked up the phone, heard a male voice ask, "Yes?"

"This is Major Lahav. I want to place a call to Jerusalem. The number is—"

"Is this an official call, Major?" the man asked.

"No, personal."

"I'm sorry, Major. No personal calls can be transmitted over Bashra's lines. Orders."

"Whose orders?" Saul's voice bristled.

"Orders from the deputy minister of defense and General Judah

Rosental," the man retorted, then added brightly, "If you wish to confirm, I can try to reach the deputy minister for you."

"No. Never mind." He hung up, frustrated, wanting very much to talk to Shana, explain that this one, like his last leaves of absence, had been definitely canceled and was gone for now.

Stripped down to shorts and lying on the uncomfortable cot in his cubicle, plagued by the dim light thrown by the single low-watt bulb set into the ceiling, he gave up trying to reread the memorandum. There were no more questions he could conjure up regarding its contents and he wondered what Judah's thoughts would be on the subject. No answers to that question came to him at the moment. Tomorrow might, or might not, provide one when he would meet with the general in Tel Aviv.

He thought again, as he often did in such moments alone, of the past. Of Miri. Of Dov in the early days of his growth. For two yearts, stationed close to Tel Aviv, home frequently, life was pure joy with Miri and Dov; watching his son develop from the stage of infant helplessness into a child of meaningful actions—feeding greedily at Miri's breast, investigating the miracle of his own fingers and toes, reaching for a small toy, the spoon that held his food. And still later, learning to crawl, stand, take his first proud steps. Feeling a deeper love for Miri and an overwhelming sense of pride as husband and father.

A year later, Judah Rosental, now a lieutenant colonel, requested that Saul be transferred to Military Intelligence headquarters in Tel Aviv. For several months there, his duties were principally in the area of linguistics, acting as interpreter, listening to intercepted tapes, evaluating radio transmissions, learning intricate codes, interrogating prisoners. Later, he was schooled in antiguerrilla tactics, an operation which required close cooperation with border patrol, police and other intelligence services.

With the increase in terrorist activities, Saul was away from home much of the time now, working with investigative units along the Jordanian, Syrian and Lebanese borders. There were numerous brushes with infiltrators from the outside as well as from terrorists within Israel's borders and principal cities, escalating at a frightening pace.

Bombs were thrown at moving buses and trucks, planted beneath cinema seats, in open markets and on the shelves of supermarkets, in department stores, post offices, bus stations and other public buildings. Men, women and children were maimed or killed indiscriminately. Infiltrators sneaked across borders to attack kibbutzim while Syrian artillery in the Golan Heights shelled farm villages in the valleys below.

Israelis retaliated as they could with what limited arms and forces were then available, but the losses mounted and there was no way to defend against the Syrian artillery. Many terrorists were killed, others captured, interrogated, charged, tried, convicted and imprisoned. Despite their heinous crimes, they remained alive. There was no death penalty in Israel.

Saul Lahav continued to play an increasingly heavy role in the interrogation process, acting as liaison to coordinate the overall information for Rosental. Constantly on the move from one sector of action to the next, he was often away from home for weeks at a time. On those infrequent occasions when he returned to Tel Aviv to make his reports in person, wearied by long and strenuous hours of work and travel, he began to awaken to the fact that he and Miri were drawing apart.

Miri had Dov and her home to care for and had resumed her studies in art and world history, but showed scant interest in the history or traditions of her adopted country. It distressed Saul that she had discontinued her studies of Hebrew beyond the need to shop for necessities, and which made it difficult for her to make close or intimate friends.

Because he knew of no way he could help Miri overcome her spoken, more often unspoken, differences and resentments, Saul nevertheless tried to understand her ambivalence toward Israel. For himself, he was able to accept its favors with unrepressed joy, its hardships with equanimity, its wars and attacks from outside as a necessary evil and way of life he had been familiar with from childhood.

But to Miri, Israel remained a land of contrast and contradiction. America, even during World War II, had been safe from bombing attacks and, therefore, remote from the battlefields of Europe, the Pacific and Asia; a nation at war, yet enjoying a certain peace at home. She seemed unable to accept the fact that Israel had been born of necessity and became strong by that same need. Living between conflict and tension, walking bravely, yet nervously, the Israelis had learned to bear the terrible cost of constant preparation for wars yet to come, always with one ear close to their radios to hear everything said or done in Washington or Moscow, in Cairo or Damascus, that might bring on the next holocaust.

Religious and irreligious, cosmopolitan and rural, literate and illiterate, Israelis lived side by side, yet eons apart in culture and philosophy. Ultra religious Hasidim scorned the modern Jew and were in turn scorned by the super-religious N'turai Karta who, like the millions of Arabs who surrounded the infant nation, refused to recognize Israel as a nation; insisting that Jews would get back the Promised Land only when the true Messiah arrived to return it to them. They refused to use Israeli currency, serve in the Israeli Army, or vote. Coming from abroad, they balked at flying on an El Al plane because it was owned by a government which, to this rigid-minded, unrelenting cult, did not exist.

These and other anomalies. more and more, became disruptive factors in the personal lives of Saul and Miri Lahav to such a degree that soon, neither dared mention them out of fear that to do so would open wounds which could not be healed. Restive, unable to solve this vexing problem, Saul came to realize that from the very beginning, he had unconsciously felt that Miri had cared far less for him than he had for her; that she had permitted him the privilege of loving her. Perhaps their initial introduction, under dramatic hospital conditions, he the wounded soldier, she the bearer of comfort, had been a strong influence in what had brought them closer together and eventually into marriage. It occurred to him, as he looked back into the past, that she had never, other than those times when they were engaged in the sexual act, expressed her love for him as he had so often voiced his for her.

Now, sex between them became an infrequent act, with Saul eager, Miri submissive, expressing no pleasure or delight. She complained of their repressive life, of a lack of true cultural atmosphere, of the inferior quality of merchandise and foods, of high prices and taxes, of the inconveniences of living in Israel. And despite his affection for, and closeness to Dov, Saul soon began to look forward to returning to duty.

In mid-July of 1956, when it became a near certainty that a new war was imminent, Miri, urged by her parents, flew to Los Angeles, taking Dov with her, her first trip home since before her marriage.

And now, with the increased demand for experienced manpower in the field, Judah Rosental asked for temporary active duty and was assigned to a tank battalion, one of his military specialties. Saul at once requested assignment to his unit and Rosental agreed and arranged for it. At once, he entered into intensive training and was later assigned to the Fourth Armored Brigade.

In its first major action, the Fourth captured Kusseima, then continued on to link up with a paratroop unit that had been dropped at Mitla Pass. There, joining up with other tanks, half-tracks, gun carriers and jeeps, they drove head-on into a trap laid by the Egyptian Army, which had taken up positions in the caves that lined the wadi. Once engaged in fierce battle, the remainder of the brigade was sent rushing to assist the trapped column. For eight bitter hours the battle raged, much of it in hand-to-hand combat. General Dayan declared it a most heroic example of determination and bravery, despite certain faults of misjudgment and errors in transmission of orders.

Bloodied in battle, the brigade turned its attention to El Arish in support of infantry operations and witnessed the swift retreat of the Egyptian Army from that field. Dayan, on the scene, became Saul's idol and inspiration. In the heat of increased action, Saul became separated from Rosental's Fourth and was ordered to join the Twenty-seventh in the assault on Gaza. The Egyptians again showed little resistance and Gaza fell on November third. But Saul was out of it now. On that morning, standing up in one of the lead tanks for a clearer view, he took a rifle bullet in his upper right chest.

After emergency treatment at a field hospital, he was removed to Tel Hashomer Hospital in Tel Aviv and spent four weeks there before being given convalescent leave, the 1956 Sinai campaign now a vivid memory.

During Miri's absence, he had received two letters from her, both brief, expressing her joy at being home, of her parents' delight with Dov, now six years old. With time on his hands, he wrote her at length, omitting the fact that he had been wounded, asking when she would return.

In February Miri and Dov flew into Lod, unannounced. Saul had been sent to the Golan area where the Syrians were continuing to shell the kibbutzim in the valleys below their fortified positions in the Heights. Two months passed before he was reunited with his wife and son.

*   *   *

He was ready shortly after dawn when Rosental's helicopter arrived to take him to Tel Aviv. He was met by his driver, Asad Hasbani, who drove him to headquarters. He went directly to Rosental's suite, past the receptionist who greeted him with the word that the general "is in conference with the chief, Major, but Colonel Kohn is in his office."

He went to the door of the general's deputy, knocked and entered. Omri Kohn looked up from the Daily Activities Report printout and waved a hand to the visitor's chair. "*Shalom*, Saul. Sit for a minute. Coffee?"

"*Shalom,* Omri. Yes."

Kohn spoke into his intercom and ordered the coffee. Moments later, while Kohn concluded reading the report, the receptionist brought the coffee. The deputy initialed the report, handed it to the receptionist and swiveled around to face Saul. "The general is in conference with General Bartok and the defense minister. I don't think they'll be much longer.''

"Something important?'' Saul asked.

"When the minister comes visiting with the chief, usually everything becomes important. But don't run off. Judah left word that he is anxious to see you.''

Saul grimaced at the implied enforced inaction. Conferences had a way of lasting for hours. "What about the two from Adamit?''

"We're holding them here until we can get something from them that makes sense.''

"Nothing yet?''

"The usual gibberish.''

"Names?''

A shrug. "Yes. Probably false. As usual, they carried no identification other than some inexpertly forged papers. We ran their prints through R and I. The files are downstairs but you won't find anything helpful there. Would you like to try it while you wait?''

"Why not?''

"Good. I'll notify Records and Security. Incidentally, something we didn't let out to the press. The truck they were driving and which was partially destroyed by fire, was loaded with more arms and explosives than we feel the men knew were aboard.''

Saul pondered this for a few moments, then said, "If that is the case, and since they could hardly have crossed the border in a truck, it is most likely the truck was supplied to them after they crossed over.''

"Obviously, and the load of extra equipment was already on the truck, probably from a stockpile somewhere in the north, using these dupes to transport it to their destination, wherever that might be.''

"Makes sense. Have them put in separate interrogation rooms next to each other while I check their files.'' As Saul rose, Kohn was on the phone, transmitting the orders.

On the level below, Saul checked in with Records and the young woman in charge handed over two new files, each with a set of fingerprints clipped inside. Besides that, there was only the report of the action written by the border patrolman who had survived.

"Nothing more than this?'' Saul asked.

"Nothing. They're clean otherwise.'' She smiled and added, "You'll be on your own, Major.''

Her smile annoyed him and he said, "That amuses you, Corporal?''

She reacted stiffly. "I am only amused by the idea that every fedayeen captured must have a police or prison record, Major. It's that simple."

"Nothing is as simple as you make it sound, Corporal, not the seduction of boys to become murderers nor of a woman to share a man's bed."

She flushed at his rebuke and began to turn away. "I'm not finished, Corporal," he said admonishingly.

"What more can I do for you, Major? You have your records and I am not a candidate for your bed."

Saul laughed lightly. "Wait until you are invited, Corporal. I want two dossiers, anybody's, as long as there is more in them than in these."

"Anybody's?" she asked, puzzled.

"Anybody's. Something to hold in my hand that is more impressive than these while I interview them." To soften his earlier snappishness, "They will never see what is in the files, only that some record of some kind exists."

The corporal shrugged her eyebrows and returned to her files to give Saul the desired folders. In the basement, a security guard sergeant directed him to the interrogation area where armed guards stood before two doors. Saul entered the room nearest him and closed the door. The room was small, without windows. It had bare gray-painted walls, lighted only by a wire-enclosed bulb in the high ceiling, which did little to brighten the room, its switch mounted on the hallway wall outside. A six-by-six-inch panel of shatterproof glass was set into the door at eye level.

There was a table with two wooden chairs on each side of it, a tin ashtray in the center. On one of the chairs sat one of the prisoners. Saul had two names, but no way of knowing which one this was. The Arab looked up and Saul stared at him for a moment, saw the angry defiance, or fear, in his eyes. Perhaps both. Slender, his arms, chest and shoulders showed fair musculature through the tight shirt he was wearing, evidence of some physical training. His features were clean and purely Middle Eastern, with dark, alert eyes and longish black hair.

The Arab looked away. Saul opened the files and looked through several pages of each, then said, "You are Mousa Awad or Zayim Samdat?"

The boy looked up, but did not answer. "Which one?" Saul demanded sharply.

"Samdat."

"Where were you born?"

"In the Garden of Allah."

Saul dropped the files, reached across the table and pulled him up out of his chair by his shirt front. "Listen to me, boy. I have no time to waste with people like you. Answer my questions or else—"

Samdat pulled back suddenly and Saul found himself with a strip of shirt in his left hand. He moved quickly around to the other side of the table and grabbed the remaining ends of the shirt, then slammed Samdat against the wall hard. As the terrorist bounced back off it, Saul threw his right forearm actoss the boy's throat and held him pinned there. "Talk, Samdat, or you will leave this room on a stretcher."

Samdat nodded, unable to speak with Saul's arm across his throat. Saul released him and pushed him down into the chair, then went to the opposite side to face him across the table. He sat down and picked up one of the files and turned a page.

"Where were you born?"

"Magdal Kroum."

Saul nodded, as though this information confirmed what was in the file. "And from there?"

"My family moved to Acre."

"When?"

"When I was nine years old."

"You went to school in Acre?"

A nod, his eyes on the table.

"Look up at me when you speak." Samdat's eyes looked up without moving his head.

"Where did you get the truck you were riding in when the border patrol engaged you?"

"It was given to us after we crossed the border."

"At Adamit?"

"At Adamit."

"How many were with you when you crossed?"

"We were six, but three left us to return to our camp. They became frightened and said they would go no further." Angry contempt crept into his next words. "Cowards. They were children."

"Where were you going with your load of submachine guns, revolvers, grenades and explosives?"

"I don't know." Samdat suddenly became passive. His head fell on his chest and his eyes closed tightly.

"Answer me. What was your destination?"

"I have no more to tell you. Do what you want with me. I will tell you nothing more."

"Very well, brave one, we will see." Saul went to the door and called the guard inside. "Stay here with this one while I talk to his friend in the next room," he ordered.

Dossiers under his left arm, Saul went out. Instead of entering the second interrogation room, he went back to the security guard's station and asked the desk sergeant if he had any of the weapons found on the two prisoners. The sergeant unlocked a small storage room and returned with two revolvers, each bearing an identification tag. Saul removed the tag from one, asked for six cartridges, which he placed in his jacket pocket.

Now he entered the second interrogation room where Mousa Awad sat. Awad was shorter than Samdat, more heavily built, more muscular, with darker skin, stronger features and piercing eyes that were as black as his hair. As with Samdat, there was anger in him, a firmness of lips that bespoke sullen arrogance.

Saul tucked the revolver into his waistbelt and scanned one of the dossiers; slowly, contemplatively. When he closed it, Awad said, "There is nothing in there that concerns me. I have never been arrested before."

"So. Then let's get on with it. What is your name?"

"You have it in your records, no?"

"Tell me so that I can verify it."

"Find it out for yourself, Jew. Don't waste your time on me. I will not do your work for you."

"Very well." Saul removed the revolver from his waistbelt. Holding it loosely in his right hand, he said, "This gun, and others, were found in a truck you were driving, along with a quantity of submachine guns, grenades and explosives. For possession alone, you are facing twenty years to life in prison at hard labor. How does that make you feel?"

Awad turned his head and spat contemptuously on the floor. Saul shifted the revolver to his left hand, then took the six cartridges from his pocket and began inserting them into the weapon. Awad's eyes began to follow every move with increasing apprehension. Saul then went to the door and summoned the guard who, when he saw the revolver in Saul's hand, started to speak, then closed his lips tightly, a questioning look in his eyes. Saul returned to stand opposite Awad across the table. He raised the revolver and thumbed the hammer back. Awad started out of the wooden chair, eyes wide open with fear. "Wait . . . wait . . . what are you—"

Saul turned to the guard and said, "You saw him attack me, didn't you?"

The guard grinned. "Oh, yes, Major, yes."

Saul moved the barrel a few inches to the right and downward, then pulled the trigger. The gun roared and bucked as the bullet hit the concrete floor where the two corners of the room met. And over the roar came the piercing shriek from Awad's mouth, "Ah . . . no. *No!*"

When he finally realized the bullet had not been intended for him, Awad fell back into his chair, sweating heavily, mouth open in surprise. Or relief.

Saul walked to the door, the revolver in his hand smelling richly of cordite. To the guard, he said quietly in Hebrew, "Keep an eye on him. Don't let him talk or raise his voice."

Outside, he walked back to the first interrogation room where he had left Zayim Samdat. He entered and ordered the guard out, then returned to face Samdat across the table. The Arab youth sat at the table gripping its edges with both hands, his face pale and bathed in perspiration, widened eyes on the revolver which Saul held at his side.

"Now, you," Saul said. "Where were you going when you ran into the border patrol?"

Samdat gulped. Saul raised the gun's muzzle an inch or two, then slowly thumbed the hammer back. "Where?" he demanded.

Resistance had fled. "T . . . to N . . . Nazareth," Samdat stuttered.

"For what purpose?"

"To meet a . . . man . . . there."

"What man?"

"I don't know. I swear it by Allah, I don't know."

"But Awad knew, didn't he?" The impact of using the past tense showed its effect on Samdat.

"Yes. Oh, yes. He knew. Awad was our leader."

"A leader who couldn't keep three of his men from running back to Lebanon?"

"They held their guns on us. It is the truth. I swear it."

"So. I want to know the name of the man in Nazareth and why you were taking weapons and explosives to him." And now the muzzle of the revolver moved upward slowly until it was aimed at Samdat's chest, less than six feet away. "What about the other arms and explosives in the truck?"

"We knew of no other explosives or weapons except those we had brought with us from our camp. I swear it. None of us knew what was on the truck except the crates of vegetables. We knew nothing until we were accused—"

Samdat's body had moved to the left as he spoke, but the muzzle followed the move. Perspiration beading the Palestinian's forehead broke into tiny rivulets and began coursing down his cheeks, but he seemed totally unconscious of this and his hands remained clenched together as though in prayer, bulging eyes on the tip of the gun.

"Look at me!" Saul said sharply, and when Samdat stared upward, the grim face he saw did little to lessen his fears. "Tell me, Samdat, what is the name of the man in Nazareth? You have ten seconds."

With that, Saul began to count. "One . . . two . . . three. . . ."

Desperately, "Wait . . . wait . . . please—"

" . . . four . . . five . . . six. . . ."

"No! Don't. Please. In his shoe. Mousa's shoe . . . the left one . . . a paper . . . the names—"

Saul released the hammer and shoved the revolver back into his trouser belt. At the door, he said to the guard, "Watch him carefully. If he has lied to me, I will return in a few minutes."

In the second interrogation room, Mousa Awad sat at the table, a sullen line shaping his lips into a tight grimace. Without glancing at him, Saul addressed the guard. "I want his shoe. The left one. Quickly."

Awad leaped to his feet, but the guard was more than equal to the contest and pinned him down in the chair again, arms twisted behind him. Saul reached down and removed Awad's left shoe. He examined it carefully, then used his pocket knife to pry the worn heel off. It was solid. Now he began picking at the stitches, separating the outer leather from the inner lining, and found the folded slip of paper.

It contained a list of five names. At the top was that of Hassan Atassi, with a Nazareth address and telephone number. Below that was an inch of space, followed by four other names—Ahmed Hadek, Mashir al-Habab, Hamdi Amid and Farik Said. Another inch of space, then a single sentence: *With compliments to His Majesty.*

Saul studied the list, then signaled the guard to follow him. Outside, he said, "Take this one back to his cell, then return for the other one. Keep them separated and in isolation so they can't see or communicate with each other. I will instruct your sergeant."

When he returned to Rosental's suite, the meeting was over. Colonel Kohn ushered Saul into the general's office. Rosental looked up from a document he was perusing. He removed his reading glasses, ran one hand through his unruly hair and said, "*Shalom*, Saul. Sit, sit." And to Kohn, "Some coffee, Omri, please."

When Saul was seated, Rosental said, "Up to your old tricks, Saul?" And to Saul's upraised eyebrows, "The security sergeant phoned Omri the moment he heard the shot."

Saul reached into his shirt pocket, withdrew the slip of paper with the names on it and said, "It worked, Judah." He handed it over to Rosental, who put his glasses on and studied the names, announcing each aloud. "Hassan Atassi. I know that one. A lawyer, prominent in local politics in Nazareth. Do you know any of the others, Saul?"

"None except Atassi. But that last sentence is interesting."

"Yes, of course. It obviously refers to our Jordanian neighbor—"

"And a group who, either here or in Jordan, have been designated to eliminate him."

"I agree, considering the quantity of arms and explosives they were carrying on that truck. Do you think there is anything to indicate that this operation may be connected with this UPFP thing of Collier's?"

"Unless there is much more to the Sokolnikov debriefing than we already know about, I would doubt it. I don't believe they were aware of the other material on that truck, so it must have been assembled on our side of the border, delivered to the infiltrators along with the truck after they crossed the border."

"Supplied by whom, Syria? Arafat?"

"More than likely, but it makes no difference."

A pause, then, "You still maintain your contact in Amman?"

"Yes. Nothing has changed between us there."

"Then you will take care of this matter?"

"Today or tomorrow. As soon as I can arrange a meeting with Major Halawa."

"Good." The receptionist entered with a tray and two cups of coffee, bringing with her the copy of the Sokolnikov memorandum Saul had left with Colonel Kohn before interrogating Samdat and Awad. "Colonel Kohn said you would would want this," she said and placed the envelope on the desk. When she went out, Rosental picked it up, leafed through its contents quickly, then said, "You have studied this carefully, Saul?"

"There was little else to do in Bashra last night."

"Any conclusions?"

"No conclusions, but I found some very interesting possibilities. Not too much to go forward with."

"But you believe it."

"After much thought, yes."

"Why?"

"Judah, I listened very carefully to Collier and heard the means by which they came by this document. I know that their evaluators are among the best in the business. If they are convinced that his story is authentic, I don't think we can afford not to believe it. Therefore, my answer stands. I believe it.''

Rosental sighed, sipped at his coffee while Saul lighted another cigarette. "As you said, Saul, there is so little to go on. If we accept it—''

"You don't, Judah?''

Rosental smiled wryly. "Why are you so suddenly more receptive to the proposition now when you were so hostile to it at Bashra? Was it the idea, or perhaps Collier?''

"Neither." Saul shrugged. "Maybe it was the suddenness of it. Maybe because I was tired.''

"Not because I canceled your leave?" When Saul did not answer at once, Rosental said, "I'm sorry. I didn't mean that, Saul." He stood up and began pacing the room, then returned to his desk. "For a while, with what is going on in Lebanon, I thought we might have a breathing spell, but it never lets up. As tied up as the PLO is in Beirut, they still try to infiltrate their terrorists—''

"That's too much to hope for, Judah. It isn't realistic not to expect them to keep trying," Saul said quietly.

"I suppose not. Still, there aren't enough hours in the day, never enough manpower, equipment or money to run down every rumor that comes along." He paused, then added, "Saul, has it occurrrd to you that this could be no more than a Soviet dis- or misinformation attempt to mislead us, force us to commit more than we can afford to go chasing nonexistent ghosts? Or to commit a tactical error that might bring us into a confrontation with Syria, which would negate the Sinai pact and force Egypt to live up to its commitment to join Syria in the event of such a conflict?''

"Those thoughts, and others, have crossed my mind, Judah, but I dismissed them as paranoia. For one thing, Egypt needs another war as much as we do, and will do everything possible to stay out of one. For another, according to Collier, Sokolnikov has turned over too much important verifiable information to the State Department and CIA to be a double agent. Remember that this UPFP matter came from him voluntarily and not under their questioning or pressure.''

"Clearly an assumption on your part, isn't it?''

"Judah, Sokolnikov is not entirely a stranger to us. He has always been regarded as one of their more clever operators. I think that if his goal was what you suspect, he could have put together a far better story, and without so many gaps, to keep us running around in circles.''

"Maybe yes, maybe no, Saul.''

Saul looked up, his expression questioning. Rosental said, "To set this thing up to look deeply into a vague and new terrorist organization, I would need to ask for a lot of money at a time when our budget is already strained beyond its limits. General Bartok has been insisting that all departments cut back in these times of heavy inflation and increasing taxes.''

"Have you discussed this memorandum with the chief?''

"No. At the moment, he and the other heads of security and intelligence services have their hands full with problems concerning other vital matters.''

"So we drop it?''

"No, we don't drop it,'' Rosental replied somewhat testily, as though resenting what he believed was implied criticism. "For now, we put it aside until we have more evidence of the existence, or presence, of such a menace to us. But we don't forget it.''

The finality of his voice outlawed further argument or discussion. Saul drank the last of his coffee, stubbed out his cigarette and stood up, waiting to be dismissed; even hoping that Rosental might relent and permit him to resume his leave of absence. "Is that all, General?'' he asked, returning to formality.

"No. Sit down.'' When Saul resumed his seat, "Since you were not scheduled to take part in other arrangements for later this week, I want you to take care of this matter with Major Halawa. If he shows any inclination toward gratitude for our cooperation, you might try to sound him out on the treaty between Jordan and Syria, how matters stand there. And Saul,'' Rosental waved a hand over the litter of reports, letters, teletypes, memoranda and newspaper clippings that lay on his desk, "here are at least a dozen active projects that need our more immediate attention, all definite and in progress. Let us concentrate on these first.''

"Yes, of course.'' All hope of resuming his aborted leave was now abandoned.

Rosental handed him the Sokolnikov file. "Take this with you for now. Put it in your file for future reference, when some of these more pressing matters are out of the way. But don't forget it.''

"Yes, of course.''

In his own office, Saul's first act was to place a call to Shana in Jerusalem. Since she might still be on leave, he tried her apartment first and found her in. "Shana?''

"Yes, Saul. Where are you?''

"My office in Tel Aviv.''

"I was hoping you were back in Sharm el Sheikh.''

"No such good fortune. Definitely cancelled.''

"Ah, well. I took an extra day off, but I think I'll report back to work in the morning.''

"As you will, and I'm sorry. I will be busy here for a day or two. As soon as I can get away I'll come to visit."

"Do that."

"I'll call you first. *Shalom*."

"*Shalom*, Saul."

Twenty minutes later, Saul's secretary, Sergeant Leah Barak, had located Sergeant Asad Hasbani and informed him that he was wanted in Saul's office. Hasbani reported in, knocked on Saul's door and entered, moving directly to a side chair while Saul concluded a telephone call.

In civilian clothes, few outsiders would have taken Hasbani to be what he was; a former member of the Israeli police department, now working as an investigator for the Antiguerrilla Branch of Mossad. The son of a Palestinian father and Jewish mother, his loyalty to the state of Israel had never been questioned, nor in doubt. Both of his parents had been killed in a terrorist attack while shopping together in a food store in Haifa.

Asad, whose name translated into "Lion" in Arabic, had been fifteen years old then and was in school at the time of that incident. When he was called out of class and informed of the deaths of his parents, he received the word so coldly that there was some fear he might break under emotional strain. But Asad remained under complete control and not until his mother's brother, an Israeli police sergeant, came from Tel Aviv to take him there into his new home, did Asad break down and weep; and then, out of sight of his uncle, aunt and cousins.

In 1958, his schooling completed, Asad chose to join the police force instead of entering into army service. Because of his rapport with the Arab community, he soon became invaluable as a plain-clothes officer, ferreting out information in the Tel Aviv and Jaffa underworld, that was otherwise difficult to obtain by Jewish officers. As the years passed he rendered assistance to other intelligence services for which he was highly commended and subsequently promoted. Still later, after assisting a team of intelligence agents in breaking up a major spy ring operating out of Jerusalem, Asad was tapped by Mossad for antiguerrilla duty and assigned to Saul Lahav's group.

Physically, Hasbani hardly lived up to the name "Lion." He was slight in stature, for which he compensated by becoming expert in the art of karate, on the weapons range, and with arduous exercises. His features, inherited from his Arab father, were strongly Middle Eastern; thin nose and lips, deep-set black eyes, olive complexion, jet-black hair. He smiled only infrequently, remained a bachelor, and lived in a small apartment in an Arab quarter which he shared with a Moslem girl.

There was little formality between major and sergeant as Hasbani lit a cigarette, crossed one leg over the other and waited. Lahav hung up and handed the slip of creased paper over. Hasbani examined the Arabic script closely. "Atassi," he commented simply, shaking his head. "Troublemaker."

"What of the other names?"

Hasbani again shook his head negatively. "They aren't in our records?"

"No, none of them."

"Where did this come from?"

"From Mousa Awad."

"Awad?" Hasbani's forehead wrinkled into a perplexed frown. "I was present when he and Samdat were searched. Later, I assisted in the interrogation of both."

"It was in one of his shoes. What does this look like to you, Asad?"

A shrug, then, "Another attempt on King Hussein's life."

"It would seem so," Saul agreed. "I would like to arrange a quiet meeting with Major Halawa."

"It can be arranged. When?"

"Tonight, if possible. If not, then tomorrow night. Say nothing more than that it is important. And we will keep this between the two of us."

Hasbani returned the slip to Saul, nodded and went out. Saul rang for Leah and asked her to bring him the daily computer printouts on terrorist activities during his three-day absence, and the reports filed on each action. When she returned with a sheaf of papers and file jackets, he began reading the recapitulation printouts together with each pertinent file.

Two hours later, Hasbani was back. "It is arranged, Major," he announced.

"When and where?"

"Major Halawa is engaged for tonight, but he has agreed to meet you tomorrow night, nine o'clock. Six kilometers east on the road to Na'ur."

"Good. Keep yourself free. I will want you to drive me."

He continued to work, making notes, dictating a summation into a recording machine, occasionally making a phone call to check on a particular item. He then took up the dossier that Leah had brought him from Records and Identification on Hassan Atassi, the Nazareth lawyer.

Atassi was Palestinian-born, from the village of Kfar Kasim, in

1920, the son of the *mukhtar*, who had sent his son to Damascus to study law. By the time he returned in 1946, Hassan saw little in the way of opportunity in Kfar Kasim and after two years, moved to Nazareth, leaving the future of his father's farmlands in the hands of two younger brothers.

The record showed indisputable evidence of Hassan Atassi's close association with known and convicted terrorists, whose cases comprised the greatest number of his clients. Atassi's legal efforts on their behalf were not by any means restricted to Nazareth. However, there was no criminal record attached to his name; only observations and suspicions. It was also noted by immigration authorities that Atassi, on frequent occasions, had traveled beyond Israel's borders to Damascus, Amman and Beirut, twice to Europe, to defend captured Arab terrorists in Paris and Amsterdam.

Back in 1956, there had been an Arab-Israeli incident in Kfar Kasim, which lay close to the Jordanian border in a direct line east of Tel Aviv. A number of Israelis and forty-three Arabs were killed, including Hassan's father and a younger brother. The dossier offered little more than a record of Atassi's subsequent legal activities on behalf of terrorists.

At four o'clock, Saul placed a second call to Shana and told her he would be free for the evening. She at once invited him to share supper with her at her apartment and he accepted. He left then, driving his personal car and, a little more than an hour later, parked in front of her apartment house.

Shana placed the bottle of wine he had brought in the refrigerator to chill, then went about preparing their meal. Saul lounged in the small L-shaped living room, one area set apart by a screen for dining purposes. When she called that she was nearly ready, he put down his newspaper, turned the radio volume up a little in order not to miss the next news broadcast, then set the table and drew the cork from the bottle of wine.

4

It came as no surprise when, early in 1967, Gamal Abdel Nasser began lighting a fire to inflame the Arab world, promising that he was prepared to lead Egypt, and any Arab army that would follow him, in a final war that would drive the Jews into the sea and turn it red with Jewish blood.

These threats escalated as time wore on, thundering into Israeli ears by day and night from Radio Cairo, joined by Syria's Radio Damascus, followed by Nasser's order to blockade the Tiran strait. At which point there was no longer any doubt that the Egyptians and Syrians, encouraged and aided by those other Arab nations that surrounded Israel, were deadly serious. The Soviet Union, chief supplier to the Arab principals of every modern weapon of war, approved and awaited eagerly the demise of the upstart nation, which would enable it to step into preeminent stature in the Middle East.

On Thursday, June 1, 1967, Major General Moshe Dayan had become Israel's defense minister, which did little to lessen the tension and fears that had been steadily mounting throughout the tiny nation. From north to south, east to west, its major cities, towns, small villages, moshavim and kibbutzim heard the threats emanating from Egypt, Syria and other Arab nations, all seeking the bloodletting destruction of Israel and its people. The Israeli government, military, business communities and people in the streets had heard Arab bombast before, but never in such strident, violent bluster.

And while they waited, they prepared. Fighter, bomber and transport planes were brought up to their peak in readiness. Every tank, half-track, personnel carrier, truck and jeep was checked, rechecked, fuel tanks topped off. Ammunition of every type was issued, equipment inspected. Plane, tank and artillery crews slept close by their vehicles, on full alert around the clock, ears attuned to their radios for the word to roll out.

Reserves called up by code designation for each unit were on standby. And suddenly, men and women began leaving their offices, stores, farms and homes to report to predesignated stations; walking, hitchhiking, or being picked up at their homes by unit comrades. Buses, taxis and commercial vehicles were drafted into service to bring Israel's part-time warriors to their gathering points.

At his base in the Negev, Saul Lahav, recently promoted to the rank of captain, studied the battle plan which had been outlined to all tank unit commanders by Brigadier Mendel Ben-Golub. Having committed the orders to memory, Saul set up a blackboard and reviewed each movement and possible alternative with every man under his command. Later, he personally inspected each tank for readiness and instructed the crews to fire up and make short runs to prove their capability to spring into action when he gave the word, Roll out!

Early on the morning of Monday, June fifth, the word was flashed from Brigadier Ben-Golub's desert command headquarters. The war was on. Over the radio that relayed the word to Saul Lahav, he could hear Tel Aviv's air raid sirens in the background.

''*Roll out!*''

The drive toward El Arish, well remembered by Saul from 1956, began.

Long before they reached their objective, Radio Cairo joyously announced to the world at large, ''Tel Aviv is no more! It has been destroyed by our heroic bomber pilots!''

''The count is now one hundred eighteen Israeli planes and two hundred seventy tanks destroyed!''

And over the Israeli communications network came a cheerful feminine voice that sang out, ''Don't believe a word of it. We are still in business. Tel Aviv lives!''

But Israeli anger heightened eagerness to do battle and it became necessary for Lahav to issue constant warnings of restraint to those tanks beside and behind him not to pass his lead vehicle.

Before long, Cairo, Damascus, Amman and the rest of the world knew the true story. By Thursday, with the Egyptians, Jordanians and other token Arab forces thoroughly trounced, the Holy City of Jerusalem finally under Israeli control, they turned toward Syria. In his lead Centurion tank, Lahav ordered his unit into a frontal attack on the high ridges of the Golan to shield bulldozers that were frantically carving roads under massive artillery attack from the Syrian flank positions. Under heavy retaliatory fire, Israeli infantry, mounted on halftracks and on foot behind their tanks, advanced to face Syrian firepower. Supported by planes, they moved into enemy territory.

On Friday, June ninth, a 7:15 A.M., standing beside his Centurion studying a newly-arrived battle map with his crew, a Syrian artillery shell exploded close by. Lahav's gunner and driver were killed instantly, Saul and several others severely wounded. All were quickly moved to a nearby mobile field hospital and given emergency first aid. Saul, with shrapnel deeply embedded in his back and upper right leg, was helicoptered to Hadassah Hospital, where a team of surgeons worked over him for six hours.

On the fourth day, after he had undergone two more operations, Miri was permitted to visit him. Under heavy sedation, with tubes supplying food and blood to keep him alive, there was little more than a silent greeting, an exchange of glances between them. Then, ''Dov?'' he whispered.

''He is fine.'' Tears moistened Miri's eyes as she spoke of their son, now in his seventeenth year. ''He wanted to come. He is working as a medical aide at Tel Hashomer.''

Saul's eyes closed and tears began trickling down over his cheeks. The effort to keep them open was too much. They remained closed and when, later, he was able to open them, Miri had gone.

It was well into July before he was off the critical list. Dov, released from his hospital duties, came to Jerusalem to stay with friends and visited Saul for brief periods every day. Miri drove up on weekends.

Again, there was that dreaded silence between Miri and Saul, an emptiness that was almost visible, with no words that could fill the vacuum. Saul saw, and envied, the closeness between Dov and Miri and was determined to close the gap that existed between himself and his son.

In Miri's absence, he felt certain that a new warmth was beginning to emerge. Dov had grown tall and straight, an excellent student. He talked of his future, determined to become a doctor, encouraged by Miri in that goal. Himself the son of a physician, Saul could find no objections to Dov's ambition and added his own to Miri's encouragement.

Later, doubts increased when Dov revealed to him Miri's plan to have him take his further medical training in Los Angeles, where Robert Hirsch could guide his career and future. It occurred to Saul that should this come to pass, Miri would surely return to America with Dov and remain there, their marriage, a fragile thing at best, at an end.

What more, at this point, did they share but Dov? They had not slept in the same bed, by silent, mutual consent, in over six years;

nor shared their innermost thoughts or feelings, not even companionship. Only Dov's presence had kept them together this long. Both, possibly all three, were aware of the estrangement but none could bring up so important a subject for discussion.

Had Miri wished to leave against Saul's will, he knew she must leave Dov behind, and that would have been an unthinkable course to take. But if she could convince Dov—with Saul's permission—to take his internship and residency in Los Angeles, she would win both her freedom from Saul and Israel as well as maintain control over their son.

Saul convalesced in their home in Tel Aviv, spending much of his day in the sun, driving to the beach alone while Dov was absorbed in his studies at school, visiting army friends at military headquarters. Miri, preoccupied with volunteer hospital work, found ample reasons not to accompany Saul.

Then in January of 1968, fully healed, yet lacking in strength, Saul was summoned by Judah Rosental, now risen to the rank of brigadier general, who convinced him to accept an assignment that would remove him from direct military service—the Antiguerrilla Branch of Mossad, Israel's top intelligence service, a counterpart of the United States C.I.A. The AGB worked closely with its parent organization as well as with AMAN (Military Intelligence), SHIN BEIT (International Security), Foreign Ministry Intelligence, Border Patrol and National Police.

The full-scale operations of AGB appealed to Saul's sense of challenge and, since Rosental was in command, left him little choice. He accepted at once.

For the entire year that ensued, Saul was on the move, studying and analyzing border situations, working with highly skilled investigators and undercover operators as an observer. The work was arduous and demanding, yet the most intriguing he had ever undertaken. On call around the clock, he moved into trouble areas when and where the situation occurred; by car, helicopter or plane; to Eilat, the Negev, Sinai, Galilee, Golan, to the Lebanese, Jordanian and Syrian borders as necessity dictated.

Later, with forged documents and in disguise, he penetrated beyond those borders, making contact with Mossad agents in Iraq, Libya, Egypt and abroad to East and West Berlin, Amsterdam, London, Paris—wherever Arabs were at work planning, training, operating against Israeli embassies, consulates and individual Israelis; returning with valuable information.

*   *   *

On his return to Tel Aviv after a long and exhausting investigation trip abroad, Saul busied himself with a detailed report on various guerrilla groups posing as exchange students in East Berlin who were undergoing strenuous military and sabotage training. Elsewhere in Europe, similar groups were accumulating vast stocks of weapons, ammunition and explosives of every type, which were being shipped to them from their respective homelands in boxes labeled HOUSEHOLD GOODS.

After submitting this evaluation to Rosental, Saul experienced an emotional letdown. The year was 1969. Dov was nineteen and in medical school, deeply immersed in his studies. The situation between Miri and himself had not bettered; in fact, the silences between them had increased in depth with neither able to bring himself to discuss the problem.

Saul's seven-day leave ended and, gratefully, he returned to duty. His first act, on reaching his office, was to read a letter of commendation from the chief of Mossad, General Bartok. Awed, he got out a copy of his massive report and reread it. When he reached the last page, he began to prepare a rather remarkable document.

Considering the population and area that was the state of Israel, and the vast populations of the lands of the enemy which surrounded it, he methodically recorded facts and figures obtained from military files, books, magazines and newspapers that showed precisely what Israel was faced with in terms of manpower, planes, tanks, artillery and the huge supply base that was Russia. No item was too insignificant to be omitted. And once having committed those facts and figures to paper, he next began to outline a plan whose enormity shocked even himself—a plan that admitted to Israel's vulnerability and possible defeat; even total destruction.

He called it the Israeli Underground Resistance Plan (URP), and suggested it was time for Israel to face up to that extreme possibility; that steps should be taken at once to secretly provide caches and stockpiles of military equipment and supplies, to be hidden in mountain areas, in caves, buried in valleys and deserts; areas from which those who escaped would be able to fight back in the same manner that underground forces in occupied countries had fought the Nazis.

His URP foresaw the possibility that Israel might be abandoned by the Western world, the United Nations, even by its first and most ardent supporter and supplier, the United States of America, and be forced to go it alone. He even suggested that the Arab oil nations might foreseeably band together and force this abandonment program on the Western world by creating an oil embargo that would surely bring their industrial complexes to a halt.

URP proposed that a special cadre of experts be formed at once to train selected men and women in underground tactics, in sabotage and demolition, drawing upon those who had fought in the Polish, Russian, French, Dutch and Norwegian resistance movements. Meticulously, he gave minute details to its formation from strike force units to individual saboteurs, designed to expand as necessary. He outlined the logistics: methods of transport, food collection and distribution, the means to make vehicle repairs from stockpiled parts.

Once completed, there was the question of how he would present his plan and kept it hidden for two months before he could bring himself to disclose it to Judah Rosental and risk the general's ridicule. Finally one night, he made his decision. He wrapped the bulky, bound material in brown paper and took it to Rosental's house in suburban Tel Aviv.

"What do we have here, Saul?" the general asked when Saul handed him the package.

"Something that has been developing in my mind ever since I returned from Europe." Then, half apologetically, "It may be something that should be destroyed and forgotten, but I hope you will read it."

Rosental weighed the package in both hands and with a twinkle in his eyes, said, "I'll do that much, Saul, but I don't think I can have an answer for you by morning, you understand."

"No, that wouldn't be possible. Any time you can give it—"

"All right, Saul, I will read it when I have the time. Will you stay and have coffee with Toba and me, then maybe you can tell me a little something about it, give me an idea—"

"No, but thank you. If I did that, I might spoil the effect. Besides, Dov is home for the weekend and I want to be with him. *Shalom*, Judah."

When three weeks had elapsed and he had had no word from Rosental, Saul began thinking that his plan was not worthy of a report; but a few days later, he received a message from Rosental's secretary, asking him to call at his home that evening. Saul's intuition told him that the invitation concerned his URP and his spirits soared upward.

On the table in the general's study lay the URP, but it was not until Toba had brought the coffee to them that Rosental acknowledged it by placing one hand on its bulk.

"Saul," he said, "I have read your plan and studied it carefully. I have shown it to General Bartok, who sent it along to the High

Command without comment, but just to have sent it higher was a measure of his silent approval. Of sorts. I might add that all who saw it there were impressed with your contribution.'' Rosental paused and smiled, then lighted a cigarette and continued.

"For myself, I am very pleased that such a carefully thought out plan has come from someone in my own department.''

"But—'' Saul interjected, anticipating what must surely follow.

"But, of course, it was rejected.'' Again a pause, then, "Saul, the mood of the High Command refuses to accept the proposition of defeat. Israel cannot allow itself to entertain that possibility. Our whole nation, military and civilian, must gear its thinking and mood to one fact of life: to muster its total resources for the defense of our land and nothing less than victory in the event of another war.

"Your plan was given full consideration and after much debate—yes, there were some who were wholly in favor of it—was highly complimented. To alleviate any disappointment or rejection you may be feeling, let me add that on the defense minister's recommendation, copies of the URP were made for further study by various services. Also, I would like to retain this original for my own files . . .''

"Of course,'' Saul acquiesced quickly.

''. . . and offer you our collective thanks for your efforts.''

If Saul needed more to reassure himself that his URP was appreciated, it came two months later in the form of a promotion to the rank of major. And with it, a transfer into Rosental's planning group.

When the relationship between Miri and Saul Lahav had reached its nadir in 1972, he met Shoshana Altman for the first time. He had gone to the Jerusalem office of Military Intelligence to examine their file on a Syrian intelligence agent who had been apprehended in Jaffa while consorting with a known Arab terrorist then under close surveillance. In the Syrian's possession was a list of several names of Jerusalem residents which required checking into.

Saul conferred with Colonel Amos Zarbat, an American-born Israeli whose parents had moved to Israel when he was four. Zarbat reached for his phone, saying, "I'll get you together with our head of R and I. If we have anything on these people, the lieutenant will know at once.''

It was almost too much to believe that this remarkably attractive young woman was as knowledgeable and intelligent as their first hour together proved her to be. Her uniform skirt was short, revealing several inches of elegant thigh, but even more distracting to Saul was the obvious fact that beneath her blouse, she was not wearing a bra. She flashed a brilliant smile as she examined the list of names, then disappeared into a file room, returning moments later with two dossiers.

"Two out of three," she said in triumph. "Not bad, Major."

"No, not bad at all. If I can locate either of these, I'm sure they will lead me to the other."

"Good luck. If I can be of more help—"

"Thank you, Lieutenant. I'll be sure to call on you."

As the investigation progressed, other names cropped up and Saul found himself relying more and more on Shana's knowledge of Arab and foreign agents, aliases and code names, providing him with heretofore unsuspected members of the same network centered in and around Jerusalem.

Soon, their association moved beyond the mere checking out of confidential files, discussing their contents, checking them in again. At lunch together, whenever possible, they began exchanging more personal confidences and when, finally, he casually revealed that he was married, the father of a son who was studying medicine, she said calmly, "I know, Major."

"Someone took the trouble to discuss me with you?" he asked with surprise and some annoyance.

"No. My own natural curiosity. I had your military file pulled for me one day last week when I was in Tel Aviv on business. It is available to this office, you know."

"Anything beyond that?" he asked, fully aware that the files of all personnel in sensitive intelligence work were open only to their superiors.

"No," Shana admitted. "Your current file is sealed."

He leaned closer to her, smiling, and whispered conspiratorially, "Then ask me what you want to know. If it is within reasonable bounds, I'll answer your questions."

"No," she replied with a matching smile, "I think I may have gone too far already."

During his third week in Jerusalem, he found himself devoting as much thought to Shana Altman as to the investigation at hand. On that Friday evening, he decided not to go home to Tel Aviv for the weekend. He arranged to leave the MI building just as Shana was slipping on her jacket and met her on the pavement as she made her exit. They spoke for a few moments, then Saul said, "Are you busy this evening, Lieutenant?"

"No, not really, Major. A book I've been wanting to finish. A few other things that are always left for weekends."

"Have supper with me," he urged. "I'm not in a mood to eat alone tonight."

"No deep, dark investigation to follow up, Major?"

"Saul, please," he corrected. "This is a purely unofficial request."

"Saul, then."

"That's much better. And there isn't anything that won't hold until Sunday, Shana. It's Shoshana, isn't it?"

"Only on my birth, school and military records. Shana everywhere else."

"You haven't answered my question. Supper?"

"Isn't your family expecting you for Shabbat?"

"My family has learned long ago to expect me when I arrive home. And I prefer to spend this weekend in Jerusalem." It was a lame explanation and he was made aware of it by the quick raising of her eyebrows; his glib statement was not supportable.

Shana hesitated, then said, "Yes, Saul. I think I would enjoy an unofficial supper this evening." As they started toward his car, she said, "Why don't we pick up a few things in the market and let me fix supper for us at my apartment. Would you like that?"

"I would like that very much."

They shopped together, Saul exhilarated by the adventure and his own daring. He was fully conscious of the difference of some twelve or fifteen years in their ages, yet there was his extraordinary attraction to her that stimulated him into seeking a closer association.

Over the rather simple supper, supplemented by two bottles of excellent wine, she talked of her youth in Tel Aviv, the death of her parents within a year of each other when she was sixteen, left without brothers or sisters; of joining the army and her decision to remain in the service.

Later, listening to a musical program on the radio, the subject turned to himself and his own military experiences; which led to his marriage and, unaccountably, he felt a need to continue on into its deterioration, although at no time did Saul voice any criticism of his wife. He said, finally, "What puzzles me most of all is why a woman as beautiful as you has remained unattached for so long."

"A lovely compliment, and thank you."

"I am still puzzled."

"I know a dozen ways to avoid answering you," she said impishly.

"That implies a thirteenth answer. The truth."

She fell silent for a few moments, coming to a decision; then said, "I am what you call unattached by personal choice. I have had three strong attachments that ended in death. My father and mother, whom I adored—" She paused.

Saul said softly, "And the third?"

"A man I loved. A captain who was killed on the third day of the Sixty-seven War. We lived together for a year and were going to be married that same month. Since then, I have avoided any similar permanent attachment that might lead to a tragic ending. In that respect, I suppose I am a coward. Does that answer your question?"

"Not really. The obvious question is, why won't you permit yourself to live above and beyond the past?"

"I don't think I like this subject anymore."

"Forgive me. I'm sorry I intruded."

"It isn't so much an intrusion as the way things are."

Again, he said, "I'm sorry, Shana. I don't have the right, but it is because I suddenly see a certain sadness in you that doesn't seem . . . right, shouldn't be there in your eyes."

"Why would you notice something like that?"

"I don't know *why*, only that I . . . I care."

When she did not reply, he stood up and said, "It is getting late. I should be going."

She got up from the sofa, but made no move to show him to the door. He turned toward her and took her into his arms. "Shana—" he began, then leaned forward and kissed her lips. She brought her arms up and held him, returning the kiss.

"I don't want to go," he said in a whisper.

"Then don't, Saul. Stay here with me tonight."

"I want to. Very much. Are you sure you want this?"

"No, I'm not sure. I only know I want you to stay."

During the following week, Saul lived in a state of mental turmoil, rushing through each day in order to meet Shana at her apartment at night, not once conscious of wrongdoing or trespass against Miriam, only the realization that his affair with Shana would continue. Must continue. He spent the next two weekends with her and finally the case was closed and it became necessary for him to return to Tel Aviv to assist the prosecutor who would bring the four men and two women who had been arrested to trial.

That first night, a Friday, across the table from Miri, became a near silent disaster. She placed the food on the table between them and sat unsmiling, unreceptive and unresponsive to any talk about the work that had kept him preoccupied in Jerusalem.

"Where is Dov?" he asked finally.

"He is on duty at the hospital this weekend."

"And you, Miri?"

"As you see me, Saul. It is always the same with me."

"Yes," he replied, and that simple "yes" now unleashed something venal in her.

"Yes," she repeated incisively. "And how is it with your young mistress in Jerusalem, Saul?"

"Ah—" Shocked almost beyond replying, his knuckles showed white as he gripped his knife and fork tighter, face crimsoning.

"Yes, Saul. Did you think a thing like that goes unnoticed forever? That I don't have friends—or enemies—who are eager to pass on such joyful news to me? Shall I tell you of at least four telephone calls that were made to me anonymously during the past several weeks?"

He recovered slowly, staring at the look of triumph on her face, then said in a low, calm voice, "Miri, why should you even show you care? What have we been to each other for so long but acquaintances, even strangers sharing the same house, but no more?"

Pure anger flooded her face and next words. "Damn you and your damned Israeli arrogance!" she shouted. "Whose fault is it that we have become strangers? How much time have you spent at home so that we could be more than that?"

"I am a soldier, Miri. I was a soldier when we first met, when we were married. I tried to tell you what it would be like, the duty I owe my country."

"Even above your duty to your wife and son? What about other men with families? Are you the only one who must count Israel above family? To the point where you needed to acquire an army whore to fill your lonely hours? And what about me, am I supposed to go looking for a man to fill mine?"

"Miri, Miri—"

Bitter tears had begun flooding her eyes. "If only for Dov's sake—" she began, then broke down, unable to finish the sentence. Saul waited, experiencing an intolerable sensation of regret that his infidelity had been discovered, but none for his deep feelings for Shana. When Miri's tears had been wiped away with her napkin, Saul, still seated at the table, said, "If it is only for Dov's sake, Miri, what have we, you and I? Why should we be bound together when we could both be happier apart?"

With choked words, she said, "If you are . . . are . . . suggesting divorce, the answer is no. I can't hurt Dov that way and I won't make it easy for you to go live with your whore mistress. I won't!"

"Then what do you want?"

It seemed to him, from her quick response, that she had been waiting—for how long? how many years?—for him to ask that one vital question; and now, regaining full control of her voice, she said firmly, "In eighteen months, and I count each day, Dov will be ready to begin his internship. I intend to take him home with me to Los Angeles, to take it there. I have already written my father to arrange it."

"How long have you been planning this?" he asked.

"Long enough."

"And if I refuse permission? Without it, you know he can't leave the country. I have the means and power to prevent you from doing such a thing."

"Do you really?" she said scornfully. "Don't try to stop me, Saul, or I will create a scandal that will ruin you, and your mistress with you."

"So it comes to blackmail now."

"Call it whatever you wish, but don't try to stop me."

"And if I agree?"

"Then you can have her and I won't stir up anything. Only remember, Dov is mine, and when he is ready, he and I will leave together."

"And you will never let him return, which I am sure is part of your plan."

"There is that posibility, but by then he will be an adult, a doctor. The decision will be his to make."

"But only after you and your family have had him exclusively to yourselves to undermine against me, against Israel."

With an air of victory, she said, "Take it or leave it, Saul. I think you have little choice."

"I'll think about it."

She smiled grimly. "By the time you decide, it may be too late. You are more a stranger to Dov than you realize."

On the following morning, after a sleepless night, Saul drove to Tel Hashomer to visit with Dov, studying him more closely now that there was a possibility he might lose him. Dov had grown fully tall as Saul, perhaps more slender; white-jacketed, stethoscope adding to his professional bearing and dignity, fully at home in hospital surroundings. And with Miri's delicate features and good looks. They embraced, but Saul detected a sense of detachment and thought of Miri's last words to him, as strangers.

"I am sorry you came at such a busy time," Dov said. "I am on duty in the emergency room and there are many patients there to see."

"I understand, Dov. I only stopped by to tell you I must return to Jerusalem. Duty."

"Yes, of course. I know how it is."

They embraced again and Saul left. A sad, brief encounter. He began to understand now what Miri meant and the thought depressed him. The boy had become a man almost unnoticed by his father.

Dov, Saul realized, would have to be inordinately naïve, even stupid, not to take Saul's frequent absences as unusual. That his mother and father had shared separate bedrooms for years could not have gone unnoticed, even if not remarked upon. Whose fault, his? Miri's?

It no longer mattered, hadn't mattered for so long. Only the end result faced him now.

He had for long lived with fear and, in a manner, come to grips with it; but he found it difficult to live with guilt. For the next few weeks, he tried to make amends by remaining at home as much as possible, but Miri refused to soften to his awkward approaches. The years of silent hostility had opened too wide a gap between them to be closed at this stage. In time, he gave up any attempt at reconciliation.

More than a year later, Israel was once again confronted with a grave situation, the possibility of a fourth war in the quarter of a century of her existence as a state. Combined intelligence services made her acutely aware that Egypt and Syria, as in the past, had been mobilizing equipment and manpower on a large scale. Real, or threat?

The government, however, could no longer afford the political risk of taking the initiative. If she overreacted to a *threat* of war with a preventive attack on two fronts, her diplomatic isolation, she had been informed, would be further deepened, friendship with, and reliance on support from, the United States seriously imperiled.

Economically, there was an equally great risk. To fully mobilize her reserves would empty her farms, factories, universities and offices of men and women and bring vital industrial and agricultural production to a grinding halt. This, if the Arab threat proved to be only that, the cost of such mobilization of manpower and equipment would result in a tremendous economic loss.

Hung on the horns of dilemma, Israel was taken, not by total surprise, but not fully prepared at 2:15 P.M. on Saturday, October 6, 1973, when air raid sirens broke the solemn quiet of Yom Kippur, the holiest day of the Jewish year. Having been persuaded not be be found guilty of firing the first shot, lest worldwide opinion be turned against her, Israel paid a heavy price.

Mobilization came swiftly, but late. The east bank of the Suez, unaccountably undermanned, perhaps because of the High Holy Day, was overrun by the Egyptians who crossed in amphibious

BTR-50 armored carriers, tracked assault boats, rubber dinghies and self-propelled pontoons. The Israeli defenders, in widely separated strongholds never meant to withstand an all-out offensive without support, were routed from land captured in 1967. There were, in fact, only 450 men holding the line along the entire Suez Canal on that day. East of the Golan Heights, Syria simultaneously unleashed a massive attack with her planes, missiles, tanks and heavy artillery, moving in full force.

The Israelis fought back brilliantly, with the desperate knowledge that, as in her previous wars, she must win. Or die as a nation. As a people. Yet, when she had surrounded the entire Egyptian Third Army at Bitter Lake and moved tanks and manpower onto Egyptian soil for the first time in her history, the Russians argued bitterly in the United Nations for an immediate cease-fire, in fear that the Israelis would race westward into Cairo.

Pressure from Moscow, Washington and the United Nations finally forced the cease-fire and, as it had happened before, Egypt turned defeat into victory with her claims of superiority over a slice of the Sinai which had been gained for them by the political machinations of outside powers. What was of greater significance was that the Arab and Third World nations were willing to believe that enormous piece of public relations fiction.

But on Saul and Miriam Lahav, the war had a very special and tragic impact. At its outset, Dov Lahav was mobilized into a unit to set up a field hospital in the Golan Heights. He went eagerly, even joyously, to put his medical talents to use, for the first time to work with an experienced medical-surgical field team.

In that setting, working every moment of the day and night, Dov felt he had truly come of age. In the operating tents, he assisted by direction; in the emergency tents, he improvised as necessity demanded and was highly complimented by senior physicians and surgeons for his growing professionalism.

At the outbreak, Saul pleaded with Judah Rosental to permit him to return to the field with a tank battalion. Within hours, he was in the Sinai, racing toward the Suez. This time, he found, it was a far different war. The Egyptians were better equipped and far more skilled with their weaponry than they had been in forty-eight, fifty-six or sixty-seven. And, despite an unwillingness to accept the fact, the Israelis had been caught napping, reaching the fields of action belatedly.

And, finally, when the firing stopped, Saul sat within view of Bitter Lake with the guns of every Israeli tank and artillery piece looking down the throats of the entrapped Egyptian 3rd Army. Awaiting orders.

Then one came through on his radio from a rear command post. "Major Lahav! Major Lahav! Come in!"

Saul could scarcely believe that an uncoded call, under these circumstances, would be made to an individual. He snatched up the microphone and shouted, "Lahav here!"

"Colonel Philip Shapiro here, Major. You are ordered to return to Tel Aviv at once. A helicopter is on its way to pick you up. Stand by."

"Now?" Saul demanded furiously. "What can be more important than being here?"

"No arguments, Lahav," the colonel retorted testily. "Major General Rosental's orders. Turn your command over and prepare to return. Over and out."

He fumed and cursed all the way back to the city, where he was met by a driver who took him directly to headquarters. The general's suite swarmed with people in uniform and civilian dress, coming, going, or waiting while the receptionist and two assistants answered the constantly ringing telephones, questions from new arrivals, directing callers of lesser rank to the offices of staff assistants.

As he entered the bustling scene, Rosental's secretary broke off a conversation with a man he recognized as a foreign ministry officer of high rank. She excused herself and went directly to Saul.

"Major, the general asked to be notified the moment you arrived. Please wait in Colonel Kohn's office and I will ring him."

"Thank you, Hannah."

"How is it going at Suez?"

"Contained at the moment." Then with a touch of bitterness, "If only they hadn't stopped us."

"I know. Go right in, Major. It may be a little while. There are so many people waiting to see him."

In Omri Kohn's outer office, those next due to see the general waited in a less chaotic atmosphere, chatting, smoking, drinking coffee; anxiety written on each face. Then Kohn emerged from his private office and went to Saul. "Come with me," he said abruptly.

"Where?"

"The general's private room to which he can escape for a few minutes when it becomes necessary. Come."

He ushered Saul into and through his office where three men sat, then along a hallway and into a small hideaway office that contained a bare desk, leather chair and one visitor's chair, a sofa. There were no telephones, no filing cabinets. An austere retreat where Rosental could work or relax without interruption.

"He knows you are here, Saul. He will be with you as soon as he can interrupt his meeting," Kohn said and left him. Moments later, a clerk brought coffee to him. He drank it, then stretched out on the sofa and was asleep almost before his head touched the hard armrest.

He awoke to the pressure of Judah Rosental's hand on his arm and looked up into a face that showed deep weariness from the lack of sleep, darkened circles showing under his eyes.

"*Shalom*, Saul. What is the news at the front?"

"*Shalom*, Judah. You probably know a lot more than I. In a tank, we see only what is in front of us." Then, as though suddenly remembering his recall, "Why, Judah? Why call me back now?"

"I wouldn't have done it under ordinary circumstances. Calm down and listen to me."

Recognizing the subtle difference in Rosental's usually crisp, rapid-fire official tone, now gentle, the heat in Saul's voice evaporated. "What is it, Judah?"

"Bad news, I'm afraid, Saul. It is very hard to find a way to make it easier—"

Alarmed now, "*What is it*?"

"Dov. Late yesterday afternoon."

"Dov? *Killed*?"

"I'm sorry, Saul. He was working with a surgical team in an emergency tent. It was hit by a Syrian air-to-surface missile that somehow got through. Pure chance. Nine were killed, Dov among them."

"Oh, my God . . . my *God* . . . Miri—"

"I broke the news to her myself last night. I don't need to tell you how she took it. Go see her. She is under medical care at Tel Hashomer."

In her hospital room, under partial sedation, Miri lay upon her bed immersed in deep grief and shock. Her lifeless eyes were open and on Saul as he entered the room and approached the bed, but otherwise took no notice of his presence. Nor did she react when he called her name and, after several attempts to gain her attention, took her rigid hand into his own; but she drew it out from his grasp, frowning as though in deep pain, and tried unsuccessfully to turn on her left side, away from him. Failing in this, she closed her eyes and lay in a semicatatonic state.

Outside, the harried doctor he questioned shrugged and said, "Major, it is difficult to help a patient who does not wish to be helped. Your wife is in deep shock over her loss, a very understandable reaction. Otherwise, we can find nothing wrong with her. It is up to her now.''

"Isn't there something—'' Saul began, but the doctor cut him off shortly.

"Major, there are many seriously wounded men here, more arriving every few minutes who need immediate attention. I'm sorry. Perhaps in a few days, she will—'' He shrugged and was gone.

Saul returned to his house and placed a call to Robert Hirsch in Los Angeles and was told there would be an indefinite delay in getting the call through. He remained at the house throughout the day and night, waiting, mourning his loss. And, waiting, he went to Dov's room where he touched his son's personal possessions—clothing, books, mementos of his childhood and school years, the odds and ends a boy and young adult collects and treasures, takes with him into marriage, saves to show his own children some day; cherished photographs of school friends, girls Saul had never seen or known, a football, football shorts and shoes. (When, Saul wondered, did Dov play football? How was it possible he didn't know Dov had engaged in the sport? Had he known any of the girls in these photographs intimately? He hoped so.)

Sometime during the following afternoon, after phoning the hospital to check on Miri's progress, told she was doing as well as could be expected, he continued to wait, dozing next to the telephone, drinking endless cups of coffee, chain-smoking. He put together a meager supper of odds and ends he found in the refrigerator, listened to the radio without hearing or understanding the news reports that flooded the air. At two o'clock in the morning, he was awakened by the telephone. He reached for it with alacrity, expecting to hear Robert Hirsch's voice. Instead, it was Colonel Kohn, apologizing for calling at this late hour, explaining that the people at headquarters were working around the clock.

Saul, in turn, explained his own situation to Kohn briefly; that he was waiting for a line through to Miri's parents in Los Angeles, adding, "I will come in as soon as the call comes through."

Kohn said, "That won't be necessary, Saul. The general wanted me to tell you to take the time necessary to see your problem through, then phone him before you come in. Get as much rest as you can."

Saul fell asleep in the wing chair beside the phone and was startled awake at nine A.M. by the overseas operator, who informed him his party was on the line and to please limit the length of his call. Transmission was difficult, but he was eventually able to make himself understood; first to Robert, now seventy-two years old, who broke down, weeping and unable to speak intelligibly; then to Ruth, who took the news stonily, almost accusingly. Then Robert Hirsch returned to the phone and begged Saul to send his daughter home to him and Ruth, adding, "where she belongs," which Saul took as an indictment. He hung up in tears of remorse and guilt.

Later, after two cups of coffee, he showered, dressed in a fresh uniform and drove to his Tel Aviv office. He waited for two hours before the general was free to see him, then only for a few minutes. After offering his sympathy for Miri's condition, he said, "Saul, the situation at the moment is . . . ah . . . somewhat stable, in that we are waiting. Holding and waiting on both fronts. Whether we move in or pull back is in other hands. Russia, the United States, the United Nations. We are no longer the masters of our own fate."

"Shall I return to my field unit?"

Rosental shook his head negatively. "There is no need at the moment. Colonel Kohn has your orders on his desk, signed by me this morning. Seven days leave, starting today. Miriam needs you much more than we do."

During that week, he remained in Tel Aviv. Any thought he may have had of visiting Shana in Jerusalem had evaporated from his mind. He visited Miri at the hospital every day, sometimes dropping by at night, but despite word from the nursing staff that she had become more alert and responsive, she seemed no better when he entered her room, usually finding her asleep. Or feigning.

When his leave was over, he reported back for duty. Instead of being returned to his unit, Rosental sent him on a short tour of the Lebanese border to check the villages to make certain that the settlement guards, older men drafted for that duty in the absence of those younger and in the reserves, were maintaining round-the-clock vigilance against infiltrators, who had suddenly become more bold. He found the guard force alert and effective, but in need of more weapons and ammunition, which he ordered distributed at once.

On the last day of his journey, five days later, he stopped off in Haifa to telephone the hospital, as he had whenever possible; only to be surprised with the news that Miri had been discharged on the day before. Astonished, he tried to reach her at home, but there was no answer. He drove quickly to Tel Aviv, relieved greatly when he saw her car standing in the street in front of the house. It had been in the garage during the period of her hospitalization.

But on entering the house, he discovered she was gone, taking with her most of her clothes and personal possessions, the pictures of Dov and other of his mementos.

A phone call to the security chief at Lod Airport confirmed that Miri had flown out the afternoon before on a resumed El Al flight, ticketed to Los Angeles via New York. A neighbor then volunteered the news that Miri had asked him to drive her to the airport on the day before, then returned the car to where Saul had found it.

When, on the following night, he was able to get a call through to Los Angeles, Robert Hirsch answered. In a chilled voice, he informed Saul that Miri had arrived safely earlier that day, but refused to speak with him; adding that he would be hearing from her attorney shortly.

Thus the beginning of the end of Saul Lahav's twenty-four-year marriage.

5

Shana stirred, then came fully awake. Saul was still deep in sleep, lying on his left side facing her. She could hear his smooth, even breathing and, looking across his inert body, saw the first very faint streaks of dawn through the open window. A soft, cool breeze was blowing, sending the filmy window curtains billowing into the room. She turned and checked the clock on the night table: four twenty. It had been set the night before for four thirty so that Saul could get an early start back to Tel Aviv. She decided to allow him the extra ten minutes of sleep.

She studied Saul's face as he slept; the finely chiseled profile, the wave of his thick, sandy hair, with only a light touch of white at the temples; remembering the sparkle in his eyes that glinted with pleasure or flashed hotly when angered. He was an exquisite lover and a man of many moods; but essentially a kind, generous man who was quick to praise, reluctant to find fault.

For all the difference in their ages, she had known from the very start that this was a man she could respect, admire, and love. Had he been happily, even satisfactorily married, she also knew their involvement could never have happened. She had not made the mistake of asking for more than he was prepared to give and their relationship had not only endured, but become stronger. And richer.

Once it was over with Miri—.

The alarm went off then and Shana deliberately closed her eyes and feigned sleep. She felt the movement as Saul came alert, then reached out across her to shut off the buzzing alarm. He got out of bed quietly and she heard him shuffling across the carpet to the bathroom to shower and shave. When she heard the water turned on fully, she rose, put on her nightgown and robe and went to the kitchen to prepare their breakfast.

Finished in the bathroom, Saul emerged to find Shana not only awake, but busy in the kitchen, the aroma of fresh coffee sharpening his appetite. He dressed quickly. At the stove, the eggs were beginning to brown at their edges. Saul kissed her cheek.

"Pour the coffee, Saul," she said. "This will be ready in exactly ten seconds."

"I'm sorry I woke you," he apologized.

"I don't mind. The two times of day I like best are early morning and twilight, before the day begins and when it is coming to an end." She slid the first two eggs onto his plate, the other two on another plate for herself. Saul poured the coffee, the toast popped up and the meal was begun. "You can't stay over another day?" she asked.

"I'm afraid not. Back to Tel Aviv. Something I need to take care of later today."

"There is a possibility I could have some confidential reports to take to Tel Aviv later today. Will you be free?"

"I don't know, but I can't count on anything today. I'll hate to miss you if you drive in. The thing I have to do will take me across the border into Jordan. An old friend I must visit."

She smiled at that. "I know the kind of old friends you have in Jordan. Dangerous?"

"No. Just a quiet visit to exchange some friendly information that may be important to them."

"Maybe this weekend?"

"If I'm free. I'll phone you."

"Be careful, Saul."

"I'm always careful, Shana. Not always wise, perhaps, but certainly careful."

It was a few minutes before five o'clock and Jerusalem was hardly awake. A chilly land breeze stirred leaves and blew street debris into swirls that swept dust and small scraps along gutters and pavements. Here and there a few pedestrians moved along slowly, heads burrowed into their jackets and sweaters, on their way to open restaurants, shops or offices. Cars and trucks were moving into the city from the outer roads, carrying produce and other foodstuffs to markets and stores to accommodate the frenetic hustle and bustle that would commence within the next hour and continue throughout the entire day.

Saul was happy to leave the hodgepodge of homes and commercial buildings behind for the open countryside that lay ahead. The raw and cultivated earth smelled fresh with dew, a transient odor of orange blossoms in the clean, as yet unpolluted air. Green and gold shone amid limestone outcroppings; white, pink, orange and red flowers were beginning to raise their heads to greet the new day from private gardens. The ridges of nearby hills and far-off mountains glittered under the first rays of the sun.

For Saul, this was the beauty, the splendor of Israel. Looking back as he came into a wide turn, he could see the glint of the sun on familiar structures in the Old City behind its gray stone walls. This was its aliveness and vibrance, even as it stirred sleepily before coming fully awake; so vastly different from the emptiness of the desert under a blazing, relentless sun from which there was no escape.

The desert. Negev. Sinai. Mile after mile of waterless nothingness over which the ancients of history had trodden, fought over as though it were priceless, as modern men had ridden over it in tanks. And, in truth, it was priceless to Israel as a barrier against an implacable enemy who sought to destroy her. Lose it or give it up and the enemy would move in once again to aim its guns at the hearts of three and a half million people who had nowhere else to go.

And, driving along, remembering the past in fragmentary flashes, he felt the greatness of his love, a passion that bound him to this land that was stronger than any other emotion he had ever known, perhaps because of the ever-present threat to its security from so many who sought to deny Israel the right to live in peace.

Inside its borders, there were other problems, admittedly. Political, economic, personal. Independence, such as it was, had brought Israel the phenomenon of political parties; so many and so ideologically varied that the defense minister had recently quipped, "With so many political parties of our own constantly at war with each other, who needs Arabs?"

There was also the constant flow of immigrants to settle, house, find work for. Many, unaccustomed to freedom, found it difficult to blend into and accept life in a free society and were clamoring to return to their native lands. In terms of private earnings and massive taxes, most were like lost children. Also, there was the schizophrenia of those from free countries like the United States and Canada in religious matters, complicated by dual citizenship and dual loyalties; and resented by the Sabras for the tax exemptions allowed immigrants which were not available to the native-born. Many were surprised to learn that the strict orthodoxy they had expected to encounter was confined to relatively small groups; dismayed by the zealots in communities like Mea Shearim where, to drive through on the Sabbath in a car would bring down curses and even physical attacks with stones.

Despite its multiple internal and external problems, however, Israel had survived and even prospered, in a sense, and Saul loved it with the optimism of a visionary. It was a lusty land of strident voices and colors. Yemen, Africa, Turkey, Iraq, Syria, Libya, Egypt, Algeria, Morocco and many other nations were represented by its Jews seeking their own homeland, joining the Russian, American, French, German and British who had emigrated earlier. A land of strangers, speaking strange languages, of strange cultures, wearing strange garb, bound together in the hope that their descendants would not be strange to one another.

But for the moment, there remained that single missing, yet vital element—peace.

Saul reached his office shortly after the arrival of Leah Barak, whose services as secretary he shared with three other members of the department. The early edition papers were stacked neatly to one side of his desk, a copy of the morning report printout on his desk pad; a combined military, police, intelligence review, in condensed form, of pertinent activities concerning enemy activities at home and abroad.

Leah brought him a cup of freshly brewed coffee and several telephone message slips. He glanced at the slips, found nothing that required his immediate attention, and resumed his examination of the printout, searching for any item that might hint at the presence of the faceless UPFP. Without knowing exactly what he was looking for, he found nothing.

He had no need to get the Sokolnikov memorandum from his files in order to review the questions it had conjured in his mind at the first reading in Bashra. They came back to him easily, thought of as separate pieces of a jigsaw puzzle he must put together; or like a deck of playing cards with many jokers. Question: Where were the missing pieces—or the jokers—in the document?

Musing over his thoughts, he felt alone. To his knowledge, only three people in his organization knew of the memorandum—Judah Rosental, Omri Kohn, himself. Therefore, he could not discuss the subject with anyone but those two; and Judah had closed the door for now. But there was still Omri.

He went out of his office. Leah, sitting at her desk in the outer room, looked up. "Are you leaving, Major?"

"Only down the hallway to speak to Colonel Kohn."

"Your telephone messages—"

"When I return, Leah."

He was disappointed to learn that Kohn was out of his office. He and Rosental, the secretary informed him, were in conference with General Bartok and she had no indication of when they were expected to return. "Shall I call you, Major?" she asked.

"No, I'll try to see him later. It is not important."

He went back to his office and returned his telephone calls, then went to lunch at a nearby restaurant. He joined three men he knew at their table and enjoyed the respite from officialdom for the next hour. Two were from Military Intelligence, the third from the Foreign Office and none, naturally, would discuss any matter that pertained to his work in public.

After lunch, Saul went into closed session with Omri Kohn, who brought him up to date on the activities of those undercover agents working in surrounding Arab countries; supplying information on shipments of arms into those countries, planes and equipment, movement of troops in above-normal strength, maneuvers in the field, on terrorist organizations, splinter groups, and more recently established operational camps in Lebanon, Jordan and Syria. Most disturbing was the possibility of the sale of some three hundred million dollars in offensive weapons to Jordan, which Hussein reportedly stated would be used in concert with Syria in an attack upon Israel, which came on the heels of a new pact between those two countries.

Saul asked that word be passed among their underground agents to try to pick up some word, however slight or distantly relative, of any new group or organization operating under the UPFP name. Kohn agreed, subject to Rosental's approval of the request.

Later, he went to the Communications Section and made photocopies of the slip taken from Mousa Awad's shoe, then returned to his office and placed the original in a special file.

Saul ate his supper alone, in the same restaurant where he had taken his midday meal, wondering if Shana had come to Tel Aviv, regretting now that he had not made some arrangement to meet her, if only to share this meal together. He finished quickly and returned to his office, where Leah was ready to leave for the day. He applied himself to clearing away the remainder of the lesser odds and ends that had accumulated during his aborted leave of absence.

Twenty minutes later, Asad Hasbani knocked on his door and entered. "When you are ready, Major," he said in his usually soft, emotionless voice.

Saul checked his watch. "In an hour, Asad. That will give us time to spare."

"I will wait in the outer office."

An hour later, his desk cleared, they were on their way to the Abdullah Bridge, dressed in kaffiyehs and dark robes over their normal clothing. In an unmarked car, they crossed the border without incident. Hasbani slowed when they reached the six-kilometer mark agreed upon, where a sleek Ferrari Superamerica was parked just off the road that led to Na'ur. Behind the wheel of the Ferrari sat Major Abdullah Halawa, a distant cousin of the Hashimite king and a staff member of the palace guard security force; an extraordinarily handsome man of about thirty years, educated and trained for military service in England. The smart cut of his khaki uniform showed evidence of years spent in that country before returning to Jordan as a member of its famed Arab Legion, later brought into the palace for security duty. For two years now, the personal safety of his royal cousin was his principal concern.

He watched as the dusty sedan approached and parked about twenty yeards from the Ferrari. He saw the robed, hooded figure get out and begin to walk toward him. With one hand, he switched on his headlights while the other picked up a 9-mm automatic from the seat beside him. Within ten feet of the Ferrari, Saul removed his kaffiyeh. Halawa recognized him, shut off the headlights, replaced the automatic in his holster and got out to meet him.

"*Salaam aleikum*, Abdullah," Saul greeted.

"*Shalom*, Saul," Halawa replied, nodding toward the sedan. "Who did you bring with you?"

"My driver, Asad Hasbani, who arranged this meeting."

"Ah, yes. I am sorry we meet under conditions that prevent me from offering you a greater measure of hospitality," Halawa said in his well-practiced Oxford accent.

"Thank you. Another time, perhaps. For now, I have something I came across quite by accident, but which may be of some importance to you."

"So it was indicated in Hasbani's message to my adjutant yesterday."

Saul withdrew the photocopy of the slip taken from Mousa Awad's shoe. Halawa studied it under the small flashlight Saul held, then took the light into his own hand to examine the writing more carefully, his lips moving as he mouthed each name silently. When he finished reading it, he snapped off the light.

"May I ask how this came into your possession?" he said.

"Of course." Saul related the circumstances as he knew them, the defection of some members of the fedayeen group, the death of one, capture of two, the interrogation; all but the exact means by which he had obtained the slip.

"May I keep this?" Halawa asked, indicating the photocopy.

"Yes. It is a true copy of the original."

"Thank you. The inference of an assassination attempt on the king is only too clear. I think we will be able to take care of this by morning." He paused, took a deep breath and expelled it slowly.

"Is there anything, any way, in which I can be helpful to you, Saul?"

"I assume you expect to find Hadek, al-Habab, Amid and Said in Jordan, probably close to home in Amman."

"A most correct assumption, particularly Farik Said. That bloody bastard is *Captain* Farik Said, a member of the palace guard."

"How convenient," Saul commented.

"Very. But I can assure you that the moment I return to Amman, he will not be in so convenient a situation. Nor his three friends. Unlike your country, we do have a death penalty for traitors such as these."

"You are acquainted with Hassan Atassi, of course."

"Atassi. Yes, we know that one very well. A dedicated, unregenerated revolutionary, strongly identified with the PLO, PLA, and any other initials by which terrorists designate themselves. He is a lawyer of some skill, always ready to do battle in any court of law to defend their murderers.

"In 1970, when we threw these animals out of Jordan, Atassi was strongly suspected to be active in a number of movements to assassinate my cousin, the king. He was tried in absentia and the death penalty will be his reward should we find him on our side of the border. And you, Saul?"

"We have no hard evidence against him that would stand up in our courts. I have ordered a loose surveillance on him, however, and if something turns up, I will keep you informed. Until then, he is unofficially in the clear."

"To your way of looking at it, I suppose so." Halawa smiled, adding, "What would your attitude be if we decided to—"

Saul cut him off abruptly. "Whatever you have in mind, my dear friend, I would rather not know. Only be careful and tread softly. We cannot offer protection or immunity to any outside vigilantes no matter—"

"I am not asking for your cooperation, except perhaps that you drop your surveillance on Atassi after . . . let us say tomorrow night."

"Yes, well . . . I think I can see to that. One more thing, Abdullah. Have you in any way, however remote, picked up any word of a new organization that has been formed rather recently, known by the name of the United Palestinian Freedom Party, or UPFP?"

Halawa allowed the name to sift through his mind for a moment or two, then, "No, Saul. It is new to me, but you know how these splinter groups form up, choose a new name, make a strike somewhere and disappear when they suffer their first failure. However, I will make inquiries of our related services and if something turns up, I will pass it along to you. Can you give me any more information about them?"

"Not at this time, except that they are reputedly well financed by at least two oil-rich countries and indirectly by an East German supplier who is supported by the Russians."

Halawa whistled under his breath. "That reaches well beyond our normal scope of operations, but if I learn of anything that might interest you, you will have it at once."

"Well, then—" Saul hesitated, then said, "How are things progressing with the mutual pact between your country and your neighbor to the north?"

Halawa smiled. "You probably know as much or more about that than I do."

"I rather doubt that."

Halawa's smile evaporated. "As you know, there have been several rounds of talks, a visit to Damascus by my cousin, and public statements from both capitals. For myself, and from what I have heard in more intimate circles, I believe it is mostly show, no more than surface gesturings required by Syria as a symbol of solidarity."

"I understand," Saul said, "but since the signing of the pact there have been disturbing rumors that Jordan is about to renew negotiations with the Soviets, directly or through Syria, to acquire new missile installations—" Saul paused for Halawa's reply.

"Of course," the Jordanian said, "I have no way of knowing what extent such negotiations, if the rumors are correct, have reached, since I am not at that level in my cousin's confidence. It is my opinion that such arms would be used against the PLO if they should make an attempt to take over the West Bank by force." He paused to light a cigarette and continued. "Recently, even with the civil war in Lebanon escalating, we discovered and broke up an arms smuggling operation flowing into Jordan from Iraq which involved a PLO underground group led by a Syrian agent. We have kept this under wraps so far, but it suggests their determination to capture the West Bank and establish it as a Palestinian state."

Saul nodded and smiled. "We have been watching that very closely and are on top of it. If the PLO shows the slightest move in that direction, it is very possible that Jordan and Israel may be joining hands as secret allies."

"I would hope so. A Palestinian state between our countries would give neither of us any rest or comfort."

"Indeed, no, and we will never allow it to happen, I can assure you."

"Saul, thank you. You know how much I appreciate these meetings and your cooperation, which I will reciprocate in any way I can."

"*Salaam*, Abdullah." He pointed to the slip in the Jordanian's hand. "Take them all. And perhaps the next time we meet I will have the pleasure of addressing you as Colonel Halawa."

Halawa extended his hand with a warm smile. "*Shalom*, Saul. Go with God's hand on your shoulder. I hope that some day we will be able to meet in the open, in happier times."

"I hope so, too. Good luck."

Halawa waited until the Israeli sedan drove off toward the border, then headed the Ferrari toward Amman in a furious burst of speed.

On the following day, the late afternoon news broadcast from Radio Amman announced that Jordanian intelligence agents had uncovered a plot to assassinate King Hussein. Four men, one a member of the palace guard and three civilians, were taken into custody. Confessions had been obtained from all four during interrogation and had been duly charged. Trial was set for ten days later and if found guilty, all faced the extreme penalty, execution before a firing squad. The announcer left little doubt that such an execution would take place.

As he was preparing to leave his office two nights later, bidding his secretary and chief legal assistant good night, Hassan Atassi was met in the lower level hallway by a well-dressed man who addressed him by name.

"Yes. Who are you?" Atassi asked cautiously.

In a low, well modulated voice, the man said, "My name will be unfamiliar to you, sir. I come on behalf of a mutual friend, Captain Farik Said, a member of a group with which I am affiliated. His friends have raised a defense fund—"

"Not here. Let us return to my office."

The two men reentered the office just as the secretary was leaving, the legal assistant behind her. The latter, a thin man who wore steel-rimmed glasses, stared at Atassi in mild surprise, a question in his eyes at the sight of his companion. "You will require me—" he began, but Atassi waved him off.

"No, Kareem, a personal matter. Go along."

In his private office, Atassi said to the man, "You realize, of course, that I cannot personally appear in Amman for our friend."

"So I have been told, and it is so understood by my colleagues.

However, it was our thought that you could supply us with the name of a capable attorney who would work under your expert direction and guidance, perhaps using couriers whom we would supply—''

Atassi said thoughtfully, ''We might be able to make some such arrangement, but I would need to know more about the exact charges against Said and the others who are in custody. Also, those who are behind their defense.''

''Of course.'' The man reached into his inside jacket pocket and withdrew a leather wallet. From it he extracted a slip of folded paper. He replaced the wallet, then handed the paper across the desk to Atassi.

The lawyer took the paper, unfolded it, saw his own name at the top, the name of Said and three others beneath it, the message at the bottom. Startled, he looked up quickly and found himself staring into the muzzle of a small revolver, a silencer attached. The man said quietly, ''The others will be tried in our courts, Atassi. Your trial will begin and end here, tonight.''

''Wait . . . please . . . don't—'' Atassi began, but the verdict was delivered swiftly when the man pressed the trigger twice. The lawyer fell over backward in his chair, then slipped out of it and onto the floor. The Jordanian leaned over to feel for a pulse. He found none.

With a handkerchief covering his right hand, he recovered the slip of paper, replaced the revolver in its holster under his left armpit, put out the lights in that room, extinguished those in the outer office. He made certain the door was locked as he exited, wiping the knob on both sides. Moments later he was on his way back to the border.

In his office next norning, Saul Lahav noted the incident on the police printout, then sent for Asad Hasbani, who read the three-line entry and observed coolly, ''He who lives by words may also die by the sword.''

Shetula, Israel, April 27

In early morning darkness, the farm village of Shetula, lying close to the Lebanese border, slept peacefully under the somewhat less than watchful eyes of two civilian volunteer guards who were working members of that community.

On the eastern edge, Eliahu Barzan, a stolid, hardworking man of fifty-four, sat wearily on the tailgate of a produce-laden truck, one of several scheduled to start moving toward a cooperative distribution center when the first streaks of light would appear in the sky. On the extreme western edge of the village, the second guard,

Shlomo Zislov, thirty-two, stood watch within sixty yards from where his wife, son and daughter slept in their small house.

It was nearing two A.M. and both men had taken their midnight-to dawn watch after a hard day in the fields. Neither was comfortable nor warm in the chilly wind that knifed over Shetula's orchards and fields and down its single street. Of the two, Zislov was less protected from the wind that bit cruelly through an inadequate jacket which he wore over a thin sweater.

His hands were numbed and as he blew warm breath over them, chided himself for having neglected to take with him his woolen gloves; too sleepy to remember when Chaim Shalak woke him at eleven forty-five to take over his tour of duty. So now, Shlomo left his station, went to his house to retrieve his gloves, saw the coffee pot on the kitchen stove and was tempted to heat some; then remembered that the border patrol jeep was due shortly and rejected the notion, unwilling to be reported to the district commander for neglecting his duty, in which all male members of Shetula over the age of sixteen were required to participate.

Zislov returned to his station, only a little less cold with his gloves on. He leaned his army-issued rifle against the wall of Karl Linsky's bakery shop, lighted the last of his cigarettes as a substitute for the hot coffee he longed for, and which he would get once the patrol passed through. The thought gave him some small comfort.

Looking eastward, there was little he could see in the night shadows. No light showed in any house or building and the single street light in the center of the village was of extremely low wattage. He stared over the dark outlines of ghostly houses, shops and the synagogue toward the barns, packing and storage sheds and, at the eastern edge, the huge water tower that rose above all other structures on its four strong steel legs that were set firmly in reinforced concrete.

Surrounding the entire village were the fields that the community farmed, producing fruits and vegetables much sought after by the market centers to which they would eventually be trucked by the cooperative. These fields ran a considerable distance in every direction and, in the darkness, were indiscernible beyond a few yards.

Zislov, rubbing his arms to drive out the chill, was tempted to walk toward Eliahu Barzan's station, perhaps to see that the older man would be awake when the patrol came by, but again decided to remain where he was supposed to be.

Earlier, shortly past one A.M., five shadowy figures, dressed in dark military-type fatigues and kaffiyehs, drove a small black sedan and a Volkswagen station wagon within a hundred yards of the border, where they parked in a wadi from which they could not be seen from Israeli territory.

Each of the five men carried a rucksack slung over his left shoulder, a short-barreled machine pistol over his right. At the side of each hung a revolver with a stubby barrel affixed to its muzzle, unmistakably a silencer. Four of the men wore a buttonlike earpiece clamped to his right or left ear, attached by a thin wire to a receiver that he wore in his jacket pocket. The fifth man, apparently the leader of the group, carried a walkie-talkie in one hand as a means to issue instructions to the others when they were out of voice range.

Once inside Israeli territory, the five men crouched and ran stealthily southward for a distance of no more than six hundred yards until they reached the edge of Shetula's cultivated farmlands. Here, they paused only long enough to receive final orders from their leader. Those orders delivered, the four followers scattered within the fields, separated widely. When twenty minutes had passed, the leader spoke a single word into his hand instrument. *"Now!"*

Dipping into their rucksacks, the four men withdrew blocks of plastic material, about three and a half inches square and one inch thick. From the outer pocket of the rucksacks, they then removed thin cylinders, no thicker than a pencil. These cylinders were inserted into the plastic squares to full depth, which left no more than an inch protruding. The plastic block was then attached to anything that grew above the ground, tree trunk or stalk, then the top of the thin cylinder was twisted counterclockwise. When this was done, a tiny bulb inside the top of the cylinder began to glow a faint green.

Working swiftly and efficiently, the four men seeded the entire growing area north of the village proper with their plastic squares. Within the hour, they rejoined their leader to report this part of their job had been completed. Now he bade them lie down and rest, eat some food from their rucksacks, drink from their canteens, but enjoined them not to smoke under threat of severe punishment, which the others took to mean death.

When they had eaten, the leader checked the time and bade his men wait until he returned. He then moved westward and beyond the edge of the village. At a certain designated point, he was met by an Arab youth of about fifteen who had been waiting there impatiently.

"What do you have for me?" the leader asked in a whisper.

"All is clear," the youth replied. "The regular patrols have been moved east toward the Syrian border. By day, this road is patrolled by helicopter. At night there is a jeep patrol, two men pass by every four hours. The next one is due to arrive at two o'clock. After they talk to the two guards, they will continue west. That is the pattern they have been following.''

"Good.'' The leader reached into a pocket and withdrew some Israeli pound notes. "This is for you. You have done well. Now go home and sleep.''

The leader returned quickly to his group, lay down beside them and whispered, "Two o'clock. We have twenty minutes before the patrol is due. When it has passed through, we will move in.''

They heard, but were unable to see, the patrol jeep when it arrived at the eastern edge of the village some twenty-five minutes later. It made its scheduled stop, then moved to the western edge, stopped again, apparently to check with the guard there. After a few minutes, it continued on westward and when its motor could no longer be heard, the leader whispered, "Fifteen nimutes, then we move.''

At the appointed time, they proceeded through the fields they had seeded earlier, testing the ground in advance of each step in order to prevent the crackling of broken branches. When they reached the rear of the houses that lined the main street, the leader signaled a halt. Singling out two of his men, he said, "Karim, the one on the east end. Fayez, the other one. You know what to do. Be careful.''

Karim Gamla and Fayez Sada grinned, happy to have been chosen for this critical task. Each unslung his rucksack, checked his revolver and moved out, creeping between the houses, one toward the east, the other to the west.

When he thought he had gone far enough, Karim turned right and crept toward the main street between two houses. Peering out, he saw his target sitting on the tailgate of a truck. He waited to give Fayez time to reach the western edge, since he had a slightly longer way to go. Barely breathing, he raised his weapon and found Eliahu Barzan in his sights. Carefully, he squeezed the trigger, heard the soft *wh-h-h-t!*, felt the slight recoil and an immense satisfaction as he saw the man fall over to one side, then drop into the road where he lay still.

At almost the same moment, Shlomo Zislov had decided he could safely return to his house and get the coffee he wanted so much. He turned, took four steps and fell dead in the street, victim of Fayez Sada's impeccable aim.

No one had heard, nothing but the wind stirred. Karim and Fayez rejoined their three comrades, glowing with pride of accomplishment.

"Now,'' the leader said in a pleased voice, "let us get on with it. Quickly!''

As they had done it in the fields, they now moved toward the structures. At each corner of each house, store, barn, shed and warehouse, they attached a block of the gray-green plastic material, inserted the cylindrical actuator, its cap turned to show the dim glow, an indication that the tiny battery inside each instrument had been properly activated and was in working order.

At the large water tower, the leader himself packed a triple portion of the explosives to each steel leg, then moved to the trucks and nearby farm vehicles. By three ten A.M. the five had used up all their materials. Satisfied that they could do no more here, he ordered, "Back to the cars."

Through the fields and across the barren stretch of ground, they ran as fast as they could, unheard, unseen. They crossed the border and continued on beyond to the wadi where their two vehicles were parked. The leader now removed his kaffiyeh and fatigues, under which he wore the shirt and trousers of a farm worker. He placed these in the small sedan, ordered his four companions into that vehicle and said, "You have done well. When I return, I shall tell Falcon of the excellence of your work. Go back now. Show no lights for the next five or ten kilometers. Report what we have done, then wait for further instructions. *Salaam*."

When the small sedan pulled out, the leader went to the rear of the Volkswagen station wagon and opened it from the back, retrieved a warm jacket and put it on. With a screwdriver, he next removed a floor panel that lay beneath the carpeting, revealing a secret compartment under the floor and over the petrol tank. Into this cavern he placed his rucksack, machine pistol, revolver, a pair of binoculars and two boxes of unused ammunition. He checked to make sure the dozen plastic squares and an equal number of the cylinders were safe where he had left them. He then picked up his walkie-talkie unit, raised its long, thin antenna and depressed the talk button.

"Come in, Falcon. This is Leader One. Come in, Falcon. This is Leader One."

*   *   *

Five kilometers to the north, three men sat in a large black Mercedes sedan, waiting in the darkness. The two who wore immaculate khaki uniforms were Arabs. The third, dressed in a conventional business suit was, by his flat facial features, Russian. The two Arabs chatted easily, but the stolid, phlegmatic Russian paid little attention as he sat on the rear seat and smoked a seemingly endless chain of long cigarettes wrapped in brown paper. The taller of the two Arabs, as the soft voice came through the walkie-talkie lying on the seat between them, reached for it, got out of the car and raised its whiplike antenna as far as it would reach.

"This is Falcon, Leader One," he said into the unit. "Report."

"I report success, Falcon. Shetula is ready. The others are on their way back to camp."

"Well done, Leader One. Proceed as planned and report. Over and out."

The other two men had heard the exchange. The Arab inside the car looked inordinately pleased. The Russian stared bleakly and remained silent.

Now Leader One placed the walkie-talkie unit, which was one of a pair, into the secret compartment, screwed the floorboard securely into place and got in behind the wheel. The second such unit was placed beneath the front seat. He started the motor and drove westward over rough ground until he came to a downhill grade, where, having scouted the area the night before, he knew he could cross into Israeli territory and would be about two kilometers west of Shetula. He crossed, drove over a field until he found the dirt road, then continued in a westerly direction for another full kilometer, where he found a small clearing beside the road. He pulled into the clearing and parked.

From the glove compartment, he now removed a small calculator-type device and depressed a button that activated it, showing a tiny red light. He then raised its built-in antenna and began depressing its numbered buttons in various combinations.

Shetula slept on, its two dead settlement guards lying where they had fallen. The time was now 4:35 A.M.

Suddenly, the fields to the north erupted in flames, spreading swiftly, engulfing the entire area, moving southward behind the wind toward the village proper. Almost simultaneously, houses, buildings, trucks and other farm equipment were torn apart by violent explosions, filling the air with wood, cement, metal, flames and dense smoke. On the eastern edge, the strong steel legs of the water tower were ripped loose from their concrete base and it crumpled, unleashing thousands of gallons of water into the main thoroughfare and side roads leading into the fields, yet unable to quench the fierce flames that were hungrily consuming everything that grew there.

Screams of the injured and dying came from the houses and barns that were being swiftly reduced to flaming rubble. Several burning figures were either hurled outside by the force of the explosions or had been able to run into the open, trying to escape the holocaust, but soon fell to the ground, consumed.

Within minutes, the entire community of Shetula, inhabitants and animals alike, had ceased to exist.

The devastation was total.

And three kilometers to the west, Leader One felt a tremendous surge of exhilaration as the dark sky over Shetula began to glow, as though bathed in a reddish fog, while adrenalin sent blood pounding through his veins. He watched as the color deepened with each successive explosion, which he could not hear from this distance, then diminished, staring in near disbelief that it had really worked; far better than the experiments he had witnessed and participated in at the UPFP training camp. Truly, it was Allah's miracle of miracles.

Satisfied finally, he picked up the walkie-talkie unit, extended its antenna and spoke excitedly. "Come in, Falcon. This is Leader One."

The reply came back at once. "Falcon here, Leader One. Report."

"It is done, Falcon. The sky over Shetula is red."

"Yes. We have moved closer and can see it. Well done, Leader One. Your unit is to be congratulated. You will now proceed according to plan. I will send new instructions to you by Hawk. Over."

Leader One replaced the walkie-talkie and calculator device beneath the front seat and strapped both securely in place. Gaining the road again, he continued westward for a short distance until he found a grove of trees and brush where he could hide the station wagon from observation of any passing vehicles.

He parked there and closed his eyes, but sleep would not come in his present state of excitement. Moments later, he heard sirens that brought him to full wakefulness. He got out of the Volkswagen and crept as close to the edge of the road as he could and still remain hidden by the brush. And saw two military vehicles, then a truck filled with armed, helmeted Israeli soldiers flash by, followed by two ambulances; further evidence, if he needed it, of the success of his mission. Then silence. He returned to the car, got in and was now able to fall asleep.

When he awoke next, it was broad daylight. And quiet. He was in no hurry to move out and waited for a while before exiting the VW. He walked down to the road and looked to the east and west. All was clear. He went back to the car and got out a transistorized radio from the glove compartment and turned it on. Although his understanding of the rush of Hebrew from the Israeli newscaster was good, it came too fast for him to interpret it clearly; yet he understood from its anguished tone that the damage to Shetula had been massive. Now he could hear the motors of all manner of vehicles passing on the road below him and decided to wait before attempting to make his way farther west, as the original plan called for.

He rested for a while, then opened the secret compartment again, ate the balance of the food in the rucksack and slept for several more hours. Late in the afternoon, he started the motor and eased out of the grove, onto the road, which was clear at the moment, and headed westward at a normal rate of speed. Soon he was overtaken by a truck, then two passenger cars and another truck. Several other vehicles approached from the west, some military, the rest civilian, but this was normal traffic and gave him little concern. At this point, he would not expect to find a roadblock or checkpoint, and there were none. In his mind's eye was a picture of the map he had memorized carefully back at the camp; the location of the farm he must reach before the next road juncture where there would most certainly be a checkpoint.

He had been traveling in a southwesterly direction for a while and, at a small dirt road on his right, found the marker: a three-foot-high wooden stake with a yellow rag tied near its top. He turned into the rutted lane, and within seventy yards came to the entrance of the small farm on Ibrahim Riad. House, barn and open shed fit the description given him and he breathed a deep sigh of relief.

It was a primitive farm with no mechanical equipment in sight other than an aged pickup truck parked outside the barn. As he approached the house, a bearded man of about sixty came out and stood in front of it, waiting. Leader One stopped beside him and said, "*Salaam aleikum*. Can you tell me how many kilometers it is to Haifa?"

The man studied Leader One with cautious eyes, then replied, "You have many kilometers before you yet. I do not know exactly how many."

"But my direction is correct, is it not?"

"Yes, brother. You are welcome. Drive your car into the barn where we will cover it."

Again sighing with relief, Leader One drove into the barn and parked it at the rear, then he and the man covered the VW with a canvas tarpaulin and many sacks of grain, covered the sacks with loose hay until no part of it could be detected.

The task completed, Leader One said, "You are Ibrahim Riad, yes?"

"Yes. And how are you called, young one?"

"Assaf Hafez. I am hungry and thirsty. And in need of sleep."

"Then come. My woman will feed you and give you a pallet and blanket. I have two sons, but they will be working in the fields beside me. You will not be disturbed.''

"Thank you. You know about Shetula?''

"I heard about it on the radio earlier. A huge success. There is no more Shetula. Everything gone.'' The man grinned, displaying two rows of large, square teeth between his mustache and beard.

"As it was planned by Falcon," Assaf Hafez said, returning the grin. "In a while, I don't know when, a courier will come with instructions for me. He is known as Hawk. He will ask the same questions of you and you will know it is he.''

"I will remember.''

First to arrive on the scene were a handful of men and women from neighboring settlements who had been startled awake by the series of explosions, then looked out timorously and saw the reddened sky over Shetula. Some took the time to dress, others leaped into cars and farm trucks in their night clothes, the men armed with whatever weapons they had on hand; rifles, handguns, pitchforks. They came at almost the same time the first border patrolmen arrived, two young men in a jeep who, after a horrified glance, radioed the word back to their base camp, from which the general alarm was immediately broadcast. Then others appeared, coming from the east, west and south.

They stood on the periphery of the disaster area in stunned shock, unable to comprehend or believe the enormity of the sight before their eyes; then came the first low wails of grief, rising into shrieks and shouts of anger as they began to move in through the mud, smoke and flames, feeling intense pain as the victims themselves may have felt it before they died. Rocking back and forth as though in prayer, leaning upon each other, shuddering, weeping, their cries reached out to the new arrivals; border patrolmen now in greater numbers, army personnel, firemen from nearby and distant villages, ambulances with doctors and nurses, trucks carrying volunteer laborers to assist in whatever would be asked or required of them, helicopters depositing military and government officials, departing at once to return with more. Their anguish was not private. It enveloped everyone present.

The military men took charge, organizing working parties. They moved everyone out of the immediate area, sealed it off, then began a methodical search through rubble and mud for any possible sign of life. They found nothing but the torn, shattered bodies of fifty-six inhabitants; men, women and children who had gone to bed the night before with the expectation that tomorrow would be little different from the previous day.

Only those who had been away trucking produce to various distribution centers, to the marketplaces in Acre and Haifa, off visiting friends and relatives, serving in the military forces, or away on other business or personal matters, a very few at best, would become the survivors of a settlement that no longer existed.

As time passed, it became necessary to call in more army personnel to set up barricades to prevent the increasing numbers of local settlement residents from forcing their way into the affected area; furious men and women who had heard the first and succeeding broadcasts on their radios. Not permitted access to the village proper, they stood at the barricades and hurled curses at the army, the border patrol, the government itself, demanding answers from the ranking officials now on the scene and in charge of the activities; and who had no answers to give.

General Judah Rosental and Major Saul Lahav were among the first officials to arrive by helicopter; then came others, along with the newspaper, radio and television crews of reporters and cameramen, laden with equipment, rushing about to locate any eyewitnesses, of which there were none. Only the sightless, mute, mutilated dead.

Recovery of the bodies had become the primary need and search teams were deployed to wade through the mud from one ruined structure to the next; removing burned lumber, huge chunks of stone, plaster, smoldering debris of household furniture and goods to uncover the burned and mutilated corpses. Hospital and ambulance crews placed the recovered bodies in individual green plastic body bags and carried them to a cleared space beyond the south edge of the main street where they were laid out in precise rows. Identification would be difficult and must come later, after relatives and residents who were fortunate enough to have been away at the time would return.

More of Rosental's staff flew in with technical teams to seek for evidence and the means by which an entire community could be destroyed so quickly, so efficiently, leaving no trace of the perpetrators, or witnesses, behind. They were followed by the arrival of Defense Minister Moshe Goren, his chief deputy, Aron Davidov, and Rosental's chief, General Yigael Bartok, who were at once besieged by the news media men and crowds of civilians through whom a path had to be made in order to allow them to reach the interior scene.

Moments later, the prime minister arrived and the cries and wails of grief from those behind the barricades rose into shouts and screams of angry denunciation.

"Where was the border patrol?"

"Where was the army?"

"Why are you not out destroying those bastard fedayeen?"

"Kill ten, a hundred, for every life taken here!"

The Minister of Information, Yoshua Feig, when he arrived only moments later, became the target for the media men as soon as he was sighted alighting from his helicopter, totally unprepared except by the scanty radio reports he had heard en route, none of which had come directly from Shetula. He fought his way through the jungle of microphones and pressing reporters to relative safety inside the barricade and began questioning the senior military men present, but heard nothing that he knew could satisfy the news-hungry reporters or angry civilians.

After a few minutes of consultation, it was decided to permit a pool of three newspaper reporters, two photographers, one radio man and a television crew of two to enter the disaster area. *Ma'ariv, Ha'aretz*, Jerusalem *Post* and the senior members of the prestigious Tel Aviv *Star*, Simon Bardosky, led the way inside to witness at firsthand and photograph the rows of bodies, shattered homes, shops, barns, burned fields, dead animals, wrecked trucks and other farm equipment, then centered their attention on the huge water tower that lay burst apart on the ground with its steel legs twisted into a grotesque shape not unlike an abstract prehistoric monster animal.

The reporters, ignoring the minister of information, went directly to the beleaguered defense minister to question him. "A statement, Minister," Simon Bardosky, the pool spokesman, called out.

Moshe Goren stared at him blankly. "I arrived here only a short time ago," he said vacantly. "You have seen what I see. What statement can I possibly make at this time. Like myself, you will have to wait . . . wait—"

"Wait for what, Minister?" Bardosky persisted.

"For the investigation to be completed. Please do not impede it. Give us more time."

"Where is the prime minister?"

"With the investigating team, surveying the cost in lives, the damage. You will not be permitted in that area. What evidence exists must not be destroyed by trampling feet."

"Who is in charge of the investigation, Minister?"

"Major General Judah Rosental."

"Give us a statement for our readers, listeners and viewers, Minister," Bardosky pleaded.

"I will do my best in this trying moment, Bardosky. Later there will be one or more of official nature from the prime minister and other cabinet members."

"Yes, sir?"

"We share with you, with everyone, your grief over this sense-less, brutal attack by terrorists on Shetula. Over fifty sleeping men, women and children have been slaughtered in their beds, a village totally destroyed. Your sorrow is our sorrow, your pain our pain, but I can assure you that these innocent victims will be avenged. I urge everyone to join us in our prayers for them and that you remain calm. As you have in the past, you must now rely on your government to take what steps are necessary—"

Goren's voice choked, unable to continue. Through visible tears, he stared at Bardosky and the grouped reporters, seeing them through a watery veil. Then he said, "That is all I can . . . say . . . for now, gentlemen. Please . . . excuse me."

As the reporters began pressing for more, Saul Lahav broke through the tight circle and whispered a message to General Goren. The defense minister nodded and went at once to where the prime minister, his deputy, Generals Bartok and Rosental stood talking with members of the investigating team. Saul turned to follow, but Simon Bardosky called out, "Major Lahav! Saul!"

Saul turned and faced the group of eager reporters. "What can I tell you, Simon, that you don't already know?"

"A statement, Saul. Anything that we can build on."

"All right, but unofficially, and don't use my name. Agreed?"

"Agreed," Bardosky said, and this was echoed by the other pool members.

"Very well. No previous terrorist attack, in our experience, has been so thorough, so conscienceless, so well planned and executed. We have as yet uncovered no evidence of the means used but we are continuing the search. No witnesses were left alive, nor is there any physical sign of the perpetrators. Only the results are here. I am sure, as you must be, that there will be some form of military retaliation. For now, we will concentrate on our search for clues, remove and examine the bodies, then see that they are properly identified and buried. End statement."

So the search continued, the bodies removed. For three more days a pall of smoke would hang over the rubble that was once Shetula.

BULLETIN
ATTACK
JERUSALEM (AP)—A SERIES OF EXPLOSIONS,
SOURCE UNKNOWN THIS TIME, REPORTEDLY DE-

STROYED THE AGRICULTURAL VILLAGE OF SHETU-
LA, SOUTH OF LEBANESE BORDER EARLY THIS A.M.

JERUSALEM
ADD ATTACK—SHETULA (72)
EXPLOSIONS REPORTED VARIOUSLY AS ROCKET
/MISSILE AND/OR ARTILLERY SHELLING. LATTER
UNCONFIRMED AND DISCOUNTED BY AUTHORITIES

JERUSALEM
ADD ATTACK—SHETULA (73)
RELIABLE SOURCE INDICATES STRONG TERRORIST
INFILTRATION RESPONSIBLE. VILLAGE TOTALLY
DESTROYED. 56 MEN, WOMEN, CHILDREN KNOWN
DEAD. SEARCH CONTINUES FOR MORE. NO SUR-
VIVORS. ALL INVADERS ESCAPED UNHARMED.
MOST SUCCESSFUL, DEVASTATING RAID IN ISRAELI
HISTORY.

The AP flash, first among foreign news releases, was picked up
in Europe, the United States and throughout the Middle East. Even
while the Israeli press screamed MASSACRE AT SHETULA! 56
SLAUGHTERED AT SHETULA! in heavy red and black banner headlines, spokesmen for al-Fatah, the Popular Front for the Liberation
of Palestine, Popular Democratic Front and Black September were
each quick to take full credit for the Shetula operation; but most
knowing officials refused to accept such disjointed claims from
multiple organizations that barely recognized each other. Perhaps
one, but not in the aggregate. The Israeli public, immersed in deep
grief and anger, could care less which terrorist group shouted
loudest in claiming credit for the strike. In the mind of every Israeli
all were equally guilty.
    Despite the presence of heavily armed PLO and Syrian troops in
Lebanon, retaliation came swiftly. Israeli forces struck hard in
reprisal. On foot behind armored vehicles, they stabbed across the
border into known terrorist camps on search-and-destroy missions
blowing up water pipes, electrical and telephone systems. In the
villages where the terrorists expected such raids, the Israelis found
only deserted houses. Charges were set and these were leveled to the
ground.
    Jets swept over other inland camps, reducing them to rubble.
Two ammunition and petrol storage dumps were blown up and a
number of fleeing trucks destroyed. The toll in lives could not be

determined. From predawn into darkness, the attacks raged on. Then silence.

Radio Damascus at once filled the air with threats of retaliation in full force if the raids continued and called upon all Arab nations to join her in a full-scale war on Israel. In particular, the spokesman vented his anger upon Egypt, calling on its president to renounce the Sinai pact and live up to its agreement with Syria to join her in strong reprisals. Radio Cairo at first reported the raids on Palestinian revolutionary camps, then responded that Egypt was in no way required to live up to her agreement with Syria since that nation had not been attacked by the Israelis.

Radio Beirut, preoccupied with its own raging civil war, remained silent; but leaders of the Christian, Moslem and PLO forces condemned the raids and called upon the United Nations to denounce Israel as the agressor. In the United Nations, Russia, joined by the conglomerate Arab nations, China and Third World representatives, vociferously demanded censure of Israel as an agressor nation and a threat to world peace, reparations in the billions of dollars, trade boycott and dismissal from that august body at once if it refused to move back to its pre-1967 borders.

Western members, repelled by the senseless, brutal massacre, turned a cold shoulder to those demands.

But to the prime minister of Israel, sitting at his desk late at night with his defense minister, Moshe Goren, the retaliatory raids were but a small strip of adhesive tape to cover a massive, gaping wound that had been inflicted and would bleed for a long time to come. By demographic comparison alone, the deaths of fifty-six Israeli citizens were equal to some 2,800 Arab lives, and the useless death of any human being was repugnant to him, who had seen so much violent death in his lifetime.

"It is not enough," Goren grumbled.

"What would you do, Moshe," the prime minister asked, "throw everything into this and start an all-out war, perhaps even World War III?"

"If it comes to a war with our neighbors, Herzl, the world at large would not become involved. What is more, we would win it," the defense minister declared emphatically.

"Moshe, Moshe, at what cost? Tell me how many lives we can afford to throw away in order to win still another war? And if the superpowers permit us to win it, how will we have improved our position or furthered the chances for a lasting peace?"

When Goren remained silent, his face clouded, the prime minister said, "We are of the same generation, old friend, with the same backgrounds. When I held the position you now hold, my instincts and attitudes were much the same as yours are now. But when one sits in this chair behind this desk and is accountable to his cabinet, the Knesset, the safety of three and a half million people and preservation of a nation, the view becomes much different.

"We have won wars, yes, out of need to survive, but in each, we have been seriously wounded, physically and economically, victims of our successes. We are in a state of perpetual convalescence and cannot afford to be wounded again by an unwanted war, economic drains, loss of life by this new terrorist threat which we must somehow unearth and destroy by some lesser means."

Goren grunted. "By talking it out of existence, Herzl?"

"No. Tomorrow morning, I want to schedule a meeting with you and Yigael Bartok. . . ."

"Ah, Mossad," Goren interjected softly.

". . . at which time I hope we can agree on some action that will give us a solution to this new threat."

Goren sighed heavily. "I will be here, of course. But short of a full-scale effort, I doubt if I will be able to contribute very much to that conference."

"Then I will be forced to place full responsibility for the problem in Bartok's hands, but I want you to be present so that you will have my decision firsthand."

Goren rose to his feet, a tall, forceful figure. "Until tomorrow morning," he said simply. "*Shalom*, Herzl."

"*Shalom*, Moshe. Sleep on it and wake up with a clear mind."

6

The prime minister sat listening to his weekly briefing by the chairman of his Economic Advisory Council, Haim Singer, but his mind was on the two men in the outer office who were waiting for him. Unwilling to discourage the tall, distinguished-looking former professor of economics whose credits in world matters of finance were prodigious, he toyed with a letter opener to hide his impatience and wished the session would come to an end.

Singer, it was evident, was attempting to lessen the impact of Israel's depressing situation by highlighting Egypt's dilemma, citing the most recent evidence his people abroad had been able to bring up to date.

". . . now faces a three-billion-dollar trade deficit," Singer was saying, "with a rate of inflation of better than thirty percent and still climbing. Government employees as well as the military are demanding pay raises in increasing volume. It is apparent that Egypt cannot sustain itself with its own agriculture, since most of the land is desert and too far from the Nile to be feasibly irrigated.

"With a seriously damaged economy, Sadat has been forced to resort to short-term loans at high interest rates and its deficit financing has become extremely expensive, embarrassingly so. Its exports, mainly cotton, have been committed as barter to the Soviet Union in payment of its war debts, which the Russians are demanding. Now, thirty-six million Egyptians, some six million compressed into Cairo, are living under austere conditions and any cutback in spending will increase the unrest. Without additional financing it will be most difficult to maintain its military strength and stature.

"Add to this the pact signed between Libya and Russia, Minister, with a heavily armed Libya on her west, Israel on her east. Also, the one between Syria and Jordan—"

"I am well aware of the military implications, Haim," the prime minister said with a smile as he put the letter opener down. "This has been extremely interesting and I will review your written report later with those members of my cabinet who are directly concerned. I am afraid I am running late now, and—"

Haim Singer handed the report to which he had been referring to the prime minister and stood up. "Thank you, Minister. You will find this as complete as possible, with charts, demographs and analyses prepared by the council."

The prime minister nodded and as Singer went out, depressed a cam on his intercom and said, "Ask Generals Goren and Bartok to come in, please."

The defense minister and chief of Mossad entered, but the prime minister directed them toward the small conference room next to this one so that none would be distracted by the trappings of the larger, more comfortable office.

On the table lay the most recent editions from the presses of the country's leading newspapers, some from abroad, each prominently displaying banner headlines that updated the Shetula massacre, supported with photographs of the dead encased in plastic body bags, the broken water tower, the total destruction of homes of the once prosperous agricultural community. As they entered, an aide was placing a tape recorder on the center of the table. He plugged it into a floor receptacle and exited quietly. The prime minister picked up the phone receiver and said into it, "Hold all my calls until I notify you." He sat down heavily in the chair at the head of the table, the horror of what he had witnessed at Shetula visible in his drawn face and weary eyes.

"Earlier this morning I gave a fresh statement to the press," he said, opening the meeting, "and refused to take their questions, for which I knew I would have no answers at this time. We all know that no statement I can devise can bind the wounds or salve the pain created by this massive tragedy, nor satisfy the demands for far-reaching revenge the public in the streets is calling for.

"To you in this room, I will speak openly. I cannot imagine a more vicious, calculated blow than the one directed at Shetula. What makes it more unbearable is that this was an act in which we were taken wholly by surprise, unable to defend against it, and resulting in the wholesale slaughter of an entire community, yet leaving us helpless to strike back at the actual perpetrators who escaped unseen and without harm.

"There are three and a half million of our people scattered throughout Israel who look to this government for the safety and protection of their lives and property and, gentlemen, we have failed them. This tragedy is second only in magnitude to a new, unannounced war.''

"If they want war,'' General Goren began, but the prime minister cut him short with an abrupt slap of his hand on the desk.

"I cannot, will not, entertain any suggestion that war is the inevitable answer to Shetula!'' The prime minister paused to allow that emphatic statement sink in, then added musingly, ''War. Because earliest man could not learn to negotiate his differences with his neighbors, he invented both murder and war and handed down our oldest, longest-lasting legacy. We have had our own wars, I need not point out. We are sick and tired of them, increasingly unable to support them. Therefore, we must look for a new means, invent one if necessary, to combat this new threat.

"We have, short of war, retaliated with an action against known terrorist camps in Lebanon, but our main objective, the action group which accomplished this outrage, has gone scotfree and will presumably be encouraged to strike again elsewhere with perhaps even more devastating results.

"Let me remind you that outside these doors, our own critics are lined up in force with demands for more than token revenge. Gush Emunim alone was able to bring twenty-five thousand supportive followers to demonstrate in the streets of Jerusalem in protest against the Sinai pact. The Likud party, with thirty-nine votes, National Religious party with ten, Torah Front with five, and others, total more than our Labor Party's sixty-eight in the Knesset. If nothing to satisfy that need demanded by the public is done, and done soon, every newspaper and the opposition will be demanding our heads. And at a time when Israel can least afford it, this government must fall.

"I will listen to any proposals you wish to make.''

The defense minister and chief of Mossad exchanged glances. Bartok nodded to Goren, who spoke first, with surprising mildness. "We must all, of course, agree with your assessment of the general response from all sides,'' he said, "which we can expect will become even move inflamed by the press, and for good reason. Since you oppose stronger military action beyond that which we have already taken, I don't know what more I can offer, Minister. Without knowledge of the location of the actual perpetrators, our strikes have necessarily been in the general area of known guerrilla camps. Nor can we remove the bulk of our armed forces from their present strategic locations for the purpose of strengthening the Antiguerrilla Department—''

The prime minister wig-wagged a hand in Goren's direction, cutting him off. "I am not suggesting that, Moshe, and if my tone is

critical, it is not for you alone. I don't want to hear rationaliza-
tions, but positive suggestions so that this thing will not, cannot,
happen again.'' He turned quickly to General Bartok. ''Yigael—''

Bartok leaned forward in his chair and laid down the pencil he had
been twirling between his fingers. ''What has happened at Shetula,
no matter the criticisms of press, public or opposition party, even
among our own, can't be undone. Fifty-six innocent lives have been
taken and we are accountable.''

Drumming spatulate fingers impatiently on the table top, the
prime minister said, ''Yigael, we are fully aware of what you are
saying, but I want to hear something constructive.''

''Let me finish, please,'' Bartok replied starchily. ''I am aware
as you are, as General Goren is, that the border patrol and Mossad's
Antiguerrilla Branch are seriously undermanned to undertake total
and continued surveillance of our long borders. Therefore, to merely ask for more trained manpower, even if it were available, will not
solve this pressing problem.

''In my considered opinion, Minister, we must create a special
group, apart from the regularly constituted armed forces, border
patrol, police and Antiguerrilla Branch, to concentrate wholly and
solely on this matter, to the exclusion of all other duties. It should be
staffed with trained people drawn from any service branch which
has a man or woman with the experience or qualifications this group
would require.

''To put it in the most simplistic terms, the purpose of this elite
group would be to seek out what is obviously a new and more
sophisticated, well-trained and effective terrorist organization and
take every necessary means to destroy it.''

Goren said, ''Simplistic indeed, Yigael. I assume it would be
directed by Mossad?''

''Yes, in that we already have personnel trained in antiguerrilla
activity, but only indirectly, Moshe, as far as control is concerned.
As I see it, this group should be headed by a man with experience
not only in that specific field, but who has a military background as
well as one in intelligence activity, here and abroad; a man able to
put such an organization together, staff it with people drawn from
the ranks of our sister organizations, one here, two there, and which
would in no way weaken any single branch, but give strength to the
newly created group of specialists.''

''Who,'' the prime minister asked, ''could put such a group
together? And how soon? Immediate action is imperative.''

Bartok smiled wearily. ''With your permission, Minister, I will
confer at once with my staff, name the man and draw up as complete

a plan of operation as possible within . . . say forty-eight hours from the time you give your consent.''

For the first time since the meeting began, the prime minister seemed to relax. He turned to Goren and said, "Moshe?"

Goren's frown indicated some reluctance to accept Bartok's suggestion, but lacking a counterplan which could conceivably involve a massive movement of troops and equipment he could not stretch thinner, said, "If this can be made workable, I agree. It will at least be something to feed to the press and public for the time being."

"No!" Bartok exclaimed explosively. "In no way will I agree to make public the news of such a special group. I must insist that for the time being it must remain in the background and given a free hand in any direction necessary without public announcements to the enemy of its existence."

"I agree," the prime minister said shortly, dismissing Goren's suggestion. "I will instruct my chief deputy to keep in close touch with General Bartok and keep me informed of his progress." And directly to Bartok, "Yigael, you know how important this project is. I will support you in any way necessary to accomplish our objective. I ask only one thing, that this be organized in Jerusalem where, if necessary, I can be close to it and its operation, but without interference."

"Will there be any problems with money or the requisitioning of personnel?" Bartok asked.

"When you have submitted your plan to me in person, and if it meets with my approval, I will see the finance minister and find the necessary funds somewhere for you. I will also direct the heads of all services to cooperate in the matter of your personnel needs."

When no further comment was offered, he said, "Thank you for your attention and support. I think that will be all for now. I have a full day of conferences ahead of me and must be on hand tonight to placate a long line of demanding cabinet and Knesset members. *Shalom*."

Tel Aviv, April 30

The staff meeting, conducted by Colonel Omri Kohn in the absence of General Judah Rosental, came to a close at six thirty P.M. The subject of Shetula had been brought up and discussed, but not in great depth, considering the fact that laboratory experts were still sieving through the gathered debris for clues. As the four section heads rose to leave, Rosental entered the conference room with an apology to all present for having been delayed by the hurriedly called meeting with General Bartok earlier that afternoon.

Kohn began assuring him that the conference had been routine
but the general, dropping heavily onto the sofa, said, "Never mind,
Omri," and as Saul Lahav reached the door on his way out, called,
"Stay, Saul."

Saul returned and sat in a chair facing Rosental while Kohn took
the seat beside the general, both waiting expectantly, knowing that
his meeting with the Mossad chief must certainly have concerned
the vital question of the day, Shetula. Kohn lighted a cigarette and
offered the pack around. Rosental and Saul took the proffered
cigarettes and lighted them. The general was in a deeply contemplative mood, sober-faced, forehead crinkled under a canopy of sandy
hair.

"Would you like some coffee, General?" Kohn asked in an effort to break the silence.

"Yes, Omri. Have it sent to my office, please." Kohn rose to go
to the intercom on the conference table, but the general added, "If
you are otherwise occupied, Omri, this needn't hold you up. I want
to discuss something with Saul. I'll bring you up to date on it later."
And to Saul, "Let's go to my office. We'll be more comfortable
there."

To Saul, Rosental seemed to have aged greatly during the past
few months. New lines appeared in his sun-weathered face, older
ones more deeply engraved, more white showing in his unruly hair.
Even his vigor seemed somewhat lessened. He was twelve years
older than Saul but now appeared much older.

In his private office, Rosental removed his jacket and looked
more relaxed in his comfortable chair behind the litter of paperwork
spread out over the desk. A clerk brought the coffee and left.
Rosental sipped at his cup, then put it down with a wry smile that
gave Saul no indication of what was to come.

The close rapport between Rosental and Lahav was easy, more
like that between intimate brothers than general and major when
they were alone together. Earlier, this casualness had caused some
resentment among the other members of the staff, but they soon
came to understand that Rosental played no favorites; in fact, Saul
had often been handed assignments that others were willing to
avoid.

Saul said, "I assume it was the Shetula matter with the chief."

Rosental nodded lightly without answering and Saul recognized
that his superior had not yet fully formulated his thoughts on the
subject he intended to discuss; unusual in itself because the general
was noted for his quick grasp of a situation and his swift decisions.
He relaxed and waited.

Then Rosental waved a hand across the newspapers of the day

that were heaped in a pile on one corner of his desk. "You've seen these, of course," he said.

"Most of them, yes," Saul replied. "Not much different from yesterday's output, or the day before."

"Simon Bardosky. The *Star*. He hits hard."

"A newspaper man has a job to do, too, Judah."

"You saw his editorial today?"

"Not yet. Is it so different from the others?"

Rosental picked up the *Star*. On the front page, enclosed within a blood-red border, was a list of all too familiar names: LOD, MUNICH, QIRYAT SHEMONA, MA'ALOT, SHAMIR, NAHARIYA, BEIT SHEAN, TEL AVIV, JERUSALEM—and now, SHETUAL! And below the list that included other names in smaller print, a single line, asked "*How much longer, O Lord?*"

"Listen to this from Mr. Bardosky," Rosental said, turning to the editorial page. "He is demanding greater security measures, more men, more arms, more patrol vehicles, surveillance from the air by day and night to protect our cities, villages, moshavim and kibbutzim. Let me quote:

Where are our planners, our innovators who fought valiantly in the streets, on the battlefields, and defeated huge armies in four wars? Have we grown so fat with success that we cannot defend against small groups of conscienceless murderers who continue to penetrate our borders and enter our villages at will?

"Are we, who stood off Russian-equipped armies, far superior to ours in numbers, to bend our knees to rabble terrorists, unable to protect our men, women and children from being slaughtered in our streets, in their beds, in homes that have become death camps?

"Where are the antiguerrilla forces that served us so well in the past? These murderers are not ghosts, nor are they invisible. Why can they not be sought out and destroyed before they strike? Retaliation by air and artillery, by infantry and tanks, is not the answer. By the time retaliation is exercised, the deadly deed has been committed.

"Is it possible that our leaders have grown old and weary, our military too complacent, leaning on rusted laurels, our security agencies too dispirited to combat these zealots who are slowly eroding our morale and, in fact, our young nation? Have we indeed been overwhelmed by Palestinian *chutzpah*?

"And more of the same, Saul."

Saul said, "If one listens carefully, it seems to fit the voice of the people in the streets, Judah."

Rosental sighed deeply. "I am fifty-seven years old. Today, I feel like I'm seventy-seven."

"When things go badly, we all feel older."

Rosental's smile was cryptic. "Yes, don't we." He sipped more coffee, then said, "I'm sure you have often thought of death, Saul."

Taken unaware by the rhetorical remark, Saul hesitated, then said, "Often, Judah, as most of us have."

"Do you fear it?"

"I don't welcome the thought, but I don't fear it. I can't waste time thinking about an event, the final act of life, over which I have no control. To defend against death by violence, yes, of course. To contemplate it philosophically is to me a useless exercise."

Rosental nodded in the manner of a man who had not really been listening. Now that subject, too, seemed closed. A momentary silence hung in the air between them, which left Saul wondering what was really on the general's mind, waiting for him to broach it. Rosental said suddenly, "Anything from the laboratory yet?"

"Nothing yet. It is too soon. They're still combing the debris, sifting ashes. raking through truckloads of whatever they brought in. So far there is no trace of the explosives used, no clues anywhere. We don't know how much the water from the tower may have washed away. Only the bullets recovered from the bodies of the two settlement guards. One from each. Nine-mm, hollow-nosed. Instant death. They never had a chance."

"And nobody, evidently, heard those two shots."

"Not if they used silencers, which is very likely."

"Such sophistication. Unusual with the common garden variety of terrorist, wouldn't you say? Even remarkable." He paused, expelled a deep breath and added, "Bartok hit me with a lot of questions I couldn't answer."

Saul stood up, turned toward the door and said, "Excuse me, Judah. I'll be back in a minute."

He walked quickly down the hall to his own office, unlocked a steel cabinet and removed a manila folder. He then relocked the cabinet and returned to Rosental's office and placed the file on the desk before the general, who read the label on the cover: SOKOLNIKOV MEMORANDUM—TOP SECRET—DO NOT REMOVE; Rosental then looked up at Saul with weary, troubled eyes. "I thought it was this that you would bring back," he said.

"It has been lying in my files and on my mind since Collier gave it to us at Bashra almost a month ago, Judah. I am convinced, more than ever now, that Shetula gives us no choice but to accept this as fact, not fantasy, no matter the cost."

"I hadn't forgotten it, Saul. Nor the cost."

Saul's lips compressed into a grim line. He pointed to the copy of the *Star* and ran his finger down the listed names, stopping at the words, "and now, SHETULA!"

"How much, apart from the fifty-six dead, can we say Shetula has cost? And how much will the next Shetula cost in lives and property, in grief and sorrow?"

Rosental felt a near hint of criticism in Lahav's blunt words and stirred uncomfortably in his chair, swiveling away from the tormenting question without answering. In a voice now softer with contrition, Saul said, "Bashra will take care of the cost."

"Bashra," Rosental replied with a sigh. "Everybody sees Bashra oil as the answer to all our problems. Lower taxes, higher income, greater employment, even the end of terrorism. Well, Bashra has already cost more than a billion pounds and we still don't know for sure how much we'll ever get back."

"You're being pessimistic, Judah. Every continuing report, on top of what they are producing daily, confirms the expectations of the geologists, engineers and—"

"All right. I've seen the reports, too, and admit the results so far are good, but there are no guarantees how much more lies there beneath that desert."

Saul shrugged, unwilling to prolong that avenue of discussion. Pointing to the Sokolnikov file, he said, "So what do we do with this? Do I put it back while we sit around and wait for the next Shetula?"

Rosental reached over and picked up the file. He riffled through its several pages quickly, its contents so well-known to him, then handed it back to Saul. "No, we don't put it back in your file. I am sorry now that I didn't take quicker action on it before this."

On that note, Saul looked up with interest. Before he could ask his next question, Rosental said, "All right, Saul, let's get down to it. I have just come, as you know, from General Bartok's office. This morning, he attended a meeting in Jerusalem with Goren and the prime minister. As a result, he has handed me a very difficult assignment and for the moment, I am going to put it squarely on your shoulders."

"What is it, Judah?"

"Action. Fast action." Rosental's voice had changed, his mood now charged. "Saul, you're exceptionally good at writing operational plans, so I am going to put your talents to work on this new project. As of now, I am relieving you from all other duties. I want you to drop everything else and concentrate on this. I want an analysis of your thoughts, why you believe the UPFP, if it really exists, was behind Shetula. It isn't necessary to convince me as much as General Bartok. And if it satisfies him, the prime minister.''

Saul said eagerly, ''How far do you want me to go with this, Judah?''

''All the way, as far as you can take it. I want you to draft an operational plan designed to search for, locate and destroy such an organization. On paper, you will staff it, supply it, organize and submit a supplementary list of its needs. Go as far abroad as you feel is necessary, in any direction. By tomorrow morning, I must have something to take to Bartok. If he approves, he will then present it directly to the prime minister. If the prime minister approves—''

''What about the funding for such a project, Judah, an operational budget?''

''Concern yourself only with what I have asked for and leave the funding to others. Take it one step at a time, first things first. How soon can you get started on it?''

''At once, if I can turn over certain of the things I am now working on—''

''I told you to drop everything. That means exactly that. Leave what you are now working on to me. Go now. You have a big job on your hands and I have a lot of thinking to do before morning.''

Saul tucked the Sokolnikov memorandum under his arm and stood up. ''You'll have something by morning, Judah, enough for a discussion with the general,'' he said.

''Very well. I'll phone Bartok's office now and arrange an appointment for eleven o'clock tomorrow morning. And stand by, I may want you to go along with me for that discussion.''

It was nearing six A.M. when Leah Barak, at Saul's request, arrived at the office where he had worked throughout the night. He handed her twenty-four pages of handwritten matter to type into presentation form for Rosental's and Bartok's perusal. Before the general arrived in his office at six thirty, Saul was curled up on the conference room sofa fast asleep.

Tripoli, Libya, April 30

Hatif Tobari lounged comfortably on the shaded balcony of the plush apartment that overlooked the Mediterranean coast to the north. It was not yet eight o'clock and despite the bright morning sun, a refreshing breeze came in from the sea bringing the fragrant odor of lemon leaves with it. Within an hour or two, the temperature would begin soaring to uncomfortable heights.

With only a thin silk robe over his long firm body, he sipped at the strong coffee the young servant girl, employed to see to the comfort of his mistress, Adele Salah, had brought only moments ago. He sipped, inhaled deeply, then drew on the long American cigarette he preferred to the Middle Eastern or European product, feeling immensely relaxed in postcoital euphoria. It had been a night to which he had looked forward for six long, difficult weeks.

At the moment, he felt secure and confident. Every piece in what had been a complicated jigsaw puzzle of his master plan was ready to fall into place. The smaller pieces had been carefully assembled during the past year and a half; eighteen months devoted to moving toward his ultimate objective—proof that the money spent thus far was fully justified—and now the final piece, most important of them all, had dropped precisely into place, the picture complete at last.

Another full day and night with his lovely Adele and he must leave for Iraq to meet with his principals to discuss ways and means to proceed in the only direction possible; onward and upward. By now, they were fully aware, as the rest of the world was aware, that an entire Israeli community had been infiltrated, attacked and utterly destroyed with impunity. The reports from Radio Israel claimed fifty-six dead, but what was most important and far different from all previous reports, was the omission of the fact that the infiltrators had escaped without injury, death or capture.

Only one point annoyed Tobari, yet in a minor way, since it was possible that it would work in his favor; that was the fact that those parasite fedayeen organizations in Beirut, Damascus and elsewhere, hiding in their holes, were claiming that they, the PLO, PLA and PFLP, in separate and unrelated communiqués, had been solely responsible for the attack on Shetula. This, of course, was a small irritation since Tobari had wisely brought along Colonel Afik, deputy chief of Iraq's Army Intelligence and the Russian observer, to be witness to the perfectly planned and executed attack.

And in good time. At this point, his personal funds as well as those advanced him by the Libyan and Iraqi governments were nearly exhausted. Aside from organizational expense and the purchase of the apartment in Tripoli to maintain Adele, his reserves were down to less than four thousand Swiss francs. But after tomorrow—.

He sensed, rather than heard, Adele as she came out on the balcony, then felt her hand caress his smooth, suntanned cheek. She dropped lazily into the chair beside him, smiling and loving, and took the cup of coffee from his hand and sipped at it. "You are up early, Ali," she said.

"Yes. I have much to think about before I leave tomorrow morning for Baghdad."

An expression of disappointment clouded her lovely face. "Tomorrow morning? So soon?"

"Yes, and with regrets."

"Then put your business aside and stay, Ali."

"I wish I could, Adele, but this is very important. I will be away for a month, perhaps a little longer, but soon after that . . . soon—"

"Always it is 'soon,' " she pouted prettily.

Smiling, exposing brilliant white teeth, one hand coursing over her elegant thigh, "Yes, but this time, when this trip is over, we will take a longer vacation together, away from here. Would you like to see the French Riviera, Saint-Tropez, Cannes, Monte Carlo?"

"Oh, yes, yes! I have always dreamed to be there. I have heard so much about the Riviera from my mother. She loved it so much there. A paradise, she called it."

"Then we shall see it together. And soon, I promise."

She took a cigarette from him and puffed it alive. "It is difficult, your business, Ali?"

"Do not become too curious, Adele."

She frowned and smiled simultaneously, childlike in her beauty. "I think you keep it a secret from me, your business, because you know it excites my curiosity. Is it dangerous, what you do?"

"Only in the sense that any business involving international finance and very large sums of money must be kept secret so that others cannot interfere with one's plans. It is nothing personal, my love. When you are older, you will better understand the need for secrecy in important money matters. In everything else, I trust you completely."

"That is nice to know." She leaned over and kissed his mouth and felt his eager response, then drew back. "I will behave like a good girl should."

"I can ask no more. Shall we have breakfast now on the balcony, then take a drive and swim at a beach somewhere?"

"Yes. There is a beach I discovered on the road toward Baidi that is almost untouched. We will have it all to ourselves."

"Excellent. Tell the girl to serve us here while the morning air is fresh and cool."

"Yes, at once." Adele kissed him again, then went back into the apartment to order their breakfast.

Hatif Tobari, who was known in Libya as Ali Fathy, and in his United Palestinian Freedom Party training camp only by the code name Falcon, relaxed again, feeling the closeness of his mistress, savoring it. Adele was his opiate, his release from the tensions of intrigue, from the dangers of exposure to the schizophrenia that was so much part and parcel of his maneuverings in the psychotic world of Middle Eastern politics. Always, he must live with the possibility of assassination by envious fedayeen leaders whom he despised as disorganized, incompetent, ill-trained rabble, forever engaged in bickering, taking unilateral action without regard for their lives as well as those of others.

Living in hovels, always on the run and at each other's throats, depending on the charity dispensed in small amounts by the oil-rich, who preferred to stand to one side with clean skirts and allow others to submit to danger, hoping to emerge as leaders. Of what? Refugee scum unable to pull themselves out of their poverty and hunger? Tobari considered them beneath contempt.

Adele. His safety valve. He had known many women, known them intimately from early youth in his native Cairo, later in England, France, Algeria, everywhere he moved. Women were attracted to him as iron filings are drawn to a magnet, but none had ever touched him, reached so deeply inside him, like Adele Salah.

She was the illegitimate issue of a French officer of noble birth, Jules Dessez, whose hatred for Charles de Gaulle had driven him to join in an assassination attempt that had failed, resulting in Dessez's execution along with six of his fellow plotters. Thus he had never known his daughter, born five months later to her Lebanese mother, Kamilla Salah, in Beirut.

Kamilla, the daughter of a middle-class shopkeeper, left the Salah home in disgrace when it was discovered that she was pregnant. When the funds left with her by Dessez ran out in Adele's second year, Kamilla accepted the largess of a Libyan financier, who was followed by a succession of lovers until her death in Adele's eighteenth year; a suicide after a deep love affair with a Saudi Arabian prince who abruptly discarded her when, after three years, he was ordered to return home to Riyadh.

After a brief period of mourning, Adele coolly evaluated her assets, physical and financial, then took the only course open to her. Possessed of Kamilla's beauty and sexual appeal, she entered into an affair with the son of a Syrian financier, then with an older, wealthier Lebanese importer, but with little capability to feel deeply for either. During the next four years there was a succession of men, all in excellent financial circumstances, but with none of the pleasure she knew Kamilla had enjoyed in her alliances, until she met the man known as Ali Fathy; handsome, apparently wealthy, accepted among the social elite and affluent of Tripoli, and who had at once become attracted to her.

To Fathy, she had a certain animal attraction that awakened a spark of carnality previously unknown. Thus, in their first intimate encounter, he found himself giving more than he had been willing to give to any woman before. And for the first time in her young experience, Adele found love; with it, a need beyond all other needs to be loved by so worldly a man, serving him as he desired, moving into the apartment by the sea that he had bought to share with her. She found him not only kind and thoughtful but extravagantly generous, providing her with a servant, clothing from the most exclusive shops here and abroad, a car of her own, a bank account from which to draw funds during his absences, arranging for her to charge other needs to his accounts.

Yet, in over the two years of their association, she knew little of him other than that he was of Egyptian origin, well educated, a man of means who was involved in matters of international trade beyond her comprehension or knowledge. There had been several trips abroad together, to Paris, London and once to Zurich, each rewarding and sexually fulfilling. And what more could any woman, married or unmarried, want from life?

In a remote area less than thirty kilometers northwest of Kirkuk, Iraq, lying at the base of a low mountain range that extended well into the desert and across outcroppings of massive rock formations and deep wadis, stood the headquarters building of the United Palestinian Freedom Party. From a tall staff rising out of its well-tended grass lawn in the foreground, the national flag of Iraq flew above another which bore the UPFP insignia; a warlike falcon with a rifle clutched in one talon, a lance in the other, ready to strike.

At a distance of about sixty yards to the rear stood a small guest house and perhaps another hundred yards beyond, a series of other buildings—barracks, a large warehouse and a number of utility and repair shops, around which were parked several military trucks, cars, jeeps, two half-tracks, an armored personnel carrier and a few motorbikes. All were painted in severe black and carried the UPFP insignia.

To the north of this grouping lay open training grounds where several small units of five men, each with its own instructor, were engaged in strenuous physical exercises which included infiltration tactics through rolls of barbed wire, demolition drills, negotiating difficult obstacle courses among the rock formations and over wide deep ditches that had been dug in the desert sand. In the distance, one unit was engaged in target practice, using the latest model Russian paratroop automatic weapons. Another such unit was engaged in learning to use flame throwers.

At the headquarters building, which was of far better construction than the others, three men exited and stared intently over the mountain ridge to the east where a helicopter had cleared its top and was now beginning its descent into the valley. Of the three men on the ground, two were in crisp khaki uniforms, short-sleeved bush jackets and straight trousers, revolvers dangling from cartridge belts. The third man wore dark green fatigues. The taller of the three turned to the one in fatigues and said briskly, "Salim, the limousine."

Salim, younger than his two colleagues, ran to the rear of the building and returned at the wheel of a large black Mercedes. The other two got into the rear and were driven out to the training area where the helipad was located. All three got out and waited. The helicopter came in and landed easily, though noisily, its blades causing a veritable dust storm. The pilot cut his motor and remained inside while his two passengers exited and were greeted by their host with warm embraces and smiles. The limousine pulled up now and brought them to the headquarters building where Salim leaped out to open the doors. When the four men entered the building, Salim remained outside.

The tallest of the four men, burned a deep tan by the sun, was the Egyptian, Falcon, leader of the United Palestinian Freedom Party, and its creator. He stood a scant inch over the six-foot mark, rangy and slender in build, but whose body was graceful and strong. His face was pleasantly aristocratic, even handsome, as he moved with casual and familiar ease to his immaculate desk.

The man with him when he met the two new arrivals was Colonel Hakim Afik, deputy chief of intelligence for Iraq; stockily built, with a soft round face, full mustache and small, bright eyes. Afik had been the man with Falcon on the night of the Shetula affair.

Of the two·visitors to the camp, the taller man was General Mahmoud al-Hakemi, Iraqi minister of defense. In his bemedaled uniform, he was a truly impressive figure, both in size and imperious manner, standing at an even six feet and weighing close to two hundred and fifty pounds that were equally distributed to give him an almost heroic stature. The man who accompanied him was also in uniform, also liberally sprinkled with colorful ribbons and medals that befitted his rank and position. General Hassan Saif was Libya's minister of war; a short, slender, almost effete man with swarthy complexion and knifelike features. He carried a silver-handled riding crop and smoked a cigarette held in a long ivory holder with intricate carvings.

But it was Falcon who went immediately to the chair behind the large desk and at once occupied the commanding position while the others accommodated themselves in the three comfortable leather chairs that faced him.

The room was unusually impressive in so remote an area where everything that surrounded it seemed austere by comparison; paintings and two tapestries decorated the walls, one large and two small Oriental rugs on the floor, paneled walls, carved desk and cabinets, urns with colored feathers and tall vases with artificial flowers, and exquisite draperies added touches of unexpected softness and luxury. Behind and on either side of the desk stook the flags of all Arab nations, giving off the subtle, but fictitious aura of total unity among those nations. On the wall behind Falcon hung the framed photographs of Iraq's and Libya's chiefs of state. Significantly absent were those of Egypt and Syria.

On a table against the wall to Falcon's right, as though on display in a salesroom for armaments, were a number of implements necessary to the operations to which the UPFP was dedicated; two Kalashnikov automatic rifles, two machine pistols, two similar paratroop rifles, two revolvers with silencers attached, a pair of binoculars with night lenses, a set of long range walkie-talkie units. In the center of this display lay a dozen blocks of the plastic explosives used at Shetula, an equal number of the pencillike cylinder inhibitors and the calculator-type electronic remote control detonator devices.

But what immediately attracted the attention of Saif and al-Hakemi were the newspapers, Arab and Israeli, whose headlines blared out the Shetula story, accompanied by photographs, which lay on the otherwise immaculate desk top. General Saif pointed the tip of his leather riding crop toward the papers and smiled.

"Congratulations, dear boy," he said. "I hope you rewarded the men who took part in this . . . ah . . . affair."

Falcon returned the smile and replied coolly, "No special rewards, General. These men expect none. Success is their reward."

"Ah . . . yes. You know, of course, that the PLO, PLA and others have already claimed credit for Shetula," Saif said.

Falcon laughed easily, waved one hand loosely. "Let them. It will only confuse and divert the attention of the Israelis in their direction, away from us."

Al-Hakemi leaned forward, elbows on the arms of his chair. "That is good, of course. What now?"

Falcon's expression and voice now became serious. "I am sure you have had favorable reports from our Russian observer, Generals. Colonel Afik can also attest to the impeccable performance of five men who, six months ago, were living aimless lives in refugee camps in Jordan and Lebanon. Here, under my command, they were trained by experts, inspired and instilled with determination. They performed as expected and returned safely. The evidence," he said, pointing to the neat stack of newspapers, "is indisputable."

Al-Hakemi acknowledged with an unsmiling nod. "True, true, but this was a small, relatively undefended farm village, more or less an, shall, we say, experiment?"

With Saif's head bobbing in agreement, Falcon replied smoothly, "An experiment, of course, General, and our first effort in enemy territory. But those five men, with the others now in training will, with further experience, form the cadre that will become the force to achieve our ultimate goal, the destruction of Israel. Not by such attacks on small villages, but on their vital industries, thus creating mass unemployment, damage to their economy beyond repair, causing public panic and the inevitable collapse of not only their government, but nation."

Again, al-Hakemi nodded acceptance. "But you must remember, dear boy, our purpose is to establish a Palestinian state in which Arabs and Christians, even Jews, those who remain, will be able to live and work side by side in peace."

General Saif smiled. "In theory, at least," he commented, "considering how they are getting along in Beirut at this moment."

"First," Falcon resumed, "it is necessary to destroy that which has given the Jews power; their economy. Inflation and the rise in cost of living is helping. Even the civil war in Beirut is an advantage, shielding our activities from the Israelis. But it will require the expanded UPFP to apply the *coup de grâce*. With limited funds thus far, I have established this camp and placed people inside Israel in certain positions of strategic value to our cause. As more money is made available, there will be additional manpower to help us take out every important industrial complex, their docks, shipping and other vital institutions, destroy them just as Shetula was destroyed."

"In all of this," al-Hakemi responded, "I am curious as to how you plan to cope with Arafat, Habash and the others?"

Falcon stood up, looking supremely confident, exuding remarkable restraint. Calmly, sensing their appreciation for the picture he presented, he said, "Generals, I will speak bluntly on this subject."

He paused for a dramatic moment; then, "In assuming total command of the UPFP, I will not tolerate interference from any outside organization. As I stated in my original outline to you, if they wish to join with me, it will be only on my terms. If they resist, they will be eliminated once and for all. It can not be any other way.

"As for the men who call themselves leaders, what have they accomplished besides killing a few handfuls of Jews and losing the men sent to kill them? A few planes hijacked, some El Al planes fired at and missed? Hit-and-run attacks on apartment houses and hotels, bombs thrown at buses and into stores, most of them dying in the attempt or languishing in prisons?

"Generals, suicide actions are repugnant to me. My men will be trained to be skillful. Our investment in them will be too great to send them on missions from which they cannot return. They will be trained to *survive*, as the five who were at Shetula survived, to return and repeat their successes again and again."

"Your plan, you realize," al-Hakemi said, "is highly ambitious, to say the least."

Falcon smiled with grace. "No more ambitious than when I first proposed it to you many months ago. At that time you thought sufficiently well of it to advance the necessary funds to bring us to this point. And if it is ambitious, it is because mine is an ambitious nature."

Saif looked up sharply. "Just what, may I ask, is your ultimate ambition?"

Softly, yet concisely, "To prove to our Arab nations and the world beyond that all Arabs are truly brothers in spirit and unity; that we will preserve our way of life without permitting alien Jews, Russians or Americans to establish a foothold on our soil, on our seas. This land of our ancestors will remain Arab until eternity and Arabs will decide its course."

"Unfortunately—" al-Hakemi began, but Falcon cut across his words.

"I know, General al-Hakemi. It is has been too often said, and repeated by others, that Arab unity is a dream, an illusion. Yet, I am certain that if by one means, through a single source, it can be proved that Israel as a state can be destroyed, wiped out by Arabs, this without outside aid that others beg from the Soviets, Arab unity will become fact in their minds, in their beliefs, in their hearts. They will *know*. They will follow. Rich and poor alike will march together side by side in unity."

Al-Hakemi shifted his bulk into a more comfortable position. Saif lighted another cigarette. Colonel Afik, the silent observer in the presence of superior rank, sat quietly. Falcon waited for some response and and resumed his seat, a faint smile on his lips. The next move, he felt, must come from al-Hakemi. He was correct.

"My government," the general said finally, "is highly pleased with the results at Shetula. We are prepared, and I am authorized, to finance the next step in your plan, provided you can demonstrate your effectiveness on an important industrial complex. If that is successful, you can count on unlimited funds to support the balance of your program."

General Saif's head bobbed up and down in agreement. "And from my government as well."

Falcon's smile broadened somewhat, restraining an urge to stand up and shout for joy. "I have a number of such projects in mind," he said, "any one of which might satisfy your request. May I ask if you have one of particular importance to you?"

"Yes," al-Hakemi replied without hesitation. "Our intelligence sources indicate that much progress is being made in the Bashra oil fields. The activity has increased tremendously there, both in construction and added manpower. Since the discovery, there is no longer any mystery why the Jews were agreeable to return the Abu Rodeis and other oil fields on the east bank of the Suez as part of the Sinai pact with Egypt. Also, Bashra will make the Israelis self-sufficient in oil reserves and give them additional strength both industrially and militarily, a position we find intolerable. That oil belongs to the Sinai, which they misappropriated from Egypt in 1967. We cannot allow it to remain in their hands to be used against Arabs."

"Ah, Bashra," Falcon said. "It is high on my list of prime targets, Generals, but because it lies there in the open Sinai, heavily guarded, it will take special planning to infiltrate with people able to accomplish the necessary preliminary work. It will be difficult and costly, but I can assure you it is possible.

"As I already know, Bashra draws its labor pool from Gaza, Khan Yunis, El Arish and other areas, Arab brethren who are legal Israeli citizens and members of their Histadrut, with equal pay and privileges, which, for us, is truly fortuitous. Among them, we will find willing supporters."

"And if you were to put Bashra at the top of your list of priorities, how much do you estimate this operation will require?"

"I would estimate roughly between five and seven million Swiss francs."

Al-Hakemi nodded his acceptance at once. "You have it," he said. "Let Bashra be your next operation. We will authorize the transfer of seven million Swiss francs to your account in Zurich."

Saif added, "Yes. Our governments are agreed on this project."

"Excellent, Generals. I will start at once to order the equipment I will require from Dresden," Falcon said with elation.

The conference was over. Falcon, Saif, Afik and al-Hakemi were then driven to the helipad by Falcon's aide, Lieutenant Salim Tabet, who recognized from the warm, genial attitudes toward Falcon that success had been achieved. Tabet remained behind the wheel of the Mercedes while the Libyan and two Iraqis embraced Falcon, entered the helicopter and lifted off the ground. When Falcon got into the rear of the limousine, he said, "It went well, Salim. We are on our way."

"I am happy, sir. Will we now begin to extend our recruitment plan?"

"Yes. I want you to prepare to leave as soon as you can to meet with Hafez and give him instructions for the Soulad woman. It is important that she impress on Zuheir Masri the need to recruit only the most knowledgeable mechanics and workers to be sent to seek employment in the Bashra oil fields. To those, she is to offer double pay and a bonus at the completion of the project. Hafez is to remain in the Haifa-Acre area to assist Masri in any way he requires." He broke off as they neared the headquarters building, staring beyond it along the dirt road that led to the entrance gate. "Is that a car I see arriving?"

"Yes, sir. While you were in conference, a call came through from the security man on duty at the gates. It is Amon Sadani. I ordered his car held there until the helicopter left."

"Good judgment, Salim."

Tabet parked the car at the building entrance, but Falcon did not get out—not until the small sedan arrived and parked next to the Mercedes and he could recognize the man who emerged, carrying a suitcase and an attaché case. His face lit up with a broad smile as he saw Falcon coming toward him and walked into the taller man's warm embrace. "Amon! You are a delight to my eyes!"

"As you are to mine," Amon Sadani replied.

"You have arrived at a most auspicious moment. Come in, come in. I have much to tell you." And turning to Tabet, who had followed them, "Salim, have the luggage taken to the guest house and tell the cook I will have a special guest for supper. Our finest wines, eh?"

Amon Sadani walked arm in arm with his host into the building. Side by side, they presented an almost startling contrast, Sadani a good three inches shorter, stockier built, with little of Falcon's elegant, soldierly bearing. He wore thick-lensed glasses in heavy black frames, a full beard and mustache that obscured most of his lower face, his hair windblown and unruly. The suit he wore, although well made, hung loosely on his blocky body in a way that gave him a permanently rumpled look.

Pouring a glass of sherry for his guest, Falcon said, "Well, Amon, a rewarding trip?"

"Possibly. The economic conference in Paris was dry and dull as usual—"

Impatiently, "What about Dresden?"

"I had a long discussion with Eisman, but he found it necessary to get approval from his party superiors, which took an extra day. He is now prepared to furnish our requirements on an initial down payment of one and one half million Swiss francs for the necessary raw materials, parts and labor alone. The balance of one and one half million is to be paid into his Zurich account prior to delivery. Which presents a problem since our own account is now down—"

Falcon slapped Sadani's shoulder with a chortle of glee. "We have it, Amon, and more. Much more. Up to seven million for now, as much as we'll need in the future when we have our next success behind us."

Sadani's look was one of total gratification. With a wide smile, "That is the most welcome news I have heard in a long time. How soon? The drain on our current funds, I don't need to tell you, has been tremendous and has me scraping the bottom to keep our internal organization together."

"That problem, happily, no longer exists, Amon. On your way back to Israel, you will go by way of Zurich, where you will find our account richer by the seven million. Pay the one and one half million into the EismanOptiks account, then withdraw another two million for your internal operational needs, which will leave three and one half million in the general account."

"Then they have agreed to back us fully?"

"Let us say conditionally, to the extent of the seven million."

"What conditions?"

"Nothing we can't live with. Hear me, dear friend. As you arrived, they left, al-Hakemi, Saif and Afik, completely satisfied with the results at Shetula and slavering for more. The condition? One more example to satisfy their masters that Shetula was no lucky accident. The Bashra oil field is to be our next target."

Sadani's eyes widened as his head rocked slowly from side to side. "It will not be easy, Hatif."

"Easy projects will never loosen the money we will need to go forward, Amon. It can be done and I can do it. And when I have brought it off, we will have many more millions to accomplish our goals. Then it will be ours. All of it." Tobari paused to take a deep breath, eyes glittering. Coolly, his features immobile, he spoke again with the voice of a mystic visionary.

"Think of it, Amon. First, Palestine and the Holy City. That alone will bring the Saudis and their oil-rich brethren flocking to us with a fortune in money. Syria will regain her lost land, but for a heavy price in military equipment from her Soviet supplies. Next we will rid ourselves of that mouse, Hussein, and annex Jordan into our new state of Palestine which, with Allah's help, I will rule.

After that, who knows how far we will reach when we rebuild Bashra as our own?''

"Easy, easy," Sadani cautioned. "Let us not run too far too fast, Hatif. We must not only consider the envy we will create, but there will be Egypt to settle with. Our need for military hardware in vast amounts—"

"Once we are in power, Amon, we will make our own deals with whomever we please. Egypt will be no problem. We will deal with the Soviets as an independent nation and they will deal with us without suffering the humiliation Egypt has shown them. It will be ours to do with as we please, to—"

"To create enemies among those who have thirsted for what we will have achieved, even those who are supporting us now? Can we afford to overlook that possibility, Hatif? Their loss will—"

Tobari's expression was one of disdain interlaced with supreme confidence. In a softer voice, he ticked off a stream of names. "Who, Amon? Those disorganized fanatics, Arafat, Habash, Hawatmeh, Kayyali, who in over twenty-five years failed to bring even the tiniest sense of unity to the millions of Palestinian refugees? And as for our Libyan and Iraqi friends, once we are in power, what can they do? Our presence will be recognized by the entire outside world as an established fact. Can they allow it to be known that they were responsible for the growth and domination of the UPFP and be condemned by their brethren in Egypt, Syria Algeria, Saudi Arabia and elsewhere? No, Amon, in no way will they permit this to be made public. Ours will become the true force and voice, situated in the most strategic position in the entire Middle East, outflanking Egypt. We will use the Russians as we have used the Libyans and Iraqis, as the Israelis have used the United States and built a military organization second to none. Don't underestimate me, Amon, as Sadat once did. I know my strengths, my destiny."

When Sadani did not reply, Falcon leaned over and patted his heavy knee gently. "We have come a long way together, Amon. We will go a lot farther the same way. Trust me."

Preparing for bed in his private quarters later that night, Hatif Tobari reflected on the events of the day with near sexual gratification, a feeling he always experienced when he could see himself close to achieving the power he sought; the power that only the ruler of a nation with full military strength could possibly know. In this moment of approach to his eventual, and in his eyes inevitable, goal, more than anything else, he longed for Adele Salah. Not that he could share this good news with her; nor could he permit her to visit him here in Iraq. Only for the release and comfort her body would bring to him.

Lying awake, he reviewed his conversations with al-Hakemi and Saif in minutest detail and felt richly rewarded with the results of eighteen months of planning and labor that had gone into this creation of his brain, the UPFP.

Life was indeed ironical. Since his exile from Egypt, he had lost all faith in Pan-Arabism, saw no great leadership in its claimants to that role in the entire Middle East and respected only the wealth and power of those oil-rich rulers who knew the true strength such wealth could generate, but lacked the wisdom to put it to effective use. At this moment, they held the power to bring the industrial world to its knees but were afraid to apply full pressure. Even without oil, he would achieve what he wanted, but he would have to face up to the need to arrange secret talks with Russia.

For that moment, when it came, he had yet another plan in mind; one that would eliminate the need for the Soviets to continue pouring war matériel into Egypt, Libya and Syria by concentrating on the new Palestinian state headed by himself. But that would come later. For now, he must win the next step, Bashra.

Born forty-two years ago in Cairo, Tobari was the product of wealth and certain influential power. His father, Fawzy Tobari, was head of the largest textile mill in Egypt, employing thousands of men and women, and which supplied printed cotton goods to international and local markets. Much of his success as an industrialist had come through the connections of his wife's cousin, Hamid Sadani, a director of the Bank of Egypt and personal financial adviser to King Farouk.

The Tobaris and Sadanis lived side by side in the fashionable Giza section of Cairo where Hatif was born one year later than his cousin, Amon Sadani. Both had been educated in private schools and, since both were expected to deal in international markets, were later sent off to England to further their educations. With additional tutoring, Hatif managed sufficient credits to enter Oxford simultaneously with Amon.

In England, Hatif, the extrovert, entered an exciting new phase of life. Extremely good-looking and tall, well supplied with money and introductions to his father's British connections, he took advantage of his position in the social world and treated it as his personal playground. Enjoying sports, he took to car racing, cricket, tennis, fencing and sailing, which soon found him caught up in a far livelier world than Egypt could provide.

Amon Sadani, on the other hand, was far less personable, and an academic plodder. Concentrating on economics and finance left him little time to devote to social adventures, participating only at Hatif's insistence; thus he was introduced to young, willing girls he could not otherwise win by himself and who accepted Amon in order to be closer to Hatif.

In 1952, the exile of King Farouk hit both Hatif and Amon very hard, Amon with devastating effect when the elder Sadani was summarily dismissed from the Bank of Egypt by General Mohammed Naguib. In the case of Fawzy Tobari, however, the dependence of the economy on his widespread textile operations was too great to tamper with; thus the Tobari situation remained intact and undisturbed. Then in 1954, when Naguib was replaced by Gamal Abdel Nasser, who had been strongly backed by Tobari, the family fortunes soared while those of the Sadanis, the memory of Hamid's closeness to Farouk still strong, worsened despite Tobari's efforts to have his friend and relative restored to his former position.

So, in 1957, when Amon Sadani began his advanced studies at the London School of Economics and Hatif was ordered by Fawzy to France's Ecole Polytechnique, Hamid Sadani fell into a state of deep depression and committed suicide. Amon's mother fled to London to share an apartment with him, supported financially by Fawzy Tobari, and she died there of heartbreak a year later. When his grief abated, Amon moved to Paris to be close to Hatif.

Not an admirer of the French people in general, whom he felt were arrogant and impossibly superior with little reason, Hatif sought friendship among the members of the flourishing Arab Student League. Before long, he and Amon joined as members and donated liberally to their cause. Soon, Hatif took an active leadership role in the organization and became widely known among its other branches throughout Europe. Suffering the pangs of humiliation by defeat in two successive wars at the hands of the Israelis, he became obsessed with the need to eliminate this tiny, yet powerful, thorn that festered in every Arab heart. Hatif had found a new mission in life.

In the ensuing year, he underwent extensive leadership training with his newly found group, undertaking strenuous physical exercises as well as learning to use every type of weapon from knife to machine gun, explosives, time bombs, and developing new techniques in sabotage. During the summer, after a visit to Cairo, he returned to Paris to become chief liaison officer with similar organizations operating in Germany, both East and West, then became affiliated with the International Council of Arab Students, made up of the extremist Maoist, Saiga and PDFLP throughout Europe, and who were opposed to the more moderate elements connected with al-Fatah.

Always stimulated by action, Hatif moved to Albania and later to Algeria, where he found able instructors in terrorist activities and tactics among former underground freedom fighters from those countries. In Algeria, where they were fighting for independence from France, he came to know death by violence among men dedicated and willing to lay down their own lives for a cause.

In 1962 when, to the mortification of France and the immense satisfaction of Hatif, that war came to an end, he returned to Cairo for a warm reunion with his parents. Amon, his postgraduate studies concluded in Paris, also had returned. Hamid Sadani had left a considerable fortune, banked in Zurich, and the two, with Hatif as always the dynamic leader, renewed an active social life, sharing an apartment in the city as their base of operations.

To Hatif's surprise, he learned that his activities abroad had not gone unnoticed. That discovery came in the form of an invitation to call on President Nasser's chief of internal security intelligence at the palace. The interview was cordial and pleasant and ended with General Walid Sabah's offer of a commission as lieutenant on his palace staff, which Hatif accepted without hesitation.

Handsome in his British-cut uniform, wealthy, and with access to palace functions, Hatif was provided with an everbroadening social life, into which he plunged with all the vitality of his youth and not inconsiderable strength. With support from his father and General Sabah's influence, he was able to procure an excellent position for Amon on Nasser's economic advisory staff.

For five years, the two cousins led an enviable life, marred only by the death of Fawzy Tobari in 1964, and the decision of Hatif's mother to move to Paris to live out her final years with a widowed sister there.

Three years later came the rustling winds of war as Nasser's belligerent voice sounded across the Arab world, demanding the total extermination of what he termed ''that cancer known as Israel that keeps gnawing at Egypt's stomach and heart.'' Supported and encouraged by Syria, Libya, Iraq and a host of other allies, and with vast amounts of military hardware pouring in from Russia, Nasser's threats heated up as the world moved into 1967. Ranting, raving, promising to turn the sands of the Arab world red with Jewish blood, his voice became the voice of all Arabs in a universal cry for a swift, decisive victory.

History, of course, recorded his abysmal defeat, witnessed his tears in failure, heard his resignation as president of Egypt. The Tiger of Faluga had been reduced to the Lamb of the Sinai, a crushing blow to his ego and stature in the Middle East. And then, to the amazement of all the outside world, the Egyptian public responded by demanding that their idol rescind his decision to resign and remain as head of state. Nasser, of course, heeded.

Now a captain and close Nasser aid, Hatif had not participated actively in the war, to his deep regret, but had been kept on duty at the palace under General Sabah's orders. Nor had Amon Sadani, who could not have cared less for physical action. At its conclusion, however, Hatif was ordered by Sabah to enlarge his already broad connections in Europe and the Middle East among men who had used terrorism as a prime weapon in the OAS struggle against France.

So adept did Hatif become at this form of underground activity that he became principal training officer in the art of clandestine warfare. Early in 1970, he was named chief instructor and strategist and on his own initiative, created and developed a virulent plan—a concentrated program to infiltrate Israel secretly with sufficient trained manpower and matériel for the purpose of eventually destroying its most important industries. He guarded his plan carefully, discussed it only with Amon Sadani, who added brilliantly to it by devising the ways and means to move people inside Israel so that detection would be almost impossible. These people would live and work in Israel as Israeli-Arab citizens, to surface at a later date when needed by Tobari.

Together, Hatif and Amon perfected their plan to present to General Sabah first, later, hopefully, to Nasser himself for approval, adoption and implementation. Fate decreed that this was not to be. On September twenty-eighth of that year of 1970, Gamal Abdel Nasser died suddenly of a heart attack and plunged all Egypt into the depths of despair that was hardly assuaged when Anwar Sadat, virtually a nonentity in the political hierarchy, moved from the vice-presidency to become president. In the emerging turmoil and national sadness, there arose the perplexing question: Who would really rule Egypt?

That question was answered by Sadat himself, who quickly took hold of the government reins and, through intricate political maneuvering at which he showed himself to be masterful, granted concessions to most of Nasser's loyal followers, placated those all-important generals with promises and managed to hold firm, pleading for loyalty and compassion from the vast mourning public. To the surprise of opposing factions, he emerged victorious.

This came as a severe disappointment to the coterie of palace stalwarts of which Hatif Tobari was a member, who despised Sadat as an ineffectual compromiser who would eventually disgrace Egypt by submitting to stronger voices in Syria, Iraq and Libya; possibly even to Israel, which now occupied the entire Sinai, had taken Egypt's oil fields on the eastern shores of the Suez, their guns trained on the Strait of Tiran, the Suez itself now a graveyard of ships where a once thriving and income-producing shipping route lay in idleness. Now, more and more, Tobari came to see his destiny—as a leader among those who must eliminate the ineffectual successor to Nasser.

Thus, Hatif put aside his master plan and began another—a coup to depose Sadat in favor of General Walid Sabah, who had fought beside Nasser at Faluga and to whom the name of Nasser was almost synonymous with that of Allah. Amon Sadani was drawn into the plot to assist Hatif in organizing and recruiting sympathizers for the takeover. Months passed before they were ready to present the plan to Sabah and those army colleagues who were loyal to him.

The presentation was made to Walid Sabah in private. The general listened, questioned and, after three days of considering the plan, finally approved and applauded its author. He then proposed that Hatif deliver the outline to his chosen junta members on a holiday that was to occur four days later, when all would be free of their duties and excite no curiosity from prying eyes. In an exuberant mood the three men parted, Hatif and Amon in possession of the master plan in order to make sufficient copies to pass among those who would attend the secret meeting.

On that very night, however, General Walid Sabah made a mistake that was to prove fatal. He celebrated the occasion with his young, attractive secretary and mistress who, having first been sworn to secrecy, learned of the plan that would make Sabah head of the nation. In the morning, after having consumed much wine and engaged in prolonged sexual exercises, Sabah had little recollection of his indiscretions. However, his talented secretary-mistress, an ambitious woman who was a member of the army counterintelligence corps, recently placed in Sabah's office for the purpose of exploring the possibility of a palace revolt, passed the word on to her superior within an hour after reporting for work. Even before Sabah was in full control of his wits, he and his erstwhile junta group were locked behind bars in the Bab-al-Khalik prison and a quiet alert was broadcast for the arrest of Captain Hatif Tobari and his fellow conspirator, Amon Sadani, who was enjoying a holiday respite in the country with two female companions.

On their return to the city that night, Hatif became suspicious at the sight of several unmarked but recognizable security cars in the vicinity of the apartment he and Amon shared. With a plotter's prescience, or intuition, he knew the game had somehow been lost. He continued on past the apartment building and headed eastward, then north. Along the way, it was decided to abandon the car. They bought some clothes from a peasant farmer who took them, hidden beneath a load of farm produce, into Port Said. Four days later, they bribed the captain of a small freighter to take them to Cyprus. From there, they took another ship to Naples and rode a bus to Rome, where Sadani had funds in the Bank of Rome.

Weeks later, they learned that Sabah had committed suicide in prison, his fellow plotters sentenced to life terms. He and Amon had been declared enemies of the state and exiled for life, death to be their reward if found on Egyptian soil. There was also the likelihood that underground agents would be seeking to execute them in some other part of the world.

Hatif had friends in Rome and Amon had family banking connections. Soon, both were caught up in a round of gaiety that, after a month, began to pall on them. Drawing on funds in Zurich, they decided on a change of scenery and flew to Beirut, where life was easy and pleasure cheap in this center of Middle Eastern intrigue; and far more to Hatif's liking. Within a short time, Hatif had been invited to join with several terrorist organizations with which he had connections; but after close examination, decided that most were no more than disorganized mobs without proper order, training or leadership. Undisciplined rabble.

Then, during their fifth week in Beirut, Hatif made the contact he was searching for; in the bar of an exclusive club where he was the guest of an expatriated Egyptian financier. Introductions to other political figures were made, then a foursome went to a dining club for a late supper and entertainment. This latter consisted of four enticingly lovely girls who spent the balance of the night with them. Their host on that occasion was a Libyan, Halil Sheraf, about fifty, a cosmopolite and a man of apparent wealth. And intrigue.

Two days later, Sheraf called upon Hatif, met Amon, and after lunch and much roundabout conversation, surprised the two Egyptians with a bit of extraordinary intelligence; he knew much about Hatif's background and involvement in the abortive coup to depose Sadat. "From my sources in Cairo," he added, "I have also heard that you have a plan which you were unable to put into force, one which I think my principals would be willing to listen to if it is one of practicality."

"There is no plan," Hatif informed him. "It was hidden in a safe place which I was unable to reach before I left Egypt, in, as you have guessed already, a hurry."

"Of course, and understandable, but as its author, you know its details and can reconstruct it, no?"

"Naturally, but only as long as there are certain guarantees made to us."

"As to financing," Sheraf said with a smile, "there will be no problems."

"There are others."

"Such as?"

"First, that I will head the organization the plan proposes, with full autonomy. Second, that a substantial fund be placed at my disposal through my Swiss bank to permit me to recruit necessary manpower, instructors, etc. Third, that a training camp be established close enough to Israel, either in Lebanon, Syria or Iraq. Fourth—"

Sheraf held up a hand at that point. "So far, your demands are neither impossible nor unreasonable to me. However, I am not in a position to give you a definite affirmation. Let me propose this: tomorrow, you and I will fly to Tripoli for a meeting with certain ranking officials. You will outline your plan. Guarantees, if it meets approval, will be given. You should have an answer within three or four days. Agreed?"

"One point," Hatif said. "If your government is in this alone, it will not work. It will need the cooperation of others, and I must have the same guarantees from them."

Sheraf smiled expansively. "My government and that of Iraq are irrevocably aligned in this venture and I can assure you of indirect cooperation from Syria and Lebanon. Does that satisfy your needs?"

"A final question, then. Would any other known Palestinian fedayeen organizations be a part of this?"

"Only if your plan includes them."

"It does not in any way include them, or anyone else."

"Then I am sure that can be agreed upon." Sheraf smiled and withdrew his wallet, from which he extracted a sheaf of currency. "To show good faith, here are five thousand Swiss francs for immediate expenses. Be ready to leave at eight o'clock tomorrow morning. My car will call for you then. You alone." He turned to Amon then. "My apologies, but that is how it must be."

Amon nodded his acceptance of Sheraf's terms, content to remain behind, feeling he could contribute little to negotiations in which Hatif was far more skilled. As usual, he preferred the role of follower.

At a private, well guarded seaside villa in Tripoli, far grander than any Tobari had ever seen in the Middle East, Halil Sheraf introduced the Egyptian to General Hassan Saif and left them together. Tobari's first reaction was disappointment, assessing his host as an effete dandy, and he was immediately determined not only to remain firm in his demands but to raise his sights higher. However, as the two men shared a delicious meal on the broad veranda overlooking the sea, he came to realize that Saif was not only a man of unusual insight and intelligence, but knew exactly how such games were played.

Therefore, when his plan was outlined in the briefest of terms, more in a manner of salesmanship than in detail, Saif occasionally dropped a comment into the discussion that was more than adequate to prove his understanding of the overall design. Yet his attitude remained one of restrained interest as he posed thoughtful questions that concerned methodology, without displaying undue eagerness. The evening passed on that note and without either affirmative or negative decision.

Saif left Tobari at sundown to return to the city, indicating that a second meeting would take place after lunch on the following day. An apartment had been placed at Tobari's disposal at the villa and, after an impeccably served supper, he lay in a sunken tub and soaked away the tiredness of travel and his long discussion with Saif.

He had risen late on the next morning, was served a light breakfast, after which he went for a swim, lay in the sun, then dressed for his meeting. After lunch, Saif appeared with two uniformed generals and two civilians. In the resplendent library, the six men sat around a carved table and Tobari repeated his limited proposal. From the deference shown Saif by his colleagues, Tobari became soon aware that the minister of war was the power here—the key spokesman for President Qaddafi.

Now Saif pressed the Egyptian harder and Tobari opened up a little more, but stubbornly resisted any changes in his demands. The two generals and two civilians did little more than listen to the exchanges between the two principals. Smilingly, Saif continued to urge Tobari to disclose more. Finally, Tobari considered it unwise to withhold any more lest negotiations be broken off and he would be left with nothing more than an empty plan. He thus revealed his project in full, even to the method by which he intended to build an internal organization within the borders of Israel, and without which no plan such as this could hope for success.

The Libyans were obviously satisfied with his disclosures and appeared willing to make certain concessions, except on the point of total and absolute autonomy. Saif agreed that a training camp would be provided in Iraq; funds for recruitment of necessary manpower and instructors would be forthcoming upon agreement with his chief of state. But before the plan would be accepted in full, solid evidence that Tobari's objectives were attainable must be clearly demonstrated or support would be withdrawn and the project abandoned. The question of autonomy would rest upon such proof.

On the third day of discussions, Tobari agreed to Saif's amendments. He and the general then flew to Baghdad to meet and confer with General Mahmoud al-Hakemi. After two full days of meetings, total agreement was reached and a down payment of half a million Swiss francs would be deposited to Tobari's credit in Zurich to commence operations. At such time when the new UPFP organization would prove conclusively that it was capable of carrying out a successful mission inside Israel, further funds would be forthcoming. Al-Hakemi also insisted that until that time of proof, his deputy chief of intelligence, Colonel Hakim Afik, must be included in all operations as an official observer.

Having little choice in that direction, Tobari agreed; and also to the presence of a Russian observer at the time of the first mission.

Hatif returned to Beirut with certain doubts still plaguing him. With most of the obstacles removed, he felt ready and able to begin putting his organization together, but there were certain values he felt the Libyans and Iraqis were unable to understand. Tunnel-visioned, they were able to concentrate on a single target, but little beyond that. For instance—

Hatif understood the inbred desire to destroy Israel, but not in the total, bloodletting destruction that Nasser had intended or encouraged, which was what he was now expected to accomplish; if not at first, later. Deep in his mind, he reasoned that since 1948, nothing in its centuries of history had cemented Moslem and Christian Arabs so firmly together into a unified family as the birth of the state of Israel, providing them with a single common goal, its destruction.

Unity, in realistic terms, was another Arab fable, a fantasy dream. Egypt, by entering into the American-inspired Sinai pact, had shown the Arab and outside world how fragile and meaningless was that word. Even if Israel were to be conquered, its Jews obliterated or otherwise dispersed, that unity, frangible thing that it was, would fall apart at once, with all Arab nations embroiled over its partition. When that occurred, who would accept—even tolerate—the multi-thousands of Palestinian refugees along with their poverty, diseases and whining complaints, and for whose fate Israel had become a necessary and welcome scapegoat?

If this question was to be solved, it must be done in one way. First, the UPFP must take over all that land called Israel, with its buildings, improvements and industries that remained, and dominate it by right of conquest, yielding nothing to any other claimant. Once reestablished as the state of Palestine under one rule, it must refuse to recognize the jackals now clamoring for it—the dozens of splinter groups of terrorists who would be tearing at each other's throats within minutes of Israel's defeat. They, rather than the Israelis, must first be destroyed, and the defeated Jews driven into the Sinai to live as refugees themselves. Later, they would be offered a choice: to live under Arab rule and work for the good of the state of Palestine or live in extreme poverty until the Zionists in the United States or elsewhere could force their governments to accept the Israelis.

Beyond this, to solve the Palestinian refugee problem, he secretly planned an even greater goal, which would involve the one Arab nation he considered to be most vulnerable to takeover.

Jordan.

The Hashimite king had long been a thorn in the side of Tobari's idol, Nasser, holding back on his agreement to attack Israel in force during the 1967 and 1973 wars, contributing nothing to draw Israeli troops away from the Suez, supporting no one but himself, whining, complaining of a lack of air support. Hussein's diplomatic antics and overtures to the United States were a personal affront, putting on a show of doing battle with the ragtag PLO in 1970, driving them out of Jordan. Thus, Tobari saw a portion of Jordan which he would allocate as a proper home for the refugees and with that solved, the extinction of al-Fatah and the other irregulars as a threat.

*   *   *

Lying low in the water well south of the Lebanese border and some forty-five kilometers west of the Israeli coastline off Achziv, Seraf Nuri's aged fishing boat, its motor cut, rose and fell lazily in the soft swell of the Mediterranean. Muri sat hunched forward on the starboard rail, a gaunt man with skeletal frame and thin features, gnarled hands and soured expression. His young nephew, Nafech, who had removed the wooden hatch over the motor and laid out an assortment of wrenches and other tools, a fiction in the event a passing craft or patrol plane became curious, leaned against the hatch and smoked a cigarette. Soon it would be sundown and such precautions would no longer be necessary.

Nuri looked out over the blue mirror of sea around him. It was almost impossible to define where the sea ended and the sky began. The day had begun in the predawn hours in order to leave port unnoticed and they had thus had to kill time, stopping now and then, proceeding slowly, to reach this point at this hour. He pulled a sweat-dampened rag of a handkerchief from his hip pocket and wiped the moisture from his forehead and face, which gave him little relief.

It gave him some small comfort when he thought of the six men who were crowded together in the forward cabin, bathed in their own sweat and without sufficient headroom to stand or move about; four on the short, wooden benches on port and starboard side, two sitting cramped on the floor. Each was armed with a submachine gun and pistol, hand grenades pinned to their jackets, extra ammo clips jutting from their pockets. During the entire day none had been permitted out of the cabin to stretch their muscles or catch a breath of fresh air, nor would their leader, Salah Jihadi, permit the cabin door to be opened. Like a furnace in there, Nuri thought.

"How much longer, in Allah's name?" called Jihadi from inside the cabin.

"Soon, soon," Nuri replied. "The sun is lowering. When it falls below the horizon we will move southward. Not before."

There was a chorus of grumbling and curses from the cabin, but Nuri and Nafech exchanged grins as they looked around them over the empty sea and sky. Let them curse. Jihadi had urged Nuri to move faster, faster throughout the day. Now, lying dead in the water, there was little air to breathe. For his needless haste, let them sweat. Once he landed his human cargo off Nahariya in their rubber boat, he and Nafech would be on their way back to their home port, Tyre, under safe cover of darkness.

Once he dropped them, he had no intention of lingering. If these fools wished to commit suicide, Nuri did not intend to become a part of such nonsense. But the money for delivering them here was good. He had listened to their talk and reckoned their chances for success and escape to be impossible. How they could expect to hit the largest hotel there, the Carlton, and get out alive, was beyond comprehension. As in the case of the Savoy raid in Tel Aviv, he knew the Israeli police and army would storm in and slaughter them regardless of the cost.

Forty minutes later, although there was still some light in the sky, Nuri passed the word to Nafech to start the motors. Taking the wheel, he began moving slowly in a southeasterly direction. He would use no running lights on the approach. Those that would appear on the shoreline later would guide him toward their target.

In their light two-seater patrol plane, pilot Joel Nachman and his observer, Chaim Laboff, had reached the end of the northernmost leg of their run and banked left over Kfar Rosh Haniqra for the final run back. Routinely, Laboff reported his position by radio to base camp, then picked up his long-range binoculars and swept the sea to his right.

Below, the sea had turned from blue to dark gray and from their height they could barely see the thin upper rim of the sun that was about to disappear below the horizon. On the run north, Laboff had seen nothing to excite interest along the entire coastline.

Now, to break the monotony, Nachman swung west away from the coast over the darkening sea and began a gradual descent. After fifteen minutes on that course, he banked easily to his left to return to the coastline and, as he began to gain altitude, Laboff called out, "Joel!"

"What?"

"There, off to my right—"

Nachman dipped the nose of the plane and swung right. "What is it?"

"A wake. A boat, running without lights."

"I don't see it."

"Drop down. I'll turn on our landing lights."

Nachman began to circle the area, losing altitude. Laboff switched on the powerful landing lights and there, in the center of the circle, was the fishing boat, barely moving in the water. As they swept over it, they could see two men, one bending over the uncovered hatch, the other standing beside him. Fishing gear littered the deck. Both men looked up, then waved in a friendly gesture.

"What do you think?" Laboff replied. "They were moving at a fair clip moments ago, so their motor is running. And why are they working over the engine without a light to see by, or without running lights. If their electrical system is out, they would be unable to move at all and would be signaling for help."

Without further discussion, Laboff picked up his radio mike and reported his suspicions and location to base camp and asked for a patrol boat to investigate. Base camp acknowledged and ordered the plane to fly cover until the patrol boat arrived on the scene. Laboff then switched on his loud speaker system and bellowed the order to lay to. The fishing boat acknowledged the message and cut its motor.

"Turn on your lights!" Laboff ordered.

The taller of the two men waved his hands from side to side and shook his head negatively, indicating that they had no lights, possibly the reason why they had been running without them. The boat began to drift slowly as the plane continued to circle it.

*   *   *

Just as dusk had fallen, Lieutenant Baruch Cohane and his crew had begun their tour of duty in the new patrol boat that had been delivered to Coastal Command after a full week of shakedown runs. Tonight would be its first regular patrol assignment and the entire complement was eager and alert. Cruising south and west of Shavei Zion, her radio chattered its call letters and Cohane replied immediately, and received his first order. He gave his quartermaster the course change and ordered full speed ahead. There was a certain electricity in his voice as he gave the command for the two heavy machine guns to be uncovered and charged, the huge searchlight forward turned on.

Racing in a northwesterly direction, with every pair of eyes straining to pick up first sight of their objective, Cohane made radio contact with the patrol plane, giving it his location, direction and rate of speed.

Back came word from the patrol plane; that it must soon abandon its position and return to base camp before running out of fuel. Cohane checked the position of their target with Nachman and acknowledged. Within a few minutes, the patrol plane was overhead, signaling its presence by flicking its landing lights on and off, then disappeared in the blackness overhead.

Aboard the fishing craft, Salah Jihadi emerged from the cabin as soon as Seraf Nuri advised him that the plane had departed. "Then why are we waiting?" Jihadi asked. "Let us move on. We have a long way to go yet."

"We are not going to move on," Nuri replied firmly. "In all too short a time, a patrol boat will be breathing down our necks."

"We have come this far—"

"And we will go no further."

"Damn you, head north quickly!"

"It is no use. We won't be able to outrun their patrol boats. The best you can do, and at once, is to inflate your rubber boat and get your people into it. If you are lucky, you will be too low in the water to be seen."

"You ass!" Jihadi thundered. "You have been paid to take orders, not make decisions. Start your motor!"

Nuri turned away, pointing. "Look there," he said, "and tell me who is an ass. The faint light you see there is heading in our direction. It is an Israeli patrol boat and—"

"Move, I tell you!" Jihadi roared.

"It is already too late. We cannot outrun them. By now, they have us on their radar screen. You still have time to do as I say. Get your rubber boat inflated—"

Jihadi pulled out his revolver and rammed its muzzle into Nuri's belly. "Start the motor and get out of here. Quickly!"

Nuri nodded and Nafech started the motor. With surprising ease, the craft responded. Jihadi prodded Nuri toward the wheel. "You damned coward! Head north and west!"

Now the other fedayeen had emerged from the cabin and stood indecisively, aware that all the plans they had been discussing for the postmidnight infiltration into Nahariya had been for naught. In every mind was the silent, nervous assessment of their chances for escape.

Running at full speed, the fishing craft was hardly a match for the oncoming patrol boat, whose searchlight grew larger and brighter by the minute. To his guerrilla colleagues, Jihadi shouted, "Get down out of sight. Lie flat on the deck behind the bulkhead. When they come within range, commence firing. Use your grenades—"

"It is useless," Nuri shouted, gesticulating, trying to make himself heard over Jihadi's shouts and the roar of the motor. "If you fire even one shot, they will sink the boat and kill every one of us. You are a fool—"

"Shut up and do what you were told, fisherman. I am in charge now. I will not be taken into a damned Israeli prison!"

"Then we will all die here tonight."

"So be it."

The searchlight behind them was now sweeping the sea from side to side, the lookouts eagerly scanning the surface through binoculars. Cohane, of course, had suspected that the target craft would have begun moving soon after the patrol plane departed, and stood beside the quartermaster, changing course to widen the circle of search. It was then that the starboard lookout caught the wake of the fishing craft in his binoculars and shouted his sighting. Cohane steadied his binoculars and ordered a course change to starboard. The two machine gunners threw the safeties off their weapons and were ready. And now, at full speed, the patrol boat moved in on the target, siren activated, bullhorn ready to issue the command to lay to.

As it cut speed and approached, Cohane could see only two men in view. He raised his bullhorn and shouted, "Cut your motors, turn on your lights and lay to! We will board for inspection!"

The fishing boat throttled down but did not cut its motors. Nuri, with Jihadi's gun aimed at him from the deck, went to the side and shouted back, "I am having motor trouble! If I shut down, I will not be able to start up again!"

"Cut your motor at once or we will open fire!" Cohane shouted.

Then, suddenly, the Israelis were taken by the surprise of seeing six figures rise up from the deck and begin firing their submachine guns. First victim was the searchlight. Second was Rudi Shalhana, the starboard gunner. As the second gunner opened fire, the fishing craft leaped out and, after a brief straight burst of speed to open some distance between them, began a zigzagging course northward.

The patrol boat raced after it, opening a circle to take it out of range of the submachine guns, yet within striking distance of its own heavier machine guns. On board Nuri's boat, two men had fallen, Nafech and one of Jihadi's men. The others, except for Nuri, who remained at the wheel, had dropped below the solid rail and continued to rise and fire sporadically at the patrol boat. Cohane shot ahead and, with superior speed, began to circle the moving fishing craft. And now his machine guns were depressed farther, firing into the target's waterline. Coming around on the port side, the two gunners swept the afterdeck, then concentrated on the starboard waterline. And now, Nuri, realizing the futility of further attempt at escape, reached up and cut the motor. The craft shuddered and wallowed to a stop.

"Start the motor!" Jihadi screamed.

"It is useless. We are taking water. We will sink, you fool!"

Jihadi fired twice and Nuri fell to the deck, dead. The Arab leader rose and began tinkering with the starter, unable to find the correct switch to turn, then smashed the console with the butt of his revolver in total frustration. And now the patrol craft nosed in closer. A flare had been fired and night turned into day; then a second flare added to the brightness. The fedayeen were on their feet now, but with two heavy machine guns looking down their throats, with water beginning to lap at their ankles, none made any further attempt to raise his weapon. No grenade had been thrown. Even Jihadi saw the senselessness of continuing the action. He dropped his weapon and sat down heavily on the wet deck, head held between both hands.

Two boat hooks drew the fishing craft alongside the patrol boat and four fedayeen came aboard. Two Israelis boarded the fishing craft and herded Jihadi ahead of them. They searched the vessel, gathered up the weapons and handed them across to the patrol boat. Then Cohane radioed in with word of the capture and for instructions.

He signaled two more of his crew aboard the foundering fishing vessel. The dead were then handed across and charges were set. The boarders returned to their own vessel, the order given to move off. At a point some six hundred yards away, they stopped and waited. A few minutes later, the time charges exploded, flaming the sea and sky for a few brief minutes. When the fishing boat sank beneath the surface of the sea, they continued toward the coastline.

* * *

General Yigael Bartok looked up wearily from the mass of paperwork that lay strewn across his desk, smiling forlornly as he pushed his thick-rimmed glasses up over his forehead to rest on a thinning carpet of gray, curly hair. "Come in, Judah," he called out, then peering through squinted eyes, "Ah . . . Lahav . . . Saul, isn't it? Come in. Sit down." He spread his muscular arms, hands with palms upward over the cluttered desk. "Papers," he said morosely. "Letters, cablegrams, teletypes, reports, reports and more reports. Without paper, there would be no wars."

Rosental and Lahav took chairs facing the chief of Mossad's desk. "There were conflicts and wars," Rosental observed laconically, "when men were still writing on stone tablets and the walls of their caves."

"True, Judah, true." As Bartok began scavenging through the desk litter, he added in an undertone, "Except for the invention of paper and more sophisticated weapons for men to destroy each other, I often wonder how far we have come from those days." He began rustling through a number of bound documents, pushing papers aside, and with a victorious "Hah!" held up the copy of Saul's report. "Here it is."

"Have you had a chance to review it?" Rosental asked.

"Yes. Yes, of course. I put it ahead of everything else."

"And?"

"Well." Still grasping the material in his right hand, "Considering the shortness of time you were allowed, very good. A comprehensive proposal." Peering first at Rosental, then at Saul, he directed his next remarks to the junior officer. "I take it this is the product of your labors, no? Reading it, I was reminded of a report that Judah submitted quite a long time ago which dealt with a very detailed underground resistance operation."

Saul grimaced. "I had hoped that one would have been buried and long forgotten by now, General."

"No, no," Bartok protested mildly. "I recall that it showed excellent thinking and imagination, even though it was rejected as being . . . ah . . . in conflict with our policies and goals."

"I have long since changed my viewpoint on that subject, General," Saul said.

"Yes, so I assume. Reading this proposal," waving it toward Saul, "I considered that some of the same imagination was still at work." He flipped over the first introductory sheet to the copy of the Sokolnikov memorandum which had been included. With his head turning from Rosental back to Saul, he said, "Now, as to this UPFP matter from the Russian defector—'' Bartok broke off and looked back to Rosental.

Sensing some possible doubt in the chief's preliminary opening, Rosental rushed to head off what might well be an abrupt dismissal of the suggested project. "General," he said, "I fully concur with Saul's analysis of this new and threatening situation that confronts us and with his plan to deal with it. I don't think the possibility of its existence, as exposed in the Sokolnikov memorandum, should be taken lightly. We believe strongly that the danger is clear and present and I support Saul's feeling that it was the UPFP that was behind Shetula.''

"So I gather from this document, Judah, but is your judgment based on allegations by a Russian defector, handed to you unofficially, clandestinely, and not substantiated by supporting evidence of any kind?''

"General," Saul interposed, "if in the past we had been forced to sit and wait for positive proof that an enemy action was imminent—''

Bartok waved that aside with a broad flat hand, showing signs of impatience. He stood up and began to pace back and forth behind his desk, forehead wrinkled in deep thought.

He was not impressive in stature, standing no more than seven or eight inches over the five-foot mark, broad-featured and showing thick musculature in his arms, chest, and shoulders. His face, neck and hands, with the texture of desert sand, were burned permanently brown by years in the outdoor sun. From his earliest years, brought to Palestine from Poland at the age of seven, he had known marauding Arabs close at hand, had defended his kibbutz in the Jezreel Valley as a member of the *shomerim* guards, served with the British Army during World War II, against the British in pre-1948 Haganah, as an infantry officer in Israel's first national army, commanded a paratroop unit, and later moved into tank command.

Following the 1967 war, in which he distinguished himself, Bartok left active field duty to become deputy chief of staff of Mossad and, on the death of its chief, was chosen to head that senior intelligence service, holding that position under two prime ministers.

The aggressiveness for which he was noted in the field had become considerably subdued by the nature of his present duties. He had become an intelligent listener who absorbed details and facts, catalogued them in proper order of importance and made swift decisions. When he did so, he became dynamic in movement, pacing, gesticulating to dramatize a point. He seldom stood on ceremony with subordinates and was inclined to address them by first name rather than rank, and encouraged them to reply in kind. Few did, yet the effect was one of intimacy and openness; but underlying all, each knew better than to assume softness on Bartok's part. A good friend, colleagues called him; and a very tough enemy. But no one had ever challenged his abilities in matters vital to the survival or safety of his beloved homeland.

"I have studied the Sokolnikov memorandum, the American analyses, together with your collective opinions," he said now while continuing to pace. "I have also reviewed our own dossier on this Russian defector and find some hesitancy on my part to readily accept his casual story, which Mr. Collier reports was unasked for and given wholly voluntarily. Certain questions arise in my mind; *if* there is some connection between Sokolnikov and this Egyptian, Falcon; Falcon's connection with the alleged UPFP; and the UPFP, *if* it in fact exists, with Shetula. What I see are large gaps that are not clearly related.

"Putting those questions aside for the moment, there are other considerations that must be taken into account, but first, I must ask this: how far can we trust this Lee Collier? Were he and his colleagues taken in by Sokolnikov? Is there more behind this than meets the eye?"

"What are you suggesting, General?" Rosental asked, bridling.

"I am not entirely sure, Judah, but certain possibilities come to mind and I would like to explore one that is of primary concern to me. As you know, I was in favor of the Sinai pact from the very start, in face of rather strong opposition from other quarters, including General Goren, who objected to our withdrawal from the Mitla and Gidi passes strongly. However, despite my approval, I have always felt that the removal of our troops from those passes would strongly intensify terrorist activities on the part of Arafat, Habash and other elements who suffered a terrible defeat and swore to step up their attacks on us, as they have.

"Russia, also losing considerable face by the signing of the pact, has been pouring unlimited military stores and money into Libya, Syria and Iraq, along with other aid to the Palestinians, at once regaining strength which it had lost in Egypt. Their propaganda machines in the United States have been playing a very familiar tune; that aid to Israel, in any form, is creating another Vietnam situation, bringing them to the precipice of a war that will involve American lives in a hopeless effort."

"General," Rosental interposed, "isn't that stretching matters far beyond the subject we are here to discuss?"

"Not if you study the reports from Foreign Ministry Intelligence,

Judah, with copies of American newspaper editorials, statements made in the Congress, letters to editors from the public. The climate there, since withdrawal from Vietnam, has been one of total opposition to involvement in any war or internal politics abroad. Understandably. Also, there is an enormous reluctance to offend the Arab oil countries in the face of a continuing and critical energy crisis.''

"But Bashra will eventually relieve that situation, won't it, General?''

"Eventually, Judah, is not today. We have given up Abu Rodeis and Bashra is still not producing enough to supply all our needs. In time, perhaps, but not yet.''

"So?''

"So we are faced with a multiplicity of problems that still remain unsolved. You are aware, of course, that a main objective of the Palestinians is to involve us in a war with Syria, in which case the Sinai pact would be voided by previous pact and Egypt would be obligated to come to Syria's aid. In which event, we must ask ourselves these questions: Will the United States continue to resupply us with much needed military equipment as our own becomes depleted in such a war? Or will it take months of debate in the White House, Senate and House of Representatives before a decision is arrived at? And finally, will the decision be favorable or unfavorable to us?''

Bartok paused, almost breathless, then sat down. "If I seem to be placing undue emphasis on issues that go far beyond the subject we are discussing, Judah, Saul—''

"If I may, General,'' Rosental said, "I think you are. I don't see the connection between the UPFP and total war in the future.''

"Possibly, Judah, possibly, yet one must try to look into that future. To go even farther afield, we are still at odds with Syria over the Golan Heights situation. Syria's strong differences with Iraq over sharing the waters of the Euphrates will have no bearing on their relationship if a war erupts between Syria and Israel. She also has a pact with Jordan. Even Libya would settle its differences with Egypt if a unified war showed the possibility of the destruction of Israel. After which, God forbid, they would again resume their own wars.

"So, Judah, all the parts and bits go to make up the sum total, and each part, no matter how small, must be taken into account. Since the birth of our tiny nation in 1948, we have lived through wars, threats, diplomatic pressures, boycott and blackmail, and we have survived, however barely, and are, as always, prepared to use every means available to us to continue to survive. There is serious talk that if, in our next war, we are unable to contain or defeat our enemies by conventional means, we will surely do so by . . . ah . . . unconventional methods. If Israel goes down, she will not go down alone. Cairo, Damascus, Amman, Tripoli and Baghdad will keep us company."

"Ah," Rosental said, "the nuclear threat."

"It goes far beyond mere threat, Judah, and we are obligated to understand the implications." Bartok paused for a moment, then continued. "To get back to our primary subject, how can we accept this new bit of information wholeheartedly without exploring its reliability or looking for valid proof that such a danger really exists?"

The last question seemed to be addressed to Saul, as author of the proposal to take action against an unknown terrorist organization. He shot a quick glance at Rosental, saw no immediate reaction there, then realized it would be up to himself to further defend his position.

"General," he said, addressing Bartok, "I am fully aware of the situations which you have outlined, but in all fairness, I feel that much of it is not applicable to the matter presently at hand. Despite what transpires in the rarefied atmosphere of high-level politics and diplomacy between Israel and other nations, I see this as a situation for local consideration and action, not involving a total commitment of military forces.

"I undertook to propose a certain course of action because I do not believe a man like Lee Collier, who has worked with General Rosental in the past, would be used to pass on useless Soviet disinformation that would put Sokolnikov in the position of a double agent, designed to embarrass us. My question is, why such an excessively roundabout method when there are less extravagant means to accomplish that same goal?"

When Bartok nodded, signifying a silent request for Saul to continue, he said, "As for positive proof of the existence of the UPFP, and its connection with Shetula, there is none, admittedly, but the sophistication with which this attack was accomplished is great enough, in my mind, to speculate that a remarkably new advance has been made in terrorist tactics and technique that is beyond the capability of present similar organizations as we know them.

"As to our American friends, I largely suspect that what Collier has given us is in the nature of a friendly act on the part of some in Washington, even possibly at lower levels, with whom we have exchanged valuable information on an equally unofficial basis in the past. There is also the need to take into consideration the oil fields of Bashra, a definite asset to America as long as they are in our hands, an embarrassment to the world energy crisis if they fall to Egypt.

"Take note that we have been requested to keep Washington out of this in order not to compromise their own precarious position in the Middle East and with the OPEC nations with whom they must deal on the question of oil prices and possible embargoes. Further, General, I like to think I am somewhat of a judge of character to this extent: I believe Collier is an honest man who sincerely believes the opinions of his department's evaluators, therefore I accept the Sokolnikov memorandum for what it is."

With a smile, Bartok said, "And how do you feel about what we have just heard, Judah?"

"I not only support Saul's judgment in his proposal, but also as it pertains to Lee Collier," Rosental affirmed. "I have known Collier for a long time and have worked closely with him in the past. I trust him implicitly."

"So," Bartok said, still smiling. "I am glad to have your opinions. Understand, I am not entirely opposed to your views. Sometimes I ask questions and project negative thoughts in order to force those views into the open, pro or con. To delve deeper into this, as you must realize, will create manpower and monetary problems, but a great part of any cure is to be able to first know and name the disease. That much will have to come next. There is also a time factor involved and it seems that time is no longer on our side. Like the Arab nations, aided and supported by Russia, and with money from their sources of oil, and opposition to us by Third World nations, time has become our enemy."

No reply had been called for and none was forthcoming from Rosental or Lahav. "So," Bartok said with finality, thank you for your efforts. I will take this matter up with the prime minister and ask for a decision."

"When?" Rosental asked.

"Since time is the controlling factor here, Judah, at once. One way or another, hopefully, I am sure we will have an answer by tomorrow, no later than the day after. I will be in touch with you as soon as I have it."

Late on the following afternoon as Judah Rosental sat at his desk reviewing and analyzing Saul Lahav's suggested list of requirements necessary to establish the proposed Special Operations Branch, he was surprised by a visit from General Bartok; a rarity, since Bartok would normally have had his secretary summon a subordinate for a conference, even a chat. Rosental rose, stubbing out his cigarette, but Bartok motioned him to resume his seat. "Sit, sit, Judah. Am I interrupting?"

"No, no, General. I was only reviewing Lahav's plan, just in case—"

The older man dropped into the visitor's chair with a sigh. "Just in case the plan is approved? And what if it is rejected?"

Rosental pursed his lips. "It has already been decided?" he asked.

"No, not yet. Not conclusively. I have discussed the matter with the prime minister at length. He was receptive and is discussing it with his chief deputy, Davidov, and some of his cabinet advisers. By tonight, I think I can expect to have an answer."

"I hope it will be a favorable one."

"After selling the plan of Lahav's to the prime minister as well as I think I did, I think I succeeded in selling it to myself as well." He paused to light a cigarette, then said, "Judah, I am convinced. This thing must not be allowed to be talked out of existence. Sixty-four acts of terrorism and sabotage last year and we are well on our way to break that record so far. In the matter of deaths, we are far ahead of last year's total."

Rosental merely nodded acknowledgment of statistics that were only too well-known to him.

"So," Bartok resumed, "what about Lahav to head this proposed Special Branch, Judah? From the little I have seen of him, I like him, but I don't know too much about him."

"Saul? I would find it hard to recommend anyone over him, General. His credentials are the finest; in the field, and in my department. I have known him since the early days of Haganah, into which I recruited him as a young boy. He is experienced, stable and a dependable, dedicated man."

"I have examined his official record and can find no fault there. He is married, I noticed."

"Well . . . yes and no. His wife, Miriam, returned to America soon after the seventy-three war and remained there with her parents. Last year, she finally filed for a divorce there."

Bartok emitted a sibilant, "Ah—" as though he had discovered a flaw; then, "There are children?"

"There was a son, Dov. A medical student. He was on duty in the Golan during that same war. He was killed there. It brought a final end to a marriage that had been deteriorating for a long time. Let me add, General, that I can't fix any blame on either Miriam or Saul."

"Then what brought it about, this deterioration?"

"Two things, I think. Miriam's inability, for an American-born woman, to adjust to a much harsher way of life than she had been exposed to before, and Saul's total dedication and sense of duty to Israel."

"There was no scandal, no other woman involved?"

Rosental hesitated before answering, then said, "General, are you making a particular point?"

"Yes, I suppose I am. Since yesterday, I have made some private inquiries. I understand that Lahav is involved with a lieutenant in Military Intelligence, a Lieutenant Altman. You know about this?"

"Yes. Toba and I know about it and know her very well. And only in the most complimentary terms. She is a good officer—"

"And," Bartok interrupted, "I suppose if Lahav is given command of this new branch, he might even ask for her transfer?"

"If he does, I will give his request my full approval."

"I see. And from our point of view, do you consider this is a wise move, safe?"

"I think this, General. From our point of view, his arrangement with Lieutenant Altman will be advantageous in permitting him to live a normal life, what he can spare from his duties, and will in no way interfere with his primary purpose, which is to seek out, locate and destroy this new menace. His duty has always come first, which is perhaps the true reason for the failure of his marriage."

"And if I can't see it that way and reject his request to have her follow him into the new branch?"

"I would hope you won't do that. If you do, I suspect that we will have to look farther for someone to head that branch."

"And you would not, I take it, want that."

"No. If the branch is established, as I hope it will be, I want the best man possible for that job."

"All right, Judah. In deference to your judgment, I won't bring the matter up. But what if a higher authority does?"

"General, let me put it to you this way. What I am concerned with here is Lahav's performance. The other does not enter my thoughts. Toba and I have entertained Shana Altman and Saul Lahav in our home on many occasions and I can find no reason to drive these two people apart from a relationship I consider is their affair and theirs alone."

"Do you think Lahav would defy the prime minister, Judah?"

Rosental laughed briefly and grimly. "In this case, yes. Let me clear the picture a little better for you. I think we need him more than he needs us. Lahav is a man of considerable financial means, money he inherited from his father that has been wisely invested and grown. I honestly believe that if his relationship to Shana Altman arises as an official matter, he will ask for retirement, or resign, which would be Israel's loss."

"I see." Bartok stood up to leave. "Well, Judah, I will let you get back to your work. As soon as I have word on the prime minister's decision, I will be in touch with you.''

While the discussion between Judah Rosental and Yigael Bartok was taking place, Saul Lahav was at his desk poring over a list of names, men and women he felt qualified to fill the positions he had enumerated in his original proposal for the organization of the Special Operations Branch. Some had served with him in the field, others known to him by casual association, the rest by reputation only.

It was a worrisome chore in that his top choices were from other service branches and he must therefore exercise caution in order not to offend the heads of those other services; in which case, further cooperation, vitally necessary, would be indeed hard to come by. Yet, he knew that if the recommended list was approved by Rosental and other higher authorities concerned, the prime minister's order would override any objections by the service heads.

Thus, he struck out a name here, substituted one there, added new names to his list. When he was finally satisfied with the pared down assortment of names, he worked out a second list of assignments and began pairing names with jobs.

Soon, afternoon slipped away into night and it was nearing ten o'clock when he finally compiled what he believed to be a reasonable selection of field and staff personnel. Only then did it occur to him that there remained one position in the entire makeup that lacked a name; that of the man who would head the organization. He pondered over the omission for a while, reluctant to propose his own name for that ranking position, then threw down his pen, scooped up the papers and locked them in his desk drawer until morning. He was tempted to place a call to Shana, then considered the hour and decided against it. At eleven fifteen, he left to get a full night's sleep.

At two ten, his phone rang persistently and finally awakened him. He responded with a sleep-thickened voice that was barely recognizable. ''Lahav.''

''Major?'' came the perplexed voice. ''Major Lahav?''

''Yes. What is it?''

''Adam Solomon, Major. Night duty officer.''

''What is it, Adam?''

''We've just had a call relayed to us from Coastal Command's detention center at Kerem Maharal. They've taken four survivors in an attempted terrorist attack on Nahariya from the sea. The senior officer is requesting someone to handle the interrogation. Colonel Kohn advised me to give it to you.''

Saul muttered an imprecation under his breath. "All right, Adam. Order out a helicopter and have it stand by, then phone Asad Hasbani and have him meet me there."

"At once, Major." Saul hung up, groaned his way to the bathroom, then began dressing.

The sun was beginning to rise when Saul completed his interrogation of the four surviving terrorists, learning little more than they had been first trained in Syria, then sent to Tyre under orders to avenge the most recent retaliatory attack on a Lebanese fedayeen camp by the Israelis. Salah Jihadi steadfastly refused to answer any questions put to him and would not even admit to his name, which Saul had obtained from one of the others.

Asad pleaded with Saul to permit him to question Jihadi alone, but Saul knew they would gain nothing more at this time; disappointed that he could find nothing to link this abortive attack with the elusive United Palestinian Freedom Party. After three solid hours of effort, he decided there was nothing here to interest him.

After a quick breakfast with the camp commander in the mess hall, they checked the weapons and ammunition taken from the fishing boat. All were of Russian or Czech manufacture, familiar and not out of the ordinary. These were placed in cartons to be taken back to Tel Aviv with them. Hasbani was sealing the last carton with tape, marking it for identification, when a sergeant summoned Saul to the commander's office to take a call from Colonel Kohn.

"Good morning, Saul."

"Good morning, Omri. I hope you had a good night's sleep."

Kohn chuckled. "Sorry, Saul. I had little choice. Was there any possible connection with UPFP?"

"No. This was no Shetula operation. Al-Fatah, standard weapons. The leader won't talk yet, but one of the men told us they were going to hit the Carlton Hotel, take hostages like the Savoy thing some time ago. Otherwise, nothing out of the ordinary."

"When are you planning to return?"

"We're just about ready to wrap up and leave."

"Good. The general would like to see you as soon as you get back. Lunch. Agreeable?"

"Affirmative. I'll be there."

After dropping off at his house to shave, shower and change into fresh clothes, Saul drove to Rosental's office and arrived at twelve fifteen. Rosental smiled and said, "You look a little tired, Saul. You should try to keep better hours."

It was a standard, well-worn joke between them and Saul wondered over Rosental's apparent good humor and mood. "Maybe I will, Judah, sometime when I can get a full night without an emergency call.'' Then added, ''Or a leave of absence that isn't canceled on the second or third day.''

''You'll never let me forget, will you. Let's hope it will come to pass. Omri tells me there was nothing interesting at Kerem Maharal.''

''Only the usual. Four prisoners. Three others dead. We lost one dead, one wounded, not seriously. Coastal Command will notify the dead man's parents and make all the necessary funeral arrangements.''

''Ah yes. Regrettable. Well, let's get out of here. Ready for lunch?''

''I'm starving.''

In the restaurant nearby, patronized principally by military and government personnel who worked in the large blocks of adjacent buildings, Saul and Judah were seated in a rear booth away from most of the hubbub of voices. They had finished their meal and sat over coffee and cigarettes in casual conversation dealing with the work at hand, but Saul could feel there was something more involved to come. At a table in the near center of the room, four men were similarly preoccupied in sober conversation, when one, a short, stocky, balding man with black-framed glasses rose and started toward the rear. Rosental looked up, caught the man's eye and returned his wave of recognition.

To Saul, ''Mordecai Aarons, a member of the Economic Advisory Council, an expert on budgetary matters. You know him?''

''I've seen him,'' Saul said, ''but never met him.''

Both rose as Aarons reached their table, a hand extended to Rosental, which he took, exchanging ''*Shaloms*.'' He then introduced Saul to the newcomer.

''Ah, yes. Major Lahav. I have heard of you, Major, many excellent things.''

''Thank you.''

Aarons turned his attention back to Rosental. ''It has been a long time, Judah.''

''Yes. Months, Mordecai.''

''I don't get down to Tel Aviv often, then only for a quick conference and back again.''

''And today?''

''Only time for lunch, a conference, then back to Jerusalem. How is Toba?''

''Fine, fine. And Suzi?''

''As usual, fine. Judah, we are having some friends in for an evening, tonight. Perhaps you and Toba will join us? Also,'' pointing to his table at Morris Lurie, the Inspector General of Police, "Lurie, Broder and Aronsky will be there."

"I think it may be possible, but I must first check with Toba to see if there is something else. I'll phone you later, either way, if that is all right."

"Of course. And," Aarons suggested, "perhaps Major Lahav can join us as well?"

Saul, surprised by the suddenness of the invitation, hesitated for a moment, then said, "I'm afraid I won't be free this evening, *Adon* Aarons. Duties, you understand."

"Ah, duties. I understand, Major. Perhaps another time." And to Rosental, "Eight o'clock if you can make it, Judah?"

"If we can make it, Mordecai, and thanks."

Seated again, Rosental said, "That was not very diplomatic of you, Saul. Aarons will have a lot to say about any budget request for a Special Operations Branch to handle this UPFP thing."

"The minister has approved it?" Saul asked with quickening interest.

Rosental smiled. "You have so little faith in Bartok's powers of persuasion, Saul?"

Eagerly, "That is really good news, Judah. Who will head it?"

Still smiling, "The minister and Bartok made a number of excellent suggestions."

"Some of their former army friends, I suppose."

"Some, but an amicable decision was finally arrived at."

"Who?"

"You, Saul." And as Saul's face lit up with pleasure, "But it took a lot of convincing by the chief."

Momentarily stung, "Judah, if the minister thinks I am not qualified to—"

"No, no. He knows you are qualified, Saul, but that wasn't the question."

"Then what?"

"There was an . . . uh . . . personal, a moral question."

Indignantly, "A *moral* question?"

Rosental nodded. "The prime minister, it seems has heard rumors of an . . . ah . . . affair between you and a certain attractive lieutenant in Military Intelligence, and that you are still married. It came up in the discussion with General Bartok."

"You know the divorce is in progress—" Saul broke off angrily. "Listen, Judah, I'll accept any assignment I'm given and do my job. I'll put up with every known inconvenience, as I have for years. What I won't stand for is interference in my private life, what little privacy is left in it, and I'll tell that to Bartok and the prime minister in person.''

Rosental smiled again. ''So relax, relax. Bartok told the prime minister exactly that. Remember, Saul, he is the prime minister because he is a flexible man, not only in military matters but in his judgment of people.''

''So?''

''So as of this morning, while you were at Kerem Maharal, you were officially promoted to the rank of colonel in charge of the new Special Operations Branch, which will be technically under my supervision for administrative purposes.'' And as Saul continued to stare, ''You will pick your own staff from ours and other intelligence services as your proposal outlined. Each service will be directed to cooperate, but don't overdo it. However, you will have to move to Jerusalem, where you will be closer to ministerial observation. Your new headquarters will be the old abandoned police station at number seventeen Rehov Ben Gurion.''

That evening, Saul did go to Jerusalem, but not to attend the social evening at the apartment of Mordecai Aarons. He drove directly to Shana's apartment to break the news to her and, while she prepared supper, he telephoned Yoram Golan, a colleague of Shana's at Military Intelligence. That call concluded, he phoned Dov Shaked of Shin Beit, with whom he had often worked in the past. After a light supper and while the four bottles of imported wine he had brought were cooling, Yoram and Aanat Golan arrived almost simultaneously with Dov and Dorit Shaked. Saul drew the cork from the first bottle and poured six glasses.

''To what?'' Yoram asked.

''To Saul,'' Shana offered. ''Colonel Saul Lahav, head of the new Special Operations Branch of the Antiguerrilla Department. *L'chayim.*''

They drank and congratulated Saul on his promotion, then clamored for an explanation of his new assignment. ''I can't tell you very much now, dear friends, and only if you, Dov, and you, Yoram, will accept my invitation to join me in the SO branch. If you agree, I will make official requests on Military Intelligence and Shin Beit for your transfers.''

''Done,'' Dov Shaked said with enthusiasm.

''Done,'' Yoram Golan echoed.

Hands were shaken, shoulders slapped. Dov said, ''Like old times again. When, Saul?''

''At once. Transfers will be effective almost immediately. Aanat and Dorit, you will both be pleased to know we will be headquar-

tered here in Jerusalem. I am also requesting Shimon Navot from
Mossad and Uri Yerushalmi from border patrol to round out my key
staff. I will take your recommendations for other agents we will
need to fill our vacancies and see how it fits in with my list. And
now," he turned to Shana, "the one I have been holding back for
last. Shana, how would you like to transfer from Military Intelligence to head our Records and Communications Section?"

The others applauded and began urging her to accept.

"Wait, wait," she exclaimed, elated. "You know how much I
would love it, but I don't think that Colonel Zarbat will approve my
transfer."

"He will have little choice, Shana," Saul countered. "I have the
highest priority from the minister himself. My first act tomorrow
morning will be to submit my list of key personnel I need from the
various services. Within a few days, all your chiefs of service will
be informed, Colonel Zarbat along with the rest."

"When will all this happen, Saul?" Shaked asked.

"By the end of this week. On Monday, I hope we can all report to
our new home, seventeen Rehov Ben Gurion."

Shaked groaned with dismay. "That hole?"

7

The building at number 17 Rehov Ben Gurion, surrounded by small business establishments on a street known by another name until the death of Israel's first prime minister, was an ancient two-storied building of stone that had outlived its usefulness as an area police station. From time to time thereafter, it had served as a warehouse and storage depot for old police records and unusable equipment. More recently it had been rented to a furniture manufacturer who had moved out when he found his operation required more working space. At present, it had been vacant for a period of five months.

Now a labor force of cleanup crews, painters, carpenters and electricians swarmed through its interior to renovate its two floors and basement. On the street level next to the entrance door, a sign painter was lettering its new identification: SHOMERON IMPORT-EXPORT CO., but the device fooled hardly anyone; yet neither neighbors nor passersby stopped to ask questions or otherwise satisfy their curiosity.

On the rear parking lot, trucks arrived to unload desks, chairs, tables, filing cabinets, typewriters and more sophisticated types of office machinery, cartons and crates. On the rooftop, a crew was busy installing a system of highly complicated antennae. Greatest attention was directed to the upper level where offices and working cubicles had been marked off and walls erected. Glaziers inserted glass dividers between cubicles from waist-high to ceiling while telephone technicians installed outlets where a blue-chalked "x" had been marked on floors and partition walls.

Whereas the offices and cubicles were arranged to line the east and west walls, the entire center of the second level remained an open working area with desks forming aisles and file cabinets used to separate the various interoffice sections. Along the south wall,

161

which faced the rear parking lot, Shana Altman was supervising the installation of radio communications and computer equipment which would operate in conjunction with Records and Communications, plus a bank of teletype machines for instant contact with other intelligence agencies in Jerusalem, Tel Aviv and Southern and Northern Commands as well as police and border centers.

The entire north wall, facing out on Rehov Ben Gurion, had been divided into a private suite; a reception office at the head of the stairway, Saul's private office, and a large conference room. The ground level, opening onto the street and parking lot, was divided into smaller offices and storage space, with a guard stationed behind a counter at the front and rear entrances. In the cavernous basement, the rear section had been outfitted by Dr. Sara Levitt as a technical and scientific laboratory where she and three assistants would tend their criminalistics duties. The front half of the basement contained six steel-barred detention cells, two full-doored isolation cells, two interrogation rooms, bathroom and kitchen facilities.

General Rosental paid his first visit to number 17 when the improvements were completed and after a quick inspection, voiced his approval. There was little to discuss at the moment, although Saul could feel a sense of urgency in the general to get matters moving. A good deal of money had already been spent, equipment and vehicles borrowed from other services, experienced personnel likewise requisitioned from sister organizations over numerous protests and objections; but which were quickly overridden when requests were confirmed by ministerial directive.

Rosental had insisted on personal security for Saul, but Saul refused to allow any unnecessary importance be attached to him that might mark him as a natural target. To temper his refusal, he agreed to a driver-bodyguard and chose Sergeant Asad Hasbani for that assignment. Asad was delighted to serve Saul in that capacity and at once moved his mistress into a small rented house in the Arab quarter in East Jerusalem.

The first staff meeting was called on a Sunday morning, a full working day. Yoram Golan, Dov Shaked, Uri Yerushalmi and Shimon Navot were the first arrivals in the conference room. Leah Barak, who had moved from Tel Aviv to become Saul's secretary-receptionist, served coffee while the men examined the huge aerial photo map of Israel and the Arab nations that surrounded it. The map occupied the entire length and height of the west wall. On the east wall was a map of Israel alone, shown in multicolors that divided the nation into police and military districts. Here, each major, secondary and minor road was carefully marked and code-numbered, every city, town, village, moshav and kibbutz clearly identified, all borders sharply defined.

In the center of the room stood a long table with five chairs on each side, one at each end. Other chairs, a sofa, side tables and a stenographer's desk, along with a standing blackboard, made up the balance of the furniture. At six of the places on the table, Leah had placed a lined yellow notepad, ballpoint pen and an ashtray.

Despite open windows, the conference room was stuffy with the odor of recent paint. The four men were jacketless, tieless, in short-sleeved shirts that were open at the throat. The air that entered from outside did little more than add to the inside heat.

Yoram Golan and Dov Shaked were friends of long standing, having served together in the same army unit; the former of British parentage, born in London and emigrated to Israel late in 1948. Golan was tall, blond, with even features and a certain reserved manner. He was thirty-eight years old. His wife, Aanat, who was thirty, had been born in Amsterdam and had escaped Holland with her widowed father in 1940, aided by Dutch friends who had shepherded them to neutral Sweden and from there to Haifa.

Dov Shaked was Golan's age, a Sabra like his wife, Dorit, both born in the Galilee. Dov was shorter than Golan, more ruggedly built and had studied law for two years after his required military service before finding academic life too dull to his taste. Upon rejoining the army, he began taking a keen interest in intelligence work, which eventually led to his recruitment by Shin Beit.

Uri Yerushalmi was forty-one, known to Saul and the others only by reputation. A lieutenant in border patrol, his knowledge of the northern and eastern borders, and experience with infiltrators, was vast. Outwardly, he gave the appearance of a quiet, taciturn man who weighed his words carefully. He was married, the father of five children, and kept his private life strictly apart from his work, spending what time he was allowed with the single hobby of his lifetime, archaeology.

Shimon Navot was innocuous in appearance, a man who could easily be overlooked in a crowd, ignored when moving about alone. There was little that was unusual or outstanding about his five-foot-eight-inch height, 160 pounds, and tawny complexion to attract attention. He was clean-shaven, hair cut short, with ordinary features that were perhaps his greatest assets. He seldom looked anyone directly in the eyes, as though unwilling to be stared at in return. Navot, however, could name streets, buildings and alleys in most Middle Eastern cities where he had worked underground, recall telephone numbers, faces, names and aliases without hesitation. He was forty-five years old and had never married.

At eight fifteen, Saul and Shana entered the conference room together. Behind them came Asad Hasbani, carrying a number of folders which he placed on the table in front of Shana's place. As he started to leave, Saul said, "Stay, Asad." Hasbani went to the sofa, but Saul added, "At the table with us, Asad."

To the others, "For those of you who have not met him let me introduce Sergeant Asad Hasbani, a former member of the police department's investigative branch and a six-year member of Mossad. Since General Rosental insists that I need a bodyguard, which I have resisted, I have compromised by asking Asad to move from Tel Aviv to Jerusalem to become one of us. He will be assigned officially as my driver, but I will find many other uses for his special talents."

All present acknowledged the introduction with brief nods and a smiling wink from Navot. "To continue," Saul said, "you have met my secretary, Leah Barak, who will take notes at this, and subsequent staff meetings. For future reference, Leah will know at all times where I can be reached when I am not here at headquarters. At other times, the day or night duty officer will be given that information. For the rest of you who will be operating in the field, Dov, Yoram, Uri and Shimon, you will let the day or night duty officer know where you can be reached, day or night, whenever you check out of this headquarters. Is that clearly understood?"

Those named nodded in agreement. "So, we are ready for the business at hand. Today is the official birth of the Special Operations Branch of Mossad's Antiguerrilla Section. I have spoken to each of you privately and at length. You know my reasons for having chosen each of you for this job; Yoram and Shana from Military Intelligence, Dov from Shin Beit, Shimon from our parent organization, Mossad, and Uri from border patrol. You have now met Asad, who will be assigned to various duties by me personally. I think my choices should be obvious to each of you and I am very happy to welcome you here today as a unit. We also have other personnel, requisitioned similarly from various services. Others will be added. All are capable men and women with special talents and I will look to you present here as my key planning and operational staff.

"From this morning on, we in this room will be working closely together. We will eventually come to work and think alike. Later, I will discuss separate divisions which each of you will head. For now, the first assignment is Shana's. She will head our Records/Identification/Communications Section. We will make our rules and regulations as we find need for them, but I will mention several here and now.

"No one will be addressed by his or her rank in the SO branch. There will be no uniforms worn on duty or off. On entering this building, all personnel will wear a special identification badge where it will be visible to all. On leaving, the badge will be removed. So much for minor matters. Now to our purpose.

"I have discussed this subject with each of you personally and informally. Let me now explain it to all so we will have the same meaning. In simplest terms, our purpose is singular: to seek out, locate and destroy an enemy organization of terrorists presently known to us only as the United Palestinian Freedom Party, or UPFP, and about which we know little more than that it very likely exists. Our suspicions in that direction are closely tied to a top secret memorandum which you have not yet seen, and which will shortly be disclosed to you, and linked to the recent Shetula massacre, which we believe with good reason was committed by that terrorist organization."

Uri Yerushalmi raised a hand. "Yes, Uri?"

"Are we to disregard the claims of responsibility made by Fatah and other organizations for Shetula?"

"I think we can discount those claims as pure boasting. Nothing as sophisticated as this operation has ever been known at their hands in the past. Reportedly, the UPFP has no affiliation with any terrorist group known to us. Beyond that, we know only a little more, but enough to give the prime minister reason to authorize this organization of ours. Therefore, we must first discover and identify it, this UPFP. That is our primary objective for now, our *raison d'être*.

"Shana will hand each of you a copy of the top secret document we know as the Sokolnikov memorandum. I think some of you will recognize that name. Attached to this memorandum, you will find an analysis by me which will explain how we obtained it and the explicit dangers to Israel that if suggests. Study this material carefully and make notes for our next discussion session. It is probably the most effective and diabolical plan yet devised by our enemies to cause the total destruction of Israel as a nation, as a people. When you have absorbed this material, we will consider its implications together and try to come up with the means to prevent it.

"One question before we dismiss: Who among you knows Egypt best, has served or lived there?"

A moment of silence followed during which each man present considered the question, then Shimon Navot, the Mossad man, said, "I think most of us here have been in Egypt at one time or another, Saul, but for any deep knowledge, I would suggest Eitan Drory. He was born in Egypt, schooled there, and worked undercover for Mossad until his cover was blown and he was forced to escape to Israel.''

''Where is he now, Shimon?''

''I don't know. On his return here, if I remember correctly, he transferred into Foreign Ministry Intelligence.'' With a shrug, ''He could be anywhere; East Berlin, Brussels, Damascus, Teheran—''

Saul turned to Shana, who sat with pencil poised over her notepad. ''Shana, contact Foreign Ministry and see if you can persuade them to give us some information on the whereabouts of Drory; then I will see what can be done about having him transferred to us on temporary assignment. If there is a problem, let me know and I will take it up directly with the foreign minister.''

To the others, ''That is all for now. Get your offices in order and study the memorandum. We will meet here again at eight A.M. on Tuesday.''

Late that same evening a small, nondescript farm pickup truck turned into the rutted dirt road that led to the farm of Ibrahim Riad. The driver stopped at the partially closed gate, got out and opened it, then drove inside and closed the gate again. As he was about to reenter the truck cab, Riad came out of his house and stared at the intruder, then started walking toward him. Dangling from his right hand, which he held behind his right thigh, was a revolver.

The driver of the pickup truck waited. He was young, about twenty-five, taller than Riad by a full head, slender in contrast to the older man. He was dressed in a pair of khaki work pants, blue shirt and a sweater that had seen better days. He was clean-shaven and wore his thick, black hair combed smoothly back from his forehead. His features were clean, eyes bright and alert and his lips began to curve upward in a smile.

Riad stopped about six feet from the man and said, ''If you seek work, there is nothing here for you.''

''I do not seek work, but information. How many kilometers to Haifa? I am a stranger in these parts.''

Now a new look of intensity came into the older man's eyes. ''You have many kilometers before you yet,'' he replied.

''But my direction is correct, is it not?''

''Yes, brother.''

''You are Ibrahim Riad?''

''Yes. And you?''

''My name is of little importance, but I am known as Hawk to some.''

''Ah, yes. You are welcome, Hawk.''

"I wish to speak with Assaf Hafez."

"Yes. Drive your truck into the barn. I will walk."

Riad started toward the barn while Hawk got into the truck, started it and followed slowly. At the barn's entrance, Riad waved him inside, where Hafez, who had witnessed the entire scene, waited. When Hawk got out of the truck cab, recognition was instantaneous. Hafez braced himself into stiff attention. Hawk, who was Lieutenant Salim Tabet, turned to Raid and said, "Thank you. Now permit us to speak alone."

When Riad was gone, Tabet said, "Stand at ease, Hafez. Away from camp there is no need for these formalities."

Hafez relaxed. "You have orders for me, Lieutenant?"

"Yes. First, Falcon's compliments on your leadership at Shetula. He asked me to express his pleasure and has rewarded you with a promotion to the rank of sergeant."

"Thank you, Lieutenant. I am very happy."

"You will be even happier with your next assignment. Now that the military roadblocks have been removed, you will proceed to Haifa, where you will contact our principal agent there." Tabet withdrew a wallet and extracted a small photograph. "This is her photograph. Study it and remember it." He turned the photograph over. "Her name is Tahia Soulad and her address is there. Commit it to memory also. I cannot let you keep this."

Hafez repeated the name and address several times, implanting it in his memory, then turned back to the photograph of the sensual face. "She is beautiful," he said.

"Yes, but do not let that come between you and your sense of duty. She is older than you and a well-known dancer, which is an excellent cover for her activities there."

"I understand. What are my orders?"

"The equipment is safely stored in the station wagon?"

"Yes."

"Then you will make contact with Tahia on your arrival. She will introduce you to the leader of a group of sympathetic brothers, legal citizens of Israel who are employed in various industries in the Haifa-Acre area.

"When you meet this man, you will display the equipment to him and explain to him how it was used to destroy Shetula, and thus demonstrate that our objectives can be achieved without detection to himself and those who will be working with him in the future. This is very important to our organization. Once this is done, you will wait until you receive further orders from Falcon, through me. You will find a room in Haifa in which to stay for the time being. Tahia will help you find one, but you must be sure not to contact her unless it is her wish that you do so. This is necessary in order to protect her safety and yours as well.''

"I understand. It will not be difficult."

"Do not become overly confident, Hafez. You must always be aware that as we seek to destroy the Jews, the Jews are seeking to destroy us. Be most careful at all times. Keep in mind one thing: if something does go wrong, say nothing, tell them nothing that can be traced back to Falcon or the UPFP. Above all, do not mention names, Tahia's in particular. That is of utmost importance."

"I understand. I will not fail you."

"Good." Tabet now removed a thick envelope from under his shirt. "Here is some money, all in Israeli pounds. Also, a new set of identification papers. From this moment on, you are Jamal Dhalad, an Israeli-Arab citizen from Jaffa. Now, empty your pockets. I want your old identification papers, currency other than Israeli, anything that will identify you as other than what you appear to be."

The exchange completed, Tabet said, "We will stay the night here. At dawn tomorrow, you will start for Haifa. I will follow behind until you reach there safely, then go on to Jerusalem where I have other business to attend. Now let us see if Riad can find some food for me."

On that same night, a drenching rain that had been falling on Hamburg, Germany, during the late afternoon had lessened in its intensity by eight P.M. Shortly thereafter, Nasri Fouad, a ranking member of the Arab Students League in that city, left the house where his terrorist cell maintained its headquarters, carrying four packages wrapped and tied in brown paper. The package on top was prestamped and addressed to:

> Honorable Benyamin Scheib
> Consul General
> Consulate of Israel
> Paris, France

and the printed return address label was that of *Freiheit Verlag*, a well-known publisher in Hamburg. The other three packages, each with the same return address label and required postage, were addressed to Israeli consulates in Amsterdam, Brussels and London.

Fouad placed the four packages on the front seat of his Volkswagen van, started the motor and allowed it to warm up before activating the windshield wipers. Satisfied finally, he turned on the headlights, shifted into drive position and pulled away from the curb.

Half a block behind him, a small, dark Opel moved out of its parking place and followed at an easy pace. Its driver was not unhappy with the falling rain, now misting with fog; if it was difficult for him to keep up with the van ahead, he reasoned that it would be even more difficult for its driver to take note that he was being followed.

At the first corner the van took a right turn. The Opel followed, saw that the VW had speeded up on the wider thoroughfare and accelerated to maintain proper distance, remaining in the right-hand lane. Within the next mile, the VW made a left turn into Bahn-strasse, which was more heavily trafficked and a better situation for the Opel driver, who moved up closer, yet permitting a single car to remain between him and the VW. Six blocks later, Fouad came to a stop at a traffic signal. When it turned green, he made a right turn into a one-way side street and pulled up on the left curb in front of a branch post office that was closed for the night.

The Opel took the same turn and parked at the curb on the right side of the street. The driver cut his lights, but allowed the motor to continue running. At this point, he was less than fifty yards from the VW van. In the Opel, Eitan Drory, a slender, sharp-featured man with swarthy complexion, reached under the raincoat that lay folded on the seat beside him and brought up a Uzi revolver whose barrel was further extended by the silencer that had been screwed onto the muzzle.

Holding the weapon in his lap, he waited coolly until he saw Fouad get out of the van, carrying the four packages toward the curbside mail receptacles. As the Arab lifted the top package to deposit it into the mail receptacle, Drory rested his weapon on the window ledge, aimed it at the three remaining packages in the crook of Fouad's right arm and fired a single shot.

The result was astonishing and remarkable; an explosion of tremendous force that instantly destroyed Fouad, the three mail boxes, set the VW on fire, shattered the immediate pavement and street, along with a number of the glass doors and windows in the post office building.

At once, Eitan Drory threw the Opel into gear and raced through the falling glass and debris to the corner of the next street, where he made a left turn on two screeching wheels that barely missed a parked car, and another left at the next street, which brought him back into Bahnstrasse, where he slowed down, made a right and melted into the traffic pattern, long before police and fire vehicles reached the scene of the bomb blasts.

On the following morning, Eitan Drory awoke at his usual hour and, after dressing for the day, left his rooming house and walked three blocks to a restaurant, where he purchased a morning newspaper and ordered breakfast. The headlines and photograph of the destruction of the night before added a certain zest for food and after a third cup of coffee, he turned the paper to an inside page and left it on the table. He paid his check and went to the nearest corner where he boarded a bus.

Thirty minutes later, he entered a building in a busy commercial section of the city and took the elevator to the tenth floor. He opened the door marked MITLA TRADING CORP., nodded to the reception clerk and walked down the corridor to the last office on the left. He knocked twice and a deep voice answered, "Come in."

Behind the desk sat an older man with graying hair and gold-rimmed glasses. The man smiled and said, "*Shalom*, Eitan," and pointing a finger to a copy of the same paper Drory had read at breakfast, "Well done. Well done."

"This time," Drory said phlegmatically, "he was carrying four packages."

"So we have prevented four possible executions in our consulates and embassies."

"Yes," Drory agreed, "but this will not stop them, you know, not here or elsewhere. I would like to—"

But the man had picked up a telex form and handed it to Drory. He said, "I'm afraid that will be all for now, Eitan. It seems your services are needed at home for something more important. I will turn this assignment over to someone else. You are booked for Paris and Tel Aviv. Your plane leaves in three hours."

Nearing midmorning of a bright, sunny day, Assaf Hafez had passed through Acre in his VW station wagon without any problems. In his rearview mirror, he caught occasional glimpses of Salim Tabet's pickup truck, which gave him a deeper sense of confidence. The road, a main coastal thoroughfare, was smooth and well-trafficked with private cars, trucks and occasional local and tour buses traveling in both directions.

He came into Ein Hamifratz, the next town south of Acre, overlooking a sweeping curve that formed a huge bay with Haifa and the Carmel hills in view. And then, coming around a bend in the road that would bring him into Kfar Masaryk, he came upon a scene that startled him by its sudden appearance: a police checkpoint. Sixty yards ahead, waiting for inspection of identification papers and contents of cars and trucks, was a line of waiting vehicles.

Police cars were angled in a manner to force all approaching vehicles from the north into a single lane, barricades marking the lane through which each must move, stop, be examined, then continue south—unless something was discovered to excite police attention.

And, suddenly remembering the equipment cached in the hidden compartment beneath the floorboards over his petrol tank, Assaf Hafez first grew confused, then fell into a panic.

Reacting to his fears, Hafez braked the VW sharply, causing his brakes to screech. The VW skidded, came to a halt, then made a sharp U-turn and began driving northward toward Ein Hamifratz and Acre. Behind him, some twenty car lengths, Salim Tabet stared in astonishment at Hafez's sudden, inexplicable move. Quickly, he pulled to the right side of the road, stopped, got out and raised the hood over his motor, just as Hafez flashed by without glancing at him.

Back at the inspection line, an alert Israeli policeman looked up at the sound of squealing breaks and saw the VW make its incautious move. For a second, he hesitated, then called to a colleague, who joined him in his car and raced northward in pursuit, blue light twirling, siren wailing.

Tabet, standing beside his pickup truck helplessly, could only stare in stunned surprise, momentarily disoriented by the amazing turn of events.

In the VW, Hafez now realized the enormity of his lapse, but was well aware that it was too late to attempt any correction. Ridden with new anxiety, his only desperate thought was of escape and survival. Dim in the background of his mind, all but faded, were his hopes of a heroic future in UPFP. He tore past a number of north-bound passenger cars and trucks with his foot pushing the accelerator to the floorboard. At one turn, he sideswiped a southbound passenger car. In his rearview mirror he could see the police car in pursuit and it appeared to be gaining on him.

They were north of Eim Hamifratz now and, coming into a sharp blind turn, Hafez shot past a passenger car and into a head-on collision course with a huge, heavily laden transport trailer truck coming down the southbound lane. Sweating profusely, Hafez cut his wheel hard to the right, into the path of the passenger car he had passed only seconds before. Its driver, wrestling with his wheel to avoid the wagon, slammed into its left rear. The VW, off balance now, flipped over on its right side and skidded for about twenty yards, sending up sparks where metal scraped concrete, then rolled over into a shallow depression beside the road. Fortunately, there was no explosion or fire.

The couple in the Fiat that had rammed the VW were unhurt, but shaken and highly vocal in their anger and distress. The police car raced up, ground to a halt, and the two officers leaped out and ran to the station wagon, lying on its right side, its two left wheels spinning wildly in midair. One officer leaped up onto the body and peered inside. The occupant lay on his right side, bleeding from a head cut and motionless.

Traffic piled up, blocking passage in both directions. The second officer got on his radio to ask for assistance and an ambulance, then tried to effect some crowd control and get traffic moving again, with little success.

But others had come to the first officer's aid, holding the left door open while he leaned inside the VW and hauled the victim up into waiting arms. Other police cars from the checkpoint were on the scene now and traffic eventually began to flow again. Hafez was laid out on the ground, still unconscious, but seeming to have survived beyond several cuts and bruises on his forehead and face. Then an ambulance rolled up, summoned from Acre. Attendants examined Hafez, bandaged and taped his cuts and placed him in the ambulance. Seconds later, a police tow truck arrived to set the VW upright, and haul it into the Acre police station compound.

In the passing line of traffic was Salim Tabet in his pickup truck, now heading back toward Acre to try to learn what Assaf Hafez's unaccountable indiscretion would lead to.

Shortly before one P.M., Saul Lahav and Asad Hasbani arrived by helicopter and were driven to the Acre police station, where they were shown into the office of the chief of police, Meir Halevi. On the chief's desk lay the equipment that had been discovered in the hidden compartment of the wrecked station wagon, and which had impelled Halevi to report the unusual find to General Rosental's office in Tel Aviv which, in turn, had reported it to Special Operations Branch.

"A good find, Colonel," Halevi commented with pride. "See for yourself."

Item by item, Saul examined the display: one Kalashnikov submachine gun, a most recent model produced for paratroop use; one heavy-duty attack rifle; a revolver with silencer attached; one box of a hundred hollow-nosed bullets; one pair of binoculars fitted with night lenses; one canvas rucksack containing twenty-four squares of plastic compound, undoubtedly explosive material; an equal number of pencillike cylinders, not identifiable; one pocket-size calculator-type device, not identifiable; and one long-range walkie-talkie set with extra long antenna extenders.

But what Saul found equally as interesting as the items themselves was the distinctive "E-O" marking on the walkie-talkie set, the binoculars, and calculator device. Also, that same trademark impressed into each block of the plastic compound. Here was a definite link with EismanOptiks of Dresden in East Germany, undeniable evidence of the manufacturer and supplier. And even more vital a discovery—a first link to UPFP. Saul could hardly contain the excitement that was rising within him.

"And the prisoner?" Saul asked finally.

"Other than a few cuts, bruises, some sore, possibly cracked ribs, he is in good condition."

"Have you interrogated him?"

"We tried, but got nothing from him, only the papers and two thousand Israeli pounds from his pockets. Then we received orders from Colonel Kohn in Tel Aviv to hold off until you arrived. He is in solitary confinement with two men guarding him."

"Good."

"You wish to question him?"

"Only briefly. Meanwhile, I want everything found on him and in his vehicle packed for us to take back to Jerusalem, along with the prisoner. Have a receipt made up and I will sign it for you. And an extra copy for me, please."

"I will have him brought into an interrogation room for you."

"Thank you."

In the small, bare interrogation room, Assaf Hafez sat on one of the two wooden chairs placed on either side of the scarred table. A bulb in the ceiling provided the only illumination, which was scant. There were no windows. The terrorist sat with his eyes on his manacled wrists, waiting.

He had regained some of his wits during the past few hours and knew, of course, that the police had found the incriminating evidence in the VW. For that alone, he was in serious trouble. Now he realized that if he had any chance at all to survive, that chance lay with the UPFP, but only as long as he refused to answer any questions or reveal anything about the UPFP or its involvement in the Shetula matter. He would be placed on trial, certain to be convicted of possession of dangerous weapons and explosives, sentenced to—what, ten years? Twenty?

The news of his arrest, through Hawk, who had witnessed his misfortune must soon reach Falcon, who had a vital interest in his silence. So, Hafez reasoned, Falcon must take immediate steps to secure his freedom; either through UPFP agents in Israel or by taking an important hostage to bargain for his release. Only, he told himself over and over again, do not talk. Tell the Jews nothing.

When the door opened and the guard ushered in two men he had not seen before, Hafez glanced up quickly, then lowered his eyes to the handcuffs on his wrists. The newcomers moved to the opposite side of the table and stared at him. The guard said, "Is there anything else?"

"Yes," Saul Lahav said. "Remove those manacles."

The guard did so and went out, closing the door behind him. For almost thirty seconds, neither Lahav nor Hasbani spoke, but merely observed the prisoner. And while they did so, Hafez was more determined than ever to keep his hands steady, to show that he was not in the least nervous or apprehensive. Unafraid.

Then the taller of the two men spoke. "What is your name?"

Hafez neither looked up nor answered.

"Your name," Saul repeated.

Still no reply. Then Asad leaned across the table, grabbed the two ends of his open shirt collar and hauled him to his feet. "When you are spoken to, answer," he admonished Hafez harshly.

Again, Saul asked, "What is your name, boy?"

"It is in my papers—"

Hasbani slapped him twice. "You will answer the questions that are asked you. Do you understand that, boy?"

Hafez twisted out of Hasbani's grip, a move that tore his shirt wide open. "I am not a boy! I am an Arab freedom fighter, a soldier of honor! I am not a traitor to my people like this one," indicating Hasbani with a finger. "I spit on him, on you, on all Jews, who are no more to me than camel dung!"

As Hasbani lunged toward him, Saul said, "That's enough for now, Asad. He has had his turn, we will have ours later." And to Hafez, "Very well, soldier of honor. We will take you back to Jerusalem with us where we can better persuade you to be more cooperative. Asad, have them prepare him for the journey."

Salim Tabet parked his pickup truck near a small house in an Arab quarter in Haifa. He got out, looked around carefully without taking special notice of the house itself, then walked to the end of the street. He entered a coffeehouse, ordered coffee, drank it and went out again. He turned up the side street until he came to an alley, turned left and continued on until he came to the rear of the house near where he had parked his truck. He knocked on the door and an old crone of a woman opened the door and asked brusquely, "Who are you? What do you want here?"

"Tahia, little mother," he said. "She is home?"

"Who are you?"

"Tell her it is Salim. I am a friend." When the woman tried to close the door, he pushed it open and entered the kitchen and closed the door behind him. "Go tell her, little mother. There is nothing to fear from a friend."

Moments later, Tahia Soulad came running into the kitchen, arms opened wide to welcome him. "Salim! Salim! How happy I am to see you!" Arms encircling him, holding him tightly in her embrace, "It has been so long, too long. Why didn't you let me know you were coming to Haifa?"

"It has been long for me, too, Tahia, but I have been busy with the training program. It has not been easy. There is a problem, a serious one that happened only today."

"Oh. I wasn't even expecting you. I had word last week that you were sending someone to me—"

"Yes. He is the problem. On his way here, he became confused, crazy. He saw the checkpoint at Kfar Masaryk and turned and ran. The police caught him and took him to Acre. Can we move out of the kitchen?"

"Yes. Come up to my room."

He motioned his head toward the old woman. Tahia said, "Don't worry. She is all right. She is with us."

"Tahia, Tahia," Salim repeated as they moved along the narrow hallway, touching her arm, her back.

"Ah, Salim, how nice to feel your touch again."

Tahia's bedroom was a reflection of herself, with posters on the walls showing her in the costumes of a belly dancer, sensual figure liberally exposed, face in a provocative, inviting smile, the single name, TAHIA, splashed across the top. Tucked into several mirrors were dozens of photographs of friends, of herself, interspersed with snapshots; but none were of Salim Tabet. There was a certain feminine disorder everywhere; costumes and other wearing apparel lying on chairs, across an Oriental screen, on the bed. On her well-rounded body she wore a short robe that fell to midthigh and it was at once obvious that there was nothing but herself beneath it.

She was not a tall woman, but her voluptuousness gave her the illusion of height; full-bosomed, slender-waisted, with long legs and well-fleshed arms. Her complexion was a sultry beige and her long-lashed, slightly slanted eyes added a certain mysterious quality to her face. She moved with the lithe grace of a cat, smoothly and sensually, which was her principal attraction as a dancer. Even her voice, low and soft, seemed to hint an unvoiced promise.

She closed the door and stepped into Salim's embrace, sharing a deep kiss. Then she pulled back and said, "This man you sent me, he was one of the Kirkuk group?"

"Yes. He had the makings of an excellent unit leader, but today—"

Light scorn tinged her voice as she said, "These are the kind of well-trained, disciplined soldiers Falcon puts his faith in, who run at the sight of a policeman's uniform?"

"A slight miscalculation in character, Tahia. We will not make that mistake again."

"But Salim, if you sent him to me, he knew my name, my address. They will force it from him."

"I don't think so. By now, I am sure he has recovered his senses. We put him and the others through the most severe physical tests in Kirkuk. He stood up to numerous beatings and would not talk."

"If he does, I am in danger. Great danger."

Tabet kissed her. "As long as I am nearby, Tahia, you will never be in danger. You are too precious to me. Trust me."

She hesitated, frowning, wanting to accept his assurances. "And what now?" She removed some garments from a chair and said, "Sit. Let me look at you while you talk," and sat on the edge of the bed, holding one of his hands in her own.

"What time do you leave for the club?"

"Not for three hours. Can you stay overnight?"

"No, I'm sorry. I must leave for Jerusalem, to the farm."

"At once?"

"After dark."

"Then stay with me until then."

"Yes, of course."

"Tell me, with your man caught, what now?"

"For now, go about your work as usual. Do not attempt to contact Zuheir Masri or any of the others until you hear from me. Later, when this thing here is settled, we will have Masri begin to recruit workers for the oil fields in Bashra."

"Bashra? That will be the next strike?"

"Yes. I shouldn't be telling this to anyone, but it will be Bashra." Eyes glowing with anticipation, "We will cripple them for months, even years to come. Then the Haifa refinery, the docks. And then—"

She tugged at his hand, drawing him toward her. "Ah, Salim," she said softly, "I am more interested in now. Here." She went to the door and locked it. Returning to him, her robe parted and Salim's blood began pounding through his veins. He stood up and began to remove his clothes.

On Saturday, Saul and Shana spent the morning adding some finishing touches to the apartment he had been able to lease, with an option to buy, through the influence of Judah Rosental's older brother, Yehoshua, who was prominent in the real estate and investment business. It was a two-bedroom affair, new, and located in the quiet, upper middle-class neighborhood of Beit Hakerim, within a twenty-minute drive of 17 Rehov Ben Gurion.

Together, they unpacked and placed new utensils and appliances, hung curtains and pictures, rearranged furniture. Everything glittered and sparkled with newness except for the few pieces shipped from Saul's house in Tel Aviv, closed temporarily. They had shopped for food and incidentals on the previous day before the markets and shops shut down for the Sabbath, and shortly past noon the apartment took on livable shape.

In a holiday mood, they decided to drive to the Old City to have lunch and spend the free afternoon wandering among its ancient shrines and conglomeration of shops in the world's most famous tourist center. Saul parked outside the Jaffa Gate and they strolled into the bustling mixture of humanity; every possible race, color and culture from almost every nation on earth. They ate in a small, crowded restaurant where the proprietor greeted them with a smiling, *"Miyet marhaba."* A hundred welcomes. My poor house is honored by your visit. To which Saul replied in Arabic, "To be welcomed here is an honor." A greeting between friends who had known each other for a considerable time.

They ordered *tehina* and *hummus*, then *kibbeh*, an Egyptian combination of wheat and lamb, topped of with *fetir*, a cross between strudel and noodle pudding, and strong coffee.

To both, as to the hordes seeing it for the first time—or the hundredth—the Old City was a pure delight. Cradle of Judaism, Christianity, Muhammadanism. Ruled by Jews, Persians, Macedonians, Egyptians, Ptolemies, Maccabeans, Romans, Byzantines, Arabs, Seljuks, Crusaders, Mongols, Mamluks, Turks, British, Jordanians and, since 1967, Israelis. Having been ruled by so many, it truly belonged to all the religions, faiths and peoples of the world. And now, an open city to all.

They strolled slowly past the golden-domed Omar Mosque on Mount Moriah; the slivery dome of el-Aqsa Mosque; David's Tower; the Church of Christ's Grave; Calvary; past the Garden of Gethsemane; following priests, pilgrims and guided tour groups with their inevitable cameras clicking away; along the Via Dolorosa, the route taken by Jesus as He carried the cross, its stations clearly marked. Here He fell. Here He paused. Here He cried out. "Daughters of Jerusalem, weep not for me, but weep for yourselves and your children."

Here Christ was crucified. Here David lies buried. Here Abraham prepared to sacrifice his son. Here Muhammed ascended to heaven. Here the hooves of Roman horses left their mark on ancient stones, still visible. Here, here, and here—. And here, the Wailing Wall, sacred to Jews all over the world, where Saul and Shana each said a silent, private prayer to their departed loved ones.

The day had turned warm under a brilliant sun as they made their way up and down narrow, crooked streets and alleyways, past ancient structures and through history. Arab merchants, standing in front of tiny, doorless shops, shrilly hawked endless mountains of foods; unbelievably fresh and colorful vegetables, fruits, sausages, lamb, dried fish, olives, dates, halvah, flat pita, peppers, Carmel wines, cheeses, pastries, coffee.

Others displayed multicolored and black-and-white robes, gelabayas, milayehs, veils, scarves, shoes, camel saddles, inlaid ivory tables and taborets, wall hangings, embroidery, local tobaccos (and to the knowing, hashish, the odor of which filtered through the air). There were elaborately carved boxes, trays, chess sets, leather goods, hand-beaten plates, urns and vases in brass; jewelry, crucifixes, icons, Stars of David, rings, bracelets, chains.

Souvenirs and oddities to be taken home to Europe, Africa, Australia, the Americas and wherever else these visitors had come from to see with their own eyes this unique walled and holy arena.

Saul and Shana moved along in the flow of humanity, nudged here, jostled there, enjoying the overheard snatches of German, Dutch, Arabic, English, French, Scandinavian, and *Ivrit*, the modern Hebrew language, as opposed to ancient, biblical Hebrew. Looking into the eyes and faces that reflected solemn awe, surprise, perplexity. And pure joy.

Faces. Saul was always intrigued by the faces of people—all people—perhaps as a matter of professional preoccupation. But mostly, the faces of the Israelis he saw at their work, in the field, the streets, or sitting at an outdoor cafe over coffee, interested him most. Of the old, who had lived through Israel's pre- and postwar days, of the young who had never known a life free of war or the threat of war. Resigned faces, apprehensive faces, joyful, relaxed faces, able to hide what nervous tensions they felt just beneath the surface.

Israeli military uniforms mingled with those of Arab policemen and civilian security guards, all aware, all seeking to avoid a sudden terrorist attack where most would be vulnerable. Women and men soldiers, El Al girls in uniform among them, enjoying their Sabbath holiday, calling out a "*Shabat Shalom*" to a passing friend or acquaintance, pausing for a brief exchange with someone encountered by accident.

Saul and Shana made a few small purchases for his new apartment, trivial accents, then rested in a small, crowded coffee shop to refresh themselves until dusk descended upon Jerusalem. They heard the muezzin's call, taped, from a nearby minaret and it was time to leave.

As they got into the car, Shana looked back and said, "The Old City. There is nothing like it anywhere in the world. There can't be, can there, Saul?"

"No," Saul agreed, "and please God it will remain an open city to all the world, for all times."

Back in Saul's apartment later, preparing supper together in the kitchen, Shana said, "What about this boy from Acre, Saul? Is he truly a part of the UPFP, the Shetula massacre?"

"I was never more certain of anything in my entire life, Shana. Everything points to his involvement, the weapons, the equipment and explosives we found in his car."

"But you haven't really interrogated him, have you?"

"No, except for a few minutes in Acre. I've decided to let him spend another day or two in solitary confinement with his own thoughts. Let his imagination work on him for a while until the laboratory reports are complete and I have something more to throw at him."

"Ah, you and your psychology."

"Sometimes," Saul said with a smile, "it even works."

"What is it abour this one? You act as though he were somehow different from the others."

"In a way, he is different. Better trained, physically and perhaps even mentally, emotionally. Not the ordinary types we have run into before. The wild, undisciplined ones."

"He shows courage?"

"Except for having turned and run at the checkpoint, yes. However, it isn't enough to show courage in the face of disaster, but intelligence in the face of difficulties that he is up against. I believe he is lacking in that quality and I will need to use something more than subtle threats."

"Well—good luck. Now go to the table. We are only five minutes away from being ready to eat and I am hungry again. Walking miles through the Old City always does that to me."

They ate their meal, discussing the possibilities of gaining firm, indisputable evidence of the existence of the UPFP and a definite link with Shetula, evidence that would justify the need for the Special Operations Branch beyond all doubt, and any necessary expansion of its future activities.

"Have you talked with General Rosental about this Hafez yet?" Shana asked.

"Of course. He wants it kept under a tight lid until we come up with something positive that he can present to Bartok and the prime minister.''

"How will you be able to sleep with all that running through your mind?''

"I expect to have help. From my assistant in charge of Communications and Records.''

"Then neither of us will get any sleep.''

"So it will become an experiment of how well we can take stress, but successful or unsuccessful, delightful.''

Later, they did sleep, but not beyond dawn. At four forty A.M. they were awakened by the shrill of the telephone that had been installed on the day before. Saul reached out for the receiver.

"Lahav here.''

"Brenner, Colonel, night duty officer. I have a note to call you if there is any word of Eitan Drory, no matter the hour.''

"And?''

"He has just reported in.''

"Make him comfortable, Brenner, but make sure he does not leave until I have seen him. In one hour.''

When he replaced the reciever, Shana said sleepily, ''Who was it?''

"Night duty officer.''

"Important?''

"No. Go back to sleep. I'm going to the office.''

"At this hour, for something not important?''

He was out of bed, pulling on his clothes. ''Important for me, not for you. Eitan Drory is here. I'll see him alone first. You'll hear all about it later.''

Eitan Drory came as a distinct surprise, far different from what Saul had imagined he would be. His slight build, swarthiness and sharp features, together with rumpled clothing, could have easily marked him as an unemployed Arab. He appeared to be much older than his thirty-seven years of record, and had a hungry look about him, that of a man who would remain undistinguished, unnoticed on the street, in a marketplace, almost anywhere. Reticent, almost shy, Drory remained seated when Saul entered the reception area. Seeing no one else, he said, ''Drory?''

"Yes.''

"I am Saul Lahav. In here, please.''

In Saul's office, Drory did accept a cigarette without speaking and, lighting his own, Saul stared at the man keenly, fully aware of the record of his accomplishments. He smiled and said, ''You were told why you were sent for, Eitan?''

"Only that I have been assigned here for temporary duty. I was not told why."

"Very well, let me tell you. I need a man who has a deep knowledge of Egypt and Egyptians. I have been told you are such a man."

"It is possible. Perhaps if I knew exactly what you have in mind."

"We will get to that later. For now, tell me about yourself."

Drory shrugged slightly. "I was born in Cairo. I lived there with my parents. My father owned a jewelry shop. I was educated in private schools."

"Your record shows you began working for Mossad when you were sixteen—"

"That was in 1954. With permission from my father."

"And then?"

"I was a courier between agents in Cairo, Alexandria, Ismailia and elsewhere as needed." Drory's eyes lowered and his voice dropped an octave, speaking just above a whisper; out of weariness, perhaps, or because he was being asked to relive a part of his life he had put behind him years ago.

"Go on," Saul encouraged.

"In 1967," Drory continued, "Nasser so inflamed the people that they attacked our house. The houses of other Jews. They killed my mother and father, then looted and burned the store. All this while the police looked on and did not raise a hand. I was living in a room near Tahrir Square and knew nothing about this until my Mossad contact in Cairo came and told me. There was nothing that could be done.

"After a short while, I don't know how, my cover was blown. One night, I was in my room when three Egyptian intelligence agents began to break down my door. I went out through a window and escaped. Eventually, I reached Port Said in disguise. Only a week before the war broke out, two Mossad men smuggled me out on a small boat to Cyprus, from there to Israel, the first time I had set foot on its soil. When the war was over, I was moved to Foreign Ministry Intelligence and have worked for them ever since."

"My information seems to be substantially correct then. I think you can be very useful to us here."

"In what way, may I ask?"

"I am having a master list prepared of all Egyptian intelligence officers and agents known to us. Those of captain's rank will be underlined in red for special observation by you. I will give you a copy of that list and the physical description of a man known to us only by a code name. I will ask you to study both, then try to fit that description to a single name on that list.''

"I will do my best."

"This may be the most important service you can perform for us at the moment, but there will be others. Get some sleep now, Eitan. When your head is clear, report back here to me."

When Drory hesitated, Saul said, "Do you have a place to live in Jerusalem?''

"No. This is a strange city to me."

Saul took out his wallet and handed over some pound notes. "In the meantime, take a room at a hotel until you can make a more permanent arrangement. I'll have one of our people drive you and see that you get an accommodation."

In the basement laboratory, Dr. Sara Levitt, a small, birdlike woman of about forty, observed carefully as two male technicians and two maintenance mechanics bolted a heavy lid onto a large steel cylinder that had been moved behind a concrete barrier. Hinged properly, the lid was left open while Dr. Levitt mounted a small stepladder and examined the inside of the cylinder with a flashlight.

After a few minutes she stepped down to the floor and nodded her satisfaction. "I think we are ready, Aron," she said to her chief assistant, "but let us wait for Colonel Lahav."

"I hope it is strong enough," Aron said. "I still think we should be doing this somewhere out in the open countryside."

"It was suggested and turned down. There is the feeling we would attract too much attention."

"If your calculations are correct, Doctor—"

"Enough, Aron. It is the colonel's responsibility."

They moved out of the four walls of the five-foot barricade and went to the far end of the laboratory to Dr. Levitt's office where, in a large glass beaker over a Bunsen burner, coffee was brewing. Outside the office, a large, thick sheet of steel had been mounted on a movable wooden base, a long, narrow observation window of shatterproof glass set at eye level.

Elsewhere in the large room, lighted by overhead fluorescent tubes, the laboratory was fitted with the usual maze of equipment; flasks, beakers, burners, tubing, microscopes, electronic measuring devices, ballistics and other testing instruments. One woman assistant was busily engaged at a double row of animal cages, distributing food, while another monitored a console that recorded reactions from a battery of test tubes to which it was wired.

Moments later, Saul Lahav, Uri Yerushalmi and Asad Hasbani entered to interrupt the impromptu coffee klatch. Saul went directly to Sara Levitt, took the coffee mug from her hand, sipped some of it, then kissed her cheek fondly.

"The best coffee brewed in all Israel, Sara," he complimented.

She smiled and replied, "With the finest scientific equipment available, it shouldn't be?"

"So. What do we have, Sara?"

"We are ready to introduce the material, Saul." She handed each present wads of raw cotton and instructed them to place them into their ears, then picked up a square of the plastic material with the E-O imprint and inserted the thin, pencillike cylinder into it. Firmly implanted, she twisted the cap of the cylinder counterclockwise. At once, a small bulb inside the cap began to glow a faint green.

With the others following her, Dr. Levitt carried the plastic square to the steel tank, mounted the stepladder and placed it in a basketlike carrier inside. The two maintenance men then closed the heavy lid and locked it into place.

"That's it, Saul," Sara said. "If we have miscalculated its strength, this little experiment may cost you a new lab. Maybe even a new building."

"We'll have to risk it. If we did this outside, we might have the biggest war scare since seventy-three."

"So let's get behind the steel barrier. Everybody."

From the pocket of her white lab coat, Sara Levitt took the calculator device and depressed the ON button, which turned a bright red, then raised the long, thin antenna. Assured that everyone was well behind the barrier, she warned, "Does everybody have cotton in his ears?"

All present nodded, further tamping the pieces of cotton tightly, holding them in place with their fingers. Only four were able to observe through the glass panel—Dr. Levitt, Saul, Yerushalmi and the chief lab assistant. Sara now depressed two of the numbered buttons.

There was a muffled roar that made the floor tremble beneath their feet. On the long tables, glass tinkled and a number of beakers broke. Tables moved and some of the objects on them rolled off and crashed on the concrete floor. Over the roar of the explosion they could hear the terrified screeching of the animals in their cages. They heard the cracking of metal and the thump of the steel drum as it tore away from its base, toppled over and split apart, sending flame and smoke leaping upward.

Sara Levitt reached behind her and punched two buttons on the wall. At once, four streams of heavy foam were released from a tank that hung over the concrete barrier, smothering the flames, but did nothing to control the thick, choking smoke. Aron turned on the exhaust fans and the smoke rose and was drawn out through several ceiling vents.

Sara sent an assistant and two maintenance men to the floors above to reassure the other occupants of the building and any curious neighbors or passersby. One assistant remained to try to calm the frightened animals who were trying desperately to claw their way out of the cages.

When the smoke had finally cleared, they examined the results in silence, astonished by the tremendous force compacted into one small square of explosive plastic. The steel tank had been blown apart; top, bottom and sides were ripped away at its welded seams, turned into tangled scrap metal that lodged chunks of it into the concrete barrier and the ceiling above.

In her office, Sara pointed to the E-O symbol imbedded in another block of the plastic. "Eugen Eisman," she said simply. "The man is a genius."

"What is it, Sara? What gives it so much strength?"

"I don't fully know that yet, Saul. It will take much more probing, but I can tell you this much. Eisman has been able to put together a superior combination of gelignite, thermite and other ingredients, some organic, some inorganic, to produce this amazing thing we have all witnessed with our own eyes. Pure genius."

"It explains a lot," Saul said soberly. "How an entire village could be destroyed so quickly, so efficiently."

"The inference isn't a pleasant thing to contemplate, is it?"

"No. No, it isn't. Very convincing. And frightening."

"Well, there you have it. I've got my work cut out for me to get a complete analysis for our ordnance people."

Present in the conference room for the next staff meeting were Shimon Navot, Dov Shaked, Uri Yerushalmi, Yoram Golan and Asad Hasbani. In addition were four other agents recruited into the unit from various services: Dan Kaspi, Moshe Tal, Eliahu Darvit and Yossi Zeitel. And Saul Lahav.

On the table before them were the articles that had been taken from Assaf Hafez's station wagon. Each item had been tagged, closely examined, and passed along to the next man until all had seen and handled it.

Saul stood then and addressed them. "I have here a report for each of you that accurately describes the effect of these squares of plastic. Uri, Asad and I witnessed the results. So now we need no longer search for more proof of the existence of the UPFP or its presence here in Israel, nor of the type of weapons and equipment they have available to use against us."

He waved one hand over the exhibits. "These destroyed Shetula. They can also destroy Israel." Saul paused to allow that statement to sink in; then, "You have studied the Sokolnikov memorandum and know how few clues we have to go on. I will name them for you.

"We know the source of these items, from EismanOptiks in Dresden. We know that the Egyptian leader of the UPFP, known only by the code name Falcon, is an even six feet tall, fair to dark complexion, about a hundred eighty-five pounds, strongly built, black hair, brown eyes, full lips, prominent nose, attractive. He is reputed to be well-educated, intelligent, probably of good family background, a linguist and a former captain in Egypt's intelligence service. The Russian defector gave little else in the way of information, but we are checking to learn more.

"We also have a prisoner in an isolation cell who has had four days to contemplate his uncertain future without seeing or speaking with another human being, not even the guards who slide his food and water through the slot in his cell door. I intend to begin interrogating him at the conclusion of this meeting. Hopefully, I can convince him to cooperate."

Saul paused to light a cigarette. Some of the others did likewise. "Very well. You know what we need to do, the basics. Get out and make contact with your informants. Check on everybody with a past history of sabotage or terrorism. On the streets, in their homes and hangouts, bars, whorehouses, nightclubs, in jails and prisons. Bring in for questioning anybody whom you suspect may have knowledge or a connection with any terrorist organization. A hint, a clue, no matter how slight, may lead us to the UPFP.

"Pass the word along to your colleagues in your former service branches in Tel Aviv, Haifa, here in Jerusalem, along every border, in occupied territories. Use the local police to assist you, but leave no stone unturned, no grain of sand untouched. I want daily logs kept and a weekly summary of your activities on the report forms Shana will give each of you. For the time being, Dov Shaked will take charge of making those assignments and be responsible for logs and reports.

"I am also preparing a roster for night duty in this headquarters. Each of you, and the people you have working with you, will take regular turns as night duty officer. No matter the hour, day or night, the duty officer will know where I can be reached as long as I am in Israel. If there is a break anywhere, I am to be notified immediately by telephone or radio.

"Dismissed."

*   *   *

When the guard propelled Assaf Hafez into the small, dank, windowless interrogation room at the end of the cellblock, he squinted at the brightness of the overhead ceiling light and stared at the green walls, then at the small oblong table and two chairs that faced each other across it. There was nothing else in the room to relieve its drabness.

"Sit there," the guard ordered, pointing to a chair. "Someone will come soon."

"A cigarette, please," Hafez said.

"Ask the colonel when he comes."

The guard went out, clanging the steel door shut. Hafez sat in the hard chair, allowing his eyes to become accustomed to the light, fingering his shirt that had grown damp and musty with perspiration in his badly ventilated isolation cell. And, waiting, he began to feel anger; with himself for his moment of inexplicable panic at the checkpoint, with his plight now. Chosen to lead a unit, he had carried out his dangerous mission with a measure of brilliance, and for which he had received both commendation and promotion from Falcon himself; only to have failed so ignominiously without real cause.

For four days and nights, unable to tell one from the other, he had pondered his desperate situation, seeking alternatives, but could find none. In the hands of the Jews, he now considered that he might well be written off by Falcon, by Hawk, by the UPFP. His ruminations were cut off by the sound of feet outside the door, flooding him with increased apprehension. Now it would begin, the ruthless questioning, pain inflicted, even death. He rose to his feet and stood behind the chair, his back resting on the wall. Then the door was flung open and the man entered, the man who had interrogated him in Acre, the first familiar face he had seen since that day. The colonel, the guard had said.

Saul Lahav went to the opposite side of the table as the guard closed the door and left them alone. He stood facing the sullen-faced Arab for a brief moment, then riffled through several pages of the file folder he had brought with him. He placed the file on the table and said curtly, "Sit down."

Hafez remained standing, unresponsive and defiant.

"Don't try my patience, boy. Sit down!"

Hafez reacted to the incisive order by sliding into the chair slowly. "What is your name?" Saul asked, resuming a normal tone.

"You know my name. It is in the papers your Jew police took from me in Acre."

"Let me hear it from you. Your true name this time."

"I have nothing to say to you."

"Then listen carefully to what I am going to say to you. You were found with certain illegal weapons and explosives in your possession, for which, alone, you can be charged, tried, convicted and sentenced to a minimum of twenty years at hard labor. Do you understand that?"

Hafez remained silent, a look of contempt on his face. Saul sat down and leaned forward, arms resting on the table. "Very well, Jamal Dhalad, or whatever you wish to call yourself. The papers taken from you in Acre were forged. We know from your fingerprints that your true name is Assaf Hafez, that you were born in Nazareth. At fifteen, you were arrested for burglary and possession of stolen goods. At seventeen, for burglary and attempted rape. At eighteen, for assault with a deadly weapon while attempting to steal an automobile. At nineteen, on suspicion of terrorist activities, dismissed for lack of evidence."

The recitation, somehow, seemed to give Hafez a sense of importance, of accomplishment. He looked up with an arrogant half smile and said, "You can't kill me, Jew. There is no death penalty here."

"Fortunately for you. So far, for your misdeeds, you have seen only our jails. Prison for convicted terrorists may be something very different, perhaps even worse than death for one so young as you."

Angrily, eyes flashing, Hafez slammed a fist down on the table. "I spit on your prisons!" he shouted. "I spit on all Jews! Soon we will take over all your jails, your prisons, houses, your women, too! I will be freed by my own people, our freedom fighters! And I am not a *boy*! I am a *man*! An Arab soldier of honor!"

Coldly, Saul said, "A soldier of honor who murders innocent men, women and children in their beds at night while they sleep? That is the act of a *man*? A *soldier*?"

Hafez leaned back in his chair and regarded Saul with a cool, amused half smile. "Why is it, Colonel, that only Jews are murdered, while Arabs are merely killed?"

"To the dead, Jew and Arab alike, there is little difference in the meaning of the words." Saul removed a pack of cigarettes from his shirt pocket, lit one, saw the hungry look come into Hafez's eyes and handed it to him. He lit another for himself, watching as the Arab sucked hungrily on his own, looking relaxed.

"You have parents?" Saul asked. "Sisters, brothers?"

Hafez studied the question as he puffed on his cigarette, then with eyes moistening slightly, "My father is dead. My mother, two younger sisters and a brother live in a dirty shack in a refugee camp.

Someday, they and all other Arabs living in that filth will live here, on the land stolen from us by you Jews.''

"If they do," Saul said, "it will not be through the kind of thing you are involved with." There was silence while they smoked their cigarettes, then Saul said quietly, "How many were with you on the night you and your comrades attacked Shetula?"

Hafez's head jerked upward, eyes meeting Saul's directly, flooding with anger. "Why should I talk to you? I know nothing of this place, this Shetula!"

"You are lying, Hafez."

"Prove it!"

"When the time comes, I will."

"Then why do you need to question me?"

"Because there were others, those who were with you, those who sent you on your mission. I want to know where you came from, who the people behind you are—"

Hafez leaped to his feet, leaned forward with both hands flat on the table and spat on the file folder lying there, at the same time unleashing a flood of screaming curses. Saul lunged forward and grabbed the Arab's shirtfront in both hands, pulling him across the table to within two inches of his face. Biting each word off sharply, he said, "You will talk to me, boy, or I will nail your lying tongue to the wall!"

Hafez's teeth began to chatter, eyes rolled back into his head, trembling in Saul's hard, tight grasp. Then he was shoved backward into the chair, which slammed against the wall on its two back legs and settled down again on all four, leaving Hafez shaking. Saul sat back in his own chair and lit another cigarette. When Hafez was restored to some sense of calm, Saul said, "Let us begin once more."

Hafez's head rocked from side to side, throwing off Saul's words. "Listen to me!" Saul ordered, and Hafez's head stopped shaking, eyes cast downward.

"It is time for us to stop playing games," Saul said in a low, steady voice. "We have a special place for terrorist-murderers like you, a prison where men have grown old long before their time for less than what you and your honorable soldier comrades did at Shetula. Those men work from earliest dawn to darkness, harder work than your mind can even imagine, closely guarded to prevent them from escaping by taking their own lives. They know no freedom except to eat their food, to breathe the air, to stay alive and remember what freedom is like on the outside. They sleep, only to awaken to a new day that will be the same as their yesterdays, a life without hope. They have not seen their families for years, nor have they felt the flesh of a women in all that time.

"You are young, your body firm, your mind vigorous, but you will grow old and feeble in mind and body. From early morning until dark, you will labor like a beast of burden, thinking of free men and the woman you slept with last; of your mother, two sisters and brother—"

"Don't . . . don't—" Hafez began, the words choked and barely intelligible.

"It need not be that way, Hafez," Saul continued in a more soothing voice. "Tell me what I want to know and I will see to it that the charges against you will be lessened, your sentence lightened. Jail for perhaps a year, then freedom. I give you my word."

Hafez looked up hopefully. Saul said, "How many were with you at Shetula?"

There was little resistance now as Hafez stared down at his folded arms, his mutinous indignation gone, ready to accept the promise; gone his resolve to remain courageous without the presence of Tabet or Falcon to support him. "There were . . . there were . . . five of us—" he began.

That evening, Saul and Shana dined at the King David Hotel. They had spent a long, tedious, but rewarding, afternoon in Saul's office where they had labored over the detailed questioning of Hafez while Shana recorded the confession on tape. Hafez had, in turn, responded, broken down, continued, balked, wept, hurled obscenities at his tormentors, but Saul had patiently pursued and prodded, challenged and goaded until he was satisfied beyond his earliest expectations.

"Do you think we will be able to pick out enough to make a clear copy, Shana?" Saul asked. "I need something without all the crying and shouting to present to General Rosental, who will need to take it to General Bartok, and higher."

"No problem. We can eliminate much of the extraneous matter and bring up the whispering, as long as we keep the original intact, for the record. I'll work on it later tonight and have a clear copy for you by morning. When I have that, I'll have someone transcribe it so you can have a written copy as well, and for our files."

"Good. I'll stay with you until it is finished."

He poured more wine, then began to attack the lamb dish the waiter placed before him. Moments later, he looked up and saw two couples crossing the room on their way out. As they reached Saul's table, he recognized the Inspector General of Police, Morris Lurie.

Lurie paused with a smile of recognition and Saul rose. Lurie introduced his wife, Ziporah, then the couple with them, Mordecai and Suzi Aarons, the latter younger than her husband and strikingly attractive.

Aarons smiled and said, "Colonel Lahav and I have already met."

"Yes," Saul acknowledged. "May I present Lieutenant Altman."

Aarons extended a hand and Shana accepted it. In continental manner, Aarons touched it to his lips. Lurie said, "Don't let us interrupt your meal, Saul. A pleasure, Lieutenant. *Shalom.*"

The foursome moved on. Saul and Shana resumed their meal, but Shana took note of Saul's look of undefined curiosity. "What is it, Saul?" she asked.

"Nothing," he replied with a noncommittal shrug.

"Is it Aarons or his pretty wife?"

"Aarons. There is something about him . . . I don't know what . . . a certain feeling I have—"

Shana laughed. "It's your work. I sometimes wonder if you aren't suspicious of me."

He smiled in return and said, "Of you, always," then, "It is nothing. Forget it, eh?"

Dov Shaked had paired himself with Dan Kaspi, a young man who had gone into Shin Beit from the army and was emerging as a top investigator, assigning themselves to the Jerusalem area. He teamed Yoram Golan with Eliahu Darvit for Tel Aviv-Jaffa, Uri Yerushalmi and Moshe Tal for Haifa-Acre, and Shimon Navot with Yossi Zeitel on roving assignment, on backup call to any team which might require additional assistance.

Each team studied lists of names, descriptions and, where available, photographs of hundreds of former convicted saboteurs, arsonists and terrorists that Shana had compiled from every intelligence branch, police and border patrol records. Thus armed, each team fanned out into his area of operations to locate their quarry.

During the days and nights that followed, working with local police and detectives, they searched homes, bars, night clubs, coffeehouses, whorehouses, along streets and alleys, not surprised to discover that many they sought were gypsylike in their habits, wanderers on the move or in hiding. Those they did find were questioned relentlessly in search of any sign, however slight or remote, of the elusive UPFP.

Informants were similarly contacted, money exchanged in some cases, given a telephone number to call in the event information of interest turned up. To the delight of local authorities, this concentrated effort resulted in uncovering numerous criminals in unrelated matters, leads that brought about other arrests.

The Golan-Darvit team was instrumental in breaking up a widespread prostitution ring in Tel Aviv and uncovered a narcotics operation of considerable magnitude in Jaffa, but came up empty-handed in their search for the major terrorist bank they sought. In the Haifa-Acre area, Yerushalmi and Tal, posing as longshoremen looking for work, pursued a suspect truck leaving the Haifa docks and bagged four Jewish dockworkers who were selling imported appliances, tools and auto parts to a receiver of stolen goods who had connections for resale in Jordan; but found no trace of UPFP.

Navot and Zeitel began their stint by visiting jails and prisons to interview convicted terrorists, offering reductions in their sentences in exchange for information, but came up without a single helpful lead. In the Jerusalem area, Shaked and Kaspi labored day and night in their search, following false trails that led nowhere but the brink of sleepless exhaustion. Even their most reliable informants went blank at the mention of the name UPFP. There was no reluctance to discuss better known groups of fedayeen, even individuals, which resulted in many pickups for further interrogation, but nothing that coincided with their all-important need.

Saul had ordered coded messages sent to every embassy and consulate in Europe, to every agent operating undercover in Syria, Lebanon, Jordan and Egypt, but with little more than bare description of the man known only as Falcon, there was little hope of obtaining meaningful results.

As Saul's driver, Asad Hasbani had been excluded from Shaked's roster of investigators. On his own, however, Asad circulated through areas of Jerusalem that were well familiar to him from his police days. On his eight stop that day, he found himself at the shop of Kamel el-Zumi in the Old City, a bazaar of sorts that dealt in a wide variety of merchandise, including some suspected of having been stolen: clothing, furniture, stoves, colorful cloth, ivory inlaid tables, hand-beaten copper and brass plates, vases and urns, tapestries, appliances and jewelry.

It was night and Kamel's three sons were bringing the goods displayed on the pavement indoors. Asad greeted them and they responded with little warmth. All three had, at one time or another, been arrested and questioned as receivers of stolen goods, but none had served time in jail or prison. Asad entered the store and went directly to the rear where Kamel, a robust man in his middle fifties, sat at his untidy desk counting the proceeds of the day. At the sight of Hasbani, he swept the money into the top drawer and locked it, exhibiting a broad smile. "Allah's blessings on you, young brother," he greeted. "You wish to buy something? Come, make a choice and I will give you a handsome discount."

"I am not here to buy, Kamel."

"Ah, then, if your visit is social, let us go upstairs where we can be more comfortable." Kamel shouted several instructions to his sons, then led the way to the rear hall and up ancient stairs to his home, which occupied the entire second floor of the building. The central room, off which a long hallway opened onto a series of other rooms, was large and exquisitely furnished, the floor covered with fine Oriental rugs. Numerous cabinets and tables of fine workmanship blended with comfortable sofas and chairs and were scattered throughout the room which, because of its size, showed no sign of being crowded.

"Sit, sit, my friend. My house is honored by your presence," the older man said.

"As I am honored by your gracious welcome," Asad replied with traditional politeness.

"Will you have wind? Coffee?"

"Coffee, please."

Kamel went out and returned a few seconds later. On his heels came a young girl of about sixteen, whom Asad recognized as Kamel's daughter, Leila. She carried a tray with a silver coffee service and fine china. She filled two cups silently and departed. Both men raised their cups and drank the aromatic cinnamon-flavored coffee with relish.

Asad said, "I hope you prosper, old friend."

Kamel smiled. "Prosperity and poverty are in the gracious hands of Allah, who has been kind to his servant. What can I do for my young friend?"

"You have been helpful to me in the past, Kamel. I need your assistance now."

"So. In what way?"

"I seek information about a new terrorist group—"

"Ah, there are so many—"

"This one in particular is known as the United Palestinian Freedom Party. The UPFP."

Kamel el-Zumi's eyes rolled upward expressively. "Names mean nothing, my dear boy, as you know. They change overnight as easily as I change my garments."

"Have you heard the name?" Asad persisted.

"Not that one. Others, yes, which I am sure you already know about. There are whispers, always, but no more than that."

"What whispers, Kamel? Who are the whisperers?"

"I do not know. One hears talk in the streets, in the coffeehouses, but I seldom pay attention. Who they are?" A shrug. "They pass like the wind."

"You deal with many people, Kamel—"

"True, true. In this business, it is often necessary that I deal with certain elements whom I would never invite into my home. I deal with them out of necessity, as a business man. This you know. They come with merchandise to my shop, but—"

"We are wasting time, Kamel, so I will say this to you openly. You are a fence who deals in stolen goods. Because you have cooperated with the police and have been helpful in the past, they have looked to one side and allowed you to operate within reason. Now tell me what you have heard about this UPFP group."

Kamel was genuinely distressed. "By the souls of my dead father and mother, I do not know of this group of people. I admit that in the past I have dealt with thieves, yes, but I do not deal with terrorist murderers. I swear to you that I know nothing of the group by that name."

"What is important to me, Kamel, is that you may know those who do know them. They talk, they whisper, you listen. I want you to listen more carefully and remember what you hear. And I want to know what you hear."

"I will say it again. I know of no one to whom I can point a finger, but this I will promise you. I will listen. If I hear anything about these people, I will tell you. This I swear on my soul and honor."

Asad sat silently for a few moments, then removed a card from his pocket. "I will accept your word for now, Kamel," he said finally, "but I will expect to hear from you. Soon. You understand?"

"I understand."

Asad handed him the card. "I will speak to our people in the proper places and inform them that you are cooperating with me. When you have something for me, telephone me at the number on this card. If I am not in, leave your name and no more. I will receive the message and visit you at once."

Kamel nodded. Asad rose, made the usual polite farewell and left.

In the cubicle assigned to him at SO branch headquarters, Eitan Drory continued to check the list of "possibles" Shana had compiled especially for him; names gathered from every internal source of Egyptian agents and officers known to the Israelis since and before Israel had become a state in 1948. It was very slow and tedious work, trying to match the description of Falcon in the

Sokolnikov memorandum to the long list of names on the computer printout, but Drory doggedly pursued the task at hand.

And in Tel Aviv, Saul Lahav, Judah Rosental and General Yigael Bartok listened together while the taped voices of Saul and Assaf Hafez rolled through the playback machine.

LAHAV: How did you come to join the UPFP?

HAFEZ: I was recruited in Nazareth.

LAHAV: How long ago?

HAFEZ: Eleven months. It may have been twelve, or ten. I can't remember exactly.

LAHAV: By whom?

HAFEZ: A man. I did not know his name. I was not told it.

LAHAV; Did he say why you were particularly chosen?

HAFEZ; Because he knew of me from someone.

LAHAV: He knew of your police record. That was why, was it not?

HAFEZ: (a pause, then) Yes. He knew.

LAHAV: He gave you money?

HAFEZ: Yes.

LAHAV: How much did he give you?

HAFEZ: One hundred Israeli pounds. He said there would be more later.

LAHAV: Then what happened?

HAFEZ: A week later, he sent me to Nahal Gashur to meet a man. This man took me across the border into Syria that night, then to a camp outside Damascus. There were others like me there, from other places, refugee camps. After another week, I was put in charge of four of them and we were moved to a camp in Iraq.

LAHAV: Where in Iraq?

HAFEZ: First to Baghdad. From there, we were taken to the training camp.

LAHAV: Where?

HAFEZ: I don't know where. We were in a truck that was covered. We were locked in. They told us it was necessary because if we were seen, we would be attacked by Kurds who were fighting with the Iraqis then. This way, it would seem to be a Kurdish farmer on his way home from market, and we would be safe.

LAHAV: Tell me about the training camp.

HAFEZ: What is there to tell? Except that it was good there. Clean beds, good food, clean uniforms, cigarettes. And hard work from morning until dark. But we soon became strong. We learned to shoot new rifles, pistols, machine guns, how to blow up tanks, cut fences and telephone wires, everything.

LAHAV: Who taught you these things?

HAFEZ: We had instructors. From Algeria, Germany, elsewhere, too. We learned all kinds of combat, even to run through fire. They taught us well. Very well.

LAHAV: Were any of the instructors Russian?

HAFEZ: No. No Russians.

LAHAV: And you were chosen to be a leader? They must have thought well of you.

HAFEZ: Yes. I was the best, so they chose me to be in charge of the four men who came to Iraq with me. I was the first, Leader One.

LAHAV: And the superior leader?

HAFEZ: (a long pause, then) He was known by the name Falcon. We saw him only twice. Once when we arrived and he spoke to us; then the night before we left for Lebanon.

LAHAV: This Falcon. The description you gave me of him before. Can you add anything to that?

HAFEZ: No. That is how I remember him, what I told you.

LAHAV: And you never knew him by any other name?

HAFEZ: No. Only Falcon.

LAHAV: You have given us two names and locations. Ibrahim Riad and Tahia Soulad. Can you add to these?

HAFEZ: I gave you three names. Hawk, who was assistant to Falcon. Those are the only ones I know. Since I did not reach Haifa, I never saw the woman.

LAHAV: And your instructions to her?

HAFEZ: (a pause of sixteen seconds) I was given none. The instructions were to come from her to me.

Saul cut the machine off at that point and said, "I am going to run that last back, if I may." He rolled the tape back and replayed the last question and answer, stopped it again and said, "You will note the long pause before he answered that question, as though he was trying to think of a proper answer. That pause was in the original tape, from which this one was patched to eliminate long passages of weeping, emotional outbreaks, cursing and other extraneous material. At this point, Generals, our little friend began holding back from us."

"Let us hear the rest of it," Bartok said.

Saul pressed the "Forward" lever and allowed the tape to run to its conclusion. That Hafez was holding back became more apparent toward the end.

"What do you believe he was holding back, Saul?" Bartok asked finally.

"I don't know that for certain, of course, but I suspect that if he was sent to contact the Soulad woman, it was for the purpose of transmitting certain instructions to her, perhaps to be passed along to others, and not the other way around. He was evidently holding back in order to give him some leverage toward a reduced sentence in case he needed it later on. However, I am convinced that the Soulad woman is a key person in the UPFP organization."

"And what do you propose to do about that?" Bartok said.

"I am going to have her placed under round-the-clock surveillance at once and hold Hafez for further questioning."

"Where is he now?"

"In a cell at seventeen Rehov Ben Gurion, but I intend to transfer him to Central Jail where he will be able to eat better and sleep more comfortably than in our holding cells. If we turn up something more, I'll bring him back for further questioning."

Bartok stood up and began pacing. "All right, Judah, Saul," he said finally. "With this capture of Hafez and the weapons taken from his car, plus this tape, I am satisfied that the creation of the Special Operations Branch was an excellent and necessary move. I will so inform the prime minister and replay this tape for him. Congratulations to you both. The matter is now in your hands. In the future, you need only report situations of extreme importance to me. Good luck."

Late that afternoon, Asad Hasbani drove Dov Shaked and Saul to the airport where a jet helicopter was standing by. "I'll drop you off in Haifa, Dov," Saul instructed. "Check in with the chief of police there. I have already spoken to him and he will be expecting you. I want a close surveillance on Tahia Soulad. Learn everything you can about her as far back as you can go to her birth. Police record if she has one. Where she works, lives, goes. Whom she visits, who visits her. Round the clock. Stay with it and see that the local men assigned are on their toes. I'll be back in my office by morning."

The jet put down in Haifa and was met by a police car. Less than a minute later, Saul took off. When he landed close to the Lebanese border at the Israeli town of Zar'it, he found the army unit he had ordered waiting. One jeep and one armored personnel carrier, a lieutenant in charge and ten men sprawled on the ground. Saul identified himself and said, "Mount up, Lieutenant. We have only a short way to go. This shouldn't take long."

In the jeep beside the lieutenant, Saul gave him the direction and, less than twenty minutes later, they drove into a lane and through the gate that led to the farm of Ibrahim Riad. The personnel carrier drove through the gate without stopping to open it.

The farm was deserted. Not a human or animal was in sight, nor in the house, barn or field. "Colonel?" the lieutenant said. "They were evidently expecting visitors."

"You know what to do," Saul replied. "Let's get it done. Set the charges, level the house and barn."

A sergeant supervised the setting of the charges and, at a signal from the lieutenant, inserted the handle in the hellbox he held in his hand and twisted it. The C-4 charges demolished the buildings in an instant. Within minutes, the unit was on its way back to where the helicopter waited to return Saul to Jerusalem.

That night in Haifa, Dov Shaked and police detective Zalman Harkan finished a quick meal and returned to headquarters, where a R and I clerk had the file on Tahia Soulad ready for their examination, complete with photographs in front and side views.

Tahia Soulad had been born in Haifa of Palestinian parentage, their whearabouts presently unknown. Age, 27. No record of marriage or children. One arrest as a juvenile for shoplifting, two for prostitution in her seventeenth and eighteenth years. Lived in Beirut during her nineteenth to twenty-second years, where she worked in various nightclubs as a waitress, then a dancer. Presently employed as a dancer at the Gharbieh, a nightclub in the Arab quarter within eight blocks of her given address, a house owned by the club operator. Probably his mistress. A further note added that Tahia had reached a certain peak of popularity and success as a dancer and entertainer, and had appeared in other Arab capital cities.

"Would you like to see her perform?" Harkan asked.

"What is the usual makeup of the Gharbieh audiences?" Shaked asked.

A shrug. "Tourists, Arabs, Israelis. It is not a first-class club, but it offers a lot of color and is a favorite attraction to the working class locally."

"Any chance that she could spot us?"

Harkan laughed. "In Gharbieh, you would need a flashlight to find the drink or food on your table."

They parked on a nearby side street and made their way past a crush of pedestrians moving in two directions. Music blared into the street from radios emanating from the open-fronted food stands where people crowded to buy and eat *felafel* and cooked meats, pastries and fruit, washed down with cola drinks. Children tagged along after sightseers, begging for coins. Others pleaded for an opportunity to keep a special eye on cars and police walked their beats nonchalantly, impervious to the noise and odors.

Inside, Gharbieh was packed at this hour. Shaked and Harkan stood among other waiting patrons until a table for two became available. The show seemed to be a continuous parade of dancers and singers and thirty minutes later, after a singer and group of four accompanists had completed their number, the jaunty master of ceremonies announced, "And now, ladies and gentlemen, we proudly present the lovely star of our show, and Haifa's favorite dancer—Tahia!"

She glided onstage to an orchestral flare and much applause, wearing a scanty costume that revealed far move than it concealed, glittering with sequins, seductive in movement.

"Assignments like this don't come often," Zalman Harkan commented.

"No," Shaked agreed, nodding in time with the musical beat. "I've had much worse. Have you made out your man yet?"

"At the bar, the fourth stool from the left. The other is outside at the entrance. For the next show, they will trade places."

"Good. Then I'll go back to my hotel and telephone Jerusalem and get a full night's sleep for a change."

"Rest well. We will be on the job."

"I'll check in with you at headquarters in the morning."

8

Where the dirt road came to an end some six kilometers beyond Ein Fara, which lay northeast of Jerusalem, a five-foot-high chain link fence, supported by two massive stone pillars, marked the entrance to the farm estate that once belonged to the al-Sa'idi family. It had been in the possession of the al-Sa'idis longer than any present member of the family could recall, until 1968, when its patriarch, Mahashir al-Sa'idi died in his eighty-eighth year.

With his death, his eldest son and principal heir, Kamel Ali al-Sa'idi, then fifty-three years old, decided he had been too long restricted to a rural existence. Whereupon, he put the estate up for sale and moved his immediate family to Beirut. After a few months of negotiations between the al-Sa'idi family attorney and George Hassan, an attorney from Nablus, representing one Fayez Abou Fathy, who was alleged to be traveling abroad at the time, a substantial down payment changed hands along with an agreement to purchase the property. After a brief period, the deed changed hands, but it was still known as the Sa'idi estate.

The main house was a large stone structure that was set well back from the entrance, hidden by a grove of trees and surrounded by a well tended, lawn and flower gardens. Behind it were the usual utility buildings; repair and blacksmith shops, garage, a generator that supplied its own electricity, and a large pump that drew water from one of a number of wells. A single line ran from the roof of the house to the telephone pole on the road just outside the entrance gate.

Beyond the main house lay the cultivated fields that produced acres of vegetables and fruits that were trucked to the Machaneh Yehuda outdoor market in Jerusalem as well as to a central distribution point which shipped the produce and oranges to other cities and overseas. On the far edges of the estate stood numerous shacks in which the farm workers lived, the packing sheds and storage buildings for the necessary farm equipment. In the distance, the children of the farm workers tended flocks of sheep and prides of goats that supplied meat and milk for the estate and its market customers.

Inside the main house, however, the character of the placid outdoors took on a totally different change; the al-Sa'idi estate, through Fayez Abou Fathy, who existed only on paper, had become the headquarters for the United Palestinian Freedom Party inside Israel. The man in charge, Massif Razak, was a Syrian Army major who had formerly held the position of deputy warden of the Damascus prison, on loan to the UPFP. At various times, as many as twenty members of the organization had been housed here, occupying the upper floor, which had been converted into an open sleeping dormitory, dining hall, with its own kitchen.

The lower floor consisted of a huge library-office, living and dining rooms, four bedrooms, bath and kitchen. In the basement, which was stone-lined, there were four rooms that opened into a central corridor and whose thick doors were always kept locked. An armed guard sat at a table at the bottom of the stairway at all hours of the day and night.

Inside those four rooms was the arsenal of the UPFP; smuggled into Israel from Syria, Jordan and Lebanon in farm trucks, atuomobiles, on the backs of donkeys and humans; accumulated over a period of two years. Automatic rifles, submachine and hand guns, machine pistols, small mortars, bazookas, many carried in in a disassembled state, reassembled later, oiled and ready for use at any given moment. There were also racks of bazooka and mortar shells, hand granades, sticks of dynamite, fuses, and cartridges in endless numbers.

The library-office, which was the largest room on the lower level, was comfortably furnished with Oriental rugs, leather chairs and sofas, a huge desk, lamps and tapestries. Now, at the desk, Massif Razak sat listening with a deep frown as Salim Tabet recounted the incident of Assaf Hafez's capture by Israeli police. Razak's twisted facial features telegraphed his obvious displeasure, giving him the look of an unhanged pirate. He was in his early fifties, his head shaven totally bald, with a long mustache that was carefully waxed. In stature, he was short, but carried himself with military erectness. His narrow eyes were icy cold, an indication of the cruelty of which he was capable. Those eyes now seemed to bore into Tabet and caused the younger man much uneasiness and concern.

The third man present was the heavily bearded, shaggy-haired Amon Sadani, who peered intently at Tabet through heavily rimmed glasses as he spoke. Though vitally interested in the proceedings, he was far more relaxed in contrast to Razak.

"At that point," Tabet was saying, "Hafez suddenly lost his wits. Unaccountably, he turned and ran. I say unaccountably because until that moment, he had performed every move in exact detail as he had been instructed. His performance at Shetula, in command of the others, was exemplary. Evidently, the sight of the police checkpoint, coming with such suddenness, unbalanced him. I know of no other way to explain his behavior. There was nothing I could do but wait and follow the ambulance that carried him to the Acre police station."

Sadani said, "I should have thought he would have been well instructed how to behave when coming face to face with such a situation."

Before Tabet could answer, Razak snapped angrily, "And the girl? What about her?"

"I saw her later that evening, after Hafez was taken away from the station. My informant there told me he was being moved to Jerusalem for further questioning. I then contacted Tahia and cautioned her to break off all contact with Zuheir Masri until she receives further instructions."

"But at the time Hafez was taken, he knew her name and where to contact her?" Sadani asked.

"Unfortunately, yes. I had told this to him before we left Riad's farm."

Razak and Sadani exchanged quick glances; then Razak said, "They will twist it out of him."

"I don't think so," Tabet replied. "In this, he and the others were thoroughly tested. By now, I am sure he has recovered from his fright and will—"

"A fallacy, Tabet," Razak said harshly. "We cannot rely on a man who has already demonstrated weakness. In their hands, he is too dangerous. We must get rid of him before it is too late."

"It was a lapse, I agree," Tabet offered defensively, "but he was our best unit leader. Remember Shetula—"

"Shetula," Razak snorted. "Shetula, my young friend, is in the past, over and done with. We have far greater objectives than Shetula and need unit leaders who are not subject to these cowardly lapses, which endanger all of us. The man knows too much—"

"I don't think he will talk," Tabet insisted.

Sadani said quietly, "Salim, you are naïve if you believe that. They have ways. Stronger men than your Hafez have broken down under their pressures."

"Amon is right, Tabet," Razak interposed in support. "It is better to get rid of him quickly. The girl, too."

Tabet's head jerked upward, flushing darkly, ready to object, but Sadani said quickly, "Hafez, yes, I agree. The girl, no. They have nothing on her, even if they learn her name, since there is nothing to substantiate a charge against her. She is older, far better disciplined than Hafez, and has given us excellent service in the past. I do not think she is in danger, and she is our principal contact with the people in Haifa and Acre who will be vital to us in our recruitment program for Bashra." He turned to face Tabet directly. "Can you arrange to take care of Hafez?"

Tabet nodded with a touch of reluctance. "Yes, if it must be done." Anxiously now, "And Tahia?"

"For the present, move her out of Haifa until she is again needed there," Sadani said, "but be very careful. She may be watched. Bring her here to Jerusalem. Put her in the Club Morocco where we have friends and you can keep an eye on her. Give her a new name. Let her adopt a veil to add to her dance costume. It is not unusual for a dancer to change her identity. If Hafez reveals her name, the worst that can happen, if they find her, is that they will question her and she can deny that she knows him or has even heard of him. Without proof, it will come to nothing. I'm sure she can handle that."

Razak had been overruled but remained in a surly temper. He said, "Has Falcon been advised of this latest piece of stupidity?"

"I have sent him word," Taget said. "It is too soon to expect a reply."

Razak muttered a curse. "Our people here are growing restless," he said, addressing Sadani. "They hear promises, but see no action. When does Falcon plan to move on Bashra?"

"Patience, my dear Razak, patience. First, the necessary new equipment must arrive from Dresden. Meanwhile, four units must be put together and trained as a single unit for this special project. An accurate plan must be devised and is being worked out with the greatest care. When it all comes together, there will be action enough to satisfy all."

"May Allah bless that happy day."

"Meanwhile, Razak, exercise extreme care. Let no one leave here unless he is on a truck taking produce to market, and returns by the same means. Others, myself and Salim included, will come and go only by night. The special branch is in full operation now and we cannot afford a mishap on this end. Salim, we will look to you to take care of Hafez."

"As soon as you locate him for me, it will be done."

"By morning I will know and pass the word to you through Razak here." He smiled and added, "Let the Jews concentrate where they will. We will outwit them, the best of them. Believe me."

"Well, Eitan?" Saul Lahav asked from the doorway of the cubicle where Drory was applying himself assiduously to the pages of the computer printout.

Eitan Drory placed an ashtray on the particular page he had been studying and leaned back in his chair, then pointed toward the desk top. "I have studied every name that was underlined in red. The Egyptian captains. He is not among them, your Falcon."

"You are certain?"

"Yes." There was a look on Drory's face that puzzled Saul. Certainly it was not one of utter disappointment.

"But?" he prompted.

Drory leaned forward and pointed a thin finger at a name he had circled in black. "This one, Colonel. I think he could be your man."

"Who?"

"This list is an old one. He is shown here as a lieutenant. If he was made a captain later, he was promoted after the time I knew him. The description fits him better than any other."

Saul's voice quickened. "You *knew* him, Eitan?" He stepped into the cubicle and closed the door.

"Knew him? I almost killed him once. In Cairo. He was one of the three agents who came for me as I escaped through the window, the first one through the door. He saw the gun in my hand and leaped to one side. The bullet hit the man behind him."

"So. Tell me about him. Everything you can remember. Try not to overlook anything."

"I don't know too many of the details you would like to have, but Mossad should have a dossier on him somewhere. In the underground, one of our duties was to compile every bit of information we could learn about their agents."

"Come with me."

Together, they crossed the outer room to the communications section where Shana and her two clerks were busily engaged. She looked up quizzically. "Something I can do for you?"

"Yes, Shana. Priority. Eitan will give you a name. I want you to put it on the teletype to Mossad Records in Tel Aviv and ask them for an immediate transcript. As soon as it comes through, give it to Eitan to bring to me at once."

"Right away, Saul," and to Drory, "The name?"

"Hatif Tobari, Lieutenant, Intelligence, palace staff. Mark it for the attention of the Egyptian Desk."

Saul returned to his office, where Leah Barak was placing a written message on his desk. She handed it to him, saying, "This call came in while you were out of your office. From Dov Shaked in Haifa. Sometime last night or early this morning, Tahia Soulad evaded the surveillance of two Haifa detectives and has disappeared."

"Damn! Where is Dov now?"

"At police headquarters there, waiting for a call back."

"You call him, Leah. Tell him to have Haifa broadcast a general inquiry on her. No arrest. They are to locate and inform us here. And tell Dov to return to Jerusalem at once."

Twenty minutes later, Eitan Drory brought him the information he sought, with the comment, "It is not much, Colonel."

"Sit, Eitan, while I read this.

SUBJECT: HATIF TOBARI, LT EGYPT MIL INT BORN: MAY 6, 1935 CAIRO HT: 6 FT WT: 175 HAIR: BL EYES: BR NO VIS SCARS/MARKINGS NO PHOTO DOCUMENTATION AVAILABLE SUBJECT. FATHER: FAWZI TOBARI, ACTIVE TEXTILE TRADES, WEALTHY, RESIDES IN ZAMALEK DISTRICT. FAMILY: MOTHER (MELANIE) AND SON (HATIF) ONLY CHILD SUBJECT EDUCATED ENGLAND, FRANCE, CLOSELY IDENTIFIED WITH ARAB STUDENT LEAGUE, ARDENTLY PRO-NASSER SENT ABROAD [ALGERIA, EAST GERMANY] TO STUDY GUERRILLA TACTICS AND SABOTAGE TECHNIQUES RETURNED 1964, ASSIGNED MIL INT BY NASSER UNDER GEN WALID SABAH, PALACE STAFF INT IN 1970. AFTER NASSER'S DEATH, SUBJECT WAS ACCUSED INVOLVEMENT IN PLOT TO OVERTHROW SADAT, 19 OFFICERS ALL RANKS ARRESTED. TOBARI ESCAPED. SEEN LATER IN BEIRUT, BAGHDAD, DAMASCUS AND EUROPEAN COUNTRIES. PRESENT WHEREABOUTS UNKNOWN. IF MORE RECENT WORD IS RECEIVED YOUR BRANCH REQUEST INFORMATION FOR FILES THIS OFFICE. END MESSAGE.

Saul placed the telex on his desk. "Well, Eitan, do you still feel the same about this man, Tobari?"

"Yes. It clarifies him firmly in my mind."

"And you believe he is our Falcon?"

"Over all the others on the list, yes."

"What else does this clarify in your mind? What can you tell me about him that is not in this telex?"

"Only from memory and what I heard from other agents in Cairo at the time. He was, as I recall him, a handsome man physically, a favorite with his superiors and also with women. It was said that his family and the Sadani family were close friends, that Hamid Sadani, the banker, had an interest in the friends, that Hamid Sadani, the banker, had an interest in the Tobari textile business, and that both were made rich by King Farouk. The Tobaris and Sadanis supported Nasser over General Naguib. There was talk, after Nasser's death, that Hatif Tobari despised Sadat as a compromiser and coward, who was called *Bikbachi Sah*, which means Colonel Yes Sir, and after the coup that failed, Hatif went into exile. By then, I had been forced to leave Cairo and know no more."

Saul said thoughtfully, "Added to what little we know, he does seem to fit into the pattern." He sighed and added, "So now we have a name, and what we need is the face to match it. Also, his present whereabouts, somewhere in Iraq. Or Lebanon. Or Syria. Or Libya. Or anywhere."

"It will not be easy, Colonel. It is still possible that the Eygptians would also like to get their hands on him, which would keep him on his guard."

Saul smiled without humor. "If it were easy, Eitan, the services of the SO branch would not be necessary, eh? What about Eugen Eisman, EisemanOptiks in Dresden?"

"That one I know. He was one of Hitler's eminent scientists who did much to develop the V-1 and V-2 bombs that caused so much destruction in England. He is wanted as a war criminal in the West for his experiments on concentration camp inmates to see how much electrical current they could stand before dying. We know he escaped to Dresden with the help of the Russians, for whom he has been working since."

"So I understand. Thank you, Eitan. You have been very helpful to me."

"Do I now return to my regular assignment, Colonel?"

"Not yet. I have another assignment for you. I would like you to take a trip to Dresden—"

There was a knock on the door and Yoram Golan came into the office, his expression tense. He paused on seeing Saul engaged with Drory, but Saul waved him inside. "What is it, Yoram?"

"A call from Central Jail. Assaf Hafez has been found dead in his cell. First report is that he was poisoned, probably in his breakfast food."

Saul's head rocked from side to side in dismay. "They have arms long enough to reach inside our jails and prisons?"

"In this case, there is little room to doubt that. They are conducting an investigation in the kitchens and among the food handlers. Other than the cooks, most of the other help are trusties."

"That should be a great consolation to us. Our only single contact with the UPFP, and he is snatched away from under our own prisoners," Saul added sadly. "Thank you, Yoram. Get over there and see what you can learn."

He turned back to Drory, but at that moment his private phone rang. Leah informed him that General Rosental was on the other line. He said to Drory, "I'll discuss Dresden with you later," and Drory left.

Into the phone, he said, "Saul here, Judah. *Shalom.*"

"Saul, I know you are busy, but I have just received something that may be vital to your investigation, something I must put into your hands personally. How fast can you get here?"

"I will leave at once if it is that important. An hour?"

"At once."

"I'm on my way." He hung up, called Leah on the intercom and asked her to have Asad Hasbani stand by with his car.

Judah Rosental greeted him eagerly and without apology. "Sit down, Saul. This is something I couldn't discuss with you over the phone for reasons which will be apparent to you." He opened his center desk drawer and removed a manila envelope, addressed by hand, but unstamped. "This was handed to a guard downstairs by a taxi driver, paid by an unknown man who asked him to deliver it here."

Saul took the envelope, read the name and address, then opened the flap and removed three sheets of white paper, letter size. On each of two sheets, four strips of developed 35-mm film, each strip with six exposures, were firmly taped down at the corners. The third sheet bore a typed, unsigned message:

JUDAH:
I understand Saul Lahav is handling the UPFP matter. These may be something he is looking for. Area is roughly computed at some thirty or forty kilometers NW the oil installation at Kirkuk, Iraq. Blowups will show very interesting details. Compliments Our Eye in the Sky.
Lots of luck.

As Saul finished reading the note, Rosental said with a smile, "You can guess, of course, who sent this?"

"Collier. And the CIA's satellite cameras. I had better get these to our photo lab at once."

"The sooner the better. I thought it would be more secure to let your people handle this and avoid complications of too many hands being involved. And as Collier says, 'Lots of luck,' Saul. Let me know what you find in these. *Shalom*."

In little more than an hour, Saul was back in Jerusalem, where the film strips were turned over to his photo lab man.

At ten o'clock on the following morning, after having selected the dozen best of the forty-eight blowups, eleven of which were mounted on stiff cardboard and were now pinned to the large blackboard in the conference room, Saul had Leah call in Drory, Golan, Yerushalmi, Shaked, Navot and Shana. All but Shana, who had handled the processing of the film, reflected surprise and interest at the display, each ready with questions.

"Wait, wait," Saul waved them off. "I want you to first examine each of these carefully; then I will explain everything to you."

The blowups, 11 by 14 inches in size, were remarkable in clarity. Each showed a different overflight view of what was obviously a training camp at the base of a mountain range, extending into a desert area marked with rock formations and rippled with wadis. To the west, various buildings, trucks, military vehicles, a well-marked helipad and a small house were extraordinarily visible. In the center of what appeared to be a smooth, grassy lawn, stood a large building that was surely a headquarters, showing a flagpole with two flags flying.

In several of the photographs, small groups of men, dressed in dark fatigue uniforms, were undergoing various forms of training; running, leaping, climbing, crawling. With each group of five was a man dressed in shorts and white T-shirt, undoubtedly an instructor. When they had concluded their examination, Saul picked up a pointer and directed it to one of the photographs that showed a unit working with an instructor. "Look closely here," Saul said, aiming the pointer to the T-shirt the instructor was wearing, facing in the direction of the camera. Golan, standing closest to the blackboard, picked it up at once.

"Yes. I can make it out." As the others crowded closer, Saul said, "What is it, Yoram?"

"A falcon, with something like a rifle in one claw and a lance, or stick, in the other. An insignia."

"Correct. A falcon." Smiling broadly while the others took turns peering at that photograph, Saul went to the table and picked up the twelfth photograph that he had turned face down. He went to the blackboard and affixed it above the others with two pieces of tape.

"Study this one well," Saul said. "It is the most important of the entire lot."

The photograph showed two men on the edge of the helipad, in the act of greeting two others who had just exited the helicopter with Iraqi military markings, taken from a slanted angle that clearly showed their faces as they were about to shake the hands of two waiting hosts.

Eitan Drory was the first to break the silence. Pointing to one hatless man, taller than the others, and who was smiling a greeting at the two arriving officers, he said in a calm, controlled voice, "There is your Egyptian, Colonel. Hatif Tobari. A little older since Cairo, but the same man."

In a quickened voice, Saul said, "You are sure, Eitan?"

"I am positive. I could never forget that one."

"Excellent. Excellent. Now we have a face to fit the name."

"This one—" Shimon Navot began, but Saul broke in over his words and said, "Wait, Shimon." He turned to Shana and said, "I want reprints of Tobari's face, together with his full description. Circulate it to every one of our people here and make additional copies to be distributed to all intelligence agents operating among our neighbors, with particular emphasis on Iraq. Locate and inform us, maintain careful surveillance, but in no case approach, intercept, or be discovered. Get that started now, Shana."

When she left, he turned back to Shimon Navot. "Now."

"This one," Navot said, "is Colonel Afik. Hakim Afik, the number two man in the Iraqi Military Intelligence organization. The man beside him is General Mahmoud al-Hákemi, Iraq's minister of defense."

"I recognize Afik," Yerushalmi added.

"It is Afik," Saul confirmed. "And I am sure some of you recognize the last man, General Hassan Saif, the Libyan minister of war. Gentlemen, we have a very fine package of conspirators here and we can easily guess where Tobari, or Falcon, is getting his financial support. This is the biggest step forward we have made yet and we must continue to dig, and dig harder, for more. That will be all for now, but keep what you have seen firmly and unforgettably in mind. Let us see what thoughts you can come up with."

Saul turned and saw that Asad Hasbani had joined them, and as the conference began to break up, asked him to remove the photographs from the blackboard. "Hang them in my office, Asad, on the wall facing my desk."

"At once, Colonel."

At his desk, he watched as Asad pushpinned the aerial shots to the corkboard panel that ran across the center of the south wall. When the task was completed and he was alone, Saul placed a call to Judah Rosental in Tel Aviv and informed him of their find; that he would send him a set of five- by seven-inch duplicates by special courier as soon as they could be printed. Rosental expressed extreme gratification and his eagerness to examine the photographs.

Saul hung up and turned his attention to the morning report, which consisted of pertinent information compiled from the daily logs kept by the various intelligence services at home and abroad; actions and counteractions and evaluations covering the previous twenty-four-hour period, and circulated among interested agencies for whatever value they offered. These reports, received by radio, teletype, cable, telephone and courier, some requiring decoding, were then compressed into synopsis form, marked for specific attention of the properly designated service head.

Leah Barak interrupted Saul's thoughts momentarily when she entered to drop a memorandum in his incoming tray and went out quickly. Saul resumed with his reading until he came to the end of the morning report. He walked out into the large open work area where Golan and Navot were in deep discussion with Moshe Tal and Yossi Zeitel. Yerushalmi was on the phone. Dov Shaked was in his office, on the phone with Haifa police, inquiring into their activities in trying to locate Tahia Soulad. Shana was away from her section, probably in the photo lab in the basement with the negatives she wanted printed for distribution.

He returned to his office with the uncomfortable feeling that nothing was happening to give him the excitement he wanted to be immersed in with this assignment. It was moving in the right direction, he believed now, but too slowly for his temperament. It was nearing four o'clock and on his desk lay a new batch of reports of interrogations taken by the field force, and from which he expected to garner little, yet required his attention. To each report was clipped a brief synopsis of its contents and a brief notation by the interrogator as to its value. In none did he find anything to merit deeper interest or action. He initialed each and dropped the entire batch into his file tray, then went to the south wall and studied the UPFP photographs again; and at the face of Hatif Tobari with particular attention, assessing him as his prime antagonist.

Shana phoned then to advise him that the photographs were on their way to Tel Aviv by courier, those for distribution having the identification data printed on their reverse sides. Leah knocked on his door and came in with an envelope that was edged in red and blue, many stamps affixed. "What is it, Leah?" he asked.

"From the United States, Colonel, airmail special delivery, registered and marked personal."

"Thank you." He took the envelope from her and stared at it while Leah removed the material from his desk tray and went out. Saul sliced the envelope open with the slender blade of a curved dagger and removed the single sheet of paper. He read its two paragraphs, reacting with an enigmatic, somewhat sad smile-grimace. He reread it, studied it for a few moments, then replaced it in the envelope, folded it over once and tucked it into his shirt pocket.

Later that evening, he drove to Shana's apartment, carrying a bottle of wine. Supper was already prepared and waiting. Saul removed the cork from the bottle of imported wine and poured two glasses while Shana brought the food to the table.

"French Chablis," she commented. "A celebration, Saul?"

"Of sorts. What about the photographs and descriptions of Tobari?"

"They will be printed tonight and ready to be distributed by morning. Full face on one side, postal card size, the description on the reverse side. The wine is for that?"

"Only in part. A small part."

"And the other part?"

"This." He took the envelope from his pocket, removed the letter and handed it to her. "From Miri's lawyer in Los Angeles, Sol Rosenthal. If I don't answer within thirty days, she will receive an uncontested divorce by default."

Shana finished reading the letter and handed it back. "What now, Saul?" she said.

He smiled brightly. "Thirty days from the date on the letter. Then you and I will have a decision of our own to make."

She looked up with a teasing smile. "What decision? Aren't you happy the way things are with us now?"

"Are you, Shana? You don't want more than this, living apart?"

"You're the one who is complaining, not I."

"That's another point. You've never complained. Maybe because you are so much younger than I and don't feel the need for the security of marriage—a marriage you should have."

"Saul," she said, "if we were married, the chances are you would want me to leave the service. If not, departmental policy would prevent us from working closely together. What then? Do I stay home and become a housewife?"

"The difference, my dear Shana," he replied, "is in time and timing. When this UPFP matter is over I intend to request retirement. You and I would leave the service together and we will take what is left and live it, enjoy it together."

"And," Shana said, still in a teasing mood, "if I decide to stay on in the service after you retire?"

Saul's smile matched hers now. "Then, before I retire, I will find a good enough reason to have you court-martialed and dismissed. Dishonorably, of course, for committing adultery with a married man."

"Ah, what a lovely scandal to add to your other honors, Colonel Lahav."

Lifting his glass, he said, "*L'chayim.*"

"*L'chayim.*"

Dinner concluded, Shana cleared the table while Saul relaxed on the sofa and listened to a musical program on the radio. Then Shana came in and lay down beside him, both relaxed, with little left to be said between them at the moment. When the program came to an end, Saul reached behind him and turned the radio off. Shana sat up and said, "Coffee?"

"Yes." He followed her into the kitchen and watched as she prepared to brew the coffee.

"You're very quiet," she said. "Is there something on your mind, Saul?"

"Yes. Shana—"

"What?"

"In the morning, book a flight for me to Baghdad by way of Athens and Teheran. Get me a proper passport, some Iranian and Iraqi currency and check with Mossad for the name of their agent in Baghdad. Have them arrange for him to meet me at the airport on arrival and arrange a recognition signal."

Her concern was immediately apparent. "You're going to the UPFP training camp alone?"

"I'll have our agent there with me."

"Why you, Saul? Why not Eitan Drory? This is more in his line of work, isn't it?"

"For two reasons. First, I am sending Eitan to Dresden to do some checking on EismanOptiks, with which he is familiar. Second, because I need to see this training camp with my own eyes, understand its operation and pinpoint it clearly in my mind and on our maps so that I will be able to give firsthand information to the defense minister and air force chief in case it becomes necessary at some point to bomb it out of existence. Also, to defend such an action to our friends and enemies alike if it is taken."

"I'm beginning to understand a little better how it must have been with Miri and you," Shana said.

* * *

Wearing a drooping mustache and sunglasses, in an ordinary business suit of little distinction, Saul deplaned in the small, dilapidated airport and was at once caught up in the bustle of Arab humanity. While others waited to claim their luggage and bundles, he carried his single small suitcase to the long table where he presented his Jordanian passport to a heavily built, sweating immigration official. The man asked several innocuous questions, which Saul answered in impeccable Arabic, glanced through the opened suitcase briefly and returned the stamped passport with total indifference.

On his way outside, Saul bought a local newspaper and moved to the·sidewalk, which teemed with porters and taxi men vying for customers. He moved out of range to one side and stood there peering over the top edge of his newspaper, seeking his contact man. A few minutes later, a slender, smiling man, jabbering like the rest of the porters and taxi men, plunged through the crowd and reached for Saul's suitcase, murmuring, "A beautiful day for travel, is it not?"

The recognition signal. "Yes, beautiful, if one finds it necessary to travel," Saul responded with relief, feeling the humid heat and the moisture that had formed inside his shirt.

The driver led him through the crowd of emerging passengers along the equally crowded sidewalk, past hawkers and vendors to where his ancient taxi stood at the curb; but it started at the merest turn of the key and glided smoothly into the traffic stream, a maze of small cars, trucks, motorbikes and blaring horns. Once out of the airport area, the driver said without turning, "Herzl Avron. *Shalom.*"

"*Shalom*, Herzl. Saul Lahav."

"I know the name well, but our paths have never crossed before."

"My misfortune," Saul replied. "How long have you been here in Baghdad?"

A shrug of shoulders. "I was born in Iraq. I went to Jerusalem with my parents and wife in 1954, then returned in 1958 with my wife and daughter. Other than a few business trips to other countries, we have lived here since then. We will be at my house in twenty minutes, where we can talk with less noise."

"I need to get out of Baghdad as quickly as possible, Herzl."

"Where to? I was told nothing except to meet you and to follow your orders."

"I will explain everything at your house. I assume we will be safe there."

"Safer than if you were on Ben Yehuda Street. Here I am known as Mohammed Murad. Also, I have made a few good friends with the local police."

They drove through streets that were indescribably filthy, debris and garbage clogging gutters and scattered over streets and pavements by passing trucks and cars. "We had a heavy rainfall last night," Avron commented, "but even without rain, it is not much better than this."

Ten minutes later they were in a residential district of modest working-class homes, most in sad need of paint and repair, but much quieter than the center of the city through which they had passed earlier. Avron pulled into a narrow lane between two such houses. At the rear of one was a locked shed that served as a garage. A young girl of perhaps fifteen emerged at the rear of the house to unlock and raise the garage door. Avron drove inside and stopped beside a small Fiat sedan.

The girl was Ariel Avron, Herzl's daughter, who acknowledged the introduction to Saul in Arabic, smiling shyly. Inside the small house, Anna Avron, who was about thirty-six and equally as reserved and shy as Ariel, welcomed Saul briefly, also in Arabic. A meal had been prepared, which Herzl and Saul ate alone while Saul explained his purpose, pinpointing the approximate location of the UPFP camp on a small map tracing.

"If your map is accurate," Herzl said, "there is a road I think we can take that will not require us to go through Kirkuk, which is heavily guarded by the military against sabotage by Kurd guerrillas."

"They are still active?"

"Did you think they would not be? Even though Iraq and Iran have signed their border agreements and Iran has stopped supplying the Kurds with weapons, they have not forgotten their years of struggle for the independence promised them. The revolution was crushed, yes, but no Iraqi considers himself safe in those hills."

"Then the danger persists for us as well."

"To some extent. There are Iraqi patrols and Kurdish resistance fighters between Kirkuk and Mosul and as far north as Haj Umran and the mountain valleys behind the Rawanduz front, the Pesh Merga fighters who are well armed and tough."

"Is there a chance we can get through?"

"I have a friend, Mustafa Fayed, here in Baghdad, a Pesh Merga—"

"A Kurd?" Saul said in surprise.

Herzl grinned. "Of course, but do not be concerned. In our business we sometimes sleep with strange bedfellows, as you already know. Mustafa and I have helped each other a number of times, exchanging information. Once, for ten days, I hid him in my garage while the Iraqi military were rounding up Kurd resisters. He is a lifelong enemy of all Iraqis.''

''And not of Israelis?''

'' 'The enemy of my enemy is my brother,' '' Herzl quoted with a laugh. ''Mustafa will be very helpful to us, Saul. He knows every mountain road and trail and can send word ahead to his friends that we must not be harmed.''

''When can you see him?''

''Tonight, as soon as it grows dark.''

''And when can we start?''

''You said you want to get out of Baghdad as quickly as possible. Is tomorrow morning too soon? He will need that time to send word ahead.''

''Good. Arrange it.''

''You will sleep here tonight. After I see Mustafa, we will need to decide what kind of equipment we will want to take with us for wherever you have in mind.''

At eight o'clock that night, Herzl drove away in his Fiat and returned at a little after nine with a thickset, fierce-looking man with a full, flowing mustache and a strong odor of garlic on his breath, laughing jovially as he entered the house, his bulk seeming to fill the room.

''This is my good friend, Mustafa Fayed,'' Herzl introduced him, ''and this is my good friend, Saul.''

Saul and Fayed scrutinized each other carefully, then Fayed smiled broadly and said, ''I am pleased to know any friend of my good friend Mohammed. *Salaam aleikum.*''

''*Salaam*, Mustafa. I am pleased that we will be together.''

''I hope you will not be disappointed. One never know s what will happen when we move into the northern parts, but we will be careful, eh?''

Herzl was satisfied with the encounter and, a half hour later, after initial plans were laid for the following morning, was ready to drive Mustafa back to his home. When he returned, Herzl showed Saul to his garage, which they entered through a side door, out of view of the street. At the rear, Herzl moved an end section of his workbench away from the wall. Beneath it, covered with linoleum, was a trapdoor. Using only a flashlight, he handed up two short-barreled Uzi submachine guns, two revolvers, several boxes of ammunition, half a dozen hand grenades and a pair of binoculars.

''What about Mustafa?'' Saul asked.

''He will bring his own, one he took from an Iraqi patrol he and some others ambushed a while back. Very modern, Russian.''

These were placed in the trunk of the Fiat sedan and covered with blankets, some items of clothing and a carton of tools. To this, Herzl added three large tins of petrol and two of water. He then locked the fully loaded trunk and both returned to the house. In the living room, they sat discussing their project. Mustafa knew the region well and was certain he could not only get them through into the area, but pinpoint the exact location of the UPFP camp as shown on Saul's rough map.

Now the talk turned to other matters in which Mossad might be interested. ''What information do you have that will confirm or deny reports we have had of a buildup of a Soviet naval base in the Persian Gulf?'' Saul asked.

Herzl shook his head from side to side. ''Nothing as to a naval base. I have scouted the Umm Qasr port on three separate occasions in the past seven months. There are four old piers and two new jetties that were only half completed. Nor are there any such signs elsewhere. At Umm Qasr, Soviet ships have unloaded some patrol boats, minesweepers, small rocket ships, a few torpedo and antisubmarine boats, along with supplies, but no true bases have been established as yet, and none are likely to be.

''The Iraqis do not want foreign bases here, nor would it be practical. The gulf coastline has no real depth and is therefore not useful. Besides, along the Shatt al Arab River, the Iranian refineries are in clear view from the Iraqi side and a Russian presence would not only be offensive to the Shah, but would disrupt the present uneasy truce between the two countries. Thus, the rumors are only that—rumors.''

''You have reported this to Tel Aviv?''

''I am still in the process of coding the lengthy report. You can save me much trouble if you will carry the information back with you. Including the films I have been able to shoot, but have no way to reduce them to microfilm.''

''Whatever you have, I will take with me.''

Since there were only two small bedrooms in the house, Saul slept on the sofa under two blankets with only his jacket and shoes removed. He had little difficulty in falling asleep at once.

At four in the morning, Herzl shook him awake. He put on his shoes, washed in the basin Anna brought him and ate the food she had prepared. Herzl carried a small wicker basket of additional food and two thermos jugs filled with coffee out to the car, and they drove away. Twenty-five minutes later, Herzl stopped in front of Mustafa's house. The Kurd was ready and emerged from the darkened house carrying something wrapped in a blanket. Once inside the car, he unwrapped his own weapon, a Russian-made Kalashnikov paratroop submachine gun which he exhibited proudly.

They were well out of the city before the sky began to turn light. There were no checkpoints. By noon they were within thirty kilometers of Kirkuk on a road well trafficked with heavy trucks, tankers and farm vehicles. At a branch road, Mustafa directed Herzl off onto a dirt dogleg that would skirt the large oil center and bring them into the foothills of a mountain range. Here, they turned off onto another road, hardly more than a trail, that led up into the mountains which began climbing slowly, then more steeply, running into deep ruts that forced them to stop occasionally to remove fallen rocks from their path.

In midafternoon they reached the crest where the road was only slightly better. "A patrol road," Fayed explained from the rear seat, unlimbering his Kalashnikov and inserting a long banana clip to give him more fire power, and injecting a cartridge from clip to chamber. "It is wise," he said, "to keep our eyes open here."

Saul at once regretted that his and Herzl's weapons were still in the trunk and was tempted to ask Herzl to stop so they could retrieve them; but Herzl did not seem to be perturbed, relying fully on Mustafa's ability to handle any situation they might encounter.

Then, on their left, they were able to look down into the broad valley which was sunlighted and clear. "Soon," Mustafa said. "If your map is correct, another two or three kilometers."

And, almost exactly three kilometers ahead, Herzl braked the car to a stop. There below them, Saul could make out the buildings exactly as he had seen them from the satellite photographs, but from a lower angle. "This is good," he said. "Right here."

They got out, unlocked the trunk and took out their weapons and ammunition, dividing the six grenades between them. Herzl quickly topped off his tank with petrol, added water to the radiator, then pulled the car off the road to their right into a grove of trees and brush. Mastafa chose to remain with the car, his weapon ready, in order to keep the road in sight. Saul and Herzl crossed the road and moved below its rim, from which point they had a clear, open view of the entire valley below. From a pocket, Saul removed a 35-mm camera. From another, a long lens, which he fitted into position, then inserted a roll of film.

Lying flat on his stomach, he first scanned the UPFP training center through his binoculars, focusing on the movement of five separate groups of men, five in each group, and each with a T-shirted instructor who ran beside them, gesturing and issuing orders. Satisfied, Saul began shooting frame after frame until the roll was spent. He unloaded the film, reloaded, again scanned the camp through the binoculars, then resumed shooting.

In the middle of the fourth roll, while Herzl used the binoculars to check the road leading up to the crest from the north side of the valley, the Iraqi Jew called out suddenly, "Saul!"

"What is it, Herzl?"

"Some movement coming up from the north, road dust. A car. It could be a patrol."

"Warn Mustafa, then return here. I must finish this roll."

Herzl sprinted up the hill to the crest, crossed the road and told Mustafa, who grinned and patted his weapon. "Good," he said with obvious elation. "Maybe I can get another few of these."

"Be careful, Mustafa. If they do not see us, do nothing to attract their attention. It is most important that we do not engage in a pitched battle up here."

Mustafa grinned and nodded. Herzl again warned him, then ran back across the road and crept down the steep incline where Saul lay, still engrossed in making his careful record of the campsite below. Taking up the binoculars again, Herzl swept the landscape and centered on the cloud of dust, now grown larger.

"What do you see, Herzl?" Saul called out.

"I can make them out more clearly now. It looks like an Iraqi patrol. Four men in a jeep."

Continuing to shoot, "How far away?"

"Six, maybe seven kilometers."

"Plenty of time. I will be finished here in another minute or two."

Herzl let the binoculars hang from the neck strap and moved the two Uzis up beside him, then placed their spare ammo clips next to them. Moments later he called out, "Saul, they are getting closer, no more than a minute away."

Saul took his last shot, quickly wound the reel up and removed it, unscrewed the long lens, pocketed that and the camera and moved up hill beside Herzl. Both were lying well below the rim of the road and out of sight, heads close to the earth, now able to hear the jeep as it ground along the road some sixty yards to the north and a mere eight feet above them.

Herzl stirred, bringing his Uzi up in line with the crest above him. Saul reached over and touched Herzl's arm, cautioning him not to move. "We are well below their line of vision. If they do not stop, let them pass."

Herzl nodded. Then the jeep was directly above them, growling past while churning the dirt into clouds in its wake, keeping to the center of the road. Suddenly, the stillness was shattered by a burst of fire from across the road, then another.

Mustafa Fayed had been unable to resist the target of four totally unaware Iraqi enemies; or perhaps it was his greed for the automatic weapons they carried.

The first burst killed the man seated directly behind the driver instantly and wounded the driver so that the jeep, with no hands on the wheel, veered toward the left and crashed into a huge rock. The second burst from Mustafa's Kalashnikov almost tore the wounded driver's head off. The other two Iraqis either leaped, or were thrown, from the right side of the jeep to the ground, then began returning Mustafa's fire, burst after burst in the direction from which they had seen the first gun flashes.

In the momentary silence that ensued, following the first return of fire, both Iraqis turned toward the opposite side of the road, searching for other possible attackers or perhaps to gain the rim of road for cover, crouching low, weapons at the ready; and at the rim, discovered Saul and Herzl in the act of reaching that very same rim at the crest. As the Israeli guns exploded, the Iraqis drew back quickly to the wrecked jeep where they took cover and resumed firing.

Dodging below the rim again, Saul signaled Herzl to move to his left while Saul crawled to the right; still safe from gunfire but unable to gain the road without offering themselves as targets. On the left side, Herzl shoved the muzzle of his Uzi over the rim and fired blindly in the direction of the jeep to draw the fire of both Iraqis. When he was rewarded by return fire from two guns, Saul raised up and fired from the right side. Now the Iraqis turned in that direction to answer and Herzl pulled the pin from one of his grenades and lobbed it over the edge toward the jeep. There was a stunning blast, followed by a second explosion when Saul threw one of his grenades. Then total stillness.

They waited for thirty seconds, then Saul rose from a crouch and peered over the rim, seeing only smoke and small flames from the burning jeep. Now Herzl was up on the road, walking toward the wreckage, Uzi ready, and Saul met him from the opposite direction.

The four Iraqis were dead, literally torn apart by Mustafa's automatic weapon and the two grenades, the jeep a total wreck. In the grove, they found, as expected, Mustafa, with gaping holes in his chest, half of his head torn away.

"Let's get out of here," Herzl said. "I don't know how far this noise can carry in these mountains."

"Yes," Saul agreed. "We don't know how long it will be before they are missed or when they were due to report in to their station."

While Herzl backed the Fiat out of its hiding place, Saul gathered up the weapons of the Iraqis and stowed them in the trunk along with their own. During the next hour, Herzl Avron gave Saul Lahav the wildest ride of his life.

*   *   *

Next morning Saul arrived at the Baghdad airport as a passenger in Herzl's taxi. Herzl leaped out and handed over the suitcase. Without an exchange of words, Saul paid the fare, picked up the suitcase and entered the airport building just in time to catch the seven-ten plane to Teheran.

In Teheran, he discovered that the plane to Athens would be delayed for four hours due to mechanical difficulty. It took thirty minutes of diplomatic negotiations and an exchange of cash before he was able to switch to an Alitalia, the next plane departing for Rome. Enroute, he wiped the firefight from his mind and concentrated on what he had seen in the valley below; the units under intense training, the physical properties of the camp itself, the film he had shot in black-and-white and color to convince higher authorities of the authenticity of the Sokolnikov memorandum that had been confirmed by the satellite photographs Collier had furnished. If, indeed, more proof than Shetula and the sophisticated equipment found in Assaf Hafez's station wagon, were needed.

In Rome late that afternoon, Saul deplaned and went directly to a phone booth where he placed a call to Shana. After considerable delays, he caught her at her desk just as she was preparing to leave for the day.

"Saul! How good to hear your voice. Are you all right? Where are you calling from?"

"From Rome airport. I'll explain everything later. There is an El Al out in—"

"No, Saul." Her voice rose with a sense of urgency. "I have a message for you from J. R. The material we had distributed?"

In a scarcely audible tone, "The . . . you have something on it?"

"Yes. Definite."

"What is it?"

"Khoury. Tripoli, Libya. You understand?"

"Yes, yes. What can you give me now?"

"Your Number One has been located. Khoury has positive information. J. R. wants you to contact him soonest. He suggests that you be accompanied by a woman for cover."

"Do we have someone here in Rome?"

"Negative. One will be sent to you from here on the first plane out in the morning."

"Wait. Cancel that arrangement. I want you for that."

"I would need permission from J. R.—"

"You don't need that. *I* am giving you the necessary permission and a direct order. Besides, you have the rest of your interrupted leave coming to you."

There was no argument or resistance from Shana. "I'll be on that first flight out in the morning. Where will you be?"

"The Europa."

"Under what name?"

"In Rome, my own. For Tripoli, use Syrian passports, any safe names you have on hand. Be sure to bring along some Libyan currency."

"Yes. That early flight arrives at ten fifteen tomorrow morning."

"I'll be at the airport to meet you. *Shalom*."

"*Shalom*."

In his room at the Europa, Saul ordered a light meal to be sent up from the dining room. He showered leisurely, trying to erase the tensions created by his recent experience with violent death, but only succeeded in reawakening older memories of similar violent deaths witnessed under combat conditions which he had thought were beyond recall; perhaps remembering Shana's earlier suggestion that adventures of this caliber belong to men like Eitan Drory; younger, more resilient men who could look ahead without having to look backward.

He slipped into pajamas and tried to relax until the food arrived, but became restless and began pacing the room, chain-smoking. When the waiter brought his meal finally, he dallied over it with little relish or interest except for the coffee; turning his mind toward Shana's arrival in the morning. The meal pushed aside, table rolled out into the hallway, he focused his mind on Khoury and the matter at hand: the message that he had located and identified Hatif Tobari—Falcon. The elusive kingpin. A very real and vital find.

Tobari. Khoury. Both names were now irrevocably wedded in his thoughts, with only one fact in common. He had never seen either man in the flesh.

Now he began to relax somewhat, trying to put both names in proper context, allowing them to float loosely through his mind. Tobari's face was indelibly engraved there, able to recall it at will, each feature; engaging smile, well-spaced eyes under moderately thick eyebrows, straight nose with slightly flaring nostrils, clean-shaven, strong-jawed, firm, resolute chin, overall dark or sun-tanned face and carefully combed black hair that swept forward over his forehead like a small canopy.

And Khoury. He remembered only the name and a few scant facts about the man who was head of a small Mossad network operating from his headquarters, a dress shop, he recalled, in Tripoli. Reaching deeper into his memory bank, he dredged up a first name. Emile. Yes, Emile Khoury, a cover name for one Saul had never heard or known, like those of so many who worked strictly in the netherworld of secrecy. Dress shop. The reason behind Rosental's suggestion that a woman accompany him to provide credible cover.

Over a period of years, Saul had read reports and excerpts of reports from many such shadow men stationed throughout Europe and Middle Eastern countries—men like Herzl Avron—but had had personal contact with a mere handful, and only when it had been necessary to an operation of importance. Some had been working in deep cover in a single area for years, identification and occupation supporting their secret; others for only a short period on special assignment, moving on elsewhere as needed, forwarding information back to Tel Aviv that was invaluable to national security and survival.

There was little more Saul could think about or plan ahead for now. The next act would take place in Tripoli, whose revolutionary chief, Colonel Muammar Qaddafi, resolutely held the extreme position that all-out war with Israel was not only necessary, but inevitable. To that extent, he was willing to extend multi-millions of Libya's oil dollars to support any nation or terrorist group to bring about that war. He had broken with Egypt, entered into separate agreements with the Soviet Union for aircraft and other sophisticated military hardware. He counted on Algeria, Iraq and Syria among his closest allies.

Now, physical weariness overtook Saul's efforts to concentrate on what lay ahead tomorrow. He phoned the desk and left a wakeup call, then fell into a deep sleep.

In midafternoon of the following day, Saul and Shana arrived at the Tripoli airport from Rome in a Middle East Airlines jet. Security was light and they passed through customs and immigration without difficulty after presenting their documents and answering several questions in perfect Arabic. Outside, they followed their porter to a line of dilapidated taxis and directed their driver to the Tripolitania Hotel.

"You have reservations?" the driver asked.

"No," Saul replied.

The driver shrugged. "It may be difficult. There are so many refugees from Beirut here; the fighting there, you understand. If they turn you down, there is one I know where you can find a room.''

"Thank you. We will see.''

Neither noticed, as they pulled away, that a swarthy man had been paying particular attention to them as they exited the airport building, watching as they engaged their taxi driver. The man now crossed quickly to the next lane of parked cars, where he joined another man seated in a small tan sedan. When the taxi pulled out, the tan sedan followed.

The Tripolitania had been built during the British administration in 1948, a twelve-storied edifice that stood in the center of a ten-acre park and faced the Mediterranean, perhaps the most modern building in Tripoli, although its interior had become shoddy and shopworn through neglect. As predicted by their taxi driver, it was heavily patronized, but the clerk, after the exchange of pound notes, found a room available on the eighth floor; not sumptuous, but adequate.

Shana insisted on refreshing herself and changing her dress. Saul, after a brief wash and change of shirt, waited in the lobby over a copy of the morning paper which headlined the news of another broken truce and the renewal of fighting between Palestinians and Christians in Beirut; also a terrorist attack by Palestinian terrorists on an Israeli village south of Lebanon, after which the Israeli air force retaliated with ''a massive attack upon a Lebanese refugee camp, resulting in the deaths of many innocent women and children.''

When Shana joined him, they took a cab at the door and gave the driver the address of Khoury Couture on Rue El Arz, which was familiar to the man. As they pulled away, the two men in the tan sedan followed, a not too difficult task through Tripoli's suburban traffic until they reached the more heavily crowded commercial center with its shops and *souks* overflowing with shoppers. With little regard for traffic, relying mainly on horn and brakes, the driver plowed through the teeming area of a large flower market, then made several turns to avoid the massive pedestrian traffic, cars and trucks, and emerged on a wider boulevard with far less activity. In doing so, the tan sedan had been cut off and left behind.

On Rue El Arz, the principal shopping street, Khoury Couture had the perfumed atmosphere of a Paris salon and, indeed, many of the gowns, dresses and robes, jackets and coats on display came from that center of fashion to tempt the eyes and purses of Tripoli's *haut ton* as well as the money-laden visitors from other Arab capitals. Saul and Shana walked across rich Oriental rugs to where an elegant hostess waited to greet them. Elsewhere in the subdued quietude of the shop, two women customers talked with a sales-woman while a model paraded in a sheer, multicolored sheath designed for evening wear. Another pair of women were ready to be shown into a fitting room.

"May I be of service to you, Madame, Monsieur?" the hostess asked, speaking in exquisite French. "My name is Daniele."

"Yes," Saul replied in the same language. "My wife is interested in something for day wear. And can you tell me if my friend, M'sieu Khoury, is not too busy to spare me a few moments?"

Daniele looked at Saul through slightly narrowed eyes and, still smiling, said, "I shall be happy to inquire, M'sieu." Signalling an attractive young woman to attend Shana, Daniele indicated a comfortable armchair for Saul, then went to the rear of the shop and disappeared through a mirrored door. Moments later she emerged, went directly to Saul and said, "M'sieu Khoury is not engaged at this time. If you will please follow me—"

Emile Khoury was perhaps fifty-five years old, a large, hearty man with broad shoulders and contemplative, smiling eyes, long sideburns that were tinged with gray that added a distinguished touch to his otherwise black hair. He looked almost out of place, overpowering, in the uncluttered office that was furnished in extremely good taste with a carved desk, a long table behind it, and glass-fronted cabinets that displayed small figurines in gowns reflecting the Napoleonic era. Other chairs and cabinets that made up the balance of the furniture were delicate and graceful, such as one would expect to find in the drawing room of an elegant home.

Paintings on the walls were interspersed with neatly framed photographs of friends and recognizable Libyan political figures, each of which included Khoury and was autographed to him. On the table behind the desk lay groupings of material samples and a neat array of French, Italian and British fashion magazines, duplicates of those on the coffee tables in the salon.

Khoury rose from his huge chair at the desk and smiled warmly when Saul was ushered into the room by Daniele. With a polite bow and smile, she left the two men together.

"Welcome to Tripoli, Colonel," Khoury greeted affably. "I was informed you would be arriving but hadn't expected you so soon. Sit, please. Will you take coffee?"

"Thank you, not at the moment." Saul looked around the room with curiosity and caution. "Can we talk freely here, M'seiu Khoury?"

"Emile, please."

"Emile, then. I am Saul."

"Saul. And yes, we can speak freely here. The girl who showed you here is my most trusted aide. The others employed here know nothing outside their work. This room is soundproofed and we cannot be overheard.''

Saul relaxed in his chair. Khoury leaned back and said, ''Saul. Saul Lahav. I know the name well. It is my loss we have never met before. You know Tripoli?''

''I have been here once before, long ago, on an assignment, but unfortunately, I had little time for social interludes. In that respect, it is my loss as well. How long have you been in Tripoli, if I may ask, Emile?''

Khoury smiled expansively. ''A long time, Saul. I escaped from Paris only a few hours before the Nazis moved in. I spent the rest of the war in England, working with their intelligence people, made a few drops in France to do some demolition work. In London, I made a number of Israeli friends and in forty-six returned with them to Israel and joined Haganah's intelligence unit, then into Mossad. I was sent here in 1950 under assumed Libyan citizenship.''

''And this?'' Sal waved one hand to include the office and salon outside.

''A most natural cover for me. My family, the Samuels of Paris, manufactured fine clothing for many Parisian fashion shops for generations, so I was sent here to set up a listening post, which later developed into a small network to supply information on terrorist groups, political maneuverings in other Arab states—the sort of thing I sent to you through our link man. One would be surprised at the amount of information that is passed along idly by upper-class women in the process of buying gowns. Through them, I meet many others,'' a wave to indicate the photographs on the walls, ''who can sometimes be rather careless, even indiscreet, in their talk at dinners, their clubs, their homes.''

''So. And no problems?''

''None when one knows how to conduct himself carefully.''

Saul was tremendously impressed with the man and his ease in these surroundings, a man who seemed to be fully in command of himself in a precarious occupation. ''Your message was one we have been looking forward to eagerly, Emile,'' Saul said now. ''What do you have for me?''

Khoury rose and moved toward a painting, one of several on the wall to his right. ''Hopefully,'' he said in progress, ''the man you are looking for.'' And adding as an aside, ''Eventually, the extremists all manage to come to Tripoli for one reason or another, principally for financing.'' He pressed a catch below the frame of an original oil painting. It swung away from the wall to reveal a safe dial. A few turns to right and left and it was pulled forward, swung to the left, opening a steel circle some twelve inches in diameter. From the cavern within, Khoury withdrew a copy of the photograph of Hatif Tobari that had been circulated only a few days earlier.

"This," he said, handing it to Saul, "is what I think you want. Your Hatif Tobari, or Falcon, is known here in Tripoli as Ali Fathy, a wealthy Egyptian of obscure interests, with a fondness for the gambling life and attractive young women. His current mistress, Adele Salah, lives in an expensive apartment on the road to Benghazi and is a frequent customer in this shop. Fathy moves around a lot, but visits her perhaps once a month or five or six weeks for two or three days at a time. Sometimes there is a longer gap—"

"Then he is not here now?" Saul asked.

"I am sorry to disappoint you, but I think not. If he were, I am sure I would know about it, either here with his Adele, or in one of the clubs they generally frequent."

"When was he here last?"

"To the best of my knowledge, about two months ago, perhaps a little longer. He came in to pay Adele's account, as he usually does, always in cash, which seems to be plentiful."

"Do you have any idea when he is due next?"

Khoury shrugged his massive shoulders. "When he feels the need of her, I would say, but I would guess within a week or two, since it has been quite long since his last visit." Khoury then added, "To see her, this Adele, is to understand why."

Saul's disappointment was apparent. "Yes, well—" he said slowly. "I hope you will keep me advised through regular channels of Fathy's next visit. It is vitally important that I know the moment he arrives in Tripoli. Also, is it possible to arrange for a loose surveillance on the Salah woman's apartment so there will be no time lost?"

Khoury nodded. "We have that means."

"Be careful that your man does not attract her attention. I am not interested in her movements, only in Fathy's arrival."

"My man is most experienced, Saul. How long will you remain in Tripoli? I can arrange for—"

But Saul was shaking the suggestion off. "There is a late flight back to Rome at midnight tonight, another early tomorrow morning. We will decide later which we will take."

"We?"

"Yes. The lady with me is my assistant, sent along so that I would not look too conspicuous in a dress shop alone."

"Ah, yes, of course. Then is there anything else I can do for you as of now?"

226 Jack Hoffenberg

"No, I think not. Except for the dress I am sure my colleague had chosen for herself."

Khoury laughed heartily. "Naturally, naturally. I hope your department can afford my prices."

"Only if you offer a liberal discount."

"I'm sure we can work out an arrangement to your complete satisfaction."

Shana, meanwhile, had chosen a smartly styled dress that ended at knee length, tucked in at the waist to accent her shapely breasts. Encouraged by the saleswoman's flattery and Daniele's insistence that "it was created solely for you, only you, Madame," Saul nodded his firm approval. The dress was boxed and they left to return to the hotel.

Amon Sadani, from the very first day Massif Razak appeared to take charge of the UPFP's operational center in Israel, had been opposed to the Syrian major for that position of vital trust and extreme sensitivity. He made his objections known to Tobari, who had the delicate job of soothing Sadani, although he was not without certain doubts himself. However, there was little he could do about the matter. Razak had been the personal choice of General al-Hakemi, who was aware of the Syrian's background and qualities, and Tobari was forced to agree.

That Razak had proved to be a capable organizer, although a harsh, ruthless man, surprised Sadani, even though he cared less and less for him as time passed. Razak was not unaware of the underlying resentment of the Egyptian, demeaned by the necessity of taking orders from a civilian whom he contemptuously regarded as a clerk.

Thus, in midafternoon when Amon Sadani arrived at the UPFP headquarters in answer to a coded telephone summons from Razak, he was not in a pleasant mood when he entered the office where the Syrian and Salim Tabet sat drinking coffee over cigarettes. Addressing himself to Razak, he said in a surly tone, "I have told you before that it is difficult for me to absent myself from my office on short notice this way. I am required to leave word where I can be reached at all times during the day—"

Razak snapped out, "This is an emergency, Sadani, and there was no time to play games that would cause unnecessary delays."

"Emergency?" Sadani blinked behind his thick glasses and said, "What emergency? What has happened here?"

"Not here." Razak's affected calm only exaggerated Sadani's apparent anxiety, which pleased the Syrian. "And it was not possible to give you more notice—"

"What is it, man? Don't waste my time with petty explanations."

Razak pursed his lips and said, "Just after noon today, I received a message, marked urgent and for immediate action, by radio transmission through Damascus. It is from Falcon and addressed to both of us.

"Sometime yesterday, an Iraqi patrol of four was attacked and killed by unknown assailants in the hills high above the camp. A fifth body, one of the attackers, was too badly shot up to be recognizable or identifiable. Falcon is deeply concerned that this may have been the work of Mossad's Special Operations Branch, that the camp is being spied upon. Also, the Iraqi military command is furious and has threatened to expel the entire operation if there is a recurrence, which is extremely disturbing to Falcon."

"And what does Falcon expect us to do about that here?" Sadani demanded.

"Read the translation for yourself. He has ordered the assassination of its head, Colonel Lahav."

Sadani's look was one of total disbelief. "Lahav?" he exclaimed. "I can't believe it. He can't be serious. That would be insanity!"

Razak shrugged. "Is it for you to question Falcon's orders?" He rose, went to the desk and returned with a sheet of paper. "Here, read it for yourself. It is a direct order. It leaves us no choice."

Sadani took the sheet and began reading it while Salim Tabet looked on with quiet interest at the interplay between his two superiors. "I am sure," Razak commented in a mocking voice, "that Falcon does not expect this, or any other operation he orders, to be easy, Sadani. What he expects is a well planned and executed—"

Razak had now touched a sensitive nerve and Sadani reacted swiftly. "Don't take that tone with me, Razak," he said explosive|ly, "and don't presume to interpret Falcon's orders for me. I have known and worked with him far longer than you or anyone else." Without waiting for a reply, he resumed reading.

When he had finished, he folded the sheet of paper and began tearing it into small pieces, then took them to an ashtray, lit a match and reduced the pieces to ashes without further comment.

Now a thick silence hung in the air between them which was broken when Salim Tabet said defensively, "I think I can handle this matter, if it is decided it should be done. With your approval, of course, Amon," he added diplomatically.

Sadani favored him with a bleak smile. "I am certain you can, Salim, but I still question the wisdom of such an act. I can't see what it will accomplish. Certainly it will not cause the collapse of the special branch. If anything, such an act would only tend to reinforce its activities. And there is no proof that it was the branch that had anything to do with the attack on the Iraqi patrol. It could very well have been the Kurds—''

"Still," Razak persisted, "this is a direct order from Falcon and if you dismiss it, it will be on your own responsibility." Before Sadani could reply, he added, "Such an act can accomplish two things. One, it will create havoc with Lahav's organization and cause delays in what plans they have. Two, it will serve notice that no Israeli, no matter who, where, or of what rank, will be safe from us."

Ignoring Razak, Sadani turned back to Tabet. "Very well, Salim, since Falcon has ordered it. We will have to work out a plan. We must make certain to use people who have never been here at this headquarters. In the event of an unforeseeable misadventure, we cannot afford to have anyone taken who can reveal its location or identify any of us."

"Except, of course, myself," Tabet said, "but you need have no fear that I will—''

"I am not worried about you," Sadani said quickly, "only about the others."

"I will choose carefully, only those of whom I am certain."

"Very well, Salim. Plan well. When you have it worked out, we will go over it together." Turning to Razak, he said curtly, "Give Salim what he needs, weapons, money—''

"Of course," Razak replied with a smug smile, having won a point from Sadani, who turned back to Tabet. "They are getting nowhere in the investigation of Hafez's death. A commendable job, Salim."

"It was not too difficult with so many of our people working as trusties in their kitchens."

"Nevertheless, I am very pleased. What about the girl?"

"That also has been taken care of. Two nights ago she slipped out of the club disguised as one of the cleaning women. I had a car waiting and brought her here to Jerusalem, as you ordered. She will begin dancing at the Club Morocco tomorrow night under a name she has used before. Gabriela."

"Excellent, Salim. I will report this favorably to Falcon."

"You have heard from him recently?" Razak asked.

"Three days ago. Soon he will have twenty men ready to merge into a single combat unit for the Bashra operation. Meanwhile, he must wait for the equipment to arrive from Dresden." And to Tabet, "Very soon, I will give you the word to have the girl contact Zuheir

Masri in Haifa to arrange for him to start recruiting his people, singly and in pairs, to apply for jobs in Bashra. Once they are there at work, instructions will be given Masri to prepare for action."

"As soon as the word is given," Tabet said, "it will be done."

"Good. If there is nothing else now, I must leave for the airport. I am flying to West Berlin for an economic conference and will go from there to Dresden to meet Falcon. I will return here within a week or ten days. If your plan for Lahav is completed before then, do not proceed until I have returned."

Saul had left a call for seven o'clock, made an early supper reservation for eight thirty, then he and Shana took a nap. Awakened promptly at seven by the operator, they bathed and dressed, Shana in her new Parisian frock, Saul feeling somewhat rumpled beside her in the suit he had worn all day. They had supper in the main dining room, rather quiet at that early hour, ordered a carafe of wine and idled over the balance of their meal in the pleasant afterglow of their shared intimacy.

"Are we taking the midnight flight to Rome?" Shana asked.

"Would you prever the early morning flight instead?"

"Yes. This is my first visit to Tripoli. I am enjoying it."

"Then tomorrow morning," Saul agreed.

"Will we be able to see some of Tripoli's nightlife?"

"If there is any, why not? We have the whole evening before us."

"I'll need a jacket from our room."

"Then let's go up now. I'll pick up a paper at the newsstand and see what the nightclubs are offering. Later on, we can visit a casino." He signaled the waiter, asked for the check and paid it. In the lobby, they waited at the newsstand for the line of tourists to be served, then Saul handed her the room key. "You go on up, Shana. I'll get the paper and join you in a few minutes."

"And a Paris *Match*."

"If they have one. If not, I'll find a substitute." He turned back to the line and waited.

On the eighth floor, Shana exited and went to her right to room 822, where she fit her key into the lock, turned it and entered. Even before her hand found the light switch, it was grabbed from within and she was quickly pulled inside, too surprised to cry out or put up a struggle. One strong arm was wrapped tightly around her waist and an evil-smelling hand clamped hard over her mouth. She stamped her foot down hard in an effort to find her attacker's instep with her heel, but the man's legs were spread apart and his muscular arm held her in a firm grasp, the hand more firmly pressed against her mouth, giving her no opportunity to cry an alarm or bite into its flesh.

Then the door was slammed shut by a second man and the lights came on. There were two of them. The one who held her lifted her easily and carried her to the edge of the bed. Still holding her firmly from behind, he said in Arabic, "I am going to take my hand away from your mouth. If your scream, my partner will slit your throat."

She accepted this resignedly and nodded. He removed his hand slowly, holding it cupped close to her face in the event she decided to change her mind. "Lie down on the bed. If you behave, no harm will come to you."

The other man had resumed searching through Saul's suitcase and her own bag. As Shana attempted to sit up, her assailant pushed her back so that she lay flat on her back, a not too gentle shove. He made no move when she reached out to pull her dress down as far as it would go, but reached into his pocket and withdrew a knife. A button was pressed and a wicked five-inch blade flashed up from the well in its handle. "Where is your man?" he asked.

"On his way up."

The man nodded with a tight smile. "Good. When he enters, you will lie still and remain quiet. If you call out or utter even a sound, both of you will die."

"Is it money you want? I have—"

The other man looked up from the suitcase he was examining with a brusque laugh. "How much money do Israeli agents carry with them in Arab countries?" he asked.

Shana turned to ice. "That is insane. We are Syrians from Damascus. You can look at our passports—"

The first man said sneeringly, "Arriving from Rome on MEA?"

"Yes. We went to Rome first to see our son who is in school there."

"You are lying, you Jew whore. You arrived in Rome on El Al. You spent the night with Lahav at the Europa. You took MEA to Tripoli. We were informed by our people in Rome and have had you under observation since you landed here."

There was no way in which Shana could hide the chagrin that flooded her face. "Surprised that al-Fatah's intelligence is as effective as Mossad's, Lieutenant, often better?" He threw a look toward his accomplice. "The door, Gamal. Release it."

Gamal dropped the lid on the suitcase and went to the door. He opened it, then closed it so that it would require only a touch from the outside to permit entry without a key. He then removed a flat automatic pistol from his shoulder holster and positioned himself with his back to the wall so that he would remain unseen when the door was thrown open. Affixed to the inner side of the door was a full length mirror for use of guests to check their final appearance before leaving the room.

"The lights, Gamal."

"No, Fouad. Since she is here, he will expect them to be on, and I want him to see her lying there on the bed, with you standing over her, the knife at her throat. When he leaps in, I will have him with his back to me."

At that moment, they heard footsteps scuffing along the thickly piled carpet in the hallway. Fouad, knife in hand, aimed its point at Shana's throat as he stood on the near side of the bed. Gamal had again flattened himself against the wall, the automatic in his right hand. Then the door was pushed open and Saul stood there, a paper and a slick magazine in one hand, her name broken off on his lips as he took in the scene: Shaana flat on the bed, the swarthy man looming oyer her, knife in hand and less than eighteen inches from her throat, ready to strike.

Then Shana screamed, "The door! The door!" in Hebrew.

As Fouad lunged toward her, Shana twisted away and rolled to her left, Fouad diving after her with a curse. At the sound of her voice, Saul threw his body at the half-opened door, slamming it inward. It struck Gamal and bounced off his body. As it came back toward him, Saul rammed it inward again, using his shoulder and every ounce of his strength. He heard the glass on the other side as it splintered, then heard Gamal's strangled shriek of shock and pain. Saul pulled the door back and Gamal fell bleeding to the floor among the jagged shards of the mirror. The gun lay there on the floor, out of Gamal's reach.

On the far side of the bed, Fouad had leaped as Shana twisted and rolled away from him. He landed on top of her, trying to strike with the blade, but Shana had gripped his wrist and held on with all the strength she could muster. Struggling, Fouad's weight forced her to the far edge of the bed and, when she pushd back, slid off the bed onto the floor, Fouad on top of her. As his knife arm came down close to her cheek, she turned her head and clamped her teeth into his wrist.

Then Saul was upon him, one arm around his throat, the muzzle of Gamal's automatic rammed hard against his temple. "Drop the knife or I'll blow your head off!"

Fouad went limp. The knife fell to one side. With his arm still around the Arab's neck, Saul dragged and pulled him off Shana. "Get up."

Fouad stood up. Saul turned him around to face the wall and kicked his legs apart. With the gun pressed against the man's spine,

Saul patted him down, but found no other weapons. He removed Fouad's wallet and threw it on the bed to check later.

Shana went to where Gamal lay quietly among the mirror splinters, blood spattered on the wall and carpet. She stooped over him, felt his wrist for a pulse beat and found none. "He is dead, Saul. His jugular vein has been cut."

"Change and pack while I take care of this one."

She chose a suit from the closet and went into the bathroom. When the door was closed on her, Saul said to Fouad, "Turn around." When he did so, "Do as I tell you or you will be lying there beside your friend. Remove all your clothes except your undergarments."

Fouad, his face flushed with anger and frustration, stripped down as ordered. "Now lie face down on the bed with your face into the pillow, hands behind your back."

He called out, "Shana, a pair of your stockings!"

She came out, partially dressed, and got a pair from her suitcase. "A waste," she commented.

"Twist one and tie his wrists as tightly as you can behind him." When she had done so, Saul said, "Now the other one. Tie his ankles together."

Saul tested the knots, then pulled the laces from Fouad's shoes. Slipping them under the ankle knot, he drew the Arab's legs up as high as he could, then tied the laces through the stocking that was bound around his wrists. He then rolled up one of Fouad's socks, forced it into Fouad's mouth and tied the other over his mouth and knotted it at the back of his head. He then removed the clip from the automatic and ejected the cartridge from the chamber. Now he picked up Fouad's clothing, wrapped the gun and clip inside the shirt and took the bundle to the window that overlooked the garden below, empty at this hour. He raised the window and dropped the bundle to the ground, then closed the window.

He then removed the identification papers from Fouad's wallet, searched for Gamal's, found his wallet, and went through the same process. Someday, in the future, those papers would be useful for his own people. In the bathroom, he washed his hands and face, combed his hair and was ready to leave. He carried their suitcases into the hallway while Shana turned off the lights and closed the door. In a final touch of irony, she hung the DO NOT DISTURB sign on the outside knob.

In Dresden, Eitan Drory sat in the car of his local Mossad contact, Yanos Gold, parked among a number of other similar cars across the road from the EismanOptiks plant. Behind a two-foot-high stone fence from which rose a six-foot chain link barrier topped with triple strands of barbed wire, armed security guards patrolled with sentry dogs on leashes.

Drory voiced his disappointment in a series of muttered imprecations. In three days, this was the closest they could find to park near the entrance gate, but the view from across the road was somewhat obscured and not entirely to Eitan's liking for his purpose. Gold, however, seemed relatively undisturbed. "This is as close as we can get, *chaver*, without having a gun shoved into our faces," he said. "At least, we are in front and were lucky to find such a good place."

"What good will films be, shooting through a wire fence?" Eitan grumbled.

"Shoot what you can, fence or no fence. When Eisman arrives, it will be better. The car will stop at the gate, but does not go inside. He gets out, the chauffeur drives around the left side to the car park. For five or ten seconds, he will be on this side of the fence. If you work fast—"

"Then I will use the motion picture camera."

"Yes. That will be better."

They waited for almost another hour before Gold nudged Drory. "Get ready. The Mercedes limousine approaching there."

The gleaming black car pulled up at the main entrance gate and braked to a smooth stop. The chauffeur got out and went quickly around to the rear to open the door for his passengers.

"He has company," Gold said. "One . . . no, two men are with him."

"I see them." Drory had crouched down on the rear left side of Gold's car with only the long-focus lens protruding beyond the ledge of the open window, the camera grinding away. He uttered a sound of pleasure as the two visitors turned and faced in his direction while the chauffeur leaned into the front compartment and retrieved a brown attaché case which Eisman turned to take from him. Less than ten seconds later, the three men turned and walked to the closed gate where a uniformed security man unlocked it and admitted them.

Drory stopped filming then. "All right?" Gold asked as he started the motor.

"Yes, yes. Much better than I had hoped for. I recognized Eisman at once, but the tall one was an unexpected prize. He is the Egyptian we have been searching for, Hatif Tobari. Who was the third man, the bearded one?"

"I don't know," Gold replied. "I have never seen him before."

"Perhaps we will find him in our files. Is there any point in coming back later for more film, Yanos?"

"I don't think you will get anything more than you already have. When they leave, they will go through the back to the parking grounds to get the car. That is the usual pattern. If you want to go on, I will return and try to keep a surveillance on your Egyptian and the bearded one."

"Good. I want to get this film developed and have it ready for Lahav to see as soon as possible."

9

He had slept badly and awoke at five A.M. with a painful headache pounding from both temples toward the center, so strongly that his eyes could hardly focus as he stumbled toward the bathroom for some aspirin. His pajamas were wet with perspiration. He stripped them off and stood there, holding the edges of the sink until he was dried, then wrapped a towel around his waist and went to the kitchen to reheat the coffee he had made before going to bed.

Not until they were aloft on the MEA bound for Rome had he realized just how close Shana had been to death in their room in the Tripolitania. Once aboard, she had swallowed two sleeping pills in an effort to control the trembling that had overcome her en route to the airport. Eventually, she had slept the rest of the way into Tel Aviv. During the drive to Jerusalem she had sat quietly in a half sleep until they reached Saul's apartment. While he brewed fresh coffee, she had undressed and fallen into bed, too tired to slip on her nightgown.

Now she lay in deep sleep, breathing softly. In the kitchen, Saul drank a second cup of coffee as his headache began to disappear. He smoked a cigarette, then got back into bed and stared at the windows, watching them grow lighter, trying to tie together the bits and pieces of information so far gathered; with little success.

Tobari's main objective, even with the considerable support behind him, was still a mystery. The greater mystery was how he hoped to achieve it. From the satellite photos and his own personal observations at the training camp, there were no more than twenty-five or thirty men undergoing training. Or, were there more, many more, in camps elsewhere? In Syria? Lebanon? Libya? How many more terrorists were taking training similar to those he had witnessed with his own eyes?

How many Shetulas were waiting to be destroyed?

At least, he was drawing closer to Hatif Tobari. If Emile Khoury's assessment was valid—

At seven o'clock, wide awake, he showered and shaved. Shana awoke while he was dressing, still under partial influence of the sleeping pills she had taken. "Saul?" she called groggily.

"Here, Shana."

She made a weak effort to throw the covers back. "What time is it?"

"Early. Go back to sleep. Take an extra day."

"What about you?"

"I'm going to the office. Judah will be expecting me to phone him."

"I'll get up—"

He pushed her down gently. "No. You need more sleep. If you feel up to it later, all right, but sleep now."

She offered no further resistance. Her eyes closed and she lay back, placid and relaxed.

Rosental was elated with the success of Saul's trip to Iraq, taking the firefight above the camp with his usual aplomb, but was disturbed by the incident in Tripoli. "Who were they, Saul? UPFP men, do you suppose?"

"No. A coincidence. They were probably notified by someone in Rome who had identified me. Al-Fatah and surely with no connection with UPFP."

"How is Shana?"

"She will be fine. She is sleeping now, but will probably be in later."

"I want to see the pictures you took as soon as they are developed."

"I'll have a set made for you and bring them to you. I'll have others. The lab is processing the film Drory took in Dresden. We'll screen them sometime this afternoon. If there is anything of value, I'll bring that along with me to show you."

At four-thirty that afternoon, the screen had been set up in the conference room, the projector at the far end of the table. Navot, Golan, Shaked and Yerushalmi sat in their usual positions while Asad Hasbani stood beside Ze'ev Kolner, the projectionist from the photo lab, and within reach of the wall switch that controlled the overhead lights. A few minutes later, Eitan Drory entered with Saul and a tired Shana.

As they took their places, Saul said, "Whenever you are ready, Ze'ev."

Asad reached over and hit the switch. A beam of bright light shot across the room and was quickly adjusted to the black-framed silver screen. A few feet of leader film ran through while Drory said, "You will forgive me, I am not an expert and shooting from a crouched position in a car, into the light and through a wire fence—"

Wavering pictures that looked fogged appeared on the screen, then the focus was adjusted and the scene came through with improved clarity; a central three-storied brick building surrounded by a series of one-storied concrete block affairs with slanting corrugated iron roofs, all seen through a long stretch of chain link fencing.

"What is more important will come soon," Drory said in half apology, "the people in whom we are interested."

Several cars flashed by, blurs intruding on the scene. For a few dozen frames there was only that blur, then it was cleared as the Mercedes came into view. "Here," Drory said.

They watched closely as the chauffeur moved quickly toward the rear and far side of the limousine, as the occupants exited, then caught the faces of the trio a they turned toward the camera, which now centered on the bearded, eye-glassed thickset man, next on—

"Tobari!" Saul exclaimed. "The tall one, smiling at the older man. A good shot, Eitan."

Then the older man turned to receive an attaché case from the chauffeur as he turned directly into the camera's lens. "Eugen Eisman." Drory announced. As Eisman turned toward the other two men, the bearded one again came into full-face view, the sun striking his glasses and producing a light streak. Now he turned a little to one side, as though trying to avoid the direct sunlight and his face came through in the clear for a split second.

"That one," Drory said. "Yanos Gold could not identify him. Nor can I. Neither of us had ever seen him before."

Now the trio had entered the gate and the film came to its conclusion. "Run it back, Ze'ev," Saul called to the projectionist.

When the film was run forward for the second time and reached the few clear frames of the bearded man, Saul said, "Hold it there. On the bearded one."

After a few seconds, Saul said, "All right, Ze'ev. I want some blowup prints made of that face."

When Kolner left, taking his machine and the film with him, Shana followed him out. To the others who remained, Saul outlined his trip to the Iraqi training camp, then to Tripoli, leaving out the attack by the two fedayeen in their hotel room. "I am hopeful that within a short time we will have some good news from Tripoli and possibly make our first direct contact with Tobari. In the meantime,

I want each of you to redouble your efforts here in order to discover what kind of rat's nest is operating within our borders. That is all for now.''

Back in his office, Saul returned to dictating the report he had begun for Rosental to support the films he would deliver later. That concluded, he studied the reports and memoranda that had accumulated in his absence, finding little of special interest there or in the reports of his agents' activities locally. It had been a long, tiring day and he felt drained.

Now he stood up, went to the window and looked out on the diminished traffic on Rehov Ben Gurion. Gusts of wind blew dust and debris along the street and pavement. A few pedestrians walked along slowly in the late afternoon without a glance at number 17's darkened facade. The phone rang. He went to his desk and picked up the receiver. ''Lahav here.''

''Sergeant Marik, night duty officer, Colonel.''

Saul smiled inwardly. Despite his instructions that rank was not to be used in the SO Branch, habit was too strong among the military personnel. ''Yes, Marik. What is it?''

''A phone message just came in from Sergeant Hasbani. He is at the Club Morocco. He believes he has found Tahia Soulad there, dancing under the name of Gabriela.''

''He is still on?''

''Yes, sir.''

''Tell him to wait there. I'm on my way.''

The Club Morocco, in a predominantly Arab section of East Jerusalem, carried the usual mixture of patrons; Arabs, Jews and tourists among whom the distinctly Oriental atmosphere found favor. It was several notches above the usual rank and file of lower middle-class nightclubs with a reputation for exciting entertainment. Its owner, Hamdi Bek, known as ''The Turk,'' was suspected of having dealings with known underworld characters who enjoyed the lively doings at the club. He was, on occasion, a source of information concerning certain competitors whom he wanted out of the way, thus using the police as ''silent partners.''

In other respects, Club Morocco was a popular eating place, circumspect in many ways. Thus, its prostitutes wore proper dress and were not permitted to solicit patrons directly, but through an ''agent.'' In private rooms beyond the main room, others matters of intimate business were conducted in strict privacy.

When Saul arrived, he took note of the large posters that announced the opening of an entirely new show featuring:

GABRIELA!
Dancing Sensation of Many
Middle Eastern and European
Capitals!

He also noted that the photograph used in the posters revealed an extraordinarily sensuous body, but that the face below the eyes was obscured by a lacy black veil.

Inside, most of the tables were filled and as he tried to locate Hasbani in the dimly lit room through layers of smoke, he felt a hand grip his arm and Asad found him first and led him to a small table against the right wall. A smiling waitress materialized and took Saul's order for coffee.

"How did you find her, Asad?"

"One of my frequent stops when I was with the police here. Also, the food is excellent if one knows what to order. The Turk has been cooperative at times when it serves his purpose. When the police find it necessary to make an occasional raid of the back rooms, they do so through the rear, which does not disturb the patrons inside."

"So. An equitable arrangement."

"A not unusual one. It works to the advantage of the police as well as the Turk."

"What about this girl, Tahia?"

"Gabriela," Asad corrected. "I dropped in to see the new dancing sensation. Veiled, there is a certain mysteriousness added, but otherwise little different than so many others. But at the end of her number, she removes the veil for a few brief seconds, probably a matter of personal vanity with her, but long enough for an identification."

"There is no doubt?"

"None. I have seen her photographs in the clear and her face is unmistakable. It is Tahia. I waited for the next show to make certain. Will you wait for the next show, Colonel?"

"How long?"

"Her last show ended about twenty minutes ago. There will be a two-hour wait until the next one."

"Then, no, Asad. I will go back and send Dov here to meet you. He has seen her in person in Haifa and will be able to confirm your identification. When he does, I want to pick two good men to take up the surveillance and arrange for relief teams round the clock. No local police this time. We will use our own people. What time would you say she leaves here?"

"Her last number is scheduled for two A.M. and lasts a half hour.

The club closes at three. I would say sometime between two thirty and three o'clock.''

"That gives us time enough to arrange things.''

"I'll take the first turn with Dov, Colonel, if you will arrange for the relief team to take over at eight o'clock tomorrow morning.''

"Done.''

Back at headquarters, Saul had the night duty officer get in touch with Dov Shaked and arrange for him to meet with Hasbani at the Club Morocco. He then arranged a schedule for six men, working in teams of two on eight-hour shifts, starting at eight the following morning, with orders to determine if she was living alone or with someone, when she arrived at her home, when she left, whom she saw, where she shopped.

When the music came to its end, Gabriela stepped into the wings, listened for a few moments to the applause, then came out again to take a bow. With a flick of a hand, she removed the lacy veil and waved it to her applauding audience, bringing the last show of the evening to a close. Shouts of approval brought her back several times more, which she answered with smiles and thrown kisses. It was two thirty-five when she strode down the hallway to her dressing room, small, but which she occupied alone as a symbol of her star status. The other performers shared a room next to hers; larger, but more crowded.

As she entered the room, pulled the light cord and closed the door, she was startled by a voice from behind the dressing screen. "Lock it, Tahia.''

First fright gave way to deep relief as Salim Tabet stepped from behind the screen. She turned the key in the lock, then moved into his embrace for a quick kiss, then drew back. "I am wet with perspiration, Salim.''

"It is perfume to me, Tahia.''

"How did you get in here?''

"There was no one in the alley. I came through the back door.''

"Be careful, Salim. They have their people everywhere. I recognized one, the Arab Jew policeman.''

Smiling, touching her, "Our people are everywhere, too, Tahia.''

She picked up a hand towel and began wiping away the moisture from her face, neck and arms, then started to remove the wet costume. Salim assisted her, then held a short robe for her and helped her into it.

"Can you stay the night with me, Salim?'' she asked as she began applying cold cream to remove the makeup from her face.

"Nothing would please me more, but I must get back to work out the details of a very important mission Falcon has ordered."

"Then here, now, before you leave? I have missed you so much."

"And I, you." He hesitated, looking down at the clothes-strewn chaise lounge. Tahia stood up and began removing the damp costume and undergarments from the chaise, draping them over the edge of the screen. Salim was undressing, speaking to her as he did so.

"We have work for you, Tahia. Before the club is opened to the public tomorrow, use the phone in the hallway. Be sure you are not overheard. Call Zuheir Masri in Haifa and have him start moving his people toward Bashra. They are to apply for employment at the agencies in Gaza, El Arish, Beersheba—"

"Yes, Salim. Tomorrow." She removed the robe and knelt to untie the laces of his shoes.

By nine o'clock on the following morning, Saul had glanced through the several morning newspapers and checked the morning report. Leah brought him a cup of freshly brewed coffee and with it a typed copy of Dov Shaked's report of the surveillance on Tahia Soulad, covering the period until eight A.M.

"Subject: Gabriela," it read. "Identification confirmed by me to be Tahia Soulad, recently of Haifa. Subject left Club Morocco at approximately three ten A.M. alone, under surveillance of Hasbani and myself. Subject walked six streets to an apartment building at number 217 Kiryat Cholmo, arrived there at three twenty and entered. At three twenty-three, lights appeared in second floor front window, with subject observed drawing curtains.

"Lights out at three forty-two. From alley at rear, Hasbani observed lights on, second floor rear. Lights out at three fifty-seven. No other person(s) observed. No action follows. Relieved by Moshe Tal and Dan Kaspit at seven fifty-five A.M. End report."

Saul handed the single sheet back to Leah. "Have Records make copies of this for Navot, Golan and Yerushalmi and the other members on her surveillance. Keep the original in the Soulad file."

"Drory and Kolner are waiting outside to see you. They have the photographs you asked for."

"Send them in."

Kolner laid the eleven- by fourteen-inch blowups on the desk in front of Saul. He picked them up one by one, held them stretched out at arm's length. None were as clear as the earlier satellite photos, but the first, of Hatif Tobari's smiling face, was readily identifiable. As Saul held up the second photograph, Drory said,

"Eugen Eisman, the director of EismanOptiks. There is a thick dossier on him that goes back to the early thirties."

Saul put it down and picked up the third photograph. Drory shook his head from side to side as the bearded man's face was exposed, without the slightest spark of recognition.

"Eitan," Saul said, "does anything come back to you on this one?"

Drory shrugged. "I have searched through every available picture file and my memory. Nothing comes to me."

Saul turned the picture back toward himself and glowered at it for a moment. "Damn it," he exclaimed, "if he is this close to Tobari, to Eisman, somebody somewhere should know him."

"Shall I have it reproduced and circulated?" Drory asked.

Saul picked up the phone and asked Leah to have Shana come in. Five minutes later, he handed the photograph of the bearded man to her. "I want this one reproduced and circulated over the same network as the one of Tobari, Shana."

"Yes, as quickly as possible." She gave the picture back to him. "I won't need this. I'll have it done from the negative."

"Ze'ev?"

Kilner said, "I'll get on it at once."

"That will be all for now, then. Let's get back to work."

As they filed out, Drory lagged behind, walking slowly. Shana and Kolner were outside when Saul said, "Something on your mind, Eitan?"

"That picture. Let me see it again." Shana stopped and turned in the doorway, waiting. Saul handed him the photograph and watched Drory's face as he held it up to examine again, then said thoughtfully, "It is possible, of course, that we may be looking at a disguise here."

Both Saul and Shana picked up on the remark, perhaps grasping at another straw. Shana came to the desk, looking from Drory to Saul, to the photograph. "It is very possible," she said.

Now Saul took the photograph from Drory. "Why not?" he said. "It wouldn't be the first time a disguise was used." He turned to Shana. "Hold up on the reproductions for a while. Let's try something—" He looked up at Shana. "Do we have a good artist anywhere we can call on?"

"Ze'ev is an excellent artist as well as a lab man," she said.

"All right. Put Kolner to work on this. Have him make more copies in this same size. I want him to paint out the beard in one, the beard and mustache in another, the glasses in another, with and without the facial hair. Paint out the hat and give him a few different hair arrangements, all combinations he can think of."

"I'll get him started on it at once."

Saul walked out into the reception area with Shana and Drory and found Asad Hasbani waiting there. "Why aren't you home getting some sleep, Asad?" Saul asked.

Hasbani looked up and said with a smile, "After her lights were turned off, I slept in the car until we were relieved." He trailed Saul back into his office and said, "Do you think it would be profitable to contact Major Halawa and ask if they have uncovered anything over there?"

"I see no need to make the trip across the border, Asad. Can you get the answers by telephoning your contact instead?"

"I will do that today."

Saul's private phone rang then and he answered, waving Hasbani out of the office. It was General Rosental making a routine call to inquire into any progress being made.

"I have just finished viewing the film Drory brought back from Dresden," Saul reported. "We have identified Tobari and Eugen Eisman entering the EismanOptiks plant there, together with a third, unidentified party. Also, we have located our missing Tahia Soulad and are—"

There was a rapid knock on the door and Leah opened it, a perplexed look on her face. Saul stared up at her and said into the phone, "A moment, Judah," and to Leah, "What is it?"

"A man on an outside line, Colonel. He insists on speaking to you personally. He said it is about Shetula—"

"Wait." Into the phone, he said quickly, "Something has just come up, Judah. Let me call you back."

He hung up and reached for his outside phone, activating the attached tape recorder, then placed the receiver into the amplifier box. To Leah, "Send Asad and Eitan here, quickly. Shana, too, if she is available. Then get on your phone and have this call traced." He then depressed the lighted button in the base of the phone and said in what he hoped was a normal tone, "Lahav here."

A timorous male voice replied hesitantly in slightly flawed Hebrew. "I wish to inquire if there is a . . . reward . . . for information about . . . ah . . . the terrorist attack on Shetula."

"It is possible," Saul replied coolly, "if the information you have is authentic. Who is this speaking?"

"Ah . . . I do not wish to give my name at this time, sir."

Stalling for time, "Then perhaps you can tell me how you came by this information."

"Yes. I overheard two men in a restaurant. I was in the booth next to them. They spoke with knowledge and authority."

At that moment, Shana, Eitan and Asad entered the office, able to

hear the two-way conversation through the amplifier. "You know
these men who were discussing Shetula?" Saul asked, continuing
without a break.

"Yes. I know one and have seen the other man a number of times.
I also know where one lives."

"If the information you have is of value to us, I can promise you
will be well rewarded. Can we meet and talk about it?"

"Yes, but only in a safe place. If it is known that I am doing this,
it will cost me my life. These men are dangerous and could harm me
and my family." In a near pleading voice, "I tell you, sir, if I was
not in need of money, I would not do this."

"I understand, and your safety will be guaranteed. I can have a
man pick you up at any place you—"

"No, no! That is not possible!" The agitation in the caller's voice
was explicit.

"Then where can we meet? We can't do this over the telephone."

"Let me think." There was a long pause, then, "Do you know
the village of El Jab'a?"

"Yes." Asad went quickly to the wall map, pointing out the
village, some twenty-two kilometers from the center of Jerusalem,
marked as a secondary road. "I know it," Saul added. "Is this your
village?"

"Many years ago, but I do not live there now."

"You wish to meet someone there?"

"Only you, alone. No one else."

"Where in El Jab'a?"

"As one comes into the village from the north, there is a store
with a petrol pump. It is the only one with such a pump. I will meet
you there."

"When?"

"At ten o'clock tonight will be safest. Everything will be closed
by that time, the people asleep. Come alone or I will not present
myself to you. I must go now."

"Wait, wait, please. I— " They all heard the finality of the *click*
as the caller hung up.

Drory was the first to speak. "A trap, Colonel," he said.

Asad was nodding his head in agreement, adding, "No two men
with information so dangerous would be foolish enough to discuss
the matter in a public restaurant, and if they did, they would
certainly make sure there was no one close enough to overhear
them."

"That is very reasonable," Saul said, "but what if it is a trap and
we were able to trap the caller, or whoever it is behind him? In

which case, we will have someone to take the place of Assaf Hafez for questioning. On the other hand, if he is telling the truth, we will be richly rewarded.''

"But alone, Colonel?" Asad asked with deepening concern. "Suppose there are three, four, even five waiting to ambush you?"

"Asad is right, Saul," Shana said. "This whole thing—"

Leah entered the office. "I'm sorry, Colonel. The conversation wasn't long enough to be traced."

"All right, Leah. Thank you." And to Drory and Hasbani, "Let's not dismiss this entirely. We have lots of time between now and ten o'clock tonight to consider other possibilities."

"Saul—" Shana began.

"Not now, Shana. I have a lot to think about."

When they went out, Saul replayed the tape cassette for a second time, then a third. There was nothing he could detect in the man's voice, other than it was distinctly Arab, an Arab speaking in Hebrew, to give him an insight into the man's honesty or deviousness. A reward was sufficient incentive to turn informant. There were thousands of precedents that had been richly resultful in solving cases that would otherwise have remained mysteries. Still, if an ambush was successful, there were possibly even far greater rewards for the enemy.

We must be getting closer than we think, Saul thought, pleased. Close to someone who may well be just as close to us at the same time; someone working from within who has the knowledge we need.

Who? And how? Perhaps the caller had those answers. A vagrant thought entered his mind and he dismissed it almost at once. Someone inside 17 Rehov Ben Gurion? But the people he had chosen for his staff had been too long in their respective services to merit suspicion. Even the clerks and guards had been thoroughly checked out and cleared in advance of their transfers and assignments. Not one person had been hired from outside civilian sources. Ambush or not, there was something here that Saul felt he could not afford to overlook, or lose, whatever the possibility of danger.

Mulling over several plans of action and alternatives, Saul went out for a solitary lunch, choosing a restaurant where he was certain he would not run into anyone he knew. Over his meal, he continued to ponder the situation. Send someone into El Jab'a earlier to stake out the location? Hardly possible in a small village where strangers, even a strange car, would attract immediate attention. Have a car tail him at a reasonable distance? Neither the man nor any suspected ambushers would put in an appearance. Helicopter surveillance? Out of the question.

When he returned at two o'clock, faced with the need to either commit himself to move or drop the entire matter, he found Hasbani and Drory waiting for him in the outer office. Smiling, he said, "Come in and tell me your solution to our problem."

The idea was Hasbani's, fully supported by Drory. "We are nearly of the same build, you and I, Colonel," Asad said, "and it will be too dark for anyone to distinguish between us. Eitan and I have talked withour chief mechanic and he has worked out a device that we agree will be very useful to us—"

"Us?" Saul said.

"Yes. We three. You, Eitan and myself."

"Go on. Tell me more."

At nine o'clock that evening, Drory, Hasbani and Saul walked down the stairs to the rear street level and entered the garage through a side door which prevented them from being observed from the parking lot or rear alley. They went to a black Mercedes limousine that had been confiscated by the police when it was stopped at a checkpoint and found to contain one hundred pounds of hashish intended for shipment abroad. The car was one of several that had been requisitioned by SO branch for its own use.

Asad unlocked the trunk lid and Drory, smallest of the three, got inside and lay on his side, facing the outside, knees drawn up in fetal position. Asad then handed him a submachine gun and a walkie-talkie unit. He then closed the trunk. After a moment, Asad called out, "Now!"

Inside, Drory pressed a handle. The trunk lid flew up. Drory sat up quickly, the Uzi muzzle pointed outward, ready to go into action.

"Excellent," Saul remarked. "Let's try it again." Drory lay down and the lid was closed over him. Asad again called, "Now!" and the scene was replayed. When they next closed the lid on Drory, Saul got into the rear compartment where another Uzi lay on the floor, covered by a blanket, the companion to the first walkie-talkie beside it. Saul lay on the floor with the Uzi and talk unit within easy reach while Asad covered him with the blanket. Then, wearing Saul's hat, Asad got in behind the wheel, laid his revolver on the seat beside him and drove out through the gate.

He took the main road to Bethlehem and continued on the cutoff that would take him through Wadi Fukin and Nahalin and on into El Jab'a, gauging his speed to arrive there at exactly ten o'clock. As they made the turn off the main road, Saul spoke into his w-t unit. "Are you all right back there, Eitan?"

"I have known more comfortable quarters and far better roads, but I am alive and breathing good, clean petrol fumes," Drory replied.

"Enjoy, *chaver*. We will be there soon."

They had now passed through Nahalin, a small, dark village, proceeding at a moderate speed, when a small black sedan, showing no lights, drove out of a narrow side road and began to follow, remaining a good fifty car lengths behind the Mercedes. At the wheel was Salim Tabet. Beside him sat a man who held a machine pistol across his lap. On the rear seat, the man behind Tabet cradled a similar weapon in his arms. The man to his right held a submachine gun upright, its butt resting on the floor. On the rear seat between those two lay four hand grenades.

Unaware of the tail car, Asad maintained normal speed and, with a glance at his odometer, called out, "Eight to ten minutes, Colonel." In turn, Saul relayed the word to Drory. When Hasbani looked back to the narrow road ahead, he automatically glanced into his rearview mirror and saw a black shadow moving up behind him, looming larger every second. Startled by its sudden appearance, he checked his sideview mirror for confirmation.

"Colonel! Behind us, coming up fast on our left! A car, no lights!" Simultaneously, he reached for the radio-telephone, depressed the talk button and shouted, "Commander One to headquarters! Come in!"

The reply was instantaneous. "Commander headquarters to Commander One. Clear."

"We are two kilometers south of Nahalin, five north of El Jab'a, in need of backup support! Immediate!"

"Commander One. At once!"

Saul threw the blanket aside and sat up, the Uzi in one hand, w-t in the other. "Eitan! Stand by! A possible attack from the rear. Hold until I pass the word to you."

Asad had depressed his accelerator to the floor, but the small sedan, with a surprising burst of speed, pulled up and was attempting to pass on the left side. Asad swung the Mercedes toward the left, blocking that move, pulling slightly ahead. "Colonel," Asad called out, "I think it is time. I can't lose him."

Then Saul shouted into his w-t, "Now, Eitan!"

Inside the trunk. Drory tugged at the latch lever. As the lid flew open, he sat up, braced his feet against the outer edge of the trunk and began firing bursts into the chase car. At once, two guns from the right side of the sedan responded. Saul rose up, rolled down his window and fired a burst into the chase car's windshield and was rewarded by the sound and sight of broken, flying glass. The

Mercedes was swinging back and forth to prevent the chase car from pulling up beside them, and which did little to assist Saul and Drory in their aim. Then they felt a thump as the small sedan's right bumper struck the rear of the Mercedes, throwing it to the right side of the road. As Asad fought the wheel, the sedan shot forward and pulled almost abreast. Saul let loose several bursts, but the swaying Mercedes threw his aim off badly. Then two bursts entered the forward section of the Mercedes, causing it to swerve first to the left, then to the right, wobbling and rocking erratically. Then, suddenly, it rose up on its left side, plowed up clouds of dirt and turned over on its right side, coming to rest about ten feet off the road. The small sedan continued on without stopping.

Then all was quiet except for the two left wheels of the Mercedes, which continued to spin in midair.

The first police car picked up the deep ruts torn into the dirt road in its spotlight. It continued on, then came to a hard stop where the Mercedes had gouged out some thirty feet of road and found the limousine where it lay still on its right side, about ten feet to their right. As one police officer ran toward it with his flashlight, the other was on his radio relaying the word to his dispatcher. He then joined his colleague and helped him remove Eitan Drory's crumpled body from inside the trunk. They carried him to the road and stretched him out beside the police car, checked his pulse and determined that he was alive, but barely.

A second police car wailed up and the two officers ran toward the Mercedes and clambered up its left side. They found the rear window rolled down, the driver's window shattered. Their flashlights picked out one body on the front floor, the second on the floor of the rear compartment. Neither showed any signs of consciousness.

Now from overhead came a fresh source of light. A police helicopter hovered to one side, slanting its powerful searchlight beam down on the scene. Then an ambulance roared up and two attendants began examining the body lying on the road. Four men were now on the upper side of the Mercedes. Two held the front and rear doors open. A third had entered the rear section and was lifting out Saul Lahav's unconscious form to the fourth man. A fifth climbed up and helped lower him to the ground. Saul's forehead was bleeding from several cuts and his nose appeared to be broken. He was carried to the ambulance and placed inside beside Drory, who was receiving blood plasma.

Another car, unmarked, came upon the scene and Dov Shaked and Yoram Golan leaped out. They checked and identified Saul and

Drory, then went to assist the officers who had just lifted Asad Hasbani out of the Mercedes. When he was carried to the ambulance, the attending doctor gave the signal and the vehicle raced off toward Jerusalem.

Shaked was on the radio, asking to be patched in to the helicopter's radio. In contact, he ordered the helicopter pilot to scour every road in the vicinity and try to pick up any moving vehicle and radio its location to the nearest police car. After a few minutes of examining the ground, trying to piece together what might have occurred, a police tow car arrived. Golan ordered the men to use extreme care in removing the Mercedes to the SO branch headquarters garage, where it would be meticulously checked for spent bullets, the bumper examined for paint from the attack car when it made contact. As the two truck moved off with the Mercedes behind it, Shaked and Golan drove to the hospital to check on the condition of their three colleagues. En route, they radioed the word in to their headquarters night duty officer, who recorded their report in his log.

At the hospital, they found Saul conscious, the cut on his forehead sewn and taped, suffering from mild concussion, somewhat dazed and slightly incoherent. Golan then checked on Drory, to learn that he was still in surgery, no word at the moment. Asad Hasbani had been taken to the emergency room where, under anesthesia, doctors were removing two bullets from his upper left shoulder and arm. His wounds, Golan was informed, were not serious, although he had lost considerable blood.

Saul had received an injection of Pentothal and the damage to his nose was being repaired. Shaked waited until the repair was made, then went to the desk to telephone Shana. As he was placing the call, Shana arrived with Shimon Navot. As they converged on the operating room, a doctor came out and informed them, "He will be fine as soon as the anesthetic wears off. By tomorrow morning we will have read the X-rays and have word as to the concussion, which appears to be mild. He is strong and will be functioning very well shortly."

Within an hour, satisfied with Saul's and Asad's condition, Drory still in surgery, they left the hospital with orders to a staff member to inform the night duty officer of any change in Drory's condition.

In every direction from El Jab'a, Hebron south, Ramallah north, the Jordanian border east and Bet Shemesh west, helicopters searched for any suspicious vehicles that might have been abandoned by the perpetrators of the ambush. On the ground, police and SO Branch cars roved main and side roads, through streets and villages on the same hunt. Roadblocks had been set up, but without an accurate description of the vehicle in question, or its occupants, the only lead offered was the possibility that the attack car might be damaged by the weapons of Drory, Lahav and Hasbani, which were now known to have been fired. Yet, such a damaged vehicle would most certainly not be moving about.

They found nothing.

By late afternoon of the following day, his nose taped, cuts bandaged, Saul had been driven to his apartment by Shana. He bathed, shaved as best as he could, put on fresh clothes and insisted on being driven to his office. As he entered, Leah placed a call to General Rosental, who had demanded to be informed of Saul's arrival at once. In a state of turmoil, Saul made a brief, terse report of the hapless encounter. He answered Rosental's questions in the same manner, offering little that was useful, then hung up. On his intercom, he asked Leah to phone the hospital and ask for reports on Drory and Hasbani.

He then called for the night and day duty officers' reports and studied the many entries that had flooded in and concerned the attack and what actions had followed. Leah came back with the news from the hospital. Drory was still in intensive care, in fair to critical condition. Asad Hasbani would be released within two or three days.

Shana brought in a clipboard with more recent items that had been called in by the police inspector in charge of the attack investigation. He checked each item, but found little to assuage his inner rage. At the moment, there was no trace of the hit car or its assailant occupants.

In their room at the Hotel Omier in Damascus, Hatif Tobari and Adele Salah were awakened by a knock on the door. Hatif, a light sleeper by habit, awoke instantly and, in a state of half sleep, reached under his pillow for his revolver; then laughed to himself as he replaced it, calling out, "Who is it?"

."The breakfast you ordered for seven o'clock, sir," the dining room waiter responded.

"Leave it at the door and charge it to my room."

"Yes, sir."

Adele, lying naked and face down beside him, moaned softly and curled a warm arm around his lean, hard body. "Ali, what is it?"

He drew away from her reluctantly, got out of bed and slipped into a silk robe. "Breakfast, Adele. It is seven o'clock and they will be here at eight thirty. Get up now and dress. I don't want you to be here when they come."

"What will I do this early in the morning?" she asked petulantly.

"By eight thirty there will be many shops open in Shahabander Street. It will be cool and you can buy a few things for yourself, which should make you happy. Then take a walk in the park, have coffee at a sidewalk café. Be sure you do not return until sometime after one o'clock and ring me from the lobby first. If they have gone by then, I will join you for lunch and we can spend the rest of the day together before catching our plane tonight."

Tobari went to the door and wheeled the table inside. They had breakfast together, then dressed. Adele was out of the hotel only moments before the phone rang to announce two visitors for Ali Fathy.

Massif Razak and Salim Tabet entered the spacious room with considerable trepidation, but Tobari showed neither disappointment nor anger over the failure of the assassination attempt on Saul Lahav. When Razak began an apologetic explanation at the start of Tabet's account, he said, "I would prefer a firsthand version, Massif. Let me hear it from Salim."

A humiliated Tabet began telling of the misadventure; how and why the mission had failed, citing the sudden and totally unexpected appearance of two additional defenders with blazing submachine guns, his manner forthright and without attempting to lessen the degree of his own fault. At the conclusion, Razak said, "Of course, such a move should have been anticipated. There are so many roadblocks and checkpoints now that it was difficult for us to cross into Jordan to make our way here. We were forced to take an old smuggler's route in the night—"

"Later, Massif," Tobari said, cutting the self-serving complaint short. Turning back to Tabet, "Is there any danger that those involved will be taken by the SO Branch, Salim?"

"They will find nothing, this I can assure you," Tabet replied in a stronger voice. "We doubled back quickly to Jerusalem before the first roadblock could be established. The car was abandoned in an empty garage behind a vacant house."

"And the car, its identity?"

"It was stolen four hours before we put it into use. A rental car of a tourist, taken from a restaurant car park."

"Good. The men. What of them?"

"They are in hiding with Seraf Bashir, a good man I have found use for before, in charge. One was wounded and is being cared for in the safe house on Takieh Road. Bashir is under strictest instructions not to permit anyone to leave or enter the house except after dark, and only one at a time to buy what food is necessary. When the search has died down and they are safe, I will personally arrange to bring them to the farm.''

Razak began to speak again, but Tobari shook him off with a wave of his hand. ''It was a good plan,'' he said gently to Tabet, ''but like the best of plans that sometimes go awry, we can't afford to dwell on it. I doubt now that we will be able to reach Lahav again and time is growing short.

''I am almost ready to move our unit out of Iraq. Yesterday I made final arrangements with the Syrian Army authorities here to permit me to fly them to Dar'a to start their journey. However, I will need a diversion to draw attention away from that movement. The diversion I have planned will be your signal, Salim, to report to me at Dar'a, prepared to accompany and take charge of the combat unit until they are within crossing sight of the Israeli border.''

''Who will carry out the diversion?'' Razak asked.

''It is all arranged,'' Tobari said with a tight smile, ''and we, the UPFP, will not be directly involved except that we will furnish a group of al-Fatah fedayeen with a certain amount of weapons and explosives—''

''Al-Fatah?'' Razak exclaimed in surprise.

''Yes, but they will have no knowledge that the UPFP is behind it. Through agents, we have paid them a good sum of money to carry this out along several locations near the Lebanese-Syrian borders. When they strike, they will draw the attention of the Israeli border patrol and army away for two or three days and give our unit a chance to move deep into Jordan without drawing undue attention from their spies and paid observers. After that, there should be no problems.''

Tobari then went into his plan in great detail and at its conclusion added, ''Massif, you will report this to Amon Sadani at the very first opportunity that presents itself. Once the unit is on its way and has crossed safely into Israel, I will come to Ein Fara for discussions of the final step toward Bashra. I will want you three present at that time and will send you a message of the exact time of my arrival. Understood?''

''Yes,'' Razak said. ''May Allah smile upon you in this undertaking.''

''May He smile upon all of us now, as he has in the past.'' It was nearing one o'clock. Tobari said, ''I must ask you to forgive me. I have further business to attend with my contacts at the Ladkiyeh army base before my plane time tonight.''

Razak and Tabet left a few minutes later, each expressing deep satisfaction with the plan, confident that the destruction of Bashra was imminent.

When Adele phoned Tobari from the lobby at one thirty, Ali Fathy was ready for lunch, a siesta, and a brief excursion in the city before taking off. At the airport, Adele would be placed aboard a plane for Tripoli, while he would return to Baghdad and from there to his training camp headquarters.

Two days later, Leah knocked on Saul's door and entered, carrying three pieces of paper that he recognized as telephone message slips. Saul put down the report he had been scanning. "Yes, Leah, what is it?"

"Colonel, these are telephone messages for Sergeant Hasbani. Three in one morning from the same person. The man leaves his name each time, but no message. I have obeyed your orders not to give out any information about his injury, his telephone number or the assassination attempt."

Saul ran two fingers over his taped nose. "What name?"

"Kamel el-Zumi. When I asked for an address or phone number where Asad could get in touch with him, he said, 'You will tell him I called,' and hung up each time."

"Possibly an informant contact."

"Not like the last one, I hope."

Saul smiled. "The last one left no name, remember?"

"What shall I do if he calls again?"

"Tell him you have passed his name on to Asad. Let me have those slips. Meanwhile, check the local phone books and see if this el-Zumi is listed."

When she left, Saul examined the three slips. The first call had come in at eight five that morning, the second at nine fifteen, the third shortly after ten o'clock. Evidently it was a matter of some urgency to the caller. "I'm sorry, Colonel, there is no Kamel el-Zumi listed anywhere in our phone books, nor in our records."

"Well, then, I suppose the only thing left is to phone Asad and see if he can tell us something about the man. Get him for me, please."

Moments later, Leah rang him to say that Hasbani was on the line. "*Shalom*, Asad. Lahav here. How are you?"

"*Shalom*, Colonel. Much better, and very bored with life."

"Then perhaps I have something that may cheer you up a little. Does the name Kamel el-Zumi mean anything to you?"

"Ah, yes, Colonel. A very important man to me."

"Within three hours this morning, he has called three times. No message, only his name."

"That is our arrangement, Colonel. I must go to his place of business and speak with him."

"An informant?"

"From my police days. A merchant in the Old City who in the past has dealt in . . . ah . . . questionable merchandise."

"And now?"

"And now, perhaps, but in return for hard information, the police look the other way as an . . . ah . . . accommodation."

"Then this could be important?"

"I would say yes, very important."

"Can I have someone else do this for you, Asad?"

"No, no. It is a sensitive thing with us. He will not talk with anyone else, Colonel."

"Are you up to it without injuring yourself further?"

"Yes, if I can have someone drive me."

"Then we will reverse our roles. I will drive you myself."

An hour later, Asad Hasbani, bandaged arm in a sling, mounted the stairs at the rear of Kamel el-Zumi's shop while Saul Lahav waited in a nearby coffee shop. After receiving his host's fervent sympathies for his injury, and while sipping the Arab's special cinnamon-flavored coffee, Asad said, "You have some word of the UPFP for me, Kamel?"

"Regretfully, no, dear friend, but having failed thus far in that matter, I have something in which I think you may be equally interested."

Asad's face reflected disappointment. "What do you have?"

"I have heard of the attack on your superior and yourself—"

"How did you learn that we were involved, Kamel? Our names were kept from the press and public."

Kamel's smile became a laugh. "We often hear things that are kept from the general public and press, dear boy. Sometimes even things that are whispered on The Hill have a way of—"

Asad winced at this reference to the Knesset. "Let us not waste time, Kamel. Just what is this information you have?"

"This. Since the night of the attack, it is known that the police have been searching the streets, roads, alleys, garages and, I would think, even trash bins, for a certain automobile that was perhaps involved in the attack—"

Asad's face came alive again. "You have knowledge of it?"

"I know only what was whispered to me in deep secret late last night. Perhaps it is no more than rumor, but—" Kamel now withdrew a piece of paper from a pocket beneath his robe and handed it to Asad. On it was an address and nothing else. "This is where I was told the automobile may be hidden. The house is not occupied. Behind it is an enclosed shed that passes for a garage. Until recently, the shed was open. Since the night of the attack, it has remained closed and is locked with a shiny new lock. On the inside, I am told—''

''Names, Kamel. Do you have any names to connect with this?''

''I am sorry, no.''

''The man who whispered this to you. His name.''

''I cannot give it to you, but on my oath, he had nothing to do with this. He is old and does not sleep well. From his rear window that night he saw four men put the car there and leave on foot. One, he said, appeared to be hurt. Do not press me for a name, dear friend. I rely on my informants as you do on yours, and if you arrest him, we will both lose by it.''

Asad nodded. ''For now, I will not press you. If the car is there, I will forget about him.''

Saul lost no time. He first dropped a protesting Asad at his house, then drove to his office. En route, he radioed the duty officer and asked him to locate Dov Shaked and order him back to headquarters at once. Shaked and Kaspi arrived less than ten minutes after Saul walked into his office. He handed the slip to Dov with the address furnished by el-Zumi.

''What is it, Saul?'' Dov asked.

''It is where you may find the car used in the assassination attempt. A tip from a reliable informant. Take Kaspi with you and pick up two other men. You will find it in a locked shed behind the house. If it is the car we want, call in for a tow truck and have it brought in for a complete check by our lab people. Top to bottom, front to back. Prints, spent shells, bullets fired by Drory, Hasbani and myself.''

Forty minutes later, Shaked radioed in and informed Saul that the information was correct. ''We have it, Saul. Bullet holes, some spent shells lying under the seat, smashed windshield, paint scrapings on the bumpers. The tow truck is on its way.''

''Ah, excellent, excellent, Dov. Stay with it and let's see what turns up. Leave two men there to knock on doors and ask questions. Someone who saw something may be willing to talk.''

With rising spirits, he rang Shana and was put through to the photographic section, where she was supervising the retouching job on the photograph taken by Drory in Dresden. Saul asked her to come to his office, where he passed on the news of the car find to her. ''And how is the work coming with the photographs, Shana?'' he asked finally.

''Very good, but slow. We have planned about a dozen and Kolner should be running out of combinations before long. I would say he will be finished by late evening today." When his hand moved up to caress the tape across his nose, she said, "Does it bother you as much now, Saul?"

"No. There is no pain, but the patch annoys me. The doctor expects he will be able to remove it tomorrow. Bring me up to date on the Soulad woman. Are we still on her?"

"Of course. Don't you read the daily logs?"

"I'm sorry. They've slipped by me recently."

"We're on her, but nothing unusual has been happening. What is the latest on Eitan Drory?"

"Still cloudy, but the prognosis is good."

"Well, I'll get back to my desk. My own work has been neglected—"

"Not yet, Shana. If Kolner is this close to finishing the job, stay with it, eh?"

"If you wish."

Saul called Leah in and began dictating the report to be sent to General Rosental. It was a rather lengthy affair that, with the added information regarding the hit car, took well over an hour. Toward the end, the phone rang. It was the mechanical maintenance chief calling to inform him that the hit car had just arrived. He hung up, saying to Leah, "Hold up on the report. I may have more important information to include in it. If the general should call, tell him I am out of the office and can't be reached. I'll be down in the lab checking out the car if you need me for anything else."

Saul hurried down the stairs to the ground level garage, where Dr. Leyitt had joined the group of interested watchers as the tow truck operator disengaged the two vehicles. As the tow truck pulled away, Shaked, Kaspi and the maintenance chief began their superficial examination while the fingerprint man began the laborious task of dusting the outside surfaces. As Saul and Dr. Levitt looked on, the phone rang and one of the mechanics answered, then called out, "For you, Colonel."

Over his shoulder, "Take a message and say I will call back."

"It is Altman, Colonel. Urgent."

Saul cursed softly under his breath, damning the interruption as he went to the phone. "What is it, Shana? This car inspection is important—"

"What I have here may be of greater importance, Saul."

Impatiently, "What?"

"Too important for anyone but you to see. Please, Saul."

"All right. Where, your office?"

"No, yours."

"I'm on my way." He bounded up the steps, taking them two at a time and reached his office before Shana. He lit a cigarette and began pacing. On the intercom, Leah announced, ''Shana Altman, Colonel, if you are free.''

''Yes, of course. Have her come in.''

The look on Shana's face when she entered was one of wild, hard-to-suppress excitement as she came to his desk with an armful of eleven- by fourteen-inch photographic blowups.

''What is it, Shana? Why did you have to be announced?''

''I wanted to make sure you were alone.''

''What?''

''It's crazy, Saul. Absolutely insane. You won't believe this, even after you've seen it.''

''Try me, but hurry. I want to get back to the garage.''

He sat down at his desk and she placed the photographs before him in a single stack, all face down except for the one on top, which was the original of the unidentified bearded man. ''We finished up with fifteen in all,'' Shana said. ''Look at them in order, one at a time.''

He turned the top photo face down, then turned the second one face up. Number 2 was Kolner's rendering of the same photograph with the beard painted out. Number 3 showed both the beard and mustache removed. Number 4 with glasses removed, the mustache replaced. Number 5 had the hat painted out, a full head of hair showing. In Number 6, the hair had been shorn considerably, parted on one side, glasses, mustache and beard intact. The variety of alterations continued until Number 14, in which the face was shown with glasses, beard and mustache, hair cut short and slightly balding, with a fair expanse of forehead.

Now there was a sign of some reaction stirring in Saul as he looked up at Shana quickly, then reached out to turn up the last photograph. Shana reached over and placed her hand firmly on it and said, ''I think you had better take a deep breath, Saul. You'll need it.''

Almost gingerly, he turned up Number 15 and a tremor shook him. ''My God! Oh, *my God!*''

Staring up at him was an almost perfect photographic likeness of Mordecai Aarons.

''*My God!*'' Saul repeated in shocked whisper. ''Mordecai Aarons! Intimate friend of our Inspector General of Police, of Judah Rosental, and only God knows who else.''

''And,'' Shana added, ''respected member of the Economic Advisory Council.''

''One of *them*?''

''I warned you.''

It was an overwhelming moment. Saul fell back in his chair, fingering the tape across his nose, his mind in chaotic whirl, lips moving silently. Then, "Who else knows, Shana? Kolner? Anyone else?"

"No. No one. Ze'ev is unaware of who Aarons is and no one else has seen any of these. The moment I saw this one, I stopped the project, gathered everything up and took it away. I have the original film and negatives locked in my safe."

"Good. Keep it there under lock and key. This is strictly between you and me for now. No one else, Shana."

She nodded. "What are you going to do now?"

"I'm taking these to Tel Aviv at once. I need a higher authority before I can make my next move on this thing."

In Rosental's office, the atmosphere was strained and dramatic as Saul first explained the circumstances; how the photograph had been obtained, Drory's suggestion of a possible disguise, Ze'ev Kolner's retouching efforts. No name had been revealed throughout the preliminary introduction to what Judah Rosental suspected was leading to a major disclosure. The general restrained the impulse to bring Saul to the point, drumming his fingers on the desk top, toying with a pencil, shifting position in his chair. His attitude clearly said, "Come, come, let's get to it," when Saul began to expose the photographs in the same order in which Shana had shown them to him.

When, finally, the last was uncovered, Rosental's body jerked back as though a bolt of electricity had shot through him. With paled face, eyes widened, and lower jaw dropped open, he stared at the photograph before him, unable to speak. For a full fifteen seconds there was a total silence in the room, then in a broken, choked voice, "Aarons! I can't believe it! Is this some kind of a trick, a bad joke, Saul?"

"No trick, Judah, no joke. Believe me, I am as shocked as you are."

"Aarons!" The disbelief registered in that single name, combined with the aged look on his astonished face, was monumental. "Aarons!" he repeated.

In a softer voice, perhaps in an effort to lessen the degree of Judah's visible anguish, Saul said, "I am aware, under the circumstances, that I can't make the next logical move without clearing it through a higher authority, Judah. But I seriously suggest, as a first step, that we quietly, quickly, check Immigration records on Aarons' trips abroad to attend economic conferences, or whatever other business he claimed. London, Paris, West Berlin, wherever. How long each conference lasted and how many days he was away in excess on personal leave, or for whatever other reasons he gave, no doubt using his disguise and false passports."

Still in a state of shock, Rosental replied like a man in half sleep. "Yes. Of course. I'll have Omri do that at once."

"Then we must discuss the next step we need to take."

With a pained, troubled expression of momentary indecision, "Arrest. Are you suggesting arrest, Saul?"

Saul did not reply, waiting.

"To arrest him—" Rosental began, stopped, then continued brokenly. "My God, Saul . . . that man . . . I, others . . . his connections in the Knesset . . . police, military and civil budgets discussed with him . . . internal operations—" His voice failed again. He stood up, went to the window and looked out, apparently seeing nothing, then began pacing the room again. Saul said, "Judah, we must take immediate steps."

"Yes. Yes, of course." He returned to his desk, sat down heavily and glared at the offending photograph as though in confrontation with the man himself. "He came here, if I remember correctly, about six or seven years ago. From Germany. With excellent documents, lavish recommendations, and applied for citizenship under the Law of Return. His experience in banking and finance were impressive enough to attract some important officials, who brought him to the attention of the finance minister. In two years, he had moved into our highest financial and government circles and was appointed to the Economic Advisory Council."

"Are you making a point, Judah?" Saul asked.

Rosental smiled wintrily. "I seem to be trying. And failing." A deep sigh, then, "To arrest him outright would create . . . havoc . . . a mess as great as . . . as—"

"The Lavon affair," Saul suggested, mindful of the tension of the 1963 scandal which involved Pinchas Lavon, Moshe Dayan, Shimon Peres, Haim Laskov and Ben-Gurion, which had resulted in the latter's break with Mapai and his final resignation from government.

"Yes, as great as that," Judah agreed sadly. "And when we can least afford it." He paused again, distraught with the problem that faced them. "I am sure you realize the . . . the political implications involved here, Saul. The fall of this government—"

"Judah, whatever the consequences, we can't simply do nothing about this. General Bartok, General Goren, the finance minister, Prime Minister—"

"I am not suggesting we do *nothing*," Rosental said sharply, "but to bring this to their attention at this point . . . it's just that . . . that—"

"I· am not suggesting we arrest him and put him on public display, Judah. For one thing, it would cut off all possible leads to Tobari and the rest of the internal UPFP organization, which is of utmost importance to us. And yet, in spite of what embarrassment this may cause to many others, we can't allow him to move about freely."

"No." Rosental poured some water from the carafe on his desk and drank it. When he replaced his glass on the tray, he said, "Saul, while we are looking into the Immigration angle, I want you to dictate a full and detailed report. Also, I want you to make a copy of each of these photographs in strictest secrecy and deliver them here to me personally. Then I will present the whole package to General Bartok and let him make the decision to take it as high as he feels necessary, to the prime minister himself."

"Agreed. It shall be done at once. But the moment I return to Jerusalem, Mr. Mordecai Aarons will be under total surveillance round the clock."

"Yes, of course. Of course. Put your best men on him, but I don't need to tell you that we can't permit him to discover that he is being watched."

"I understand, and you can be sure that every effort will be expended in that direction."

On his return to Jerusalem later that afternoon, Saul made two quick stops before going to his office to arrange the surveillance on Mordecai Aarons. If he were in the city, it would be a relatively simple matter to put that project into operation. If not, there would be a necessary delay until he returned from wherever he was traveling at the moment. Saul drove to the hospital, where he inquired after Eitan Drory and was referred to the doctor in charge of his case.

Dr. Charles Bergner took him to the room where Drory lay asleep under heavy sedation, but breathing with regularity. The nurse on duty handed the doctor his chart and after perusing it, he said, "He is doing well, Colonel, far better than I had at first expected. He is resting and that is what he needs most at this time. If no further complications arise, I would say he will be much more alert in another day or two and you will be able to talk with him, but I hardly think he will be able to return to active duty for quite some time. He was lucky."

"Thank you, Doctor," Saul said with immense relief. "I will keep in close touch."

From the hospital, he drove to Asad Hasbani's house and found him sitting before his radio, his left arm encased in a partial cast supported by a sling. Asad's mistress of long-standing, a shy, quiet girl of exquisite femininity and large, solemn eyes, hovered inconspicuously in the background. She came forward hesitantly, offering to bring coffee, which Saul refused with thanks. She disappeared into a rear room while Saul brought Asad up to date on the recovery of the hit car.

When he concluded, Saul was rewarded with a rare smile of gratification and the single word, "Kismet," evidence that Asad's father's religious leanings and beliefs had left a deeper impression upon him than those of his Jewish mother; the will of Allah superseded all. It was so written, the idea that everything in life is preordained; that inexorably, man was destined from birth to move toward his eventual end.

"I am sure," Asad said finally, "that someone in that car was hit when you shattered the windshield. I caught a flash, briefly, of a man in the front seat with his arms upraised in pain just as our car swerved off the road and his shot past us."

"You are correct. Our informant told us as much, and we found dried blood on the front seat. Our lab people are checking every inch thoroughly for fingerprints. If we are lucky, we may soon have some of the answers we have been searching for."

"Let us continue to hope Allah is still with us. I am anxious to return to duty, Colonel. Lying about like a house pet is not to my liking."

"Enjoy your rest, Asad. You are not to return until the doctor permits it. You have lost a lot of blood. When you are stronger, you may come to headquarters if you wish, but not until you are fully able will you go back on active duty."

"We will see."

"Yes. Take good care of yourself. I miss you. We all do."

Back in his office, Saul summoned Shana and turned the package of photographs over to her with instructions to have them rephotographed, printed in five by seven size, one copy of each, and to personally stay with Ze'ev Kolner until the project was completed, then confiscate the negatives and store them in her safe.

When she left, he drew up a list of agents who would be detailed to maintain the twenty-four hour watch on Mordecai Aarons. Meanwhile, he made a note to obtain copies of Aaron's original application for citizenship, birth certificate, supporting references and any other documentation in his original file. He would then ask Mossad's West Berlin office to investigate that alleged background in fullest detail.

In his inner mind, he sympathized with Judah Rosental's distress and realized the importance of keeping the matter, for the present at least, between himself, Rosental and Shana. And even from the surveillance teams, for whom he must concoct some credible reason for tailing an important official around the clock. Public disclosure, as Judah had been quick to point up, would undoubtedly bring on public hysteria of such proportions that it would cause the wheels of government to come to a virtual halt; during which time, other UPFP factions inside Israel's borders would go deeper underground to emerge at a more propitious time.

Thus, for the moment, he agreed substantially with Rosental that the fewer who were made aware of the situation, the better. Let Bartok decide who must be told, who must be denied the information, as long as no move was made that would alert Aarons and, subsequently, Hatif Tobari.

With that in mind, Saul began a handwritten report of the situation which would be delivered to Rosental, together with the five-by-seven reprints, for Presentation to General Bartok. In the morning, he would have Shana type a clear copy.

Kibbutz Beit Tabor lay nestled in the valley northwest of the Sea of Galilee. It had been founded in 1938, affiliated with Har Shomer ha-Za'ir. At the moment, its inhabitants numbered three hundred and seventy-six men, women and children, only a handful of elders among them who were the original settlers.

Beit Tabor had known many hardships. Its original complement of less than thirty had labored for years to dry out its malarial swamps and dig out thousands of tons of rock, meanwhile planting each small patch of cleared soil until all were eventually able to live off the land they had bought and paid for with their own, and borrowed, funds. And always, there had been present the threat of attack by marauding Arabs who lived nearby and envied the results of this hardy band of determined Jews who were slowly turning wasteland into productiveness and beauty.

Others came to join and live with the original settlers, despite repeated night raids. They took up residence in temporary quarters, if tents could be called "quarters," until more substantial homes could be built. They shared the hard labor and the defense of their hard-earned land, working the fields with *shomerim*, guards enlisted from among their own ranks, to keep protective watch over them by day. At night other *shomerim* patrolled through the fields and along its perimeter to guard their land from theft and arson.

When the state of Israel was established and its army formally organized, Beit Tabor lost a goodly number of its youth of military age to the national military service. The security of the kibbutz fell into the hands and on the shoulders of the elders; women and girls took over the night watches and the sporadic attacks continued, often with severe loss in harvested crops and animals.

During the passing years, problems notwithstanding, the kibbutz had grown in size and prospered. Today, the season of life, spring, had come to the Galilee, the constant threat of terrorist attacks largely diminished, even though the now army-trained *shomerim*, armed with more modern weapons, still maintained protective watch on their land and inhabitants by day and night, young men and women taking on this necessary duty with equal responsibility.

Thus, on this warm night, twenty of the three hundred and seventy-six were on guard inside and outside the barbed wire fence that encircled almost all of the entire kibbutz to keep the hostile world beyond its borders. On the southern sector, Menashe Katz, 23, came to the turning point of his post at the very moment when Dvora Levy, 21, reached hers. In their first hour of duty, it was the first time they had met and stopped to exchange greetings.

"How is your father?" Menashe asked, delaying their parting.

"Papa is the same, coughing all night, keeping Mama and the rest of us awake. There is nothing the doctor can do for him. And your family?"

"Strong and healthy, thank God. Will you be at services tomorrow night?"

"Of course, as always."

"And afterward?"

Dvora smiled. "If you come home with us, and after Papa and Mama go to bed—"

"We could go to the lake—" Menashe suggested tentatively.

"If you promsie not to keep me out all night like last time."

"I promise—"

Dvora picked up the rifle she had rested with its butt on the ground. "I must go now, Menashe."

"All right. Let's time it for thirty minutes."

"If nothing happens, thirty minutes."

They parted then, each going in his own direction, looking out over the fields of young wheat that bordered this section. Beyond, unseen, the fertile ground was rich with lush grasses and flowers. The end of the grapefruit season had ushered in the beginning of the orange harvest, their best money crop. The sunflower seeds had been planted and soon they would all be out working the cotton fields. This season, as did previous seasons, would bring a host of foreign student volunteers from the United States, Canada and Europe to spend their summer vacations here in *Eretz Yisrael* along with native city dwellers from Haifa, Tel Aviv and Jerusalem, seeking relief from crowded urban life and heat. It was a marvelous time to be alive, to look ahead to the future. And, to Menashe Katz, to meet Dvora Levy again on their next round.

As to Menashe, so had that same feeling of security come over Dvora. They had known each other all their lives, gone to school together as children, grown into young adulthood, sang and danced together during festival celebrations; but neither had been seriously attracted to the other until Menashe went off to do his required military service with the army. On his return, he learned that Dvora was also in uniform, with four months remaining to serve. On that momentous reuniting, both somehow knew they would one day marry, this without the subject arising between them.

Their attentiveness toward each other, however, had not gone unnoticed by their parents, who couldn't have been more happy about this possibility; until Menashe began talking about leaving the kibbutz permanently to move to Tel Aviv, where an army friend who had inherited a small trucking business from his father wanted Menashe to come in with him. Both had served most of their time in the motor transport corps, mechanics and drivers both, and an eventual partnership loomed as a possibility. The plan had run head-on into strong objections from Dvora's parents, along with the displeasure of his own, who looked upon the idea of the proposed dual defection with anguish. Dvora was an only daughter, Menashe an only son.

As she walked her post now, Dvora's mind dwelling on their problem, complicated by Menashe's urgings that she come to a decision to marry him or enter into an illicit affair, her eyes were on the well trodden path before her, seeing little else, hearing only her own thoughts. Suddenly, she heard a swift movement behind her and turned, but not quickly enough. A pair of strong hands encircled her throat and dragged her down onto the path. Struggle as she might, the hands were immovable except in the mounting pressure that cut off her breathing and any attempt to cry out. Then another man appeared and the two terrorists dragged her through another path that had been cut into the barbed wire leading into the wheat field. Before another minute passed, Dvora Levy was dead.

At a point almost equidistant from where he had met Dvora, Menashe Katz, also deep in thought, met the same fate, his life ended by a long-bladed knife thrust deep into his back with an upward motion that reached his heart before he could utter more than a gasp. Moments later, the four terrorists joined up, each armed with machine pistols and carrying grenades and thermite bombs. For a moment, they hesitated, waiting, then heard the signal shot fired on the eastern perimeter, followed by heavy bursts of gunfire that seemed to be coming from all sides.

In the main guardhouse, off-duty *shomerim*, sleeping fully dressed on their cots, leaped into action and raced toward the sounds of the firing. The electric siren had been turned on and in every house, men and women took up what weapons were on hand and rushed out in their nightclothes to fight off the attack.

Already, the wheat was on fire and there were casualties. In the darkness, except for the flames, it was difficult to tell friend from foe, yet few held back in the desperate need to beat back the fedayeen and put out the fire before the entire kibbutz became engulfed in flames.

The army had been alerted by telephone and troop-carrying helicopters were on the way while border patrolmen raced toward the scene, firefighting equipment behind them. On the outer edges of the barbed wire enclosures, armed women had taken up positions, lying low on the ground or kneeling, ready to pick off any terrorist attempting to escape; and, when thirty minutes had passed, the fedayeen leader gave the signal to retreat, a white flare that hung over Kibbutz Beit Tabor like a drifting shroud.

This, of course, was the enemy's one grave error, for that single flare gave the Israeli defenders light to see by; to see the dark-clad invaders clearly, the edges of their kaffiyehs flowing behind them as they ran. Even before the first of several helicopters, their searchlights turned on, had landed, sixteen invaders lay dead, two wounded and held captive. Among the kibbutzniks, four men and two women were dead, nine wounded.

The wounded cared for, all available hands turned to the fire equipment and began drenching the flames while others worked furiously to cut firebreaks. Sparks had ignited the roofs of four homes and two barns, but these were put out by men with water-soaked blankets. With the arrival of the army and fire vehicles, the kibbutzniks set about to care for their dead and wounded while others began assessing the damage. When daybreak came, everyone scoured the fields in search of other possible victims. Two more fedayeen, burned beyond recognition, were discovered along with several kibbutz animals that had broken out of the barns during the battle and had become trapped in the burning fields. A wagon, a cart and a truck had also been consumed.

Just before noon, Saul Lahav and Yoram Golan arrived by helicopter. After learning the casualty count, they inspected the weapons recovered from the invaders. Saul ordered the weapons and several intact thermite bombs taken from the two wounded terrorists, packed up to be taken back to Jerusalem. But what Saul and Yoram were searching for failed to show up—a single piece of equipment with the E-O markings that would identify this as an operation by the UPFP.

In the desert just north of Dar'a, lying at the southwest corner of Syria and almost touching the Jordanian border, Hatif Tobari, immaculate in his British-cut khaki uniform, was engaged in conversation with two high-ranking Syrian Army officers. Less than fifty yards behind this group of three was a Bedouin encampment of perhaps thirty-five men, women and children eating their midday meal, protected from the hot sun by their black, open-fronted goat-hair tents. Nearby, more than forty camels, a dozen donkeys and a pride of goats were being tended by a number of young boys, none older than ten or twelve.

Well to the right of the Bedouin encampment, under the supervision of Salim Tabet, a unit of twenty UPFP members were busily engaged in unloading boxes from an army truck, aided by a half dozen Syrian soldiers. The UPFP men were all young, the oldest no more than twenty-one or twenty-two, except for the unit leader, who could be twenty-six or twenty-seven. All seemed to be in excellent physical condition, far superior in appearance to the Syrians, and in much better humor; laughing and joking as they passed the heavy boxes from hand to hand. All were dressed in dark, well fitting fatigues, and wore short, stout boots that were shined and well broken in. The Syrian soldiers regarded them with envy.

On signal from the senior Syrian officer, the leader of the Bedouin family, Tewfik el Nassib, a man of about sixty, joined the group of three and became engaged in the plan that was being discussed, listening without doing much talking.

The gray-bearded, gaunt patriarch had little need to listen to the plan which he had heard three times before from the Syrian officers, and which was again being outlined for the benefit of the third man, the handsome Egyptian, who had arrived that morning in the large plane with his band of darkly clad followers. Tewfik el Nassib stood with them, nodding his head, but paying little attention. He had lived his entire life in the open and under the tents of his father and grandfather, grown to manhood as a camel trader; moving across the burning sands of Arabia, suffering its *hamsins*, its cold and heat, always in search of new grazing grounds for his goats, sheep, donkeys and camels; breeding, selling, buying, feeding and caring for his family in the tradition of ancient Bedouins living beneath their tents in the open.

Following the ancient customs to which he was born, he kept his sons and daughters, their wives and husbands and children together.

Originally, they belonged to Abu Dhabi's fiercely proud and independent Munassir tribe but had repeatedly refused the offer of their ruling sheik, who had been enriched by the discovery of much oil, to accept a modern concrete block home with plumbing, electricity and a refrigerator, schools for his young, a medical clinic, and what he considered most destructive to the moral ethic, television and motion pictures, along with the influence of foreign oil workers, preferring the outdoor way of life as his father and grandfather had known it.

Meanwhile, the truck had been unloaded. Salim Tabet examined a list he held in his hand while he checked off each box against a number, then selected certain of the boxes to be opened. These contained black Bedouin robes and black-and-white checkered kaffiyehs, which the UPFP members put on over their fatigues and heads, watched with grave curiosity by the elder sons of Twefik el Nassib.

From other boxes, they now removed goat-hair tents and eating utensils, then came the Russian submacine guns, designed for use by paratroopers, one for each man. Next came the handguns, one per man, and ammunition for both styles of weapons. The guns were expertly loaded and slung over shoulders and hung on belts beneath the black robes. The balance of the equipment—four bazookas, two small portable mortars, sheels, and cartons of ammunition—was sorted out and placed to one side, to be loaded into camel and saddlebags for loading onto the backs of the animals and be transported to their ultimate destination.

The remaining boxes contained sleeping pallets, water bags, nonperishable foodstuffs and tobacco, and these were also put aside for loading. The four elder sons of the patriarch then instructed the bogus Bedouin in the proper method of erecting and striking the tents.

This completed, the empty boxes and cartons were thrown into the army truck and on instructions from the senior sergeant in charge, driven off. Salim ordered a detail from his own unit to begin loading their goods on the backs of the donkeys. As this operation got under way, Tabet and the senior unit leader, Ahmed Hourani, joined Tobari, Twefik and the two Syrian officers for a final discussion which the elder Bedouin had insisted upon. In strident tones, the old man sternly laid down his ground rules of conduct: the UPFP men were to keep apart from his family, make no contact with anyone other than himself. This applied particularly to the female members of his family. His women would cook what food was required, but the UPFP men would eat their meals separately from the Bedouin. The UPFP tents would be erected with a wide aisle separating them from the others, across which none would be permitted to cross. Finally, Twefik was to be paid one half the agreed amount at the start of the journey on the following morning, the balance to be handed over on arrival at their specified destination, after which the Bedouin would be free to depart.

The terms were accepted. To show good faith, the money was handed over by Tobari at once. He then produced a map which had been previously marked to indicate each day or night of travel, with meal, rest, and sleeping stops checked off. The map was carefully examined until Twefik nodded his understanding and acceptance. The map was then turned over to Tabet while the old man went to his family group to inform his eldest son of the plan of movement. The two Syrian officers then bade Tobari good fortune and departed in their army sedan.

"Order the men to form up," Tobari directed. Ahmed went to where the loading operation was continuing and began issuing crisp orders. The men moved smartly, formed in two rows of ten each, which included Ahmed, all standing at rigid attention.

Tobari walked toward the formation and stood before them, looking confident and exuding that confidence as he examined the face of each man before he spoke. Standing behind him and slightly to his left, Salim Tabet looked equally confident, even regal, in his Bedouin garb.

The men had been trained by the most competent instructors money could hire, veteran Yugoslavian, Hungarian, French, German and Algerian revolutionists, and Tobari felt that these were true fedayeen, men of sacrifice, zealots who were ready to die for a truly holy cause—his.

"Stand at ease," Tobari said in a calm voice. When the unit relaxed slightly, hands clasped behind their backs, he continued: "Each of you has been carefully chosen for this special mission for specific reasons. You have been examined orally and tested physically by your instructors, their comments in your dossiers carefully examined by me personally. I am completely satisfied that each of you is qualified and fit for the task that lies ahead of you.

"I will now speak to you plainly and you must listen and remember my words. Your mission, as you have been told, and for which each of you has volunteered, is a dangerous one, but the intensive training you have received has well prepared you to face that danger. To face it, and to survive.

"That word, *survive*," he emphasized, "must be kept foremost in your minds. You will survive and return to repeat your successes again and again! *Believe that!*"

Tobari paused to allow his words to be digested. "Your training,'' he continued now, ''your excellence in the field, is what places you apart and above the common run of soldier known to your enemy as terrorists. Forget that word. You are soldiers. Honorable soldiers fighting to regain your true heritage, the lands stolen from you by alien Jews from all parts of the world who have been aided by the imperialists of the West to rob you.''

Now with raised voice, ''I am Falcon, your leader. You are the forerunners, the nucleus, of the great Palestinian Army that will rule a vast Arab nation, an empire, which will be born when we have destroyed the illegitimate state that calls itself Israel. And we *will*, with Allah's aid, destroy it, wipe it from Arab soil, out of Arab minds forever. And we, its conquerors, will rule that nation with the support and friendship of our brother nations.

''Hear me! Your mission has the favor and blessing of Allah. You will succeed and survive! Do you believe that?''

Twenty emotional voices shouted as one, ''*We believe! We believe!*''

''*You will succeed!*''

''*We will succeed!*''

''*You will return!*''

''*We will return!*''

Tobari smiled, exuding gratification.

''Good. You will take orders from Lieutenant Tabet and follow them carefully. When the time comes for him to leave you, Ahmed Hourani will command you. Obey them and your rewards will be immeasurable. I wish I could accompany you on your holy mission, but I must return to carry out another side of this project that will give you even more support when you are ready to move upon your objective. I leave you now with my blessings added to those of Allah for your total victory and safe return.''

He turned and went directly to a waiting car and drove off. Now Salim Tabet took over. ''Tonight we will spend here with our Bedouin friends. You will, from this minute on, drop your military postures. Observe carefully the Bedouin manners, their way of walking and movement, of handling their tents and animals. When we are observed by Jordanian patrols, we must appear to be Bedouin nomads and nothing else. This will be the same when we have crossed into Israel. Traditionally, Bedouin camel traders and their families are permitted to cross borders and deserts without interference, and in this manner we shall reach our destination. Keep your weapons on you but out of sight at all times. Do not let them be seen beneath your robes.

''From now on we will sleep in Bedouin tents, eat the food their women will cook for us. In your talk when they are near, there must never be a hint of our mission, our goals. Above all, remain apart from their women. This is most important, and to this extent. If anyone among you disobeys this order, either Ahmed or I will kill him in a way that will not be pleasant.

"Now let us return to the tents and do our best to wipe away the distrust the Bedouin feel toward all strangers. Remember, they have been well paid to give us their protective cover to our destination, but no amount of money can buy their affection.

"At first light tomorrow, we will load up the balance of our goods and leave here to cross into Jordan. Arrangements have been made with certain officials at the border and we do not expect any difficulties there. Tonight there will be activities elsewhere to take the attention of our enemies away from this sector. Once we cross, we will move slowly, cautiously by planned schedule, sometimes by day, sometimes by night. Above all, do not become impatient and obey all orders.

"Dismissed."

The attack on Kibbutz Beit Tabor, as planned, had taken place the night before and was the forerunner for the series of events Tobari had arranged through Syrian and Lebanese agents. On this night, Palestinian guerrillas of the Amr Ibn Jibril branch of the PFLP crossed the Lebanese border east of Chuba and attacked the Israeli village of Kfar Yuval. Israeli border patrolmen in the immediate area, alerted by a siren signal at the first shot, raced to the scene and killed three of the infiltrators, wounded two and took one uninjured prisoner before more serious damage could be done. One villager had sustained serious injury.

Less than an hour later, four fedayeen, disguised as Israeli kibbutzniks, wearing T-shirts with the Star of David prominently displayed, entered Kibbutz Shamir, about fifteen kilometers from the border, under the shadow of the Golan Heights. At the sound of the first shots fired into lighted windows indiscriminately, armed *shomerim* responded quickly. The gunfight lasted less than forty minutes in the darkness, resulting in the deaths of the four invaders and one female kibbutznik, two wounded.

Elsewhere along the border, patrolmen fought off three other infiltration attempts and broadcast alerts to all villages from the eastern border to the Mediterranean. Army helicopters flew over the area, plying their searchlights over the ground while armed jeeps and heavier armored personnel vehicles maintained nightlong patrols that lasted well into the following day.

In predawn hours, army ground troops moved into southern Lebanon, meeting resistance from heavily armed fedayeen, who were repulsed. Several guerrilla camps were destroyed before Lebanese artillery mounted a duel that lasted well past the noon hour.

And at daybreak, while full attention was being directed toward these border incidents, Salim Tabet led his Bedouin-robed UPFP across the Syrian border into Jordan.

When he arrived at his office on that morning, Saul Lahav received the reports of the previous night's incidents, which confirmed what he had heard over the radio upon rising and through breakfast and on his way to work. He at once sent for Uri Yerushalmi, the former border patrol officer, and learned that Uri had already been in contact with Northern Command and had received as full reports as were available at the moment, including casualty counts. Some of the action was still in progress.

"Get a helicopter, Uri," Saul ordered. "Take Dov Shaked with you. And Asad Hasbani. Interview as many prisoners as you can. Look for any evidence of a tie-up with the UPFP, particularly in the equipment they were carrying. And anything else unusual you can find."

"I have the helicopter standing by," Yerushalmi said. "All I need is your phone call to flight control."

Saul picked up his direct line and gave the order. As Yerushalmi went out, Leah Barak entered, flashing him a warning look that needed no further explanation; directly behind her, smiling, Simon Bardosky pushed his way past her and into the office. The *Star*'s leading columnist and editorial writer strode directly to Saul's desk and dropped a copy of his paper before him.

"*Shalom*, Simon," Saul said curtly. "I hope I haven't kept you waiting."

Ignoring the rebuke, Bardosky grinned. "*Shalom*, Saul. My belated congratulations. I haven't seen you since Shetula and your promotion to this," with a wave of his hand to include the entire structure, "elite superorganization." He pointed to the paper. "Compliments of the *Star*. I'm happy to find you in such an agreeable mood."

Leah looked on helplessly for a moment, then retreated, closing the door after her. Saul said, "My mood will largely depend on you, Simon, but let me warn you. I can spare only five minutes. I have an important meeting to attend and there are people waiting."

Bardosky tipped his hat up so that it perched far back over his shock of red hair. "And I have a million or so readers who are anxious to learn what is behind the sudden activity all along the border up north."

"Haven't you stumbled into the wrong place, Simon? I should think the army headquarters in Tel Aviv would be the place for you to make that inquiry."

"Except that I happen to be in Jerusalem and the authorities here act as though they haven't heard a word about it. I thought that perhaps my old friend might be able to fill me in."

"At this moment, I don't know any more than you do, Simon, if you have been listening to the radio, nor the why or how of it. I have just sent some men to the scene to look into it."

"Understandable, Saul, but those same million-plus readers would like to know more about what happened in the Galilee at Beit Tabor, which took place the night before and which the Ministry of *Mis*information has refused to give in detail, only that the incident appears to have taken place."

Evasively, Saul said, "One million-plus readers, Simon? Then you must have a greater audience than all your competitors put together."

"That is neither here nor there, Saul, so we needn't quibble over a matter of circulation. I want a story, not personal comments or jokes."

"Then I would suggest you go back to the minister of information and talk to him personally and persuasively. He released the story—"

"And I was there when what you call a 'story' was handed out—"

"Then what more do you expect from me?"

"This. He was not at Beit Tabor. You were. I want a firsthand eyewitness account for a decent follow-up."

"Wrong place, wrong man. I was not an eyewitness. I arrived on the scene after it was all over. What I saw, and reported accurately to the minister, was just that and no more. The story, which I have already read, said clearly—"

"He said nothig clearly, and nothing we haven't heard dozens of times before. I could have written the statement long before he handed it out. Bare details, ten sentences, and he refused to answer the questions we kept putting to him repeatedly. *How* did it happen? *How* did some eighteen or twenty fedayeen manage to penetrate our border and infiltrate Beit Tabor without being detected? *How* did they make their attack through the *shomerim* who were supposed to be on duty and awake? Or were they out in that wheat field playing other games with their girls?"

"That 'how' and your other 'hows' I can't answer, Simon. I repeat, I was not there. Why don't you go there and ask those who were?"

"I tried to get permission and was told the army is in charge and no one would be allowed to enter to talk to anyone."

"Not while the investigation is still in progress, Simon. Even you should realize how much damage can be done to evidence with dozens of newspapermen and photographers trampling over everything. Try tomorrow. For now, I have nothing more to add except that the investigation is still in progress."

"If you will excuse an American newspaper reporter's expression, Saul, bullshit. Printing that statement in my column would give as much satisfaction to my readers as if I published my wife's recipe for a *luckshen kugel*."

"The choice of what goes into your column, or your stomach, is yours, Simon. Now if you will excuse me—"

Bardosky rose, his temper rising with him. "I'll say this, Saul. As spokesman for your special branch, you are not very diplomatic."

"Simon," Saul responded with a show of weariness, "we leave diplomacy to our diplomatic corps and information to our minister in charge of that function. They, in turn, leave the work we are called upon to do to us."

"One final question, then. How soon do you expect General Bartok to call you in to explain the necessity for, and cost of, a Special Operations Branch that doesn't seem to be so very special in any operation we know about since it was formed?"

To this impertinence, Saul replied coldly, "*Shalom*, Mr. Bardosky. As always, it has been a pleasure to talk with you."

Five minutes later, still smarting from the reporter's sharp barbs, Saul entered the basement laboratory where Golan, Navot and Shana had waited for him. On the table lay the weapons used by the fedayeen at Beit Tabor, along with nine grenades and two unexploded thermite bombs. Next to these was the flare gun. Each present examined the materials carefully, but no comments were forthcoming until they were back in the conference room on the second floor.

Cigarettes alight, Saul said, "The latest word from the hospital is that one of the two wounded terrorists expired en route. The other is not expected to live through the morning. Which places the burden of any analysis of this raid on our shoulders and powers of observation.

"There is nothing clearly identifiable to connect this with the UPFP, yet there is a similarity here that gives me a feeling that there may be a connection, however remote or vague. I wonder if anyone else has noticed anything unusual or different."

Yoram Golan, who had accompanied Saul on his original flight to

Beit Tabor, looked up, but Shimon Navot, who had arrived a hour later, spoke first. "The weapons, of course, are standard Russian and as common in every Middle Eastern country as oranges. There were no explosives such as were used at Shetula, none of a plastic nature, nor similar communications equipment. But there is no doubt that this was an expertly planned attack. How they slipped across the border in such numbers, I can't begin to guess at."

Golan said, "At night, one or two at a time, it is not impossible—"

"The similarity I spoke of concerns clothing. At Beit Tabor, as well as in the other attacks elsewhere that night, the invaders were dressed alike. Dark jackets and trousers, kaffiyehs of identical pattern design, all new. This indicates they were allied somehow, part of an organized effort and not the usual terrorists we encounter whose clothing seldom matches. Their weapons, also, were new, modern, and could have come from the same source, a further hint of organization and planning. Therefore, the question: Which group? Fatah, Saiqa, UPFP?"

There was no immediate answer, nor had Saul expected one. "So," he resumed, "we have this situation on our hands. Not a Shetula, but one that will bring that one back strongly in official minds. The public as well. The press is already clamoring for answers, calling for action, overlooking the fact that the *shomerim* at Beit Tabor, in spite of the fact that they were taken unawares, did a commendable job in preventing more casualties and killing all the invaders.

"Nevertheless, the pressure from the top will fall on our shoulders. General Rosental and General Bartok are asking hard questions which we cannot at this time satisfy."

Golan said dispiritedly, "We can't manufacture answers we don't have, Saul. Do they want us to quit now and turn this branch over to the army?"

"No one has suggested we quit, although I am sure General Goren would not be unhappy if this unit were dissolved and reformed under his command. Nor should anything I have said be taken as criticism of the Special Operations Branch."

"What," Navot asked, "do they suggest we do that we have not already done, Saul? I've even tried prayer."

"Prayers are for rabbis, Shimon. Results that we are looking for come from men of action. So we continue to do what we have been doing and bear down harder. And since I can't offer much more than that, let's get back to our jobs."

It was not, all thought upon leaving the conference room, a resultful or meaningful meeting. Nor, on the return of Shaked,

Yerushalmi and Hasbani from their investigation trip in the north, did Saul find cause for elation when they reported that nowhere had they found any evidence of the involvement of the UPFP in those collective border actions.

*   *   *

On the following morning, Mordecai Aarons left his apartment at eight o'clock and started toward his official car which was parked at the curb. On the other side of the street, lounging in the lobby of another apartment house building, SO Branch agent Moshe Tal spoke into a small, hand-held transmitter. "He is walking to his car, keys in hand. He is unlocking it. Now entering."

On the parking lot behind the Aarons building, Dov Shaked responded. "I'll pick you up. Stand by."

By the time Shaked reached Tal, the Aarons car had turned a corner. Shaked slowed at the same corner, eased around it, spotted Aarons two blocks away. He picked up the tail without difficulty, allowing two cars between them. Twenty minutes later, Aarons drove into the parking lot behind the Finance Ministry building. He got out and without looking to either side, went inside through the rear door. While Tal recorded the event and time in his field notebook, Shaken radioed the information to the day duty officer at SO Branch headquarters.

At one thirty that afternoon, Eliahu Darvit and Yossi Zeitel came alert when Tahia Soulad emerged from her apartment, dressed for the street, carrying a stringed shopping bag. While Darvit remained in the car and entered the item on his log, Zeitel sauntered along on the opposite side of Kiryat Cholmo. Tahia was not a difficult subject to tail on a street that was busy with pedestrians and numerous private vehicles. Striding along, she looked only to her left into the shop windows, seldom to her right, never behind. She moved gracefully, legs flashing briskly, body swinging sensually, capturing appreciative glances of men and boys, even envious women, as she passed.

She made several stops to buy bread, some fruit, cheese, vegetables and meat, then made the return trip to her apartment. The trip was duly recorded on the log, then radioed in to the day duty officer. Darvit and Zeitel remained outside in the car, waiting for her next excursion.

At the end of the first day, the Bedouin group, moving leisurely in a southerly direction, had covered less than half the distance to

Irbid, where Tabet called a halt for the night. Tents were set up, the young Bedouin tended the animals, hobbled the donkeys and camels. The women began preparing the evening meal. Had there been anyone to observe, they would have noted a curious physical separation between Bedouin and the UPFP, although no one could have distinguished one group from the other by their dress.

Thus far, there had been no complications. When the meal had been cooked, the Bedouin ate silently together while the UPFP men took their food to their tents and hunkered down to eat and talk among themselves. The only incident of contact between them came when Tabet offered the Bedouin leader, Twefik, several packs of cigarettes, which the old man accepted with a polite "*Shukran*." During that entire day they had seen no Jordanian patrols, a fact that gave Tabet a sense of temporary comfort.

On the following day, having passed Irbid by a circuitous route in order to avoid attention from curious villagers, and now moving toward Husn, Ahmed spotted a Jordanian patrol jeep of four armed men moving northward toward Irbid, some three hundred yards east of them. As the jeep came abreast of the nomads, the driver brought the vehicle to a halt. Tabet, seeing Twefik's arm arised to halt the caravan, went to him and said, "Keep moving. We will not stop unless we are ordered to do so."

The man beside the jeep driver stood up and raised a pair of binoculars to his eyes. After twenty or thirty seconds, he sat down again and waved the driver on. Both the Bedouin and UPFP men continued on with a feeling of great relief.

In the basement laboratory at 17 Rehov Ben Gurion, Dr. Sara Levitt beamed a victorious smile at Yoram Golan and handed him a fingerprint card. As he took it with heightened excitement, she said, "Those were the only prints we were able to lift from the car. The rest were either too smudged or otherwise indistinct. Our partial print section could identify this one man out of the entire lot."

Elated, Golan said, "The name, Sara, the name."

"We file these only by number here, Yoram. It is on the upper right-hand corner there. Five-seven-eight-zero, dash, seven-five-eight-seven-three, slash A. It has been confirmed. Records and Identification will have the name on file."

Golan hurried up the two flights of steps to Shana's section and handed the card to the woman in charge of print identification. She went to a cabinet and returned with a folder. He checked the number, 5780-75873/A and signed a receipt for the file. He then went directly to Saul's office and in a triumphant voice, announced,

"We have a name, Saul, from the only identifiable prints taken from the hit car."

"Who is he?"

"Seraf Bashir, fifty-four Takieh Road. Three previous convictions, one for terrorist activity. Six years prison time."

"A good find, Yoram, but it is doubtful that he will still be at that address. Take two men with you and check it out carefully. If there is a telephone line, or other utilities, let's find out in whose name, who pays the bills. Put a stakeout on the house until somebody shows up."

"For how long?"

"For as long as it takes. If it comes down to an action, I want to be notified immediately, no matter the time of day or night. Also, I want the greatest care exercised. These people will be heavily armed and dangerous. In any engagement, I want prisoners, not dead bodies."

"Do you want to set up the schedule?" Golan asked.

"Only to put you in charge of this operation. Make your own selections. When you are relieved, remain in contact with your teams in case anything breaks, and notify me at once."

He took the file from Golan and studied the side and front views that had been made during Bashir's last arrest. "Get copies made of this picture, Yoram. Give one to each member of your surveillance teams, then hope he and his *chaverim* show up."

Shana had spent the night with Saul at his apartment and, during breakfast next morning, both listened to the Radio Israel newscaster's follow-up report on the sudden increase in terrorist activity along the Lebanese border. At this moment, all was quiet but the army, and border patrol were being kept on full alert status.

"First the Beit Tabor affair, then six separate attempts on a single night," Saul remarked. "Insanity."

Shana said, "Is even one attempt sane?"

"To us, no. To them, a need to show determination. There is always the frightening thought that perhaps Arafat, Habash and the other self-styled leaders of splinter groups may be making an effort at total unification to bring them all under a single umbrella."

Shana laughed. "If that happens, it will go down in history as the miracle of miracles. They have been at each other's throats ever since the name Palestinian Liberation was invented. If there is one thing the Palestinians need, it is liberation from their Palestinian leaders."

"Yes . . . well . . . I want full reports on those actions from Military Intelligence and border patrol as soon as we get to the office. There may be something we here have overlooked.''

''You still think there is a chance that the UPFP could have been involved, Saul?''

''From Uri's report, no, but it may or may not have been a cover for some other action elsewhere while our people were otherwise engaged. I don't want to overlook any possibility.''

''I can phone in now and get it started—''

But the phone rang then and Saul went to it. He listened, then said, ''Within an hour.'' He returned to the table. ''Eitan's doctor—''

Alarmed, ''He's worse?''

''No. In fact, much better. Still weak, but able to talk. He wants to see me as soon as possible. Something important. I'll drop you at the office, then go on from there.''

''Let me go with you, Saul. I haven't seen him since it happened.''

''Why not? Maybe you can help brighten his spirits. Let's get dressed, then call Leah and tell her where we will be, that we'll be late. Have her check with M.I. and border patrol for the updated reports I want.''

A second news bulletin, while they were en route, reported that both Radio Cairo and Radio Damascus were continuing to make simultaneous threats to ''retaliate in force if Israeli troops continue their ruthless attacks on innocent Arab women and children refugees.''

Then Yoshua Feig, the Minister of Information, came on the air briefly with a statement that ''any effort on the part of Egypt or Syria to move across Israeli borders will be repulsed with full force.'' Next came a statement from the Foreign Office representative. Conferences were being held with the American ambassador in an effort to halt any further aggressive moves by the Palestine Liberation Organizations' action groups, Egypt and Syria, to which the Israeli armed forces would necessarily respond. The news broadcast came to an end and a musical program took over.

''Have you had any word from General Rosental on the report you sent him on Aarons?'' Shana asked.

''Not a word as yet. I expect he and Bartok will be moving carefully before they decide to take it higher.''

At the hospital, Saul and Shana went directly to Eitan's room and found him sitting up in bed, his chest and abdomen heavily swathed in bandages, an IV tube in the vein of his left arm. Drory responded alertly at their entrance and greetings, his drawn face attempting a faint smile. After the initial exchange and queries into his well-being, Drory asked the nurse to leave the room. When she voiced a protest, Shana assured her it would be for a short time. The nurse left reluctantly and took up a position immediately outside the room.

"What is it, Eitan?" Saul asked.

"You have seen the *Star* this morning?" He pointed to his copy, lying on the stand beside the bed.

"Not yet," Saul replied.

"Take it. Turn to page three."

Saul turned the page and there saw a two-column photograph of Mordecai Aarons. The item beneath it, in a statement to the *Star*'s financial editor, noted that "despite the high employment rate and continued increases in industrial and agricultural production, mounting costs of imported goods, labor, and heavy military spending are the direct cause of rising inflation along with spiraling prices of food, clothing and other commodities. Most certainly," the statement continued, "this will be reflected in the council's recommendation to the government for an immediate increase in taxes."

Saul handed the paper to Shana and saw her immediae reaction to the photograph, then the intense look on Drory's face. Saul said lightly, "You are worried about the new taxes, Eitan?"

"This Mordecai Aarons—"

"What about him?"

"That picture could be the twin brother of Amon Sadani, of the Egyptian banking family, and a close friend of Hatif Tobari. I have seen them together in Cairo. The Sadani and Tobari families were close, very close—"

"Don't excite yourself, Eitan. You have mentioned that name before. Tell us about this Sadani."

"There isn't much more I can tell you except that these two, Hatif and Amon, were often seen together. The Sadani name was very prominently known all over Egypt. Amon's father was an important director of the Bank of Egypt under Farouk, but fell out of favor when the king was forced into exile, although the elder Tobari, for some reason, remained in the good graces of Naguib and Nasser, whom he supported. When Nasser died in 1970 and Sadat took over, there was a national scandal involving large loans which Sadani had made illegally to Tobari's textile mills and other friends.

"It is difficult to remember the exact details, but as best as I can recall, there was a suicide, the elder Sadani, I think. I heard later that Hatif and Amon were into the attempted coup to remove Sadat in favor of a military junta, but it failed and both disappeared into exile."

"How long has it been since you last saw this Sadani, Eitan?" Saul asked.

"Eight, maybe ten years even, but I am certain it is the same man."

"A man can change a lot in eight or ten years."

"In his figure, his hair, yes, I agree, but not the eyes behind those glasses, the shape of his face and jawlines, the high cheekbones. This man, I would swear, is Amon Sadani. It is very likely that if Tobari is anywhere near, Sadani is in league with him."

"At least, Eitan," Saul said, "your wounds haven't affected your memory. Since you have been here, we have found good enough reason to accept what you say is true. Mordecai Aarons, we have just learned, is the bearded man you filmed in Dresden together with Tobari and Eisman."

Drory expelled a deep breath and fell back on his pillow. "I had a feeling, a certain sense when I saw that large photograph, that I had seen him somewhere before, but I couldn't be sure with the beard, mustache and so much hair."

"Rest easy, Eitan. We are on him at this moment." To Drory's querying look, Saul explained that it was his, Eitan's suggestion of a possible disguise, that had led to the unfrocking of Sadani as Aarons; which placed the usually dour Drory in a good mood. Binding him to secrecy, they left on that note and returned to headquarters.

Leah handed Saul the reports Shana had asked her to obtain from Military Intelligence and border patrol. He sat at his desk studying each action along the border, trying to understand and evaluate the sudden burst of fedayeen activity in the north, finding no answer that satisfied him. Next, he checked through the surveillance logs on Aarons and Tahia Soulad. There was nothing in those to excite him. With final resignation, he placed a call to Judah Rosental, only to learn from Colonel Kohn that the general was in Jerusalem and planned to see him there.

Saul went out into the open working area, stopped to talk with Shimon Navot for a few minutes, then checked with Ehud Maron, the day duty officer, and read the current log sheet; and while absorbed in this, heard his name being paged by Leah on the loudspeaker. He returned to his office to find Judah Rosental waiting there, standing before the wall map.

"Any explanation for what has been happening up north, Saul?" the general asked.

"Nothing I can find in the reports," Saul replied, "and nothing that three of my men could find up there."

"At first, it looked like the start of a new war—"

"From Lebanon? Hardly likely, Judah."

"—or a diversion of some kind."

"If it was that, and it also occurred to us here, it has either been abandoned or has succeeded, and we still have no idea what it was. But if you are interested in some minor progress—" Saul picked up a copy of the *Star* from his desk and turned to page three. "This morning, Eitan Drory positively identified our friend Aarons as Amon Sadani, an Egyptian intimate of Hatif Tobari."

Rosental sat down with a troubled frown. "I came up last night with Yigael Bartok for discussions with General Goren. Early this morning we saw the prime minister together. I sat in on the preliminary talk and was asked to leave while they discussed strategy. Later, I was called back to hear their decision."

"And?"

Rosental squirmed uncomfortably. "I don't think I need tell you of the considerable embarrassment this affair is causing at the very top, nor the amount of pure hell it would create if it were to become public knowledge, how we were taken in by this man. Even if restricted to a select few, there is the danger of a serious leak. There are always leaks, you know. The opposition would pounce on it and there is no doubt at all that the government would topple."

"I realize how sensitive it is, Judah, perhaps more than most, but what I am more interested in than the political aspect is the final decision, how far we can move on this thing."

"Well, there were, of course, demands by General Goren for the immediate arrest of Aarons and full disclosure made to certain key members of the government, but this was argued down by General Bartok because of the complications it would create with our operations against the UPFP, which would go deeper underground the moment Aarons' connection is disclosed. The prime minister agreed on those grounds alone, but Goren continued to balk strongly. Bartok and I argued that since Special Operations is closest to the situation, it would be much wiser to leave the matter in your hands for the present.

"We finally won, although Goren wanted a military group of his choosing to step in at once and take over, but the prime minister overrode him. So, from now on, and until there is a major, positive break, no material of a critical or confidential nature will be permitted to fall into Aarons' hands. He will be assigned duties which will prevent him from leaving the country on official business to attend the various economic conferences that crop up continually. This will be worked out by the chairman of the Economic Council in a way that will give him the least possible suspicion, if any. But I am sure it will not be long before he begins to suspect that something is afoot.

"As for SO Branch, you will keep him under close surveillance round the clock and again instruct your people that they are under no circumstance to allow him to discover we are on to him. You are to report daily in writing, by special courier, to me. In an emergency, by telephone. I don't need to add that every one in your command who has knowledge of this phase of your operation must be impressed with the need for total secrecy. Is that clear?"

"Yes." After a pause, Saul added, "We will do our best, Judah, but don't expect miracles overnight. We can only take one step at a time."

"That is all I am asking for, Saul."

The Bedouin group had moved steadily southward and was west of Jarash, where they found ample water to replenish their needs and permit the animals to drink their fill, to graze and rest. On his map, Tabet, Ahmed Hourani and Twefik el Nassib planned their route ahead. They would remain west of the road to E-Ruman and Suweileh, then move farther west to avoid Amman. Below Wadi Es Sir, Twefik pointed out, they could make much better time over an old trade route he had traveled many times before while engaged in his camel trading business.

Tabet took the suggestion under consideration, then dismissed it. "No," he said firmly. "We will move according to the schedule agreed upon. To reach our destination too early would be as bad as to be too late. Moving as we are, we shall be on time and everything depends on being in the right place at the right time."

Twefik shrugged without further comment, unable to understand this preoccupation with hours, minutes and seconds. Bedouin thought in terms of months and years, or seasons. He stood up and went to see that his sons and their sons were properly tending to the needs of his animals.

On the theory that an examination of the prisoners taken during the fedayeen infiltration attempts in the north might be productive, Saul and Judah Rosental flew to the army's Camp Kadesh, where fourteen captives were being held temporarily.

These were mostly young men, ranging in age from sixteen into their early twenties who, on interrogation, seemed to be no part of any well-trained organization or connected in a major, unified operation. They had been recruited at random from various refugee camps in Lebanon and Syria, given some minor instruction in the use of weapons and hand grenades. Their orders, from different superiors whom they could not name, were to move across the border in small groups, creep into selected villages or kibbutzim, and attack the sleeping inhabitants in their homes; if possible, to return with hostages.

The fourteen prisoners represented what was left of a total of thirty-four infiltrators. The remainder had been killed during the action, except for five wounded who were questioned in the camp hospital.

The interrogations produced a singularly similar pattern in content, sadly typical. All had been born in refugee camps, all were illiterate, unable to read or write. Questions were answered in monosyllables or the shaking of heads, accompanied by frequent hand gestures.

What is your name?

Houari.

Is this your given or family name?

(A shrug, indicating *I don't know*.)

Where were you born?

(Shrug).

How old are you?

Sixteen, seventeen (shrug).

Are you a soldier?

(Grin and affirmative nod).

How long have you been a soldier?

(Holding up four fingers).

Four months?

Weeks.

What were your orders before you came to Israel?

To kill Jews.

What else?

Take prisoners.

Did you kill anyone?

(Negative shake of the head).

Did your parents give you permission to do this thing?

(Affirmative shake of the head).

Were they paid to give you permission?

They were given food.

Do you go to school in your camp?

(Negative shake of the head).

In the end, with no indication that these prisoners were linked to the UPFP, Saul said, "If this keeps up, Judah, there will be no Palestinian problem. Soon we'll have them all inside Israel and behind barbed wire."

Rosental did not answer.

On the way back, he said, "I spent two hours with Yigael Bartok last night. He was not in a pleasant mood. He wants answers I can't give him, which is why I am here with you now, trying to dig up anything I can give him to justify my confidence in the SO Branch, or for its need. General Goren has again begun to question its cost, which is another tactic to take the program over."

"Bureaucrat," Saul replied with rising heat. "I told you that miracles do not come overnight. Slow miracles take even longer and are more expensive."

"No one expects miracles, Saul." He paused to light a cigarette, then said, "If there were only some way we could force them to make a move, come out into the open."

"Well, we can always arrest Aarons and try to sweat some information out of him, but even then there is no way to guarantee results."

"No, no. I am not suggesting that. It might even drive him to suicide or, like Hafez, get him murdered, which would accomplish exactly nothing."

"So, then, patience is the word, Judah, whether we like it or not.'

A week had passed and the patience of everyone at Special Operations Branch had begun to wear thin. The surveillance teams on Aarons and Tahia Soulad had thus far proved profitless, although Saul learned from Judah Ronsetal that Aarons had begun questioning his associates and superiors concerning reports of activities in his department that were being unduly delayed. In response, he received vague answers; the reporting agencies were negligent; errors had been found that required correcting; purchases of military goods and equipment were being held up because of necessary changes in requirements and specifications, etc. Only purely routine and insignificant date were crossing his desk. Israel's participation in an upcoming economic conference in Paris had been canceled without explanation.

In that week, the Bedouin group had moved south as far as Rujmes Sakhini, heading now in a southwesterly direction in order to bypass Laban, which would bring them to Tafila. Progress was good. Occasional patrols that spotted them from the main roads had paid little attention to the nomad family that moved from one sparse grazing area to the next as Bedouin had done for centuries, a most natural part of the scene.

Routinely, the Israeli border patrol plane out of Southern Command took off from Eilat and flew north along the Jordanian border over Grofit, Paran, Be'er Tzofar and Ein Yahav. It would continue on to the Dead Sea, passing over Masada and the Judean Desert until it reached Nahal Kalya, where it would begin its return leg to Base camp.

On the approach to Neot Hakikar, the observer in the right seat of the light plane brought his binoculars to bear on a small black moving train off to the east. "Zalman," he called to the pilot.

"Something?" the pilot replied.

"Maybe nothing. A string of ants moving south and west of Laban."

Zalman swung the plane toward the right and peered in the direction of Peretz Gilon's pointing finger. "I don't see anything."

"Let's go down and take a look."

"We'll get burned for violating Jordanian air space, Peretz."

"There's nothing within a thousand kilometers of us."

Zalman Darba turned due east until he was able to make out the caravan with his naked eye, then banked to his left and returned to his normal patrol pattern. "Bedouin," he said shortly, and gained altitude for the approach to the extreme southern tip of the Dead Sea. Thus dismissing the Bedouin, Peretz Gilon nevertheless made a notation on his patrol log and marked the exact point of the sighting. On future runs, he and other observers would, in accordance with routine practice, watch the progress of the caravan if it moved closer to the Israeli border.

At the end of the patrol, the log was turned in to the operations office at base camp. The item was duly recorded by the communications clerk and put on the teletype for distribution to Air Force central command, Ground Forces control center, Border Patrol headquarters and Special Operations Branch.

* * *

Asad Hasbani, shoulder bandaged, the sling removed, and unable to take the monotony of inactivity, reported back to headquarters on the Sunday morning following his last contact with Saul Lahav. Saul greeted him with some misgivings, but Asad assured him that he was able to function at somewhere near total efficiency.

"Very well," Saul agreed. "I will assign you to temporary light duty."

"What does light duty mean exactly, Colonel?" Asad asked.

"For now, Asad, it means taking a ride with me as your chauffeur for a change."

"Where?"

"To see your colleague in distress, Eitan Drory."

At the hospital, Asad's reunion with Eitan became a prolonged and detailed discussion of the events on the night of the assassination attempt. After ten minutes, Saul left them together while he sought out the doctor who had recently taken over Eitan's case. Doctor Solomon was an owl-eyed, blond-bearded youngish man with a heavy British accent and laconic manner.

"Your man Drory, yes. Remarkable constitution, must say, Colonel. Excellent progress, healing well, soon be on full, regular diet."

"What about the body scars?"

"Not important. Not a'tall. Later, we'll see what can be done with minor surgery. No problem."

"How long before we can get him out of here?"

Dr. Soloman said, "Same question he keeps hitting me with every time I see him. Mustn't rush things, of course. Another month, six weeks, p'rhaps less. Bloody well bunged up, y'know."

"Yes, I know. Well, take good care of him, Doctor."

Solomon looked pained at the suggestion that his patient would receive other than the very best of care. Saul returned to Eitan's room where the exchange between him and Asad had slackened somewhat. Saul brought Eitan up to date on their activities, then, "Doctor Solomon tells me you're doing fine and will be up and around soon. Don't do anything to change that prognosis. We'll look in on you again very soon. Let's go, Asad."

Outside, Saul took his place behind the wheel as Asad reached down and turned on the radio to the SO Branch frequency and reported their location and estimated time of arrival at headquarters. The dispatcher acknowledged. Asad then switched over to the all-band frequency, turned the volume lower and settled back. "Eitan looked much better than I had expected to find him," he commented.

"Yes. An excellent recovery, thank God. He was lucky."

"We all were. When did the doctor say he will be able to—"

With eyes on the frequency scanner, Asad saw the light stop at the SO Branch channel, cutting off all other frequencies. He reached down quickly and turned the volume up as their own dispatcher came on in a sharply pitched voice.

"Attention! Commander One and any Special Operations Branch cars in the vicinity of number fifty-four Takieh Road. Repeat, number fifty-four Takieh Road. Backup support is requested by agent Yoram Golan. Unmarked cars only. Approach carefully. Occupants at location believed to be armed and dangerous. Police are requested to keep marked cars out of this area. Repeating—"

Saul's foot clamped down hard on the accelerator. At this

distance, well away lrom Takieh Road, he hit the siren switch to clear traffic ahead. "Get us patched through to Golan, Asad," he instructed. Hasbani got through to the dispatcher and made the request. When Yoram's voice came through, Asad handed the microphone to Saul.

"Yoram? Saul here. What do you have there?"

"We finally spotted a man entering number fifty-four with two large paper sacks, probably food. A second man opened the door from inside for him. A few minutes later, a third man was seen at the window and I make him as Seraf Bashir from the picture we have of him. I don't know how many others are inside."

"Who do you have with you?"

"Yerushalmi. Shaked and Navot just called in from close by. I told them to take a position at the rear of the house."

"Good. Hold your positions. I am en route with Hasbani. We'll be there in about eight minutes." He handed the microphone back to Asad and directed his attention to the traffic. For three minutes he maneuvered carefully, particularly at corners where the traffic was heavy, then Golan was back on the air to Saul.

"What is it, Yoram?"

"This thing may break sooner. Shaked's car pulled in behind the house and was spotted from inside. Now there are two at the front window peering out from behind the curtains and I am sure they have made us."

"Don't start anything on your own—" Saul began. But Golan called out, "Too late, Saul. It has started. Shots coming from behind the house. Over and out."

Saul needed no further urging, tearing past cars and buses, racing through intersections and barely missing several crashes. Within three blocks of their destination, he cut the siren and, entering Takieh Road, heard shots being fired. Asad called out to inform Saul he could see Golan and Yerushalmi behind the right side of their car exchanging fire with the occupants of number 54.

The street was empty of pedestrians and moving vehicles by now, but onlookers were apparent; peering out from nearby doorways, windows, from between houses and behind other parked cars. A woman dashed out of one house to grab up a small boy who had climbed into a parked car and was staring out of the windows facing number 54. At the far end of the block, knots of frightened men and women were trying to hold back the more adventurous youngsters who were in a state of frenzied excitement.

Saul braked the car to a stop at the near corner, realizing the futility of a frontal approach, then turned right and headed for the alley behind the house. The car screeched to a halt when he saw Dov

Shaked and Shimon Navot parked about twenty yards beyond the rear of number 54, crouching on the far side of their car, firing their handguns and trying to keep out of the line of gunfire coming from the rear of the house.

Saul's car came to a stop about the same distance on the near side. As Asad started to leave the car, his revolver in hand, Saul shouted, "Stay in the car! Keep out of this, Asad!" He then crawled over Asad and exited from the protected right side, ran to the trunk of the car, unlocked it and picked up his Uzi submachine gun and several additional clips of ammunition, stuffing the latter into his side pockets. Asad had gotten out of the car and was crouched behind the right side, the revolver still in his hand.

From that angle it was difficult for those inside the house to direct accurate fire through the shattered window without exposing themselves to the return fire of Shaked and Navot. Signaling to the two agents to concentrate on that single window, Saul opened up with his Uzi from the near side, blasting what remained of the window frame apart, then centered on the door, splintering its lock so that it swung inward. The two men inside had now been driven from their position. Continuing to fire, Saul advanced, gained the door, with Shaked and Navot moving up behind him, concentrating their fire at the window. Within a matter of a few seconds, the action at the rear of the house was over. Saul approached the partially opened door, nudged it fully open with the muzzle of his weapon. There was no evidence of anyone in the immediate rear of the house.

Hesitating, they could hear the staccato firing coming from the front area, automatic weapons inside the house, handguns from Golan and Yerushalmi in reply from the outside. In a quick move, Saul leaped through the door, Navot and Shaked behind him, Asad bringing up the rear. They were in a bullet-ridden kitchen, with plaster and broken utensils littering the floor. Saul moved to his left, entering the bedroom from which the firing had come. Bullet holes scarred the walls and ceiling and cartridge casings were scattered across the floor. Bloodstains evidenced the fact that someone had taken a serious hit, leading to the hallway.

Crouching, the four entered the hallway, then stood erect, backs flattened against the walls on both sides. Ahead of them were a closed door on either side of the hall, another closed door at the far end, from which came the sounds of intermittent firing. In the dimness of the enclosed area, it was impossible to trace the track of the bloodstains seen earlier in the rear bedroom.

Now it became necessary to pass the two doors in order to gain their objective, the front room which faced the street. Shaked moved ahead cautiously, Navot behind him, bracketing the door on the left side between them. Crouching, Saul moved up and kicked the door open, his Uzi ready to sweep the inside; but the room was empty. They used the same procedure with the door opposite and that room, too, was empty.

Saul waved them on to the one remaining closed door ahead, again flattening themselves against the walls in order to present the slimmest target. Reaching within six feet of the door, they could hear excited shouts and bursts of automatic gunfire from inside. Saul leveled his Uzi at the center of the door and, in the ensuing lull, shouted, "Inside the room! You are surrounded! Throw down your guns! Come out with your hands over your heads!"

For a moment there was total silence. Instinctively, the four Israelis dropped to the floor, lying flat, weapons extended toward the door. A split second later, a score of bullets tore through the door, sending splinters flying above them and down the entire length of the hall. Saul's Uzi and three revolvers chattered in response as the splinters flew in the opposite direction, curses coming at them from inside. They hugged the floor, expecting heavy retaliation, meanwhile continuing to fire.

What came instead was the thunderous roar of a grenade that exploded inside the room, evidently thrown from the outside. Then a second explosion. From the front room, other than a single shriek of pain, came silence.

Shaked and Navot leaped up quickly and went to the door. Shaked raised his right foot and rammed the door open with its sole. The splintered door swung inward, then broke from its hinges and crashed to the floor and opened on a scene of carnage. A bleeding figure staggered out of the room toward them, fell in the hall and lay motionless. Inside, the room was engulfed in smoke, flames beginning to lick at curtains, the cheap carpet and several pieces of shattered furniture. Saul leaped over the inert figure into the room after Shaked and Navot, Asad behind him. Other than the crackling of scattered flames and dense smoke, nothing moved or uttered a sound. Four dead men lay sprawled around the room, one in the hallway. Then there was a crash as Golan and Yerushalmi burst through the front door and joined them.

There was no one left alive to question.

10

The ambulances had removed the five bodies and the firemen brought the flames under control. Police were now on the scene, the entire street, front and back, cordoned off while investigators from SO Branch went through every room of number 54, searching for evidence. Outside, the bullet-ridden car that Golan and Yerushalmi had used was being towed in to the SO Branch garage.

Reporters and photographers swarmed through the area interviewing eyewitnesses, but Saul and his colleagues had left the scene before the media men arrived, leaving orders that no members of the press were to be admitted to number 17 Rehov Ben Gurion.

Secluded in his office, Saul's mind was a turmoil of mixed thoughts as he waited for Leah to put through a call to Judah Rosental. "Five possible sources of information," he said to Shana. "If we could have taken even one of them alive, we might have had our first physical contact with the UPFP since Assaf Hafez."

"We still have Aarons and the Soulad woman under observation," Shana countered by way of condolence.

"Who haven't made a suspicious move since we put the surveillance teams on them."

"Relax, Saul. Maybe this will start something fresh moving."

"If it doesn't, and soon, we may have this whole operation moved to another jurisdiction," he said glumly.

"What would that accomplish? It would still require the same amount of manpower, perhaps even more."

"Ah, Shana, Shana. By tomorrow morning I'll have Rosental, Bartok, maybe even the prime minister on my back. 'Why was it necessary to kill them all?' 'You could have used teargas to smoke them out, couldn't you?' "

"Well?"

"We were lucky enough to have one Uzi with us. I was surprised when Golan lobbed those grenades through the window. I had no idea he carried them in his car." He reached across his desk to the intercom and said, "Leah, anything on that call?"

"No, Colonel. The general is still out of his office and can't be contacted."

"Keep trying." And to Shana, "Sometime today, put out an order. In the future, all our cars will carry one submachine gun per man, in the trunk when not otherwise in use. Also, six teargas shells and a firing weapon, helmets and flak jackets."

Leah knocked on the door and came in. "What is it, Leah? Some new catastrophe I haven't counted on?"

She smiled and said, "Not here, Colonel. Police Headquarters. They are being swamped with telephone calls and reporters who want a story about what took place on Takieh Road."

"And the police can't think up some kind of a story to keep them happy?" He turned to Shana. "Think up a good one and call the police information officer. Feed it to him with a spoon and tell him to keep us out of it or the roof will fall in on his head."

Shana got up and left. "What is going on outside, Leah?" Saul asked.

"Well, the excitement is beginning to die down a little. It was pretty hectic for a while. The dispatcher was picking up as much of the radio talk between cars and broadcasting it through the building. Every bit of work stopped until the all-clear came in. Now, they won't let Dov, Shimon, Yoram and Uri alone, trying to get the story from them. And Asad, still healing from his other wounds, he's the hero of the day."

Saul grinned and nodded. "Accidents have a way of making heroes out of all of us, don't they."

"I wouldn't know. The closest I ever got to combat was in an office in Tel Aviv or Jerusalem."

"Count your blessings." The phone rang on Saul's desk and Leah picked up the receiver, then indicated it in his direction, "General Rosental, returning your call."

"Judah," he began, "we've had an incident up here and I'm afraid you're not going to like the outcome—"

In the morning, after seeing that Saul's latest weapons order had been distributed to all agents concerned, Shana turned her attention to the night duty officer's log to see if there was anything that should receive Saul's immediate attention. With nothing untoward recorded, she had a clerk make the necessary photocopies for her files, then clipped the original to the morning report printout and had a messenger deliver it to Leah.

Turning back to the compilation of field agents' logs, she began with those filed by the men on surveillance of Aarons and the Soulad woman. After lunch, her teletype operator dropped a two-page report in her INCOMING tray. Shana looked up and the girl said, "Air Patrol Report," and turned away.

To relieve some of the monotony of the otherwise eventless day, Shana picked up the report and glanced through the items on both sheets, then started to drop it in her file basket, when something triggered in her mind. Swiveling around, she called out to the teletype operator. "Neora, get me the Air Patrol reports for the last three days, please."

A few minutes later, she was comparing the reports, then got out a map to check the four reports against it. After a careful study, she picked up the map and reports and took them to Saul's office.

*   *   *

They had been on the move for a week, resting by day at times, pushing ahead by night at others, and had reached a point well below Tafila and west of the road that ran parallel to, and lay less than five kilometers east of, the *moshav*, Ein Yahav, which was several kilometers north of the village of Ein Yahav. Almost equidistant between the border and road, Salim Tabet could make out the low structures of the *moshav* through long-range binoculars from where the Bedouin camp had been set up, making this stop in mid afternoon because they had moved a little faster during the previous two nights of travel and were ahead of schedule.

Thus far, all had gone well. The men had begun grumbling somewhat about the quality and monotony of the food, which was far inferior to what they had become accustomed to in their training camp; but Tabet and Hourani had been able to keep them under tight, disciplined control.

Nor had Twefik el Nassib reason to complain. Tabet had been liberal with the tobacco and certain canned foods from their stocks, a rare treat. Generally, the men in the unit had kept to themselves. There had been one or two instances when several had attempted to engage the younger women in conversation, but the Bedouin girls, by tradition and training, were shy and turned away from the strangers. Yet, the old man had experienced certain anxieties. Soon, Allah willing, they would reach their destination in the Sinai and he would receive the second half of his money and what food and tobacco remained that these twenty could not carry with them in whatever foolishness they were engaged. Life, then, would return to some sense of normality when they were finally rid of the strangers and on their way.

To one side, Tabet and Hourani sat on a sandy incline looking across the border through their binoculars. "When do we cross, Lieutenant?" Hourani said finally.

"Soon, Ahmed. Tonight we are due to meet with Zuheir Masri and two of his men, who are coming from Bashra to take the explosives back with them. After dark tomorrow night, you will move the men across the border below the *moshav* and village, once their lights are out and they are asleep.

"When you are ready to make your move, I will return north, where I will be needed. You will then be in complete charge. The map is carefully marked, day by day. Above all, keep to the schedule. Do not be overly eager to reach your final destination. When everything is set, you will receive your instructions from Falcon himself."

Hourani's chest swelled. "It will be as you and Falcon have ordered, Lieutenant," he said. "We will not fail you."

"Are you sure, Shana?" Saul asked.

"I am not sure of anything, Saul, but I am curious. And a little suspicious, I might add." She went to the larger wall map, taking the four reports with her. Pointing out the locations as she named them, she said, "Air Patrol first mentions them here in Jordan, moving southwest of Laban. They were again seen west of Tafila. The next time they were observed, they were within a few kilometers of the border, just northwest of Ein Yahav."

"Is there anything from ground patrol?"

"Nothing, but I wouldn't expect anything as long as they are west of the border in Jordanian territory."

"I can't find anything so unusual about this, Shana. A Bedouin family on a normal—"

"If we check the times given in these Air Patrol reports of sightings, against their rate of travel, they have been moving faster than any Bedouin I have ever heard of. Why the hurry?"

"Perhaps to reach a camel trading or selling market by a certain day. Besides, who ever knows why Bedouin do what they do? What do we show west of Ein Yahav?"

"Desert and more desert. Rock formations. Hardly a normal Bedouin route. Farther west there is water and some grazing below Mitzpeh Ramon, but well off the usual Bedouin trade route."

"Well, it may be nothing, but to satisfy your curiosity, get in touch with Air Patrol and ask them to check this group regularly and report back to us."

An hour before midnight, the Bedouin encampment, except for Tabet, Hourani and four armed sentries, lay asleep. Across the border, only a few pinpoints of light showed in the Ein Yahav *moshav*. In the eerie desert silence, these six men waited, eyes turned toward the west, ears attuned for any sound of movement.

Just before midnight, the sentry directly ahead of them on the western edge of the encampment, came alert. He flashed a slender penlight back toward where Tabet and Hourani sat together. Both rose at once and moved toward the sentry's signal. "What is it?" Tabet asked.

"I heard movement, like the wind, but there is no wind. Listen."

They listened and heard the unmistakable grinding sound of feet moving through sand, the faint rustle of clothing. Tabet said, "It is probably the people we are waiting for. Ahmed, go forward and lead them in, but keep your gun handy. Call out the name 'Masri.' One should reply with the first name, 'Zuheir.' If there are more or less than three, say nothing more, do nothing. Let them pass until they reach us here."

Hourani moved forward in a wide circle. Tabet and the sentry waited, listening, straining their eyes in the darkness, seeing nothing, hearing only the movement of Hourani, whose steps voided the sounds they had heard earlier. For perhaps eight minutes they crouched close to the ground, scarcely breathing; then came the small, faint pinpoints of light from Hourani's penlight—three flashes, darkness, then three more; the signal that all was well.

Zuheir Masri was somewhat shorter and much more slender than his two companions, who were both burly and broadshouldered men. They were led to one side of the camp and given water to drink and more to fill their goatskin canteens. For almost an hour, Masri talked, describing the Bashra installation in detail, and where he intended to place the explosives to do the greatest damage.

"It will not be difficult," he said finally. "There is so much activity going on by day and night that one can come and go without being questioned as long as he carries a tool of some kind and appears to belong where he is going."

"How will you account for your absence?" Tabet asked.

"That is no problem. I am assigned to make the twice-weekly run to the supply depot at Ein Avdat. We go at night and load the supplies the next morning and return that same night. The truck is now on the other side of the border with two more of my men waiting with it. We left earlier this evening in order to make up for the time we are spending here with you, but must return to it before two o'clock, which will bring us into Ein Avdat on time.''

"Then load up and we will send you on your way."

Two cartons of plastic explosives were taken from their supply stock, opened, and distributed among three backpacks. Tabet then handed Masri a separate small carton that contained the pencil-thin actuators that were to be inserted into each block of plastic when it was in place. The backpacks were then lifted onto the backs of Masri and his two companions.

On the verge of parting, Masri said, "It is necessary that I receive word in ample time to move my people out of the danger zone."

Tabet reassured him. "It has been planned thus. You will receive no less than six hours notice of the exact time when the explosives will be detonated. It will come to you on a day when you are not scheduled to make the trip to Ein Avdat. You will hear it on the walkie-talkie instrument you have been furnished."

"What time shall I expect the call, so that I will have the instrument turned on to receive it?"

"As I have told you, six hours before the explosives will be detonated, which will take place sometime around midnight. Therefore, you will receive the word directly from Ahmed sometime around six o'clock in the evening. See to it that you are out of range of anyone's hearing at that time. Do that every evening from now on at the same time. When you finally receive the word on the given day, you will acknowledge, then shut off the instrument and bury it in the sand where no one can find it. After dark, you will have your people slip out of camp and head directly north. The explosions will come close to midnight, as I have said, giving you time to get far away from Bashra.

"On the third night that passes, you will all be picked up north of Kal'at E-Nakhal and taken to El Arish, where you will be paid your bonuses. When it is safe to move on, you can all return to Haifa, Acre, and wherever else your people came from, and there await your next orders."

Masri nodded. "Go with God's hand on your shoulder," he said.

"*In'shallah*."

"*Ma'salaam*."

Back at the tend he shared with Hourani, Tabet said, "So now we have taken another important step forward."

"And next?" Ahmed said.

"We wait here one full day, resting. Tomorrow evening, you and

I will review the balance of your journey, then I will leave to return north. You know when you are to cross the border. I need not tell you how much depends on you to keep the schedule as planned. Timing is of the utmost importance. One failure and everything is for naught."

"I understand, Lieutenant. You can rest assured that I will permit no deviation of any kind from Falcon's plan."

"Excellent, Ahmed. When this is over, we will meet again at Ein Fara. You will surely receive a promotion in rank and be given more important responsibilities. The need for leaders in our new state will be greater than ever, and those who show their leadership capabilities in these early stages will rise high in the new government."

Hourani was greatly pleased. "This unit will give no one cause to doubt our ability to carry out the responsibilities that rest on our shoulders, Lieutenant."

"For that reason, Ahmed, you were chosen."

On the following day, the camp rested, enjoying a day of idleness for the UPFP unit while the Bedouin men, women and children went about their normal chores, cooking meals, seeing to the camels, donkeys and goats. During the afternoon, Hourani and Tabet conferred with Twefik, reviewing the routes that lay ahead, the stops to be made and on which nights they would push ahead and those days when they would rest.

The routes had been expertly drawn by Amon Sadani so that once they were well into the Negev and approaching the Sinai, they would keep out of sight of all main and secondary roads until they reached their destination, Wadi Talal. Twefik was now concerned that they would be on ground unfamiliar to him, with no true knowledge of water sources or grazing grounds. The feed they carried with them for the animals would be sufficient, but water was always the more pressing problem.

When Tabet assured him that the area had been well scouted previously, Twefik was somewhat reluctant to accept his word, but Tabet's firm insistence put the old man's doubts to rest for the moment, adding, "It is easy to understand your misgivings, Tewfik, but you must realize that our mission is of such importance that we would not permit anything to jeopardize its success. You have been well paid. When you are left to go on your way, you will receive the other half of the money from Ahmed, as agreed."

Alone with Hourani later, Tabet handed over the map and packet of money to be paid to Tewfik when he would no longer be needed They then reviewed the planned escape routes and the location where they would be picked up in trucks that would be sent by Massif Razak from the Ein Fara stronghold.

Later that night, the UPFP group gathered in a half circle a short distance from the main encampment. Seated cross-legged on the ground, Salim Tabet addressed them in a low voice that lent a certain drama to the occasion. Pointing across the border where a few lights of the Ein Yahav *moshav* could be seen glinting in the darkness, he said, "Soon they will be asleep there. At approximately eleven o'clock, the Israeli patrol is due to pass through from the south. They will stop for a few minutes to make their usual inspection of the settlement guards there, then continue on. Thirty minutes later, this entire body must move across the border well below the village of Ein Yahav.

"Ahmed will take over full command. He will lead you south and westward until you are well below Mitzpeh Ramon, and from there to your final destination and according to plan. Thus far, we have been secure in our movements. Once across the border, it will be the same as long as you do nothing to draw attention to yourselves. No one will take notice of a Bedouin family on the move, since this has been a custom for centuries. I have given Ahmed these final instructions and now give them to you so that all of you will know them and keep them firmly in mind.

"When you reach a point eight kilometers north of Bashra, six from the outer edge of their restricted zone, you will make camp at Wadi Talal, in the protection of the foothills that lie there. This will take four days and two nights of movement, slowly by day with rest periods, swiftly when the plan calls for you to move at night. It will be a hard, but rewarding journey. Nothing must prevent you from reaching Wadi Talal on schedule.

"When you receive the word directly from Falcon himself by the instrument Ahmed carries, you will leave the Bedouin behind and move south to the very edge of Bashra. This will be at night and the darkness and your robes will be your cover. When the explosions come, you will be ready to make your move across the restricted zone without interference. Those who remain alive in the camp will be too busy to do more than attempt to save themselves. Thus, you will move quickly into the camp itself and exterminate everyone who may still be alive. The destruction must be total. No one must be allowed to escape. When this has been accomplished, Ahmed will lead you out to where you will await the trucks that will pick you up and return you to safety in the north."

He paused to allow this to be impressed upon their minds, watching the semicircle of heads as each nodded his acceptance. "Are there any questions?" he asked finally.

There were none. Tabet felt, rather than saw, the eagerness in them and said, ''I leave you now to return north. Allah's blessings and favors are upon you. Your cause is just and noble, your rewards, when we next meet, will be far above your expectations. I charge you to give your full support to Ahmed, for when he speaks, he will be speaking for Falcon. *Ma'salaam.*''

11

The SO Branch staff meeting on Sunday morning began with a report from the surveillance teams on Aarons and Tahia Soulad, not noteworthy except for the circumspect behavior of both subjects. Nothing from the investigation of the house on Takieh Road contributed anything useful with regard to the UPFP or its possible authorship of the assassination plan. Other reports from the field locally produced nothing of interest, nor were reports from agents operating outside Israel more rewarding.

There had been a few more interior problems with demonstrators in the Nablus area. In Jerusalem, a car parked on a busy commercial street had exploded, killing two civilians and injuring six. No arrests had been made.

"For now," Saul said, "that appears to be all. I suggest—"

"Is there anything further on that Bedouin group that was reported on last week?" Shimon Navot asked.

Saul picked up the most recent report from Air Patrol. "Only that they crossed over the border and are somewhere in the Negev, confirmed by ground patrol, but nothing suspicious."

Yerushalmi squirmed restlessly in his chair. "We're not getting anywhere, Saul. This waiting for something, somehow, to happen—"

"Waiting is always the hardest part of what we do, Uri," Saul replied softly, not wishing to place emphasis on a feeling he shared with the former border patrol lieutenant. "It is very possible that since the thing on Takieh Road, they too are waiting to see if we took anyone alive there. As far as the press is concerned, we left that question open. Until they know something certain, it is reasonable to assume they will suspend activity temporarily or move with extreme caution."

"Then we continue to outwait them," Shaked said.

"Unless you have something better to offer, Dov, we will continue to outwait them," Saul said firmly.

The meeting came to an end on that desultory note. Saul got up and began to pace in front of the wall map, sending occasional glances at it in passing. After a few minutes, he went to his desk and took out all the photographs he had taken in Iraq and those Drory had filmed in Dresden. He studied them for a while, but none produced new inspiration.

No further word had been received from Emile Khoury in Beirut, which was deepening his feeling of impatience. Then Shana knocked on his door and entered, bringing with her an Air Patrol report received a few minutes earlier. He looked up and said, "Anything, Shana?"

"They are encamped a few kilometers south of Mitzpeh Ramon."

"You still think it may be something?"

"Until I have some reason to believe otherwise, I am still curious why these Bedouin are well off the normal routes other Bedouin usually travel."

Saul showed a small degree of his impatience by not replying for a few moments, then said, "I think I'll stop by and see Eitan. I'll be on the radio if you want me for anything."

"I'll notify the day duty officer."

He drove to the hospital alone and went directly to Drory's room, where he found him sitting up, face buried in the morning *Ha'aretz*, which he put aside at once. Eitan looked much better, facial color restored, hollowed cheeks showing signs of filling out somewhat, the mass of bandages over his body reduced to mere coverings for the remaining scars that would require more healing time and cosmetic surgery. Saul had not seen him since the day of the Takieh Road event and brought him up to date on that, but could give him no additional word on Tobari or Sadani.

"Sadani," Drory mused. "He is the key here in Israel, just as Tobari is the key wherever he is."

Saul shook his head solemnly. "Tobari," he said. "We have Sadani and the Soulad woman under close surveillance, but I would almost be willing to give up both to know where Tobari is at this moment and what he is up to."

"Then you must stay with Sadani. He will lead you to your Tobari. Without question."

"Not at the rate he is moving. From his apartment to his office, from office to apartment. Lately, not even any social activities. He and his wife have become virtual recluses."

"Which in itself should raise strong suspicions." Drory paused, then said, "In the past, we have found it useful to use some device to force a man to make a move. A telegram, a phone call, something that will send him running, either under cover or to make a contact with someone we needed to discover."

"It would be useful, Eitan, except that I doubt if he would run to wherever Tobari is. He is much too clever to do anything that would expose Tobari to us. What we are doing is the hardest work of all, being patient."

But later that afternoon, while discussing the emptiness of the day with Yoram Golan and Shana over coffee in his office, Saul thought of Eitan's remark and said musingly, "What do you think would happen if we allowed Mordecai Aarons and Tahia Soulad to discover that they were under surveillance? How do you suppose each would react? More important, where do you think they would lead us?"

Shana's eyebrows shot upward in surprise at the suggestion. Golan simply stared at Saul, owl-eyed. Shana recovered first and said, "Wouldn't that run counter to General Rosental's emphatic order, Saul, with particular regard to Aarons?"

Golan's head rocked slowly from side to side. "Soulad, perhaps, but Aarons?"

"There are times," Saul said, "when achieving desired results can be more important than obeying orders. That is something I learned from Judah Rosental himself when we were both much younger."

Golan's smile was enigmatic. "Since it is not my neck on the butcher's block, Saul, I am inclined to go along with you. The way things are going, we might gain much more than we would lose."

"In the case of Aarons," Shana offered, "there is also the risk that he could suddenly decide to go underground and cross into Jordan, Syria or Lebanon and disappear."

Saul sighed. "This is a game of risks, Shana. That is the chance we will have to gamble on."

"Then your mind is made up?"

"Yes. Otherwise, we can go on like this for months."

"If that is your decision," she said with palms turned upward, "there's nothing else for anyone to say, is there?"

On the following morning, Yossi Zeitel and Eliahu Darvit were parked half a block north of the entrance to the Aarons' apartment building when Mordecai Aarons exited carrying his familiar briefcase. He went to his official car that stood at the curbside as usual, unlocked it and got in. As he pulled away from the curb, Zeitel followed.

The routine was changed now. Instead of lagging behind at least a full block, the SO Branch car was only six or seven car lengths away when Aarons braked at the corner. Zietel pulled up almost directly behind. Aarons made the right turn and Zeitel followed closely, allowing no other vehicle to pull in between them.

By the time the two cars reached the Finance Ministry building after making the necessary turns involved, Aarons was conscious that he had either encountered a surprising coincidence or that he was being tailed. He turned into the reserved parking area behind the building and took note that the tan sedan had stopped just beyond the entrance gate at the outside curb. He picked up his briefcase and hurried into the building through the rear entrance.

Darvit picked up the radio microphone and reported to the duty officer that they were on location and that he was certain Aarons was aware that he had been followed. He and Zeitel now settled down for the long wait, eyes on the Aarons car.

Shortly after the noon hour, Aarons appeared at the front of the building. After looking from side to side cautiously, he began walking toward the restaurant usually patronized by higher echelon government personnel. There, he became conscious of the tall man in a dark gray suit who seemed more intent on him than on his own meal. Only halfway through his lunch, Aarons got up abruptly, paid his check at the cashier's counter and left. Before entering the ministry building, he turned and saw the same gray-suited man walking slowly behind him.

At one thirty, Tahia Soulad left her apartment carrying her usual shopping bag. Within three blocks of the shopping area, she noticed the man in a blue suit who, across the street, was matching her progress along Kiryat Cholmo. At the next shop window, she stopped, using the glass as a mirror. The man across the street also stopped and was looking in her direction. When this occurred twice more, she hurried along, completed her food shopping errand quickly and returned to her apartment. Once inside, she went to the front window and parted the curtain only far enough to peer down on the street below. The man in the blue suit was leaning against the side of a dark gray car, glancing up at her window.

Tahia then went into the rear bedroom and looked out of that window into the alley beyond the yard. There, leaning against a fence three or four doors down, stood another non-Arab man who was looking up at her window and speaking into a small black box that looked like a transistor radio.

A few moments later, Moshe Tal reported directly to Saul Lahav by radio that he and Dan Kaspi were covering the front and rear of number 217 Kiryat Cholmo. The subject, Soulad, was in her apartment and assuredly aware of their presence.

In her apartment, Tahia was anything but calm as she put away the food she had bought. She turned on a light under the coffee pot with trembling hands, then began pacing through the apartment, glancing about her to see if anyone had entered and searched it while she had been out shopping, but found no evidence of an intruder. She returned to the kitchen and poured a cup of coffee, chain smoking nervously. She went to the rear window again, then to the front. Both men remained where she had seen them minutes ago, one at the back alley, the other now seated inside the car. She was tempted to use her telephone, but a second sense warned her it had probably been tapped.

It was too early to go to the club, where she could use the public phone in the hallway that led to her dressing room, then decided that if she had been watched over a period of time, this would be a suspicious move in itself. Instead, she lay down on her bed, hoping to nap, but sleep would not come. When another hour had passed and half a dozen more cigarettes consumed, she stripped off her clothes, bathed, dressed for work and, throwing caution to the winds, went out. Before she reached the club, she was totally aware of the one man who had followed her earlier on foot, and now of the car moving slowly less than a block behind.

Restless and frightened, she waited in her dressing room for about fifteen minutes, then went out into the hallway. Assured that no one was within sight or hearing, she dropped a coin in the telephone pay slot. When a voice answered on the fourth ring, she spoke quickly, brokenly, and asked for Salim Tabet. The man on the other end said in a tight, harsh voice, "Who is this calling?"

"I must speak to Salim. Quickly, please. It is most important."

"He is not available."

"Then . . . then Razak. This is an emergency."

"Who is this?" the voice demanded again.

"Tell him it is Tahia. I am speaking from a public phone. There is no danger."

"This is Razak. How did you get this number?"

"From Salim. He told me to use it only in an emergency."

"What is it, this emergency?"

She told him of the two men who had followed her on her shopping tour and back, then remained outside her apartment and followed her again, this time to the Club Morocco.

After a moment of silence, Razak said, "Very well. We will look into it. And forget this number. Do not call it again under any circumstances. Do you understand?"

"Yes, I understand. What will you do?"

"I will have Salim contact you later, in person."

"Thank—" she began, but the line had gone dead.

At three thirty P.M. Dov Shaked, who was due to relieve Zeitel and Darvit at the Finance Ministry, radioed in to Saul with word that he and Yoram Golan were hung up at Latrun with a water pump problem and would not be able to return in time to take over the surveillance on Aarons at four o'clock. Rather than ask Zeitel and his partner to extend their tour, Saul decided to take it over himself until Dov and Yoram returned. He had his dispatcher send a mechanic to Latrun with a new water pump, then had Leah ask Asad Hasbani to stand by with his car.

When he went below, he found Asad ready behind the wheel. "Your arm is that much better?"

"For simple driving, yes. The exercise helps."

"This may be more than simple driving. We will be tailing Aarons in his car when he leaves his office."

"I am sure I can handle it, Colonel. If I feel I can't, I will turn the wheel over to you."

"Very well. The Ministry of Finance building. We will take the parking space that Zeitel and Darvit give up to us."

En route, Saul contacted Zeitel by radio, who reported, "Nothing since he came back from lunch, but he knows we are on him."

"Good, Yossi. Asad and I will take over from you. Dov and Yoram are having trouble with their car."

"If you say so, but Eliahu and I can—"

"No. From six to four is long enough. When we arrive, pull out and we will take over your parking space. You and Eliahu go home. My present to your wives. I'll see you in the morning."

Positions exchanged, Saul and Asad sat listening to the all-band radio that was turned down low. Asad kept watch on the front entrance while Saul scanned the action on the car park. It was nearing dusk and the outside lights began to come on when Saul cautioned, "Look sharp, Asad. He knows he is being tailed and may leave on foot by the front and leave his car behind to try to throw us off. Have you ever seen the man, other than his face in the photograph?"

"No, never."

"He is shorter than you, about five feet six inches, heavier, thick glasses, probably carrying a briefcase."

Asad nodded. They waited, listening to the radio. Another hour passed, then Saul said, "I have him. The back door. He is going toward his car."

They watched together, saw Aarons glance about him with care before he got into his official car and started it, then backed out of its slot. "He is taking the south exit," Saul said. "Wait until he reaches the corner, then pick him up."

Asad pulled out and allowed the car to drift slowly for half a block until Aarons' car came out on the side street and made a right turn. Asad then moved up, turned into the side street and was in good position, with only two cars separating him from Aarons.

They moved along in traffic for several blocks before the car directly ahead made an abrupt right turn. At the next block, the second car turned off and now they were directly behind Aarons. Asad played it carefully, driving slightly to the left so that Aarons would have no difficulty keeping the tail car in his rear- and side-view mirrors. And now, Aarons turned into a wide boulevard and speeded up. Asad followed, keeping about five car lengths behind, making lane changes each time Aarons did.

Saul said, "He knows. This is not the route he normally takes to go home."

Aarons made a sharp turn into a narrow street, then another, now driving in the very direction from which they had originally come. Full darkness had fallen and traffic, both vehicular and pedestrian, had increased; but Aarons proved to be expert behind the wheel, taxing Hasbani's somewhat stiffened arm and reflexes to keep just far enough behind in case Aarons decided to brake to a quick stop, which would force them to pass.

Then Aarons returned to the wider boulevard and picked up speed again. He turned off half a kilometer later, made a left turn and, suddenly, Saul realized that they were heading toward Rehov Ben Gurion! When they reached it, Aarons made a left turn into it and in reply to Asad's sharp glance, Saul said, "At the next corner, take a left and a right and drop me at the rear parking lot. I think I am going to have a visitor. You come around to the front and park. If he keeps going, stay with him and contact me by radio. If he parks and goes inside, wait and pick him up again when he comes out."

On the rear parking lot, Saul raced inside and up the stairs to his office, past startled security guards and interior personnel. He had no sooner seated himself at his desk when Leah called to announce that Mr. Mordecai Aarons was asking to see him. Into the intercom, Saul said, "Please show Mr. Aarons in."

It was a curious meeting. Or confrontation. Aarons appeared tense, yet his outer manner was confident as he entered Saul's office, still carrying his briefcase. Saul rose and said, "*Shalom,*

Adon Aarons. An unexpected pleasure." He indicated the visitor's chair beside his desk. "Please sit. Will you have coffee?"

Aarons dropped into the chair, placing the briefcase on the floor beside the chair, expelling a deep breath. "*Shalom*, Colonel. It is good to see you again. No coffee, thank you."

"And what can we do for the Economic Advisory Council?" Saul said with a smile. "I'm afraid my knowledge of economic matters is quite limited."

"No," Aarons replied with a wan smile in return, "this is in the nature of a personal matter, Colonel. This afternoon, I telephoned my good friend, Morris Lurie at National Police Headquarters and explained the situation to him. He referred me to General Rosental in Tel Aviv. I phoned and learned that Judah was out of the city, but Colonel Kohn, his aide, suggested I speak with you about it. I had planned to do that in the morning, but something has arisen that made me decide to do it at once."

"So. And how can my department be of service to you?"

"Colonel," Aarons said soberly, "I am not an alarmist, but in view of the attempt on the lives of you and your colleagues recently, and the step-up in terrorist activities, you understand—"

"Yes, of course. Please."

"I have reason to suspect that I am being followed. At first, I dismissed the thought, but I noticed it again this morning and on my way to and from lunch. When I left my office this afternoon I was followed again by two men, this time in a different car, almost to your very door. For myself, I have few fears, but I am concerned for the safety of my wife should she be with me when and if an attempt is made on my life."

Saul's expression was one of deep interest and concern. "Of course, naturally. Tell me, were you able to see these men, possibly describe or identify them?"

"I am afraid not. It is difficult when one is driving to see clearly into a car that is following, only to observe that there were two men in each of the instances. During the lunch incident, I didn't pay too much attention, only to notice that I had been followed to and from the restaurant."

"The car, perhaps the license—"

"Not that. At first, a tan sedan. Later, a dark blue or black one, nothing to distinguish it from so many others."

"Yes, well . . . I am glad you have brought this to my attention, *Adon* Aarons. . . ."

Smiling now, "Please. Mordecai, if you will permit me to call you Saul."

"Of course."

"You understand, I am not asking for a bodyguard, which was at first suggested by Morris Lurie. That could become an embarrassment to me and my wife."

"I understand. Please leave this to me. I will look into it at once and make certain there is no present danger to you. Or to your wife. I can assure you my people will be discreet."

"Thank you, Saul. A constant surveillance can become very unnerving."

"Naturally. Let me reassure you, Mordecai, that we will do nothing to embarrass your position, nor you, nor your wife."

Aarons reached for his briefcase and stood up. "Again, thank you, Saul. And forgive me for interrupting your more important duties. *Shalom*."

"*Shalom*, Mordecai." He walked Aarons to the landing and saw him start down the stairs. Saul then hurried to the Communications Section and got Asad on the radio.

"Asad, he is leaving. Pick him up, but at a more discreet distance. He will probably be going home now. Report in to the duty officer when you get there. Shaked and Golan are on their way in. I will contact them and have them relieve you."

Saul made contact with Golan and issued instructions for Asad's relief and to be doubly watchful for any attempt on Aarons' part to leave his apartment building during the night, this without revealing their presence. Golan acknowledged, informing Saul that they had just left Latrun, giving his estimatted time of arrival at the Aarons location within an hour.

Saul returned to his office just as Leah was leaving for the day. He leaned back in his chair and reviewed his visit with Aarons, admiring the cool boldness of the man. A few minutes later, pleased with this new development that showed promise of some definite movement, he phoned Shana and asked her to have supper with him at their favorite restaurant.

If Saul Lahav believed he had lulled Mordecai Aarons into a state of false security, he could not have been more wrong. Aarons drove directly to his apartment building and parked his car in its usual place in front of the entrance. He appeared to be in no hurry as he gathered his briefcase up and got out, looked to left and right, then locked the car. As he gained the entrance to the building, he saw a car turn into the quiet street from above and, without hesitating, came down at a normal rate of speed. When it passed, Aarons noted that its single occupant looked quickly in his direction, then turned away. Aarons walked briskly to the entrance, but did not go inside, hiding carefully in the shadows. Peering out, he saw the car make a right turn at the corner. He waited, and no more than fifty seconds later, saw the same car come down the street from above. It paused for a moment, then continued for about ten or fifteen yards to a parking space and backed into it. The man then shut off his motor, but remained seated behind the wheel.

Aarons deliberated for another five minutes. The man in the car had still not gotten out of the car. Aarons then went inside to the elevators and rode up to the seventh floor. Entering his apartment, he put the briefcase on a chair in the foyer and greeted his wife, who came to him from the living room.

"You are late, Amon. Is anything wrong?"

"I am afraid so, Suzi. Sit down. We have much to do and very little time to waste."

"What is it, Amon?"

"It is over here. I will explain it to you on the way to the farm. Quickly, while there is only one man watching down below. Soon, there may be others. Gather up everything valuable to you that you can carry on your person. No extra clothing, only jewelry you can put in your pockets and purse, whatever else small that will fit. I must change and put on my disguise."

"But Amon," Suzi wailed. "My clothes—"

"Only what you can wear. Something dark and what we can carry on us. Hurry."

Suzi needed no further urging. Their way of precarious living made instantaneous obedience mandatory. While she changed from her simple dress into a more durable pair of black slacks and jacket, which would provide more pocket room, and gathered up the better pieces of jewelry and a few cosmetics, she asked. "Are we getting out of this cursed country for good, Amon?"

"Perhaps you. Hatif will want me here with him until the Bashra thing is over. If he agrees, we will get you out to Paris where you will be safe. Later, I will join you there. My usefulness is over here."

"They've discovered?"

"How much, I don't know, but that Jew bastard, Lahav, knows I am not what I appear to be. He toyed with me, but I am certain he is ready to spring a trap of some kind. I can't afford to be taken in for interrogation, nor do I want to risk your falling into their hands."

He had finished putting on the beard and mustache and was pulling on the shaggy wig. "Thank Allah I will soon be finished with this mess," he muttered. The wig set, he stripped off his trousers and got into the rumpled outfit that was more suitable for his disguise.

They were ready now and as Suzi reached for the wall switch, he said, "No. Leave the lights on. All of them."

In the empty corridor, they went to the elevator door that was still open. Amon pushed the button for the basement level. The door hissed shut and the car moved downward. On the bottom level, they exited and he pushed the button that would take the car back to the seventh floor. At the rear door, he said, "Go to the car, Suzi. Start it without turning the lights on, then drive it here and pick me up."

She followed his instructions and, when the car pulled up at the rear door, he got in quickly, sliding behind the wheel as she moved over into the passenger seat. He drove out through the side entrance, into the side street, where he made a right turn, thus avoiding the street where he was certain the single watcher was keeping his eyes on the front entrance of the building. And no doubt on the upper windows of his apartment.

Minutes later, the Aaronses were out on the main road heading toward Ein Fara.

Less than twenty minutes later, Dov Shaked made radio contact with Asad Hasbani, who reported his exact position. When they appeared, Asad pulled out of his parking space to make room for his colleagues, since both sides of the street were now solidly lined with cars.

"Anything?" Golan asked after the transfer.

"Nothing," Asad replied. "There is his car at the curb, the lights are still on in the apartment, and no one has left."

"What about the rear?"

Asad shrugged. "I couldn't be in two places at the same time. From here, I could see the front windows. Every once in a while I saw one of them pass by."

"All right, Asad, you're relieved. Take off."

When Hasbani drove off, Yoram said, "I'd better stake out the back." He picked up one of the walkie-talkie units and added, "We'll switch every hour."

"Right." Shaked picked up the hand mike and radioed their location to the night duty officer and asked for a time check. It was nine fifty-seven P.M.

At ten forty the Aaronses, now Sadanis, arrived at the UPFP farm at Ein Fara. Amon drove the car to the rear of the house and parked it inside the garage among the other cars, then both entered the house through the rear door. Amon went directly to the office where Razak and Tabet sat talking. As usual, Razak seemed to be in a surly mood. Both men looked up in surprise as Sadani entered.

"What is it, Amon?" Razak asked. "Why do you come without warning me first?"

"There wasn't time and I didn't want to use my telephone or lose valuable time getting here. Suzi is with me. Lahav is on to me and my cover is blown. A day or two longer and I would be under arrest."

Tabet's face showed deep anxiety, but he remained silent. Razak stood up and began pacing. "Lahav," he said, throwing a dark look at Tabet. "If we had taken him out as Falcon ordered—"

Sadani said, "Let us not waste time on what is in the past, Razak. I don't know how they got onto me or how much they know, or even suspect. I am sure that if they were aware of the farm, they would have been here long ago. I only discovered the surveillance team on me this morning."

"Then," Razak said, "they must know more than we think they do. This afternoon, the Soulad girl called here. Tabet had given her the number—"

"To be used only in an emergency," Tabet interjected defensively.

"What emergency?" Sadani asked.

"She is also being watched," Razak barked out. "Two men. Lahav's men, no doubt."

"Has anything been done about it?"

"Nothing yet. Tabet and I were discussing it. He had a plan to reach her without being discovered. I have told him to contact her and devise a means to bring her here unobserved." He added grudgingly, "I think it is a good plan. It should work if he is careful."

"Then do it at once, Salim," Sadani said. "We can't afford to have her fall into their hands."

"I will contact her later tonight. It will take an additional day and night to bring her here in safety," Tabet said.

"This is urgent. Go now and arrange it," Sadani ordered. Tabet got up and left the room. To Razak, "I need a courier to carry a message to Falcon at once. Have a man get ready while I write it out and code it. How long will it take to reach him?"

"He can cross into Jordan later tonight and telephone it to the Florentine Hotel in Rome. From there, they will pass it along. Perhaps by noon tomorrow."

"Good. Have him wait for the reply and return here with it as soon as he receives it from Rome. What news do we have from Tabet on the Bashra project? I will include it in my message."

"According to the schedule, they are now encamped south of Mitzpeh Ramon, map code twelve. They should be ready to move south toward Kuntilla sometime tomorrow night if all has gone well thus far.

"And Falcon?"

"He is taking care of some business in Tripoli and expects to arrive here within five or six days to take personal charge."

"Then it is all the more important that he receive this message as soon as possible."

A few minutes before midnight, Salim Tabet cruised past the Club Morocco in a Fiat sedan, wearing a black and white kaffiyeh, the ends of which were draped around his neck and lower jaw. Some of the shops on either side of the street were still open, hoping to tempt the appetites and purses of tourists and passersby with the variety of ready-to-eat foods that were exposed on outdoor stoves and stands, the air redolent with cooking odors. Youths paraded back and forth hawking every type of souvenir and others simply stood in small groups, talking and viewing the passing scene.

It took only seconds for Tabet to locate the unmarked SO branch car standing at the corner, with the entrance to the club in plain view. He observed that there was only one man in the car and correctly assumed that there would be another close by, probably at the end of the alley, where he could easily watch the side and rear doors; perhaps there was even a third man inside the club.

Tabet continued along Kiryat Cholmo without pausing. Five blocks ahead, he slowed down and looked around for any sign of a second surveillance car in the vicinity of number 217. This was a residential area of apartments and homes, quiet at this late hour, cars parked on both sides of the street for the night. Continuing on, he turned right at the next corner, then right again at the alley behind the building where Tahia lived. He made two more right turns, then drove for three blocks along Kiryat Cholmo until he found a safe parking place.

After a few minutes, during which he carefully observed the street behind him in his rear-view mirror and ahead through the windshield, he got out, locked the Fiat, and walked back the three blocks to number 217, peering into each parked car as he passed.

The outer doors to number 217 were, as usual, unlocked. He entered the totally darkened building, pressed the time-release button on the wall. The dim hall light came on and he walked quickly up the stairs. Using a key, he unlocked the door to Tahia's apartment, but did not enter until the hall light turned itself off automatically. Inside, he turned on no lights, but used a slender penlight to guide him to the bedroom where he removed his shoes, jacket and kaffiyeh and lay down to wait, his revolver at his right side.

It was perhaps three hours later when he heard footsteps in the hallway outside the door. He picked up the revolver and went quickly to the door just in time to hear a key being inserted in the lock. The door opened then and a hand reached inside and touched the light switch. Tahia stepped in and closed the door. She turned and saw Salim, the sight of him causing her to gasp in fright, but before she could utter a sound, he had one hand over her mouth and said in a hushed voice, "Whispers only, Tahia."

When her trembling ceased, he removed his hand. "Do what you would normally do on arriving home," he said.

Tahia nodded slowly. "Were you followed when you left the club?" he asked.

"Yes," she whispered. "Two men. Not the same ones as earlier today. One on foot, one in the car."

"Don't be alarmed, Tahia. I am going to move you out of here and take you to the farm, where you will be safe."

"How? It is not possible. They are here now, one in the front, the other in the back, Salim."

He smiled reassuringly. "Not now."

"Then how, when?"

"Put the light out, then go into the bedroom and turn one on there, and draw the curtain. Undress the way you usually do. Let the one in the back see only your shadow on the curtain. Then turn the light out and get into bed. We will talk then."

She did as Salim instructed her while he remained in the living room away from the windows. When the light in the bedroom was turned off, he went in, undressed and joined her in bed.

"Listen carefully to every word I tell you, Tahia," he said in a whisper. "Those below do not know I am here with you. I checked the street and cars carefully before I came up. I will remain here with you until you leave in the morning to do your shopping. When you do, they will follow you as usual. When you have drawn them off, I will leave and make the final arrangements to get you away from here. It will take several days to do this, but when my plans are complete, you will receive a telephone call from me at the club, giving you the time and day.

"On that night, after your last show, a woman will come to you in your dressing room. You will do exactly what she tells you and I will meet you at a safe place and take you to the farm. Do you understand that, Tahia?"

"Yes. On the night you tell me, after the last show."

"Yes. On that night, you will make your show a little shorter than usual, then return to your dressing room without stopping to talk to anyone, and do not allow anyone to delay you. The woman you will find in your dressing room will have instructions for you. Be sure you carry them out to the letter.''

"Yes, Salim.'' She paused, then said, "I am afraid, Salim.''

"Don't be, Tahia. Trust me. I will take good care that nothing will happen to you.''

"Oh, Salim, Salim. If we could be rid of this dirty business and be together always like this.''

He took her into his arms and kissed her, stroking, soothing, feeling her grow calmer, receptive. "Soon, Tahia, soon we shall have it all. We will be prince and princess in our own kingdom, in a palace with wealth and servants to do our bidding. Only be patient for a while longer.''

At one A.M., when Dov Shaked had the car watch, with Golan on the car park at the rear of the apartment building, he reported in to the night duty officer by radio. At two A.M., as Golan returned from his station at the rear to change places with his partner, he asked, "Did you call in?''

"Yes, at two on the dot. Why?'' Shaked asked.

"Get out and take a look.''

Shaked got out of the car and stood beside Golan, then looked up and down the street. Not a human was in sight, not a car moved. "What is it, Yoram?''

"The Aarons' apartment. The only one in the whole damned neighborhood with all its lights burning. Everybody else is in bed asleep.''

"Maybe they're up there making bombs.''

"Funny man.''

"What do you suggest we do about it?''

"I think I'll go up and see if I can hear anything from outside the door. If they're still awake, I should hear voices.''

"And if they went to bed and forgot to turn their lights off?''

"Then it will be the first time that has happened since they've been under surveillance. The logs show 'lights out' at ten o'clock, sometimes a little earlier, sometimes a little later, but never this late.''

Dov shrugged. "Go ahead, Yoram, but don't blow any fuses or we'll be standing on Saul's carpet with a pair of very red faces.''

"I'll keep it in mind, *chaver*. I'll take the w-t with me. If you see the lights go out up there, whisper in my ear.''

Golan picked up the w-t unit and crossed the street while Shaked remained on the pavement staring up at the lighted windows. Golan entered the empty lobby. Only two wall sconces burned dimly. Of the two elevators, the door to one was open, the other closed, its indicator showing it to be on the fifth floor. On the seventh, Golan stepped into the empty corridor and walked toward the front to the Aarons' apartment, which was on his left.

Cautiously, he tiptoed to the door and placed an ear to it, but heard no sound of movement from within. He listened for a full two minutes, conscious of his own breathing and perhaps the slight throbbing in his veins. He stepped away from the door, contemplated it for a few minutes, then studied the door lock. Ordinary and uncomplicated.

From his wallet, he withdrew a thin, narrow strip of plastic and worked it silently between the edge of the door and the jamb. Now he began to slide it from right to left until he felt movement. Holding the strip firmly there, he turned the knob slowly. The door opened. He listened at the crack of the opening and heard nothing, saw only the inch of light that escaped from inside.

Drawing a deep breath, he entered the small foyer, closed the door so that the lock did not catch. He peered into the living room. Empty. The lights had been left on in the kitchen and dining room as well, and which he could see from where he stood. The door to the bedroom was open. It faced the street side and he knew those lights were on, having seen them from below; and now he was certain he would find that room empty, too. No one went to bed leaving every light in the room on.

The room, he found, was not only empty, but in a state of disarray; several drawers in the double dressers were open, a suit and dress thrown carelessly across the bed, which was still made up. Golan depressed the talk button on his w-t. "Dov, do you read me?"

"Loud and clear. Where are you?"

"Inside the apartment. Radio the NDO. Our birds have flown."

Shaked muttered a curse. Golan said, "I'm on my way down. Maybe we can decide what kind of new business we can go into tomorrow. Maybe a fruit or vegetable stand in a market."

* * *

Nahum Alami, the night duty officer, took Shaked's news in the same way Dov had taken it from Yoram, with a curse; then, "Are you sure, Dov?"

"If you don't believe me, I'll let Yoram repeat it to you when he gets here."

"How in hell could it have happened?"

"Only one way. They got out before we took over from Asad, when there wasn't anyone here to watch the rear car park."

"What do you want me to do?"

"What you're supposed to do. Log it, then call the colonel and tell him how brilliant all of us are. Tell him his two prize investigators are on their way back to headquarters where we will wait until he comes in and shoots us."

Alami logged the call, then put in the call to Saul.

Shana awoke on the first ring, reached across his sleeping form, unable to distinguish the red phone from the white. When it rang a second time, she saw the red light winking in its base and knew it was the direct line from headquarters for emergency use. She removed the receiver from its cradle and nudged Saul awake.

"Wha . . . what?"

"The red phone, Saul."

He took it and said, "Lahav here."

"Alami, Colonel. A radio call from Shaked. The Aaronses have disappeared."

Now it was Saul's turn to curse. Then, "Where are Golan and Shaked now?"

"On their way in."

"I want a general bulletin flashed over the all-band network with full descriptions of both, along with their private car. If located, maintain surveillance and inform only. Take no other action. You have that?"

"Yes, Colonel."

"And tell Shaked and Golan to wait there for me. I will be there in thirty minutes." He handed the receiver back to Shana and got out of bed. "Aarons. And his wife. Gone."

"I gathered as much. Do you want me to come with you?"

"No. Go back to sleep. There won't be much we can do about it. We don't know how much time they've had."

"What about the Soulad woman?"

"I'll check on her when I get there."

"My fault," Saul said when Shaked and Golan reviewed the facts for him. "The only time they could have gotten away was during the period when Asad was there by himself. I should have sent someone with him, but I didn't anticipate they would move so quickly."

Relieved, Golan said, "What can we do now, Saul?"

"Nothing until we get some word on them. Go home and get some sleep. I'll stay here and monitor any calls that come in. Be back here by ten o'clock."

When Golan and Shaked left, Saul went through the near-empty outer office where the reduced night duty force was at work typing the handwritten notes of the day crews into readable report forms, doing the routine follow-up of filing, handling the preliminary interrogation notes of suspects brought in during the day. On the street level, several suspects taken that night were being questioned by the night teams. He went directly to the NDO's desk where all radio calls were monitored and logged in for the morning report. A typist was already compiling notes for the master copy, which would be distributed at seven A.M. in the form of a printout.

"Who do we have on the Soulad woman, Nahum?" Saul asked the NDO.

Alami had anticipated the question. "Simon Zadok and Zvi Leven, Colonel." Referring to the log, "She left the Club Morocco at three ten and walked directly to number two seventeen Kiryat Cholmo. Lights came on in her apartment at three twenty-nine, out at three thirty-three, on in the rear bedroom at three thirty-four, out at three forty-four. Zadok is in the car in front, Leven on foot in the rear."

"A nice, quiet girl with regular habits," Saul commented.

"If we go by the log since we've been on her, I couldn't ask more of my own children. Coffee, Colonel? It's fresh made."

"Yes."

Alami poured a cup from the large electric pot on the table near his desk. "Nothing on the Aarons car yet, I suppose," Saul said.

"Nothing yet. The general bulletin was flashed and relayed to all police and border patrol units, also Coastal Command. All acknowledged."

Saul finished his coffee and returned to his office. He sat at his desk and began to plan now how he would break this bit of unwelcome news to Rosental; and what fallout he would be getting from Bartok and higher authorities. The truth, he decided, however painful, would be the safest way. There was, in fact, no other way.

12

Emile Khoury's delight could not have been more genuine that morning when, summoned from his office by Daniele, he came into the showroom to greet Ali Fathy and his attractive mistress, Adele Salah, a rare flower of feminine beauty. After an exchange of polite *salaams*, Daniele took Adele off for a tour of the shop's most recent importations from Paris while Emile ordered coffee to be brought to a conversation corner where he and the smiling, handsome Fathy settled down in comfortable chairs.

Fathy, as usual in a holiday mood, exchanged small talk affably with the shopkeeper, one eye on his lovely companion as she made several selections which were held aside by a comely assistant. When Adele had chosen several sports costumes and two evening gowns for the try-on ritual and disappeared into the dressing room area with Daniele, the assistant and a third woman who would attend to any necessary alterations, Fathy turned back to Khoury.

"Whatever is required, Khoury, it must be done quickly. I will be going abroad within a few days on a business matter, but will return here within a week or ten days. Then Mademoiselle Salah and I will be leaving for a vacation on the Riviera."

"I assure you that whatever Mademoiselle Salah chooses will be ready for her well within that time."

"Excellent, my dear Khoury. I am looking forward to that trip. It has been a long time since I have had a real vacation."

"A celebration of sorts?"

"One could say that," Fathy replied with a broadening smile. "I have high hopes that my business trip will be eminently successful and richly rewarding."

"May all your hopes be attained. More coffee?"

"Yes, please."

Khoury summoned a girl and sent her for the coffee. At that moment, Daniele emerged from the dressing room area and went toward the rear of the shop. At the door to the office, she stopped, turned, and caught Khoury's eye. She went inside and closed the door. When the girl brought the coffee to Fathy, Khoury excused himself and went to his office.

"She is in a rare, high mood," Daniele said, "about a trip to the Riviera with Fathy when he returns from a trip in about a week or ten days."

"I know. That confirms what he has already told me. Call in and get a messenger over here at once while I code a message. Tell them it is most urgent."

Daniele made the call to their import agent with the news that Khoury Couture wished to return an invoice that did not agree with their latest shipment from Paris, and would they send a messenger to pick it up at once. Meanwhile, Khoury prepared his coded message, sealed it into an envelope and handed it to Daniele. He then returned to entertain Fathy while Daniele went back to the dressing room, carrying with her two more sports outfits for Adele to look over.

Twenty minutes later, when Fathy and Adele left to do more shopping, a young man began to saunter behind them. Moments later, another youth of about seventeen entered the shop. Daniele handed him the envelope which he pocketed and left at once.

Saul, after checking the morning report and newspapers Leah had brought him, called off the morning staff meeting, then spent half an hour on the phone with Judah Rosental explaining this latest mishap. Now it was in Rosental's hands and Saul could only wait for whatever flak would fall upon his shoulders from a higher authority. *Selah*. So be it.

A quarter of an hour after he hung up, Shana literally burst into his office in a state of high excitement. "A message from Tripoli, Saul. Yesterday, Ali Fathy and Adele Salah were in the Khoury shop. Indications are that he will be in Tripoli for a few days, then go abroad on a business trip. After about a week or ten days, he plans to return to Tripoli and go on a vacation trip to the Riviera with his Adele. Fathy's words to Khoury, confirmed by Adele to Daniele."

Saul's sagging spirits soared. "Call Asad and have him stand by. Book me on the next El Al to Rome, have the Rome office book me on MEA to Tripoli. Get me the same passport I used last time, Libyan currency, the other documents I will need. If Rosental or anyone else in Tel Aviv calls me back, tell them I am out of the country, an emergency, but don't tell them where or what. I'll be home packing, then stop by to pick up the passport and the rest of it.''

Two days later, barely in time for the early morning flight out, a silver Jaguar sports car, driven by a young Libyan, pulled up to the MEA entrance at the Tripoli airport. Ali Fathy, smartly attired in a lightweight British-cut plaid suit, got out and waited while the young man carried his suitcase inside and checked it through to Rome. Fathy carried a small Pan Am bag.

Directly behind the Jaguar, Saul Lahav, wearing a business suit, hat, sunglasses, and sporting a full mustache, got out of a gray Mercedes sedan and shook hands with his young Mossad driver. He lifted his one small suitcase from the rear compartment and went inside to the ticket counter, three behind Fathy/Tobari in line, presented his ticket, passport, and foreign travel documents when it came to his turn. Checked through without any difficulty, he went to the newsstand and selected a morning paper and a magazine and lounged beside the coffee counter until he heard his flight announced. He was only two behind his man when they boarded the first-class section. When the plane was buttoned up and began to taxi toward the takeoff runway, Saul relaxed.

They landed in Rome on schedule at one ten P.M. Saul followed Tobari through the arrival ritual at Customs and Immigration, neither experiencing any delays. He watched as Tobari went to a row of coin lockers, wwhere he deposited his suitcase and pocketed the key, retaining only the blue and white Pan Am flight bag. Saul at once checked his own suitcase in a nearby locker, then followed Tobari outside to the rank of waiting taxis. He took the next one in line behind Tobari's and settled back for the trip to the inner city. Once they became involved with heavier local traffic, Saul interrupted the driver's chatter by waving a 10,000-lire note over his shoulder. ''Yours plus the fare if you keep that taxi ahead of us in sight until it comes to its final stop.''

The driver needed no further urging. ''You are the *polizia*, *signore*, eh?''

''No, no. The man inside is on his way to an assignation with my wife,'' Saul replied in Italian.

''Ah, *signor*. Do not kill him here. Our jails are not fit for pigs.''

''No. All I want is evidence for a divorce.''

''Ah, *si*. He will not escape us, I promise you.''

Nor did he permit the taxi in front of him to avoid their eyes for a moment, despite the crowded streets and pedestrians who crossed them without considering the perils, screeching brakes and shrill horns. At the Hotel Lombardio, just off the Via Sistina, the chase came to an end. Tobari paid and dismissed his driver. Saul, with a hearty thanks and "*Buona fortuna*" from his driver, sent him off into the traffic maze and followed Tobari into the lobby of the unpretentious hotel.

Tobari did not stop at the desk, but went directly to the staircase and walked up to the second floor. As soon as he was out of sight, Saul ran up the steps quickly. At the top, he stopped, peered around the corner and saw Tobari standing before a door, knocking on it. The door was opened from the inside and Tobari entered.

Saul waited for a few moments, then proceeded along the hall until he could read the number on the door—114. He then returned to the lobby to ponder the situation. Since Tobari had not registered, he was evidently expected by whoever had engaged the room; and since he had checked his suitcase at the airport, it was not likely that he was planning to remain in Rome overnight. In which case, it was just as likely he would not remain in the room too long. To confer with an ally? To make further arrangements? And for what?

Saul went outside to examine exits and entrances. There was a side entrance that could be watched, along with the front entrance, from across the street. The door at the rear of the hotel was not only closed, but had a pair of iron bars X-ed across it, held firmly in place by a padlock. He returned to the front, crossed the street and selected the doorway of a tailoring shop from which to maintain his vigil.

In room 114 of the Lombardio, Tobari had removed his suit, shirt, tie and shoes. He sat at the mirror of a dressing table where, using a passport photograph as a guide, a woman had smoothed down his hair and pulled a black, curly-haired wig down over his scalp. After inserting pellets of wax over his upper gums to fill out and change the expression of his mouth, she applied a beard and mustache that gave him a particularly unkempt appearance.

Meanwhile, a man was taking careful pains with a black suit and vest, a round black felt hat, a somewhat soiled shirt and a pair of black, unpolished ankle-high shoes. The left shoe, he pointed out to Tobari, had an extra lift inserted in the heel, designed to alter his walking gait slightly.

Tobari, with a frown of distaste, got into the dark clothes, then put on and tried walking in the shoes. He took a dozen or two steps and found that he was now forced into a slight limp that also caused him to hunch forward, thus decreasing his height by at least a full inch. He put on the hat and sat down in front of the mirror again to compare his facial appearance with the Israeli passport. The forgeries were perfect. He had, within a matter of forty-five minutes, been converted into a seedy, middle-aged Jew.

He pocketed the passport along with an El Al ticket, some Israeli pound notes and additional identification documents, exchanging these for his Libyan papers and currency. With approval from his two assistants, he picked up the blue and white Pan Am flight bag and went out.

Saul, loitering in the doorway across from the Lombardio, became aware of the shopowner's annoyance when the man came out for the fourth time, silent, but with expressive eyes that said, *Either come in and buy or go loaf elsewhere.* So Saul moved back to the hotel side of the street and took up a position at the corner of the side street, from which point he could observe the front and side doors. For a while, he began to doubt his earlier reasoning; what if Tobari did remain in Rome overnight, or for a day or two? It was possible that his "business" was in Rome. In which case, it would be necessary to contact the local Mossad office and arrange for relay teams to—

His thoughts were interrupted by the appearance of an elderly bearded Jew wearing a rumpled black suit as he came out of the hotel's main entrance, limping toward the curb. Reaching it, he raised his left arm to signal one of a number of passing taxis. Saul, thinking the old man might need some help in giving directions to the driver in Italian, began to walk toward him. A green mini-taxi screeched up at that moment. The old man opened the door just as Saul reached him, heard him speak to the driver in perfect Italian. "*Rapidamente, per piacere, mi conduca all' aeroporto—*" Taken completely by surprise, Saul continued on past the man, then caught sight of the blue and white Pan Am bag dangling from his right hand. He walked toward the inside pavement, turned and saw the elderly man step into the cab and pull away.

Quickly, Saul stepped into the street and hailed the next cab and directed him similarly, not without some small doubt in his mind. A careful disguise, very likely, but what if the man he was following was not Tobari, but an accomplice employed to lead a possible tail astray? The thought of the suitcase Tobari had placed in the airport coin locker came to his mind. Could that, too, be a device to draw attention elsewhere?

But at the airport, Saul's first suspicion was borne out when the elderly Jew limped to the coin locker section, inserted his key in the proper lock and withdrew the suitcase. Studying the man carefully, trying to identify him with the dapper Tobari, Saul again found his doubts surfacing, but was now left with no alternative but to see this thing through. He at once retrieved his own suitcase from the locker in which he had deposited it and walked quickly to catch up with the old man. Now, as the trail led directly to the El Al counter, Saul began to breathe a little easier, certain that his quarry was indeed Hatif Tobari.

Bypassing the check-in counter, Saul went straight to the security section, identified himself to the chief security officer, handed over his suitcase and was permitted to go down the ramp to the boarding area. Ten minutes later at planeside, he saw Tobari come slowly down the ramp, pass between the double row of security guards and board the plane. Saul waited until two other passengers mounted the stairs, then followed. He saw Tobari take a window seat in the crowded tourist section, buckle himself in, and become engrossed at once in a copy of *Ma'ariv* which he had taken from the news rack on his way to his seat. At the rear of the plane, Saul spoke to the security man who was stationed there. The man exchanged some words with the chief steward, who seated Saul two rows behind Tobari and across the aisle.

Dusk was falling as the plane was finally locked up, the security trucks and jeeps moved out of the way. The plane was towed out and away from the building area. When the tow vehicle pulled away, the jet motors caught and the 707 glided toward its departure runway. A few minutes later, they were airborne.

The plane was crowded with tourists and Israelis returning from Europe, South Africa and the United States. Voices hurled across and down aisles, passengers roamed back and forth, stewards and stewardesses were bumped and manhandled as they tried to maneuver to serve the supper meal. Initial exuberance died down somewhat during the meal, only to come alive later with songs, led by an enthusiastic tour leader who insisted that since they were on the final leg of Tel Aviv in an El Al plane, they could now consider themselves on Israeli soil.

He was shouted down, joked down, sung down, but insisted on personally visiting each seat to welcome each passenger, Israeli or not, to *Eretz Yisrael*. Saul watched with special interest as Tobari not only smiled his appreciation, but responded in perfect Hebrew when addressed, reaffirming Sokolnikov's statement as to the Egyptian's linguistic abilities.

The congenial commotion continued and any attempt to doze or nap was futile. Not until the announcement of impending arrival at Ben-Gurion Airport was broadcasted did the passengers come under some semblance of control. Belted into their seats, the tourists at the-windows began to strain to see the first lights of Israel now that full darkness had fallen.

The security man came aft and paused at Saul's seat to inform him that his message had been transmitted and acknowledged; a car and three men would meet him on arrival. Twenty minutes later, they touched down and rolled to a smooth stop. Quickly, the plane was surrounded by trucks, jeeps and Uzi-bearing guards, the outer perimeter flooded with bright lights, patrolled by jeeps. Passengers crossed into the luggage arrival section to await their possessions, then pass through Customs and Immigration.

Saul waited until his suitcase appeared, then went directly to the chief security officer and was permitted to leave without further delay. Outside, Uri Yerushalmi waited and led him to where the car was parked a short distance away. In it, Asad Hasbani sat behind the wheel, Dov Shaked on the rear seat. Saul got in beside Dov.

Greetings exchanged, Saul said, "He will be coming out soon. Beard: mustache, black suit and hat, a slight limp. A blue Pan Am bag and a gray suitcase. Let's see who picks him up and where they take him." Yerushalmi, seated beside Hasbani, said, "We have two more cars from the Tel Aviv pool standing by just outside if you want them."

"No," Saul said, "let's play this alone. I don't want a parade that can be easily spotted. Asad, can you handle it?"

"The only way he can lose me will be if he suddenly grows wings and starts to fly," Asad replied.

When Tobari finally appeared among the crowd that began to move toward the rows of buses and taxis, a sedan pulled up and waited until he reached it. Inside were three youngish-looking men who could pass for either Jews or Arabs, all in ordinary dress. A rear door was flung open. Tobari got in and the car moved out into the traffic pattern.

"Go, Asad," Yerushalmi said needlessly. As they pulled out, Yerushalmi got on the radio and dismissed the two cars from the local motor pool. Within minutes, they were in a well-trafficked stream of vehicles heading toward Jerusalem, the Tobari car only three ahead of them, with Asad permitting about four or five car lengths between him and the car directly ahead. By the time they had passed through Ramla, some vehicles ahead had turned off and now there was only one car between, the road clear, with only a few cars heading in the opposite direction, the Tobari car rolling at a normal rate of speed. A few cars passed them, then a well-laden truck, all passing the Tobari car as well. At the Sha'ar Hagai turnoff, the car directly in front of the Mossad car veered off and the subject sedan was now before them, in the clear and some ten car lengths ahead.

And now, suddenly, either by suspicion or normal precaution, the driver of the Tobari car began a series of slow-down maneuvers, possibly to determine whether or not he was being followed. Asad, unwilling to pass, was forced to slow down, then pick up speed as the car in front accelerated its pace. Asad said, "If he does that a few more times, he will know we are on his tail, Colonel."

"Lay back," Saul ordered. "Let him put more distance between us, but watch for a sudden turnoff."

Then, approaching the turnoff at Abu Ghosh, the Tobari car shot ahead with a tremendous burst of speed, passing two cars and the heavily-laden truck that had passed them earlier. Asad's foot clamped down hard on the accelerator and the car leaped forward. He overtook the two passenger cars and shot past the truck, then sliced sharply to his right, only to find it necessary to brake down in order to keep from passing the target car which had slowed down once again.

Yerushalmi said, "If they don't know now, they've got to be blind or stupid."

"Play it out," Saul said. "If they run again, we'll close in and take them, even if everything else goes down the drain. At worst, we'll have Tobari and three of his *chaverim*."

But the car ahead was now moving at a normal pace again and a small sense of well-being pervaded the atmosphere in the tail car. Then, as suddenly as before, the lead car was running again and a surprised Hasbani moved into action. Up ahead, a crossroad opened into the main highway from the right and the Tobari car flashed past it. When the chase car was within thirty yards of the crossroad, a large truck roared out, directly in their path. Uri Yerushalmi called out, "Watch—" but before the next word could be uttered, Asad had swung toward his left; hard enough, but not soon enough.

The car screeched and skidded on burning rubber as its right side ground against the left side of the truck, then came to an abrupt stop. Glass and metal bits littered the road, water flooded from the car's radiator. The occupants were momentarily shaken up, but there were no serious injuries. Asad's efforts to start the wounded car were useless.

They got out on the undamaged left side of the car and Shaked ran to the truck, pulled the expostulating driver out of the cab to the ground. Other cars had stopped, but Asad waved them on with his flashlight, guiding them into the single lane that left passage possible. Yerushalmi was on the radio, calling for backup assistance and another car to transport them into Jerusalem.

While Shaked was questioning the Arab truck driver, Saul mounted the cab and searched it thoroughly, pulling out the front seat, throwing it out on the road. From the glove compartment, he removed a flashlight, some small tools, an oily rag and other oddments. The beam of light revealed a large tool box beneath the front seat. Saul rooted through the miscellany of items in it, then noticed another object that had lain unnoticed beside it. Recognition came swiftly. He reached in and picked it up, examining it under the flashlight. It was a walkie-talkie unit with the now familiar E-O marking. The mystery of how the truck was able to intercept them at that exact moment was only too clear; but too late. Tobari and his accomplices had long disappeared.

Dismounting, and with a sense of hopelessness, Saul went to the car where Yerushalmi was on the radio, completing a description of the target car, its license plates and the present description of Tobari. At that moment, a police car with two patrolmen came onto the scene, then a second. The first team took over the duty of traffic control while the second awaited Saul's orders. He spoke to Shaked, who handcuffed the truck driver, placed him in one of the police cars and started it off to SO Branch headquarters. Moshe Tal arrived now and after a few moments of instructions to the police, Saul and the other agents departed.

It was not, Saul remarked in a way that hardly reflected his keen disappointment with bitter self-reproach and anger, a profitable evening.

On arrival at 17 Rehov Ben Gurion, the night duty officer handed Saul a message, marked *Urgent*, that had been received earlier in the day from Judah Rosental:

> *Phone me at once on arrival,*
> *no matter the hour, day or night.*

Shaked and Yerushalmi were waiting for him in his outer office. "Where is our man?" he asked.

"Waiting in an interrogation room under guard. Asad and a security guard are with him."

"We'll see him together. What do you have on him so far?"

"His name, Badar al-Hadad, his address. Married. Two sons and a daughter. He admits ownership of the truck and a small moving and hauling business, an independent operator. I am having the information run through Records and Identification."

"Good. Wait below for me while I make a call to Tel Aviv."

Saul put the call through to Judah Rosental's home and without delay, brought him up to date on his sudden trip to Tripoli and return to Jerusalem, leaving nothing out. Rosental's short, terse questions and responses to Saul's answers were a clear indication that he was, if not extremely displeased, most unhappy.

He said finally, "We have wasted a lot of time, Saul, valuable time, manpower and money. We have had an assassination attempt, a major street shootout, and a lot of running around in circles. The sum total is that we have now lost our prime lead to Tobari, Aarons, and Tobari himself."

"Judah—" Saul began, but the general would not allow himself to be interrupted.

"Tomorrow morning, I must stand before General Bartok and with little or no ammunition, try to justify the existence of the Special Operations Branch and convince him that it should be allowed to continue on, while the defense minister is urging the prime minister to turn the operation over to him."

"Judah, if you are asking for my resignation, you will have it on your desk before you meet with—"

"All I am asking for, Saul, are the answers to the questions Bartok will throw at me, the answers he will need for the questions Goren and the prime minister will be asking *him*. So far, we have been able to suppress the news of Mordecai Aarons' absence. The story is that he and his wife are away on a combined trip and holiday abroad. How long that will hold up, I can't say."

"What do you want me to do, Judah? I am not overly proud of our recent performances, but I can't control certain circumstances. Aarons should have been arrested at once and held in strictest secrecy, but I was put off because of the embarrassment that would have caused to . . . in higher circles; a political decision in which I had nothing to say. I must assume full blame for the loss of Aarons. Tobari's escape was unfortunate and I also would assume that responsibility for not having anticipated he would be clever enough to outguess us."

There was a lengthy pause, then Rosental said, "What is your next move, if I may ask?"

"As I sit here talking to you, I don't know. I haven't had time to consider that question or alternatives. For the moment, we have the driver of the interception truck in our interrogation room and I am preparing to question him. Other than that, all I can add is, when I am finished with him, successful or not, I will gather my key people together and discuss, analyze the situation and try to come up with some suitable action."

"I hope you will have better success than when your people

allowed Aarons to discover he was under surveillance. Inexcusable."

Saul felt a tug of guilt over having disobeyed Judah's positive order, but could not bring himself to admit his deviation at this moment. When he made no further comment, Judah said, "Saul, I want you to know I understand the difficulties under which you have been laboring and am in complete sympathy with that. You must also understand that any decisions that will be made will be those from a higher authority—"

"Judah, I understand what you are saying, but you are still talking about the political effect this will have if it becomes public knowledge and the government is attacked by the opposition party as well as the press and the man in the street. Again, I can't let myself become involved in those aspects of this matter. I am interested only in practical solutions. The longer you keep me on the phone, the less time I have to devote myself to that phase."

"You have made your position clear, Colonel," Rosental said with icy formality. "*Shalom.*"

The line went dead. For a moment or two, Saul sat and stared at the receiver, then slowly cradled it.

Below, Shaked and Yerushalmi waited in the corridor that led to the cells and interrogation room, where Asad Hasbani stood with a security guard. The guard opened the steel door and Saul entered, Dov and Uri behind him. The room was small, dank and musty with disuse, beads of moisture on the green walls. The truck driver, Badar al-Hadad, sat in a wooden chair on the far side of the table. Shaked placed a tape recorder on the table. Saul signaled him and Yerushalmi to take the two chair opposite the prisoner while he stood and observed.

In better light, the prisoner was a robust, well-built male in his middle forties, well-muscled and with rugged features, piercing black eyes over a hawklike nose, shaggy eyebrows, firm jaw and jutting chin. Under his jacket, the shirt was damp with perspiration, hands clenched together on the table. Shaked activated the tape recorder and began the questioning: name, age, address, marital status, ownership of the truck, his business; all asked easily, answered in the same manner, his eyes roving from Saul to Uri to Dov, then to the machine recording his voice.

Shaked looked up at Saul, who nodded, a silent request for him to continue. Where, Dov asked, did he obtain the walkie-talkie unit found beneath the seat of his truck?

AL-HADAD: I bought it some months ago.
SHAKED: From whom did you buy it?

AL-HADAD: A man who deals in such things.

SHAKED: What man? Give me a name.

AL-HADAD: (a shrug) A man. I don't know his name. He deals from the street.

SHAKED: Stolen goods?

AL-HADAD: Perhaps. Radios, watches, rings—

SHAKED: Guns?

AL-HADAD: I think yes, if one has the price. Cigarettes—

LAHAV: You know that this talking instrument is one of a pair and is useless without the other. Where is the second instrument that matches this one?

AL-HADAD: I don't know. It was stolen from my house a week ago. I bought the pair so that my wife could use it to reach me when I was out on a hauling or moving job.

LAHAV: Did you report the theft to the police?

AHADAD: No.

LAHAF: Why not?

AL-HADAD: Because then they would arrest me as a receiver of stolen goods.

There was a knock on the door. Yerushalmi leaned back and opened it. Asad came in and handed Saul two sheets of paper, which he examined before resuming the questioning.

LAHAV: The furniture you were delivering. To whom did you make the delivery?

AL-HADAD: To a house a half mile from where the accident occurred.

LAHAV: The name of the people and the address of the house?

AL-HADAD: (another shrug) This I do not know. It was a house like many houses there. No name was given to me.

SHAKED: Then how were you able to deliver the goods there without a name or address?

AL-HADAD: It was like this. A man came to my house, a stranger to me. He engaged me to haul the furniture which he had stored in a garage. We loaded the goods on my truck and he rode with me so he could direct me to the house. It was dark when we got there and unloaded it. He paid me and I left.

LAHAV: You are lying, al-Hadad. There was no man, no furniture, no house.

AL-HADAD: I have told you the truth. You are the police. I do not expect you to believe me.

LAHAV: Could you find the house again?

AL-HADAD: I don't think so. As I said, it was dark and the house was like many others—
LAHAV: Have you been arrested before?
AL-HADAD: (hesitating) Yes.
LAHAV: How many times?
AL-HADAD: (a shrug, remaining silent).

Saul held up the two sheets of paper, then handed them to Shaked and Yerushalmi, who studied them. Badar al-Hadad's eyes squinted, watching the three men closely through narrowed lids. Perspiration had begun beading along his forehead and he wiped his nose with the flat of one hand and pulled his shirt away from his body. Shaked handed the two sheets back to Saul.

LAHAV: Your record, Badar al-Hadad, is not a very clean one. You have been convicted seven times for various crimes. Dealing in stolen merchandise, once for transporting a stolen automobile across the border in Jordan, twice for terrorist activities and released for lack of evidence. You have spent a total of six and one half years in jails and prison. Does that refresh your memory?
AL-HADAD: (a long pause) That I will not deny. But since my last arrest, four years ago, I have not been arrested. Your record will show that.
LAHAV: Only because you have become more practiced and careful.
AL-HADAD: I can see it is useless for me to convince you. I will answer no more questions; do with me what you will.
LAHAV: My friend, you will answer our questions or you will spend much of your life in a cell, all alone and in darkness, in your own filth and sweat until you are willing to talk.
AL-HADAD: You cannot frighten me. I am an Israeli citizen. My lawyer will prepare papers—
LAHAV: And how do you suppose your lawyer will know that you have been arrested, that we are holding you?
AL-HADAD: He will know. He will know.
LAHAV: Only from your friends in the car we were following when you were told on this instrument to block us at that crossroad.

Al-Hadad's mouth clamped tightly into a thin, grim line. "Be sensible, al-Hadad," Saul said. "Tell me who they were and where we can reach them."

But al-Hadad's firm chin thrust forward and Saul knew he would get nothing more at this time. To Shaked and Yerushalmi, "Put him in solitary confinement. Give him no more than is necessary to keep him alive. Remove anything from his person that he might use to take his own life. Have the guards view him through the peephole every five minutes, using a flashlight.

"They are not to speak to him unless he informs them that he is ready and willing to talk to me. Feed him twice a day, always the same food without a change in variety. There is to be no record made of his presence here. Any inquiries made on us by any outside source will be answered with one sentence: 'We have no knowledge of anyone by that name or description.' When he is ready to talk, I am to be informed."

The only reaction from al-Hadad as he heard Saul's pronouncement was a tighter clenching of his hands and closed eyes.

In his office fifteen minutes later, Shaked, Golan, Yerushalmi and Navot listened while Saul related his conversation with Judah Rosental earlier. The four agents listened in embarrassed silence as Saul moved away from his desk and began to pace in front of it, concluding by lighting a cigarette and returning to the chair behind his desk. No one spoke, having nothing to offer.

"All right, you've just heard enough to know that the general, and those others sitting above him, will not hold us in high regard when this latest fiasco is made known to them. Aarons has fled and could be anywhere. Tobari eluded us tonight, but we know that at this moment, he is still in Israel. The police, border patrol, Ground, Air and Coastal Commands have been alerted.

"With that knowledge, our secret is no longer a secret. What we do know is that this thing, whatever it is, is ready to come to a head. Tobari's presence in Israel insures that it can't be otherwise. Those are the obvious indications, but we haven't been able to pin one damned thing down. I think you will all agree with me that if we don't come up with some visible result, and very soon, we won't be given other opportunities to exhibit our clumsiness.

"Understand me, I am not throwing the blame on any of you without taking the largest share for myself, which is of little consolation to any of us."

Shimon Navot moved about in his chair with a strained expression. "You have something you wish to say, Shimon?" Saul asked.

"Yes. We still are on Tahia Soulad and she is our last possible link to the UPFP, remote as it may be, and with the possible exception of our reluctant truck driver downstairs. As long as we keep him locked up, however, Tahia is our only known avenue to Tobari, small as it is."

Uri Yerushalmi picked up on that. "Correct, in which case we should be able to come up with some means to force a move from her, one way or another."

"And soon," Dov Shaked added.

"Who is sitting on her?" Saul said.

Shimon Navot supplied that answer. "Zeitel and Darvit. They are due off at midnight," checking his watch, "in about fifteen minutes. Simon Zadok and Zvi Leven are due to relieve them until eight A.M."

Saul's mind began racing. "There's time," he said finally. "It looks as though we have little choice, so we'll go with Shimon's suggestion, but it will have to be tonight. Now. Shimon, get Zeitel and Darvit on the radio. When Zadok and Leven relieve them, they are to remain on duty. I want two men on the front and two to cover the side and rear of Club Morocco. When her show comes off, I want to know it. Also, the moment she leaves the club to go home. When she does, they are to notify us at once."

"Where?" Navot asked.

"In our cars, waiting at the front and rear of her apartment, but out of her sight at all times. Let's get our cars and move out."

Shortly after midnight, the five men arrived at number 217 Kiryat Cholmo. Saul, with Shaked and Yerushalmi, parked half a block away from the front entrance, yet able to keep it in view. Navot and Golan were parked facing in the opposite direction, the former remaining in the car while the latter, carrying a w-t unit, walked around to the alley and watched the rear from a position between two houses. Once there, Golan reported his position to Havot and Saul by w-t.

"All right," Saul replied. "Hold where you are. We're going in."

Havot and Golan acknowledged.

Saul, Shaked and Yerushalmi crossed the street and entered number 217. On the second floor, they paused at Tahia's door. Dov removed his strip of plastic and within a matter of seconds had the door open. The three men went inside and closed the door. Saul turned on a table lamp and they surveyed the living room, standing in the center; posters of Tahia as Gabriela; framed photographs of herself in costume on two of the walls, all of Tahia and alone. In the bedroom, which they next examined, dresses, costumes, stockings and undergarments were thrown carelessly on the bed, a chair, draped on the dresser. In the bathroom, other undergarments and stockings hung from a stretched cord. In the small kitchen, dishes from an earlier meal were stacked in a rack on the sink ledge.

Back in the living room, Yerushalmi commented, "She lives well, our Tahia, however messy."

Saul said, "Let's get on with it."

"Are we looking for something special, Saul?" Shaked asked.

"Nothing. Just wreck it."

Wreck it they did, and thoroughly. Not a picture, chair, sofa, table or other piece was left untouched in any room. After twenty minutes, Saul said, "That's good enough. Let's go down to the car and wait."

At the UPFP farm in Ein Fara, his Rome disguise removed, now in a smartly tailored safari suit and polished black boots, Hatif Tobari sat behind the desk in the office and held a private conference with Amon Sadani, still wearing his wig and beard, fingers drumming nervously on the arms of his chair. Morosely, he spoke in a low voice, giving detail upon detail of his discovery that he was being followed, his confrontation with Lahav, the decision to flee to the farm for safety. Hatif listened without interruption, then said, "You were right, Amon, to get out when you did, bringing Suzi with you. Neither of you could have done anything else and nothing will be lost by it. Nothing."

Sadani brightened a little, preparing to offer a suggestion that had been long in his mind, but Tobari said briskly, "We have much to do. Will you call Razak and Tabet in? We will get a few things further clarified in my mind."

Sadani went to the door and called to the two men who were seated outside waiting for the summons. They came in and took the two chairs facing the desk. Tobari greeted them with a warm smile, returning to his initial stimulated mood on successfully eluding whomever it was who had tailed him from the airport, readily accepting Sadani's suggestion that it had been members of the SO Branch. The Egyptian looked from Massif Razak to Tabet and chose to speak first to Tabet, asking for a detailed account of the Bashra-bound unit from the time they left Da'ara until they were ready to cross the Israeli border at Ein Yahav.

"Then there were no problems?" Tobari asked when Tabet concluded.

"None, sir. I left the camp at once, but waited at a distance from which I could not be observed to see how Hourani would handle the situation. I waited until they were ready to move out, then followed and watched them make the crossing safely. I then crossed alone and walked north above the village to where, by prearrangement, I was picked up by our car and returned here."

"Excellent," Tobari commended. "And tonight, your man did a very good job of intercepting the car that was following us."

"He is a professional, sir, and was well paid," Tabet said.

"He showed it. I am certain they will have arrested him and he is now undergoing questioning." It was a statement, yet there was a question mark hanging on the last word.

"No matter how much they question him," Tabet responded quickly, "he can tell them no more than the cover story I rehearsed him in. He is not a regular member. I have used him before on small things."

"Very good. The most they can charge him with is a traffic matter, a fine to pay, perhaps the damage to their car. See that money reaches him to pay what is required."

"That was promised him. I will take care of it, sir."

Tobari then turned to Razak, who rose and went behind the desk, standing at Tobari's side, looking down on the map spread out there before them, showing identical markings to those on the smaller map in Ahmed Hourani's possession. "What," Tobari asked, "is the exact position of our combat unit and the latest word from Masri in Bashra?"

"The communications link we have established with our man in Ein Avdat is working well. Hourani has reported to him by hand radio that as of last night, they are here," indicating the position on the map with his index finger, "a few kilometers south of Kuntilla, which places them within ninety kilometers of Bashra. From that point, according to the movement schedule, they should be in position at Wadi Talal, six kilometers north of the restricted zone surrounding the oil field, in three more nights.

"The location is perfect for their purpose. A high rise of rocks to the south, which will keep them hidden from view of any patrols in and around Bashra. To the north, another rise or rock formation with enough cover for them during the day. To the east and west, the stretch is open. There is water nearby, some grazing for the animals in the foothills. At night, they can sleep in the open and there are caves enough for all by day if necessary. Thus far, they have kept their movement on schedule."

"And at Bashra?"

"Zuheir Masri spoke with our man in Ein Avdat on his last trip there. The explosives have been well placed in the producing wells now operating, and those still being drilled. Also, in every piece of vital operating equipment, sections of the pipeline now under construction, garages, generators, storage tanks and the refinery framework. Others have been secreted inside the administration and engineering headquarters, the workmen's barracks, dining halls, kitchens, even the latrines. Two days from now, the actuators, which have already been inserted in the plastic charges, will be activated.''

"Then everything is set for the final action?''

Tabet spoke up. ''I would say yes, sir. By the time the unit makes its final move, Masri's people will be well out of the area, perhaps six hours before detonation; at which time, the combat unit will move in and finish off those who still remain alive, human or animal. Allah willing.''

"Excellent, excellent,'' Tobari said, beaming.

Sadani said, ''It is best not to delay, imperative to move as quickly as possible. Strike fast and get out.''

"Easy, easy,'' Tobari cautioned. "There is the schedule to maintain.''

"Yes, naturally,'' Sadani said, then, "In my situation, I am of no further use here—''

Tobari eyed him coolly. "Nonsense. Of course you are, Amon. I need you to plan our route and timing so that the schedule to Bashra—''

"I thought it would be best if Salim—''

"No. I want you with me at Bashra to witness this victory of the few over the many so both of us can vividly report its effects to our Libyan and Iraqi friends. When this is over, you and your charming Suzi will return to Iraq with me, where you will be of tremendous assistance to me in planning the political and financial future of our new nation. You are necessary to me here.''

Razak said, ''Still, we must exercise the greatest care. After tonight, Lahav's people will be moving in all directions—''

Tobari cut him off sharply. "Only, my dear Razak, because they do not know the one true direction in which to look or move. Let them run in circles wherever they will. Let them suspect whomever they wish. It is their Jewish paranoia, their nature. But in four days, we will give them good reason to suspect much more, after it is too late.''

"If the goal is set for then,'' Sadani said, "we should be moving out very soon. Even with a car, we shall be proceeding slowly on secondary roads and trails, keeping off the main highways to avoid sudden checkpoints and roadblocks.''

"Then let us get on with it, Razak, a good car. Have it checked carefully, petrol, oil, water, good tires, radio. Also, some food and water. We will leave in two hours.''

Razak said, "It will be ready. There is still another matter about which you should know."

"What matter?"

"The Soulad woman." He turned to Tabet. "Salim?"

"It is already arranged for three thirty in the morning," Tabet said. "I will have her here by no later than four thirty."

Tobari said, "Then if there is nothing else to discuss, Amon and I will eat now and prepare to leave. Massif, I will give you a list of the weapons we will want to take with us."

13

In the Club Morocco the last show was coming to its close. Yossi Zeitel waited until Gabriella had taken her final bow, then went out to the car where his partner, Eliahu Darvit waited. On his w-t, Zeitel contacted Simon Zadok and Zvi Leven, who were in position just beyond the side and rear doors.

"She came off earlier than usual," he reported. "It will take her half an hour to change for the street. By that time the club will be ready to close. Let's keep a sharp eye out for her. The first one who sees her will notify the others. Acknowledge."

Zadok and Leven acknowledged.

When she entered her dressing room, the drab-looking woman in dark robe and headdress who had been waiting since the last show began stood up and said briskly, "Lock the door."

"You are?"

"Salim sent me. Lock the door."

Tahia did so. "Quickly," the woman said. "This must be done before the club empties out so that you won't leave alone. Remove your costume and makeup."

"Don't worry," Tahia said. "The customers will be drinking for at least another hour." While she undressed, the woman took a bottle from her large straw bag and uncorked it. When Tahia was down to panties and bra, the makeup creamed off, the woman poured a dark liquid from the bottle into the palm of her left hand and began to apply it to Tahia's forehead, face and neck.

"This will come off?" Tahia asked apprehensively.

"It will wear off in a few days. It will not destroy your beauty, only darken your complexion." She daubed the liquid on Tahia's shoulders, arms and hands. This operation concluded, she removed a dark-colored dress of coarse material. "Put this on. It is not the

339

style of a dancer, but it will hide your figure.'' The dress was a loose affair that fell below Tahia's knees, her face reflecting a natural distaste for the peasant attire.

"Hurry,'' the woman urged. The dress in place, she now removed her own dark robe and headdress and held it while Tahia got into it, her face half hidden by the hood. "Keep your eyes on the ground,'' the woman cautioned. "Keep your knees bent as you walk. It will not be for long and it will change your height. Walk slowly until you are safely away from here. Carry the straw bag the way a poor woman does, close to her side so that street thieves cannot tear it from her hand. There.''

The woman, minus the ugly robe and headdress, had turned into a more attractive, younger matron in a gray dress with white collar and cuffs, hair parted in the center and drawn back into a bun at the back of her head.

"Go out now and keep to the left wall where the room is darkest. Watch for a large group to leave, then go outside together with them. Keep your head down and stay close to the wall. With all the people moving around outside, no one will pay attention to an old woman.

"This part now is important, so listen carefully. You will go to the Ras el Amud Mosque on Jericho Road. You know it?''

Tahia nodded. "You must be at the main entrance no later than three thirty. Wait inside the portals, in the shadows. At exactly that time, Salim will arrive in a car and take you to the farm. You understand?''

"Yes. Three thirty o'clock at the Ras el Amud Mosque.''

"Then go with Allah's hand on your shoulder.''

"And you?''

The woman smiled. "A friend waits for me at a table outside. I will leave with him. Be careful. Other lives depend on how well you do this.'' The woman unlocked the door and left.

A few minutes later, Tahia turned off the light in her dressing room and went down the hallway and into the main room. Final drinks were being served, checks paid, people moving toward the front doors to leave. Tahia obeyed orders, hugging the left wall, feeling strange in the unaccustomed attire that scratched her body, but was gratified that no one seemed to notice her.

At the front door, she waited until a group of eight pushed outside. She fell in with them and was sandwiched by another group following on her heels. Outside, she turned to her right, head down, body hunched slightly forward, walking at a normal pace, jostled by others seemingly more intent on reaching their cars that were parked along the curb.

She was two blocks from the club and four from her apartment when she realized it was far too early to go directly to the Ras el Amud Mosque. It also occurred to her that if she was to be taken to the farm for reasons of safety, or security of the UPFP people, it was most likely she would not be returning to Number 217. The thought of losing the costumes and clothing which she could not carry with her, the cherished photographs and posters, the money and jewelry—

At least, she concluded, she could take the money and some of the better pieces of jewelry with her, the few good pieces given to her by admirers in the past; rings, chains, necklaces; perhaps even her one best street costume would easily fit into the large straw bag. How stupid to allow these to fall into strange, uncaring hands.

The street here was empty except for the parked cars, most of them in front of houses and apartments, their windows dark at this late hour. She picked up the pace, still keeping her eyes on the pavement ahead of her.

In the car facing the direction from which Tahia was approaching, Dov Shaked stirred on the front seat, head raised. "Someone coming," he said to Saul, who was seated in the rear compartment.

"The girl?" Saul asked.

"I can't make her out too clearly . . . no, I don't think so. An old woman."

Uri Yerushalmi, sitting beside Shaked, craned his head for a better look. "What the hell is an old woman doing out this time of night?" he muttered.

"Coming from an assignation with a lover, what else?" Dov replied.

"Quiet," Saul cautioned. "Let's not have her looking over here."

They sank back in their respective seats and waited, three pairs of eyes on the only thing moving on the pavement or street. Then, from the opposite direction, a car turned into Kiryat Cholmo and raced by, its headlights illuminating the street, momentarily blocking their view of the old woman. Like a magnet, their eyes followed the car, which made a right turn at the next corner. When they turned back, the woman had disappeared. That quickly.

"Where?"

It was the question on the tip of three tongues. All three looked to the left and right, but the woman was nowhere in sight. Into which building had she turned?

Shaked opened his door and stepped out into the street for a better look; to his left, then right, then up.

He got back into the car and said, "It was her. It had to be her. She was almost opposite Number 217 when the car went by."

"If it was," Saul said, "her lights will come on."

At that moment, a dull glow came on behind the two curtained windows in Tahia Soulad's apartment.

When she unlocked the door, her hand automatically reached for the light switch. The lights came on, she stepped inside and stopped in her tracks with a horrified gasp, "Oh, God, *no!*" stunned by the sight of her vandalized apartment.

Chairs overturned, tables lying on their sides, sofa cushions and pillows strewn about, the sofa pulled away from the wall. Two lamps lay on the floor, drawers pulled out, their contents heaped in the center of the room. Posters and framed photographs removed from the walls lay scattered about on the floor.

Like a somnambulist, she walked to the bedroom. The mattress and covers had been pulled from the bed, two pillows slashed open, clothes from her closet scattered over the debris of her dresser drawers. Costumes, trinkets, underwear, stockings and robes had been thrown about as though caught up in a windstorm.

"Mother of God!" Terror-stricken, weeping, Tahia dropped the straw bag and ran from the apartment, leaving the lights on, the door open.

Waiting below in the car, Saul said to Dov, "Radio our four alert watchdogs at the Club Morocco. Tell them their bird has flown her cage. Have them drive this way, but make no contact until we signal them." To Yerushalmi, "Get on your w-t to Shimon and Yoram, Uri. Tell them we should be moving out in a minute or two, to follow our lead and remain in touch at all times."

And, less than three minutes later, Saul had the w-t in his hand. "All units. We have flushed our bird. She has just exited the building and is turning to her left in the direction of the club. Let us see where she leads us. Dov will follow on foot. Keep your cars well behind mine, no lights. Slow and easy. I will keep you informed of her position."

Tahia had turned east, walking hurriedly. A very disturbed scarecrow, the black robe flapping loosely behind her. In her anxiety, she stumbled twice, regaining her footing and continued on.

On the opposite side of the street, clutching a w-t unit, Dov Shaked kept close to the building line and well in the shadows, following at a distance of half a block. And, as Tahia reached the third street and turned off Kiryat Cholmo into E-Zahara, the three cars tailed Saul's at a slow, walking pace. On foot, Shaked made the turn and called in. "I have her in sight. She is heading toward Jericho Road."

The cars made the turn in single file and now Dov was out of their sight, but a minute later, he came on again. "She has turned east into Jericho Road, walking faster now, still in sight. Hold on E-Zahara. Jericho is empty and you will be easily spotted."

Approaching the corner of E-Zahara and Jericho Road, Saul braked to a stop. The three cars behind did likewise, waiting for the next relay from Shaked. It came fifteen minutes later. "She has reached the entrance of the Ras el Amud Mosque and is standing behind the left pillar, probably waiting to meet someone."

"Everybody," Saul ordered on his w-t, "hold where you are, don't move, show no lights, not even a cigarette tip."

Then, at exactly three thirty, some twenty five minutes later Dov's voice reached them. "A car, moving slowly west on Jericho. A small black sedan. Slowing at the mosque. Making a U-turn. Stopping." His voice rose into a higher pitch now. "The woman is running toward the car, the door is opened from the inside, she is in. *Car moving*. East on Jericho Road. Picking up speed—"

Saul's voice now overrode Dov's. "All units, move out behind me. No lights. I'll pick Shaked up. Stand by for further instructions."

As Saul drew up to where Shaked stood at the curb, Yerushalmi reached back and opened the rear door. Dov leaped inside. Saul, driving with one hand on the wheel, was on the w-t again. "Lahav to all units. This car is now Commander One. Take these designations. Navot-Golan, Number Two. Zeitel-Darvit, Number Three. Zadok-Leven, Number Four. Acknowledge."

Each car acknowledged.

"Car Two, take the street on your right. Car Three, take the street on your left. Parallel the suspect vehicle and call out each cross street as you pass it. I will let you know when to pull ahead or drop back. Car Four, I have the suspect vehicle's tail lights in sight. Stay behind me at a distance of half a street in case I am forced to turn off, then take my position. All units acknowledge when you are in position."

Thus, they continued until they reached the main highway leading out of Jerusalem toward Ramallah; and now began to run into a little more traffic moving in both directions; trucks moving southward, laden with produce for early morning delivery to markets and shops, cars heading north. Running out of parallel roads, Saul ordered Cars Two and Three to fall in behind Car Four, all with headlights on.

The suspect car was moving at a normal speed now and Saul

moved up a little closer, then ordered the Car Four to pass him, overtake and pass the small sedan. When Navot complied and was about sixty yards ahead of the target car, Saul instructed him to keep that distance and for Golan to watch for any turnoff it might make behind them.

In that order, the caravan approached Shu'afat, where the sedan braked and turned off to the right. At once, Golan called in. "Commander One, we have lost suspect's lights."

"We have him," Saul replied. "He has turned off into the Shu'afat road. Return and fall in line."

Beside him, Dov said, "We've got him, Saul. Anata is next, then one crossroad between Anata and Ein Fara, where this road ends."

"Ein Fara," Saul mused. "There's nothing there. A small village."

"If he doesn't take one of the crossroads, then there must be something at Ein Fara. There's nothing else around," Yerushalmi offered.

"Let's cut our lights and move up. I can barely make out his taillights." Saul did so, handing the w-t unit to Dov, who passed the order on to the three tailing cars.

They moved through the sleeping village of Anata, approached the crossroad that led to Hizma on the left, to Ma'ale Adumin on the right; but the sedan continued on eastward. Shaked said, "So it will be Ein Fara. There is nothing else in between that I can remember."

The small sedan slowed as it came into the village of Ein Fara, then picked up speed as it crossed the center of town on its single main thoroughfare. Saul braked to a stop and watched as the target car reached the far edge of the village and made a slight turn toward the right. His rear lights disappeared. Saul motioned to Yerushalmi to take the wheel while he ran to the other side and got in beside him. "Move up slowly," he ordered. "He can't have gone too far on this road. There should be a dead end up ahead."

Shaked said, "The old Sa'idi farm, Saul. This road runs into it and ends there. We used to go there to the farm many years ago to buy fruits, vegetables and cheeses. That's all there is there."

Yerushalmi took the right turn, a mere bend in the road. The target car was nowhere in sight. He continued on for about three kilometers until they reached a low stone fence, no more than three feet high, and continued along the rutted dirt road slowly until they came to two six-foot-high pillars of stone, which marked the entrance to the Sa'idi estate. There was no gate.

"Go past it and pull up. Now cut your motor." Saul spoke into the w-t and ordered the other three cars to advance to their position.

When they were together, Saul gathered the eight agents around him. Kneeling in a tight circle, he said, "Dov, you know this place. Tell us about it."

"It was years ago when I was last here as a child with my father, but I will try to do my best. The estate is large. About two hundred yards from here, I would guess, is the main house. I was never inside it. Behind it are the service and utility buildings. Beyond that, maybe another two hundred yards, are the packing sheds and behind those are the farm workers' quarters. That was where we would go to do our buying. That's all I can remember, except for the large fields around it, the orchards. The main house is of stone, two stories, and the entrance will face us if we go in through the gate and follow the road. There are read doors that face the utility buildings."

"All right, Dov, you are elected," Saul said. "I will need a volunteer to go in with Dov and quietly look around that house, see if there is someone on guard. If there is one, take him out, but quietly. No shooting. If there are more than one, do nothing. Return here and report. Who wants it?"

All eyes were on Shaked, the only man present who had ever been inside the grounds, however many years had passed since. Dov said, "It looks like I've been elected by a unanimous, silent vote. Who will come with me?"

Yoram Golan said, "I'll keep you company."

Saul nodded. "All right. No guns unless absolutely necessary. We don't want a new war breaking out."

"I've got a combat knife in my trunk," Golan said.

"Get it. Dov, gets yours, too. And take a w-t unit with you. Let me know when it is clear to move in."

Shaked leading, the two men climbed over the three-foot stone fence rather than go through the entrance gate. Moving in a crouch toward the house, they were lost in the darkness within seconds.

"The rest of you," Saul ordered. "Get your Uzis out of your trunks. Also, helmets and flak jackets, hand grenades. Quickly, quietly, no talking, no smoking."

In teams, Zeitel and Darvit, Zadok and Leven, Navot, Yerushalmi and Saul went to their respective cars and got out the necessary gear, along with extra clips for their Uzis. In addition, Saul got out his battery-powered bullhorn and ordered Uri Yerushalmi to carry helmets, jackets and heavier weapons for Shaked and Golan. Fully equipped, they sat on the ground, backs against the stone fence, and waited.

*   *   *

Inside the grounds, Shaked and Golan avoided the dirt road and moved across stubbled growth, through a grove of trees, then broke out into the open again. There, some forty or fifty yards ahead, stood the stone house, like a white ghost. No lights showed through the windows on either of the two floors. Nothing moved. They heard only the rustle of the light, cool wind that soughed through the trees behind them.

Shaked touched Golan's arm and motioned him to the right, which would take them toward the rear of the house, yet providing some small cover from the low-growing shrubbery there. Crouching, they circled around, stopping every few feet to make brief observations. Within twenty yards of the rear right side of the house, Shaked halted, knelt down and felt the ground with his hand and came up with a stone about the size of a child's toy ball. Golan crouched down beside him as he rose up and threw the stone so that it struck the front of a wooden shed directly behind the house. Shaked dropped down beside Golan and waited.

A few moments later, they heard movement along the path that separated the house from the utility buildings, halting steps that crunched gravel, probing. Then they saw a shadowy figure slowly come into view and look around cautiously, the shape of a machine pistol clear in his hands. Golan had his revolver out, whispering a silent curse under his breath, hoping it would not be necessary to fire the weapon and alert everyone inside the house. It was reasonable to assume, with a night sentry on duty, that he was protecting others inside. Shaked held his combat knife in his right hand, waiting for the sentry's next move.

Then they heard him take a few steps closer to the row of bushes and stop again; so close they could almost hear him breathing. And in fact, did hear him expel a deep breath when the heel of one of his shoes grated as he began to turn to return in the direction of the house.

In that split second, Shaked rose up and leaped over the low shrubs. The startled sentry turned, but was too late to bring his machine pistol up and into play. Shaked's knife entered his left chest with all the force he could put into a single thrust. The machine pistol dropped from his hands and dangled by its sling as the man died with one low, agonizing gasp. Shaked caught him and lowered his body to the ground while Golan removed the machine pistol and stood up, looking around for another possible guard. Shaked waited beside the dead man while Golan tested the rear of the house; there were no others. He returned and helped Shaked drag the body to the line of bushes, lifted him across, then carried him into the grove of trees.

They returned quickly to their previous position and together made a careful circle of the house, then of the utility sheds and service buildings behind it; and came upon the small black sedan they recognized as the one they had been tailing. Shaked placed one hand on its hood and felt its warmth. Moving behind the sheds, Shaked spoke into his w-t unit. "Commander One."

"Here. What do you have?"

"One sentry, taken out. We have a machine pistol. The car we were following is in one of the sheds behind the house. All dark. We can hear nothing from the inside."

"We're on our way in. Where can we meet?"

"A large grove of trees, about fifty yards from the house, your side."

"We will meet you there."

Within five minutes, they had joined up. Shaked and Golan got into the helmets and flak jackets Yerushalmi had brought along, slung their Uzis over their shoulders and hung three grenades on the jacket hooks. Saul surveyed the building, then issued his orders quickly and incisively.

"Dov, Yoram, take the rear of the house. Yossi, the left side, Eliahu the right. Uri, Shimon, Zvi, Simon and I will approach the house from the front. I will use the bullhorn to try to bring them out. If anyone tries to break out through the back or sides, you know what to do. Otherwise, wait for the sound of any firing from the front, then take independent action.

"Keep this firmly in mind. We can't allow anyone to escape, but we need prisoners to interrogate rather than dead bodies to count. We don't want another Takieh Road incident. Only, don't get careless. I don't like making hospital visits or going to funerals. Let's move out now and report when you are in position."

They moved out quietly. Ten minutes later, standing about forty yards from the front entrance, Saul received the last acknowledgement. Everyone was in position. He activated the bullhorn and raised it to his mouth.

"Inside the house, attention! This is the police! You are surrounded! Come out unarmed, your hands over your heads! Attention! Repeating—"

Inside, Razak was listening to a tense Tahia Soulad, whose hand trembled as she smoked nervously while describing the vandalism that had occurred in her apartment. Frowning with annoyance, Razak said, "It could have been a burglary, couldn't it?"

"But . . . but they took nothing! Nothing! They searched every

room, every closet, everywhere. They were looking for evidence. I
know it! They had been following me—''

Razak turned to Tabet. ''And how do you know you weren't
followed as well?''

Calmly, Tabet reassured Razak that the plan had worked; that he
had watched as Tahia left the club in disguise, with no one following
her. The four agents on that assignment had remained in position at
all times. Later, he had spoken to the woman who had helped Tahia
with her disguise. He recounted the exact steps he had taken to spirit
her away, having first made certain she was alone. The Syrian's
head turned from one to the other as Tabet spoke, then stood up.

At that moment, Saul's strident voice penetrated the thoughts of
all three, as well as the ears of everyone else in the house. Tabet
leaped to his feet, alarm overtaking his earlier confidence. Tahia
remained frozen in her chair, hands gripping its arms tightly, a low
wail of fright rising from her throat. From overhead they heard the
sudden rush of footsteps and raised voices calling out. Tazak turned
on Tabet and shouted angrily, ''So you were not followed, you
damned incompetent fool!''

The double doors to the office were flung open and several men
stood there, eyes desperate in appeal as they confronted Tazak,
awaiting orders. Over their heads, he could see those of more men
and women, perhaps a dozen or more. And pushing through the
crowd at the door, Suzi Sadani.

''Why are you standing there, doing nothing?'' she demanded
imperiously. ''Or do you intend to open the front doors and invite
the Jews inside?''

At that moment, Razak could have cheerfully shot the woman for
her bold insolence, yet was moved from momentary indecision into
action. Ignoring her, he shouted, ''Abdul! Karim! Get the men and
women below! Arm everyone, then return here. Quickly!'' He
turned back to Tahia. ''You. Go below with the others. Arm
yourself.'' And to Tabet, ''You see that everyone is armed. When
they are, take the women and half the men above. The other half will
remain on this floor at the windows. Turn off all lights before any
windows or shutters are opened. Start firing at the first target that
shows itself. When everything is set upstairs, I want you to return
here to me.''

Tabet took Tahia's trembling arm and led her from the room.
Razak removed a submachine gun and a dozen extra clips of
ammunition from a closet, then began extinguishing the lights.
When the room was in total darkness, he parted the heavy black
curtains at the front windows, opened one and pushed the shutters
aside with the muzzle of his weapon. Outside in the moonless night,

he could see nothing but the darker outline of trees against the barely lighter sky.

Tabet, he thought bitterly. After all these years, to be saddled with an inexperienced, inept youth, Falcon's favorite, who had now singlehandedly turned their major haven of safety into a death trap; and if it came to that, Razak knew, he would personally see that Salim Tabet paid the price of his stupidity.

*   *   *

Outside, Saul had repeated the surrender order. Behind him, standing ten yards apart in a single row, Shimon Navot and Uri Yerushalmi to his left, Zvi Leven and Simon Zadok on his right, the five men braced for whatever might come—attack or, hopefully, surrender. From the house came no indication that the order had been heard.

Then Saul raised the bullhorn again. "Inside the house, attention! This order will not be repeated! You have ten seconds to come out and—"

The shutters on the upper level directly in front of Saul were thrown open with a clatter and flashes of gunfire erupted immediately. Then from two more windows to the right came more flashes. Saul dropped the bullhorn, fell to the ground in a prone position and brought his Uzi into play, crawling forward and to right and left after firing each burst. On either side, his colleagues were following the same zigzag firing pattern. With the advantage of an open field and darkness, the Israelis rose into low crouches and advanced while returning fire at the window targets.

Now fire flashes were coming from the ground level windows in furious bursts. Glass smashed, stone chips and wooden splinters flew in the crossfire, then Zadok threw the first grenade. It exploded below a window and the flashes from that source came to a momentary end, then resumed almost at once. From above, a heavy machine gun began spraying the grounds. Five Uzis at once were directed at that window and within seconds the heavy gun was silenced; but the lighter weapons continued firing at a more furious pace.

"Move in closer!" Saul ordered.

Navot, on the far left, had gained the front wall and was pressed close to its stone facade so that the guns on the inside could not get to him without being exposed to incoming fire. From the sides and rear, heavy fire had opened up and two grenades exploded, drawing some of the intensity of return fire away from the upper level front defenders.

From the right front, Zadok had now reached the wall and began moving toward the front door in a crawl. Within twenty feet of his goal, he tossed a grenade that landed on the top step. As he buried his face in the ground and covered the back of his neck with his hands, it exploded, ripping one of the two massive hand-carved doors open. The second door hung loosely on its upper hinge, two of its carved panels shattered.

On Saul's command by w-t, Zeitel and Darvit came running from their positions on the right and left sides of the house just as Saul and Leven each hurled a grenade through the open doorway and dashed inside seconds after they exploded, the others firing concentrated bursts at every window to furnish protective cover.

Inside, through the smoke and debris and small fires started by the exploded grenades, Saul and Leven, now joined by Yerushalmi, Navot, Darvit and Zadok, scattered through the darkened lower level, calling to everyone within hearing to surrender. Shots were exchanged in some instances and there were the sounds of voices calling out to cease firing. Zeitel remained on the outside to prevent anyone from escaping through the front door or windows. When the firing inside finally stopped, he joined the others.

Yerushalmi found a wall switch and lights came on. Saul ordered Darvit to stand guard over the double doors on the left of the center hallway until the other, smaller rooms were under effective control. Navot, Zeitel and Zadok returned, herding eight men ahead of them, arms over their heads in surrender. Leven and Zeitel started up the steps, but Saul ordered them back to rip hangings from the wall with which to choke out the several small fires that had been started and were licking at the rugs, filling the lower floor with acrid smoke.

From the rear came several bursts of fire, then Golan and Shaked came into the center hallway. Saul motioned them up the stairs, which they mounted cautiously, weapons extended and at the ready. From above, they could hear running footsteps and a confusion of male and female voices, but the firing there had ceased.

At the closed double doors where Darvit stood guard, Saul approached. "Locked," Darvit said. "No one answers. Be careful, Saul. We don't know what is in there, or how many."

Saul motioned him to one side and backed off a few feet. "Inside there! It is all over! If you don't come out in five seconds, we are coming in!"

When there was no reply, Saul aimed his gun at the doorknobs and fired a single burst. At once, this was returned from inside by several repeated bursts. Saul fell flat on the floor, but Uri Yerushalmi, who had just entered the center hallway after surveying the outside front, was hit and fell to the floor as the bullet-shattered doors swung open. Darvit crouched and ran to Yerushalmi and dragged him to one side out of the line of fire while Saul rolled to his left out of range.

From that position, Saul unhooked his last grenade, pulled the pin and threw it into the office through the open door. When it exploded, the shock almost knocked Darvit off his feet. Both he and Saul rose up and fired their weapons into the room, spraying it from side to side. There was no return fire this time.

Saul turned and found Golan and Shaked almost directly behind him. "Cover me," he ordered.

Crouched low, Saul crept along the wall toward the shattered doors. As he reached the edge of the opening and nodded, Golan and Shaked moved out in front of it and opened several bursts. When they stopped, Saul leaped into the room and to one side, Shaked and Golan following on his heels. There was total silence in the smoke-filled room.

Golan's foot kicked an overturned lamp. He turned it on as he righted it. To one side of the room, one man lay dead. Behind a large desk, which had been overturned and used as a protective barricade or shield, an older man lay wounded, blood flowing from a torn right arm and shoulder. The weapons of the two men, AK-47s, were gathered up. Saul said to the wounded man, "Can you hear me?"

"Yes . . ."

"You have a bad arm and shoulder wound, possibly others as well. Remain quiet and don't try to move. I will have someone look after you."

Shaked said, "The other one is dead."

Saul pointed to the small flames which were licking at the rug and one side of a sofa, and which Golan was attempting to smother with a sofa cushion. "Help Yoram put those out. Keep an eye on the wounded one, then tell Yoram to meet me in the hallway. Let's see what this adds up to so far."

From the upper floor, the men and women who had been brought down stood in a group with those found on the lower level and in the basement, dejected, tense, some weeping and disoriented, some defiant and sullen. Saul recognized Suzi Sadani, her proud face expressing no fear, only contempt; and Tahia Soulad, tears coursing down her face, which was partially covered by a disorder of hair. But he had little time or inclination to speak to either at the moment.

Then Darvit reported that Uri Yerushalmi was dead, Zvi Leven with a gunshot thigh wound, not serious. Saul went to where Yerushalmi lay, Leven sitting beside him trying to bandage his wounded thigh with strips torn from his shirt. Saul knelt and touched Uri's face, stroked his arm, then turned to Leven. "Zvi?"

"I'll be all right. It is a slight wound."

Saul said to Darvit, "Get one of the women to look after the wounded man inside that room. Stay with her. He may be the most important one of the whole lot here."

Golan returned from making a body count. "Five dead, four wounded, two seriously, thirteen men and five women prisoners. Uri—"

"I know about him and Zvi. Is that it?"

"Except for an arsenal in the basement with—"

"Later, Yoram. Get on the radio quickly. We need ambulances for the wounded, a van to take the prisoners in, a truck for the dead."

"Already radioed in, Saul, and on the way," Golan replied, then in a more somber voice, "On the way in, I'll stop by Uri's house and break the news to Sonya if you want me to."

"Do that, Yoram, but take Aanat with you. Sonya will need someone to stay with her and the children. As soon as I am clear, I will bring Shana to call on her. Right now I want to talk to the wounded man in that room. It is very likely he is the man in charge here."

"What about Sadani's wife?"

"We'll get nothing from that one. It looks like we may have been too late to get Sadani himself. Or Tobari. Where is Dov?"

"Here," Shaked said from behind him.

"Have Shimon take charge out here, Dov. Yoram, come with me and let's see if our man inside can talk now."

Together, Saul and Golan returned to the shambles of what had apparently been the office and which now, fully lit, showed scarred walls and furniture damaged by grenades and gunfire. Papers, glass and wooden splinters littered the floor. Books had spilled out of bookcases, window curtains torn to shreds by incoming fire. The smoke of the burned rug, sofa and cloth chairs added the stench of cordite and made breathing difficult, even with every window thrown open. From outside they could hear the faint siren wails of police vehicles arriving.

Outside, the sky had lightened with approaching dawn. Along the edges of the tended lawns, Saul was surprised to see over fifty people standing at the grove of trees; these were apparently the farm workers of the estate, drawn to the house by the gunfire.

Turning back to the wounded man, his chalky-hued face showing pain, one of the women prisoners had completed binding his arm and shoulder with an underskirt that had been torn in strips, a sling fashioned to support the arm. The man sat on the floor next to a window, back against the wall, chest rising and falling with labored breathing. Blood had seeped through the bandage, discoloring it, but the flow had stopped. The man's eyes remained closed, mouth drawn into a tight, grim line.

When Saul knelt to feel his pulse, the man responded to the touch by opening his eyes and emitting a weak groan. Saul said, "Your wound is not too serious. There is the possibility of a broken bone, some blood loss, but no major artery has been damaged."

"Help me to a chair," the man said.

"You will be better off sitting where you are."

"No. I do not wish to sit on a floor. A chair, please."

Yoram and Saul lifted him carefully and carried him to the chair, one of its arms blown away, but still serviceable. Saul found another chair and drew it up in front of the other, then sat on its edge, leaning forward. Golan and Shaked now turned the desk upright and began to look through the papers that were scattered about.

Saul said to the man, "Can you hear me?"

Razak's eyes opened slightly, then closed again.

"What is your name?"

There was no response.

"Listen to me. I have little time to waste, my friend, and even less patience. *Tell me your name!*"

Razak remained silent. Golan removed his revolver and placed the muzzle at Razak's right temple. "Answer when the colonel speaks to you or you won't live to see the outside of this room," he said harshly.

Razak's eyes opened at the touch of the cold steel to his flesh, pulling his head back and to one side as he heard the ominous *click* of the hammer being drawn back.

"Ra . . . Ra . . . zak," he gasped.

Saul reacted at once. "Razak! Major Massif Razak?"

Razak nodded affirmatively. Golan holstered his revolver and Saul now sat back in his chair. "Massif Razak," he repeated. "Well, Yoram, it seems we have a real prize here." To Golan's upraised eyebrows, "You don't know Major Massif Razak? We have a long and very interesting file on him."

Staring at Razak with loathing, Saul began to recite from memory. "Major Massif Razak, formerly deputy chief warden of Sheba'im Prison, near Damascus. Known for his diligence and expertise as an interrogator par excellence, eh, Razak?" And to Golan, "Also the man who gained prominence as the interrogator who broke Eli Cohen's spirit before they hanged him in a white sack in Marjan Square in Damascus."

Now Razak's eyes were on Saul's face as he spoke, his own

flushed with sullen defiance. "Also," Saul continued, "we have many eyewitness statements from former prisoners who were returned in a fifty-for-one exchange."

Saul drew a deep breath and exhaled slowly. "Our Major Razak was especially known to his Israeli prisoners by another name for his accomplishments—the 'Blinder'—which stems from the technique he used when he was not entirely satisfied with their replies; at which time, using a red-hot poker, he blinded the man for life."

Golan, blood surging to his face, exclaimed, "*You bastard!* So you are that one!" Razak shuddered and closed his eyes.

"Indeed a very fine prize," Saul said. "Yoram, there is a smithy at the rear of the house. Find a poker or something that will serve as one. Heat it until it glows white, then bring it here to me. Meanwhile, I will have some more questions to put to our friend."

Razak slumped back in his chair, perspiration beads forming on his forehead, eyes still clamped tightly shut. Saul lit a cigarette. Razak's eyes opened and looked hungrily at the smoke Saul expelled, but Saul ignored the silent request.

Then, in a choked voice, Razak said, "I did only what I was ordered to do by my superiors."

"Of course, Razak, like the good soldier you were. In the same way the Nazi good soldiers obeyed orders and murdered millions of innocent men, women and children. Very commendable, of course, from your personal point of view, but I am sure you will understand why—"

Eliahu Darvit came in then and went to Saul. "A message on the car radio from Lieutenant Altman, Colonel. General Rosental is now aware of this operation and wants you to contact him at once."

Saul paused for a few moments, then said, "Get Lieutenant Altman on the radio. Tell her to contact the general and tell him I have some unfinished business I must take care of. I should be in my office in about an hour. What time is it?"

"Almost seven o'clock."

"Tell him I will phone him around eight o'clock."

"Yes, Colonel."

"What about the transportation we requested?"

"Some are here now, the others on the way." Saul nodded his dismissal and Darvit went out. Saul turned back to Razak. "We know your superior in this UPFP thing, Falcon, or Ali Fathy, or Hatif Tobari, is here in Israel. Also, that Amon Sadani, or Mordecai Aarons, is with him. Where?"

"I know nothing. I am only the caretaker of this farm."

"Razak, I am not a child and long past believing in childish fables. Where is your master and his brother spy?"

"I have told you. I don't know."

"Very well. You have only as long as it takes to heat a poker. I'm sure you will recognize the technique, eh?"

"No . . . no—"

"If you think I will show greater mercy than you have been known to show others, Razak, let me assure you in the firmest terms possible that you will either answer my questions fully and truthfully or spend the rest of your life sightless in an Israeli prison."

Razak shuddered involuntarily. His left hand clutched feebly at his wounded right arm, pained by the spasms of terror that ran through him. Saul lit a second cigarette and waited. He could hear the movement and voices in the center hallway as the other prisoners were being led out of the house to be transported back to Jerusalem. Then Yoram Golan was back, carrying an iron poker whose short L-shaped end glowed a dull red. Saul took it from him, turned and saw that Dov Shaked had reentered the room. To Golan and Shaked, Saul said, "Hold his head toward me."

Razak's body jerked backward and, despite the pain in his shoulder and arm, tried to pull himself up and out of the chair, but Golan pulled him down from behind and pressed his shoulders against the chair backing while Shaked held his head firmly locked between two hands. When further resistance proved futile, Razak remained still but for the trembling anxiety in his bulging eyes.

Saul said, "You have five seconds to save your sight, Razak," and began counting. "One . . . two . . . three—" and with each count, brought the red tip closer to the desperate man's eyes until, smelling the heat of the iron, and on the count, "four," he cringed, shrinking back, shrieking, "Away . . . take it away . . . please . . . I will . . . tell—"

Yoram Golan searched through the debris and rubble of the office and found a partially torn and burned map which he spread out on the table Eliahu Darvit brought in from somewhere outside. The table was moved to the chair in which Razak sat clutching his arm, grimacing with pain and fear.

"Start talking, Major," Saul, standing beside him, said. "The sooner you do so, the sooner we can get you some relief and attention for your shoulder and arm." Shaked, on the other side, nudged Razak. Golan, standing on the opposite side of the table, bent closer over the map.

With his left hand, Razak slowly traced a ragged route that began at Da'ara in Syria, ran down through Jordan, across the Israeli border at Ein Yahav, then made a halting, circular motion over the Machtesh Ramon area and stopped.

"Go on," Saul encouraged.

Razak shrugged painfully and winced. "That is as much as I can tell you. They are somewhere in that region. The rest of it was never discussed in my presence."

"You are lying," Saul charged.

"Why would I lie to you now?" Razak paused, wet his lips, then "Tobari and Sadani planned it together. Tabet also knew," pointing to the corpse lying on the floor, "and you have killed him."

There was no way they could accurately determine how much more Razak was holding back. Thus far, what he had revealed checked out with the information Saul had received from Shana's Air Patrol reports, and he now wished fervently he had put more credence in those. But for the moment, the two major pieces of the puzzle, final destination and purpose, were missing.

Shaked pointed toward the poker, cold now, lying on the table, but Saul silently rejected the suggestion. Having used it once to bring Razak to this point, he suspected that the Syrian knew they would not deliberately blind him now, but continue to question him.

"Tobari and Sadani," Saul cued.

He could almost detect a small note of triumph in the Syrian's voice as he responded. "You were late, Colonel. They left here more than two hours before you arrived."

"Their destination?"

"To meet with the unit."

Saul tried once more. "Where, Razak?"

A negative shake of his head, emphasizing his previous denials. "I have told you. For reasons of security, it has always been Tobari's way to discuss his plans only with the fewest numbers of people, only those directly concerned with an operation. I was not one of those. I am only the caretaker here. Please, I am in great pain and would like a doctor to attend my wounds."

To Shaked's and Golan's questioning glances, Saul said, "Get him out of here, Take him to the hospital with the others. Have his wounds dressed, then put him in a cell at number seventeen. Alone and away from the others. Where is my car?"

"Outside, at the front door," Golan said.

"I'll see you in my office when you are finished here. Have someone question the farm people closely. Remove the weapons and explosives from the arsenal below, then post guards in and around the house."

The sun was glinting off the Dome of the Rock, the air humid, when Saul entered his office to find Judah Rosental having coffee with Shana. She rose and poured a fresh cup for Saul, which he took gratefully as he sat wearily in the chair next to the sofa where the general sat.

"A good night's work, Saul," Rosental said softly.

Saul emitted a light groan. "Uri Yerushalmi is dead, another wounded. Tobari and Sadani got away and are on the loose, and we have only a rough idea, if Razak is telling the truth, of the general area where the combat unit is supposed to be. Not a very good night's work, Judah."

"I am deeply sorry about Yerushalmi, Saul."

"I know. I know." He sipped more coffee. Shana lit a cigarette and handed it to him, then sat down on the sofa beside Rosental. "I've given the general as much as I could piece together from the logs and radio reports between cars, Saul," she said, "but I'll need your side of it to complete a report for—"

He waved the rest of it aside. "Any report at this time will be far from complete. You were right about your suspicions of that Bedouin group, Shana. Tobari's UPFP unit is with them, in Bedouin disguise. The old Sa'idi farm at Ein Fara is their prime headquarters here in Israel. We took in Massif Razak—"

"Ah, Razak," Rosental said with a voice that was as pleased as if Saul had told him Martin Bormann had been found alive. "He should be very helpful to us, that one."

"Except that we've gotten as much as we can hope for from him for now. Little enough and hardly useful for our present and immediate needs. Shana, bring the map on my desk here to us, please."

Saul moved to the seat beside Rosental which Shana had preempted and now, with the large military map spread across their laps, he indicated the Machtesh Ramon area. "Somewhere in here, these thousands of square kilometers of sand, rock and wilderness, we have reason to believe that Bedouin group and Tobari's damned terrorists are camped, or may be on the move toward their target."

Rosental peered at the map, his eyes following the sweeping motion of Saul's hand, muttering, "What in God's name can they find of interest or value to them there? The heavily protected surveillance sites west at Gidi? Or our equally well protected airfield at—"

"Out of the question, Judah. But instead, look south to Kuntilla, then southwest, here, a hundred and eighty, perhaps two hundred kilometers—"

"Bashra! My God, the oil field!"

"Exactly. A much better target by any reasoning. Of course, we have no way of knowing for certain, nor can we expect that they will be moving on any exposed roads or through the open desert. More likely, they will have chosen a course that will make it as difficult as possible to locate them, hiding in caves, in wadis and among rocks by day, pushing on by night. Razak claims he knows nothing of their destination or exact route, nor their ultimate target, which I am sure is a damned lie, but knowing his reputation as an expert, ruthless interrogator, I am just as sure he is as accomplished at withholding information, allowing only enough to delude us into believing he is cooperating.''

"What about Tobari and Sadani?"

"In all probability, on their way to meet up with their unit somewhere in the Machtesh Ramon area. There is a slightly better possibility of locating them, since they must be in a car, still en route, and will have to stay on a road, choosing secondary and lesser types. Even then, in all that wilderness, among so many caves—"

"We can order out ground troops and planes—" Rosental began, but Saul cut across his words quickly.

"Not in mass at this stage, Judah. Whatever their plan, I am certain of one thing: Tobari will be carrying with him the instrument to detonate the explosives once they have been placed. Wherever that is, it is very likely that they have already been placed. For an operation of this magnitude, I doubt that Tobari's ego would permit anyone else to take that credit for the success of his mission."

"Then what *do* you suggest, Saul?"

"I want to order normal overflights in the area to try to locate the Bedouin group and give us a definite position, which will tell us whether or not they really are moving toward Bashra. Once that is definitely established, I will contact Major Wolf there and have him double his security guard forces around the clock and make a thorough check of all operating equipment there to see if there are, in fact, any explosives that have been planted. It will not be an easy job."

"I can order the additional security guards from Camp Herzog," Rosental said, "and have them there before the day is over."

"I think that would be in order, Judah. Then, I want you to put your helicopter at my disposal, along with your pilot, and begin searching for Tobari and Sadani. I will take Yoram Golan and Dov Shaked with me and leave Shimon Navot and Shana to run things here in our absence."

"You have it, Saul, and anything else you need. Before you go, dictate as much as you can of your report. I'll need it for support from General Bartok."

"But first, put through the order to Camp Herzog and arrange for the overflights from Southern Air Command."

"I'll do that while you are dictating your report."

*   *   *

It was full daylight when Sadani, behind the wheel of the black Fiat sedan, nudged Tobari, who sat dozing beside him. "Hatif, wake up."

Tobari's eyes opened. "What is it? Where are we?"

"Beersheba lies a few kilometers ahead. We will have to go through on the main road."

"Good. We can stop for coffee. And food. I am hungry."

"We should not waste time, Hatif. There is food in the package on the rear seat."

"We may need that for later. You are too on edge, Amon. Relax. We have plenty of time and no one is chasing us. I need something hot inside me."

"We may run into a checkpoint—"

"And the sky may fall down on us," Tobari chided. "Look ahead of you. The road is clear. No soldiers, no police. We will refresh ourselves with hot food, fill the petrol tank like any other travelers, then go on."

"From Beersheba south, we will be moving slower on dirt roads that are little better than camel trails."

"And so much more difficult for anyone to find us, particularly at night, eh?"

"It will be dangerous, traveling on such roads at night, Hatif. If we have a breakdown—"

Tobari laughed as he would at a childish remark. "Amon, you have lived too long in cities where it is more dangerous to drive or even walk on the streets. Razak had the car carefully checked. We are carrying extra petrol, water and oil in our trunk. Out here in the open, exercising a certain amount of caution, we are much safer than in the heart of Jerusalem, Tel Aviv or Tripoli. Here we are, safe in Beersheba. Act naturally and all will be well."

In Rosental's helicopter Saul, Yoram Golan and Dov Shaked, taking turns between catnaps, acted as observers while the pilot, Lieutenant Ami Sartov, headed over stretches of secondary roads searching for the Tobari car. On occasion, they flew off course to examine an oasis or small enclave of nomads on the chance that those they sought may have decided to split into smaller groups in order to avoid attention. They found nothing to confirm this suspicion. Nor had they found anything along the well-trafficked principal roads. When, late in the afternoon, the light began to fail, Sartov said to Saul, "It is useless to continue on. We'll have to land and refuel soon and night is not too far off."

"If we must," Saul agreed resignedly. "We'll start again at first light tomorrow."

"Like searching for a fly speck in a ton of pepper," Sartov commented.

"Which is one of the things we are paid to do, *chaver*," Saul replied testily.

On the ground, south and west of Kuntilla, some thirty kilometers below Machtesh Ramon, Ahmed Hourani came out of the cave where he and the others had spent the day. His men joined him in the meal that had been prepared by the Bedouin women. Now Tewfik's sons were supervising the initial stages of loading the animals for the night move. The women and girls began gathering up their pots, pans and goatskin tents, the children brought in the rest of the donkeys and camels which had been staked out in a nearby wadi, virtually invisible from even a short distance, or from overhead.

Hourani finished his meal quickly, then went to a rise and swept the area south with his binoculars, then toward the north, east and west. Nothing moved in any direction or overhead. He turned back and began to instruct his unit in the order of march.

Then the Bedouin leader approached to discuss the route they would travel during the night. Ahmed produced his map and drew a line with his finger, pointing out their one rest stop and where they could expect to find good coverage at the end of their night's travel. Tewfik was patently disturbed. "This will not be good. We must turn eastward at this point to fill our goatskins, else there will not be enough water for our next meals."

"Nevertheless," Hourani said, "we will continue according to our plan and schedule."

"No. I must protest," Tewfik began, but Hourani shut him off abruptly.

"Easy, old one. We are on a schedule from which we cannot depart, and for which you are being well paid to maintain. Ration what water you have. There will be more when we resume tomorrow night."

To argue further, Twefik realized, would be fruitless with this headstrong young leader. He should never have been persuaded to become involved with these God-cursed fedayeen who had no regard or feeling for any but themselves. Two nights after this one, God willing, and he would be rid of them; but for now, he must endure the grumblings of his own people who had, from the very beginning, been against aligning themselves with these strange men whose guns were frightening and who postured like conquerors in front of the women.

Twefik returned to assist in the supervision of the loading task and to see that the goats were ready to move out.

At day's end they returned to the Air Patrol base on the outskirts of Ma'ale Hashemar, known as Camp Shloshim. After supper, Saul and Lieutenant Sartov pored over an aerial map to plot the next day's flight while Golan and Shaked talked with various pilots to determine how many smaller roads, too insiginificant to appear on the military map, might be scattered throughout the area of their control. This line of inquiry brought little more than shrugs and explanations that there were no official roads other than those shown on the map, but that very frequently, drivers would take shortcuts across the desert and make their own roads. The sand close to the rock formations was generally hard enough to support a light vehicle.

Later, they discussed and agreed upon a flight plan for the following day, then went to their cots in the maintenance crew quarters where they slept until awakened for breakfast by Sartov. Moments after first light had brushed away the night, they were aloft. There were, indeed, numerous tracks, or ruts in the desert, some easily identifiable as camel trails, but for the most part were empty and seemed to lead nowhere.

The monotony of the day was broken only slightly by infrequent radio messages from the base camp's communications officer, reporting no sightings from the patrol planes engaged in the search. Somewhere past noon, they landed to eat a cold meal that had been prepared at Camp Shloshim and to stretch cramped muscles for a brief period before resuming the search.

In the glare of the blazing afternoon sun, ground temperatures ranging above 100 degrees, distances were deceptive, sand sculptured into uniformly patterned ridges by wind and time as it must have been for endless centuries. Even through glare-cutting sunglasses it was difficult to penetrate the shimmering motion that rose from the broad expanse of heated sand below.

During the afternoon, they spotted a small car heading toward Har Ramon and slanted in for a closer look, almost causing the driver to run off the narrow trail road in fright. The man stopped and got out of the car, followed by a woman and two excited children, the man either waving or shaking a fist at them. The helicopter veered off, gained altitude and flew back along that same road to Kal'at E-Nakhal and, within forty kilometers of Bashra, Saul decided to spend the night there, taking the opportunity to check on the security measures that had been ordered.

*   *   *

Major Yuval Wolf, military commander of the Bashra security forces, met the helicopter at the landing circle beside the narrow strip that had been laid down for light plane use. To one side, bulldozers and crews were working on a much larger and wider strip that would eventually accommodate cargo and military planes.

Golan, Shaked and Sartov were dropped at one of the mess halls while Saul and Wolf continued on to Wolf's office in the headquarters building. The additional troops ordered from Camp Shloshim, the major reported, had arrived the day before and were getting settled in and assigned to their tasks, but he added with concern, "There are problems, Colonel. First—" ticking them off on his fingers one by one, "there is housing. There aren't enough barracks and I've had to put them up in tents, which they are grumbling about. Then feeding, which is far from what they have had at Camp Shloshim. More grumbling. Next, the shortage of water, which we are still bringing in by tank trucks and there is never enough. Then—"

Saul tried to hide his impatience with Wolf's housekeeping problems, categorizing him as an administrative type. He listened with a sense of weariness to the slightly-built man who was in his late thirties, sandy-haired, sharp-featured, with a petulant voice; and wondered how much field service he had behind him. "Major—" he began, but Wolf went on without a break.

". . . and also, the engineering staff and labor foremen are now complaining about so many armed guards walking around the drilling rigs and other working areas, getting in everybody's way. With so many men and no women, no recreation but exercise and reading, there are constant fights. There are rumors of strikes—"

"Major," Saul interrupted forcefully, "listen to me. These are problems that are only temporary and which I'm sure you are qualified to cope with. I am more interested in the security of the operations in this installation. What have you found so far, if anything?"

Wolf stiffened, his face flushed. "Nothing in the two days we have been searching. I have organized work parties as ordered; two men to a team, dressed as workers in order not to raise suspicions among the technicians and laborers. They have searched in every sensitive area, the drilling sections, rigs, warehouses, generators, garages, along the pipelines, posing as inspectors, but have found nothing."

"Who else knows what they are searching for?"

"Only the chief engineer and field superintendent. But as you know, a small square of plastic such as was described to me, in an installation as big as this, is not an easy matter to find. They can be placed and covered over and—"

"I realize that, but the search must continue and a careful watch kept on the work force, common laborers, truck drivers, field workers—"

"What more can we do, Colonel, than what is being done now? It is impossible to follow every man about as they move from one area to another."

Saul thought for a moment, then said, "I want you to establish controlled working areas so that these people can't come and go as they please."

"How?" Wolf demanded. "Do I assign a guard to each man?"

"Major, I want you to issue badges in different colors to each work gang in his own area of operation. A man wearing a green badge, designated for the drilling area, will not be able to enter the pipeline area, which will require a blue badge, nor the warehouse area, where a yellow badge is needed, without a special authorization from his labor foreman. This will apply to vehicle maintenance, supply section, administration and other areas as well."

Wolf looked aghast. "You are asking for a . . . a total walkout, Colonel. These people are working under the hardest kind of conditions as it is and will not stand for this, particularly the engineering staffs."

"You will issue a special gold-colored badge that will allow them the freedom to go anywhere. We are mainly concerned with the labor force, with particular attention to Israeli Arabs. You can order the badges from Tel Aviv and put that operation in motion as soon as possible."

"You are only increasing our problems, Colonel," Wolf said.

"Be that as it may, Major, those are your orders. If you feel you cannot carry them out—"

Wolf backed down quickly. "I will get started on it. Do you have any other suggestions?"

"Yes. I want you to check through your personnel records and pull the card on every man who has been hired here during the past ninety days—"

"That could be as many as two hundred cards or more."

"Even if it comes to a thousand. Name, point of origin, previous work record, references if any. When the list is complete, send it by the mail plane to SO Branch headquarters in Jerusalem, attention Lieutenant Altman, who will be instructed to run a police check on each one."

"I will have someone start that today."

"Also, no one is to be hired on this project until further notice. Phone your employment agency contacts and suspend all hiring until you are instructed to tell them otherwise."

"The work gang bosses won't like that, Colonel. They keep crying for more, more and still more."

"Like it or not, that is a security order and has priority over everything else for the time being."

Wolf shrugged. "If you say so, Colonel," he said simply.

Saul then ordered an inspection trip around the camp, which took another two hours. He noted that the sentries were well placed and alert, the work forces busily engaged under tight supervision. For the moment, he concluded that everything that could be done was being done here. He drew little comfort from that thought.

* * *

At dawn on the following day, the Fiat, now gray with dust, inched its way off the rough dirt road it had been traveling slowly during the long night and crept in between two ridges of a wadi, which would keep them well hidden from view of any passing vehicle. As Sadani braked the car to a stop on ground solid enough to prevent its wheels from sinking too deeply into the sand, Tobari reached behind him for a canteen and drank thirstily of the warm water. "Where are we in this godforsaken desert, Amon?" he asked.

Sadani picked up the map that lay on the seat between them. He unfolded it, studied it for a few moments, then said, "Here, on the Darb el Gaza, about seventeen kilometers from Kuntilla. From here, we move southwest to the outskirts of Tarhad to spend the night. We will then be only forty kilometers from Bashra, with good coverage."

Tobari wiped the perspiration from his face and neck with a large handkerchief. "And tomorrow night," he said softly. "Tomorrow night, Amon, we will light up these skies bright enough to blind every eye within five kilometers of Bashra. Ten, even."

"If the getaway plan works—" Sadani began.

"You are growing too nervous, my dear Amon," Tobari said chidingly, a hint of amusement in his voice. "Our getaway will be simple. They will be too much preoccupied to pay attention to two mere travelers with proper papers and no suspicious weapons or equipment, which we will discard as soon as it is over. At Bashra, there will be no one left. Any help that comes will be too late to find us on the scene, or near it." He paused with a small laugh. "And think, Amon, of the rewards that will await us when our friends learn of this success. Then there will be no limits to how far we can go, how fast we can move.''

Sadani did not appear to be listening, nor did he share Tobari's high mood. Quietly, he said, ''This will be my last such adventure, Hatif. I am not cut out for this kind of work. This is—''

Tobari slapped Sadani's shoulder in an attempt to comfort him, laughing as he did so. ''After this operation, Amon, you need never set your feet on this soil until it belongs to us, with the UPFP flag flying over it. Give me another year. Just one. Think of that, Amon, and let the thought cheer you. You will be my chief planner, the architect of every action we will take from now on, while I carry out the action.''

''God willing.''

''He has been with us thus far. He will not desert us now. Let us eat now and try to get some sleep in this furnace of a desert.''

So another day had passed and as night came on, Ahmed Hourani sought out Tewfik, who sat among his people, silently brooding in his resentment. Nor did he move as he saw the young fedayeen leader approaching. With his usual arrogant military stride, Hourani walked into the circle and said, ''It would be wise to eat your meal now and load the animals. Tonight we will be traveling farther and faster than before.''

When Tewfik did not respond at once, Hourani said in a louder voice, ''I have given you an order, old man.''

Angered by Hourani's voice within the hearing of his sons, Twefik rose to confront the fedayeen leader. ''I am not in your army to be given orders like a servant. I am the head of my family and must be respected as such,'' he replied with rising heat.

''We will not debate that question now. Tell your women to prepare your food. In one hour we will move out. It will be a long night on the road.'' And so saying, he turned on his heels to rejoin his own men. When he heard Tewfik say, ''Light the fires,'' Hourani turned back. ''No fires, old man. We are too close to our destination to be discovered by your smoke and fire.''

''Our women must cook. The children must be fed as well as the rest of us. It will be a long night for them, too,'' Twefik spat out angrily.

Hourani stared coldly at the older man, then drew his revolver from its holster and aimed it at Tewfik's middle. ''I said no fires. Eat quickly and load the animals. You have one hour and no longer than that.''

He stood facing the old Arab until Tewfik turned and gave the order to prepare a cold meal, then Hourani strode back to where his own group was consuming their food. He sat with them for a while, then rose when a sentry beckoned him to join him on the rise that overlooked the ridged dunes lying to the southwest.

"What is it?" Hourani asked.

"Someone comes," the sentry replied.

"Alone?"

"Alone and on foot. See for yourself." Hourani took the sentry's binoculars and, in the fading light, made out a shadowy figure moving toward them.

"Go forward and meet him while I keep him in my gunsight. He may be from Bashra with some word, but watch him carefully. If he is a wanderer, let him come no closer to us."

Now several other of the UPFP men joined Hourani and watched as the sentry approached the man, spoke with him, then turned and waved as both men walked back toward the camp together. At the top of the rise, they saw the man more closely, then recognized him as he called out a "*Salaam aleikum*" to the watchers.

Hourani responded for all. "*Salaam*, Masri. Welcome, brother."

"It has been a long walk. I am tired."

"You came all the way from Bashra on foot?" Hourani asked with an incredulous voice.

"Only part of the way. The truck to Ein Avdat is a few kilometers from here, sitting on the road. It was necessary that I find you. There are things happening you should be told."

"What things?"

"Two days ago, more soldiers were brought to strengthen the security guard. There are now twice as many there as there were before. There are inspections taking place during the day and night, round the clock. It is fortunate the explosives were placed before they arrived."

"Did they bring heavy weapons with them?"

"None. Rifles and small arms, only what they carried. In their trucks were other supplies, but I do not know exactly what they are. Perhaps grenade launchers, ammunition. Also, a truckload of food, tents for them to sleep in. There is talk of water tankers to come and additional arrangements made for more supplies. It would seem that they are expected to be there for some time."

"Have you heard any talk as to why this is being done?"

"Nothing within my hearing, but there is much movement among the military. This—" Masri withdrew a green-bordered badge from his shirt pocket, "must be worn by me at all times, in view of the guards. It permits me to work only in the supply area.

To enter another area, I must see my superior for permission, give him a reason and receive a written authorization from him.''

"Have they questioned anybody?"

"Not yet. There is something else.''

"What?''

"There are teams of men, working in pairs, who go about inspecting different sections. The entire length of the pipeline, drilling rigs, vehicle storage yards, even the offices and sleeping quarters. This morning, they came through the warehouses and sheds—''

"They spoke to you, asked questions?''

"No. Even when I offered to help them, they refused and told me to go about my business.''

"Then how were you able to get away undetected?''

Masri shrugged. "It was time for the regular run to Ein Avdat. This they cannot stop. The supplies are necessary to their operations.''

"What will be the difficulty when the explosives are detonated? I mean before that time. The means by which you and your people can get away?''

"That part will not be difficult. There is much open space beyond the camp and it would take ten times the men they have to watch every inch of the ground. Behind the northwest tower, which I have carefully scouted, there is a blind spot where the rocks come within a few yards of the interior zone. Beyond those rocks are enough wadis through which a single man can move without being seen. In the darkness, we can move through it without being seen.''

The news disturbed Hourani as he carefully digested it, trying to appraise the meaning for such additional security measures. What disturbed him more were the search teams. He said finally, "The planted explosives. Are they secure?''

"Thus far, yes. I have talked with my people. The searchers have turned up nothing. Each block remains in place, covered carefully to avoid detection. I will tell you this: If they find even one, it will be only by accident.''

"What about the actuator devices?''

"I have them well hidden. When I receive final word that everything is in readiness, I will issue them to my men and they will be placed in the planted explosives and activated. I have men in every section where they are hidden. Since the searchers will have passed through those sections by then, it will not be difficult to do this. There is one thing, however—''

"What is it?''

"With the additional security and movement in the camp, my people are growing nervous. There are fifty-two of us in all and it is imperative that we know the exact time when this thing will be done so that I can get them out of the camp in good time."

"There is no need to worry on that score, Masri. When you return to camp tomorrow, start your men at once to place the actuators and be sure they are properly turned on. The battery in each is good for at least sixty hours.

"Tomorrow afternoon, Falcon is due to arrive close enough to communicate with me. He will then give me the exact time when he will detonate the explosives. That time should be either tomorrow night or the one following. No later, and it will come late at night, most likely close to midnight. When I receive that information from him, I will send a man close enough to Bashra so that you can receive the word from him clearly on your instrument. At six o'clock tomorrow and the next day, you should make sure you are in a well-chosen place in the open where you can receive the message without being seen or overheard."

"Yes. That will be good. Once we know the exact day and time, we can plan to leave as soon as darkness falls."

"That will give you no problem?"

"No. I have observed how they move in pairs, and when. Once they pass, we can leave by the northwest corner without being detected in the dark."

"Excellent. When you do, instruct your men to bring as much food and water as each can carry. Particularly the water. There is room for all of you to hide here in Wadi Talal until it will be safe to move you north. Three days after it is over, trucks will arrive, one at a time, to pick you up and take you to El Arish and Gaza, as you wish. From there, you will have no problem getting back to your homes in Haifa and Acre. It has all been planned so."

"We will not be able to take enough food with us to last until then, Ahmed."

"Carry as much as you can. When you reach here, you will find we have left you food from our supplies. In that cave," he added, designating the one closest to where they were standing. "Be sure about the water, Masri, else it may be necessary to ration what you bring with you."

"Ah, yes. It is a good plan. I must go now to rejoin my men on the truck. We will return to Bashra from Ein Avdat no later than four o'clock tomorrow afternoon."

"You have done well. All of you will be well rewarded when it is over. Tell your people that. Make sure they do nothing to draw special attention to themselves, nor show alarm. All will be well."

*   *   *

It was late afternoon of the following day when the first break came. Air Patrol plane Shloshim Dalet swung south on the final leg back to base camp. Already the lowering sun was casting rippling shadows on the ground surface and creating difficulty for the observer. Now, on a direct course back to the camp, the observer aimed his binoculars on twin ridges of rock with a level bed of sand between them; and took notice of movement in the cul-de-sac formed by the two major outcroppings.

As they came closer to it, the observer called out, "On my right. Movement between those two fingers of rock, Meir. It could be them."

The pilot began to turn to the right for a sighting, but the observer said, "Keep going. Don't give them any sign we have seen them or they'll slip off into the night and we'll have a hell of a time finding them again."

"Call it in, Zeev."

The observer had the microphone in his hand, glancing back as they flew over the formation below. "Base camp Shloshim. This is Shloshim Dalet. Do you read me?"

"Loud and clear, Shloshim Dalet."

"We have a possible. Between forty or fifty, with camels, donkeys and goats, moving out from between a group of rock caves and ridges. There may be more."

"What are your coordinates?"

The pilot read the figures from the plastic overlay blocks on his flight map and the observer repeated them.

"We have it, Shloshim Dalet. Will pass the information on." The communications officer cut out, then radioed the information to the Lahav helicopter.

"Chopper Alef Bayt, come in."

"Chopper Alef Bayt. I read you."

"What is your location?"

"Nineteen kilometers south of base camp, on our return leg."

"We have a possible contact for you, received from Shloshim Dalet three minutes ago. Advise you return to base camp and meet Shloshim Dalet for confirmation."

"What is Shloshim Dalet's ETA?"

"Approximately thirty minutes."

"We will head in."

Forty minutes later, Saul, Golan, Shaked and Sartov were standing before the huge area map in the camp commander's office checking the coordinates with Lieutenants Meir Ben-Asher and

Zeev Ober, pinpointing the location north of Bashra. Ober described the Bedouin group, the largest that had been seen in two full days of search.

"Those camels and donkeys were carrying weight, Colonel," Ober said, "moving slowly out of those two fingers of rocks, heading in a southerly direction. By now, you couldn't find them without searchlights."

And, checking the map again, Saul said, "It must be them," receiving hopeful nods from Golan and Shaked. "We've got to start something moving their way, and damned well before they can make a move of any kind at Bashra."

"Well," Ben-Asher said, "you've got Camp Herzog just a few kilometers west of here. Tanks, armored personnel carriers, more than you'll ever need for this bunch."

"Can you put us down at Herzog, Sartov?" Saul asked.

"No problem, if you call them first and have them clear us for landing."

"I'll call it in," Ben-Asher said. "Take off."

Within minutes they were put down at Camp Herzog and went into immediate conference with the camp commander, Colonel Aaron Pelz, who had been alerted and was awaiting their arrival. Saul outlined the situation as concisely as possible and Pelz nodded in agreement. "If," he said, "we start at once, I can order out enough manpower and equipment to surround Bashra like a fence. In the morning, we can have enough planes over the area to saturate—"

"No, Colonel. That would not only be like using missiles to destroy an anthill, but would send the two men we want most into deep cover, to do damage elsewhere later."

"Then what are you asking for?"

"Two half-track personnel carriers, each with ten men, plus two machine-gun mounted jeeps, each with three men. My group will use our own helicopter to continue the search for Tobari and Sadani while your people move in on their main body."

"Anything else?" Pelz asked.

"Only the operational schedule and the briefing of the men. I would first like to talk with the officer who will be in command."

"Let me get Lieutenant Yariv in here. One of my best young men."

Lieutenant Baruch Yariv was about twenty-eight, a little man of average height, clean-shaven, with intelligent eyes and the easy smile of one who was looking forward with high anticipation to something more than a routine field maneuver or exercise. He listened carefully to Saul's explicit briefing, checked locations and routes on the large wall map, asked proper questions, made cryptic notes on a smaller map he would carry with him. When he finally folded it and placed it in his shirt pocket, Saul felt that Colonel Pelz's choice of a young leader was justified in Yariv.

"We will be ready to pull out at four in the morning," Yariv said. "If I may be excused now, I would like to pick the men, brief them and see that our vehicles and equipment are in order."

At three thirty, a sentry woke Saul. He went outside to watch the last minute inspection of the men and equipment being conducted by Yariv, in full battle dress, with Colonel Pelz and his captain-aide looking on as observers. At exactly four o'clock, Yariv gave the hand signal to roll out. The two jeeps and personnel carriers fired up and headed northward out of Camp Herzog. Saul, Pelz and the captain then walked over to the mess hall and had coffee together.

They had pushed hard during the night, but lost time during the one stop Hourani had allowed when Twefik refused to be hurried through the meal, insisting that his people needed more time to rest. Again, he had protested the order against lighting fires for cooking purposes, and a long, bitter argument ensued; but after numerous threats and counter threats, Hourani's authority asserted itself. The meal was eaten cold, deliberately slow in defiance.

Then another incident erupted when three of the UPFP men were refused water from the Bedouins' dwindling supply. This was a more serious situation and the fedayeen, despite the weapons they carried and displayed, found themselves faced with an aroused group. Fearful that matters might get too far out of hand, Hourani was compelled to order his people from the camp center to cool their tempers.

Thus it was three hours before he was able, by threat of refusing to pay Tewfik the second half of the money due him, to get the encampment started toward their final destination. And as dawn approached, Hourani found that in order to make up for lost time and enable them to reach their final jump-off point, on schedule, they would be forced to travel approximately nine kilometers in daylight, a situation that did not please him.

To each demand from Hourani that Twefik urge his people to move faster, the Bedouin sullenly replied, "Do not speak to me. Speak to the camels and donkeys." And with the Arab's adamant refusal to cooperate, Hourani was forced to give in. At this stage, he could not afford more delays. However, they were now well off any beaten path, far from road or trail, and on the edge of numerous towering rock formations where they could, in an emergency, take cover. The principal danger lay in being seen by a patrol plane overhead, but they had seen only one since crossing into Israeli territory four days earlier; the one that had flown over on the evening before had shown no indication of having noticed any movement below. If it had, Hourani reasoned, they would have circled back and dropped down to investigate.

With one man a hundred yards ahead on point, flanked on the right and left by two others at a distance of forty yards, a fourth acting as rear guard a hundred yards behind, the party continued southwesterly. Wadi Talal was marked on Hourani's map by an encircled "X" in red, easily recognizable from a distance by its characteristics clearly described to him by Salim Tabet, who had personally scouted the location.

Once arrived, Ahmed Hourani regarded the area with deep satis-faction; an excellent choice. To the left, a sheer wall of rock with sawtooth ridges rose from the desert floor to provide concealment from the east. Two rugged spines sloped downward to meet the empty desert that lay open to the west. There were sufficient caves in which to hide everyone, with some grazing beyond the north slope for the animals, where they would be hardly discernible from above while feeding in the shadows of the rocks. Or sleeping.

Even better was the protection they would receive from the south. There, that spine of rock stood as a shield in the direction facing Bashra, some forty feet high, where Hourani at once ordered two men to take up their guard post.

They were now six kilometers north and slightly east of the near border of the restricted zone of Bashra's oil field, eight from its exact center. And sometime late on the following night, according to the plan, enough explosives would be triggered to blow it out of existence. With the help of a merciful, generous Allah. Then he would move his men in to finish off every human and animal remaining alive.

No sooner had Hourani called a halt and drawn his flankers and point man in, than Tewfik approached and, in strident tones, spoke to the fedayeen leader. "You, I must speak to you."

"What is it, old man?" Ahmed demanded, annoyed by the interruption. "Can't you see I am busy?"

"I will take the other half of my money now. This is as far as we are required to go with you. I have ordered your goods unloaded and set apart. When this is done, we will depart."

Hourani regarded the Bedouin with stony contempt. "Old man," he said angrily, "we will remain here together until you will be of no further use to us. When we are next ready to move, you will then receive your money, take your people out, to hell, if you please. But not until then."

Bristling, Tewfik shouted, "We have brought you here safely as was agreed with your commander at Da'ara. Whatever evil thing it is you intend to do is no business of mine. I will not endanger my family—"

In one quick motion, Hourani's hand was under his robe and came up with a revolver, which he thrust under the older man's beard. "The danger, my friend," he said coldly, "will be far greater if you try to leave this camp before I give permission. Now get on with your unloading and keep out of my way."

When Tewfik backed off, Hourani holstered his revolver and called for his men to help unload the equipment and ammunition from the laden animals. There was no further resistance from a thoroughly cowed Tewfik or his sons. The boxes were unloaded and opened, their contents removed and apportioned out so that each man would know exactly what he would carry into Bashra on his back; spare cartridges, banana clips, grenades to hang from belt and shoulder straps, revolver ammunition in each cartridge belt, two bazookas and shells, two portable mortars.

By now, the animals had been staked out and hobbled beyond the north ridge, the goats kept apart and tended by the children. The water supply was dangerously low and what small amount remained was being carefully guarded by the Bedouin in an atmosphere that had now become openly hostile. It took all of Hourani's control capabilities to prevent his men from taking the remaining water from the Bedouin by force. He had each man empty what remained in his personal canteen into a goatskin water carrier and reapportioned the total collected equally.

"Let this do for now. Use it sparingly. When we move into Bashra, there will be plenty of water for all. Once we are organized here, lie down and remain quiet until it will be time to move on. Place pebbles in your mouths and suck on them. It will reduce your thirst."

As usual, the Bedouin remained closely together in a tight circle. The fedayeen on guard duty were split into three groups, one toward the south, one toward the north, the other to the west.

In that way, they rested and waited for the safety of darkness. It was long in coming; a hot, restless day of waiting.

After an early breakfast, Colonel Pelz's adjutant brought in a large, detailed map of the eastern Sinai area, which was spread out on a cleared table for examination by Saul, Lieutenant Sartov, Golan and Shaked. Checking the coordinates carefully, Sartov located the exact spot where the Bedouin group had been sighted by Ben-Asher and Ober on the evening before.

From that point, Saul and Pelz decided, the fedayeen would more than likely continue in a more or less direct line toward Bashra, keeping closely toward the east where the rock formations blended with the desert and would afford some protection from possible overflights. On that assumption, Lieutenant Yariv would head his attack unit north. Late in the afternoon, he would split the unit in half, sending Sergeant David Chesler in one armored personnel carrier and one jeep west until it reached the eastern border of Bashra, then head north again.

Yariv, meanwhile, would continue north from the eastern side until he reached a point parallel to the last sighting of the Bedouin group, head west for approximately two hours, then cut sharply southward. In the predawn hours of the following morning, hopefully, the fedayeen would find themselves trapped between the split units.

At four o'clock, Air Patrol was due to make a reconnaissance flight over the area in an effort to locate the Bedouin group and pinpoint its exact position for Yariv and Chesler by radio, and allow them to coordinate their efforts in effecting the interception.

They were interrupted by the arrival of a messenger from the camp communications officer with a radioed report from Yariv. After four hours, the unit was progressing on schedule. Pelz handed the slip to Saul, who read it aloud, nodded to Shaked, Golan and Sartov and said, ''Let's go.'' Within minutes they were airborne to continue the search for the black Fiat, this time with a sense of mounting urgency and desperation.

Although two full days of concentrated effort had been fruitless, it was Saul's firm conviction that Tobari and Sadani must now surely be within, or close to, communication range of the UPFP group in order to coordinate their planned strike against Bashra. He was now convinced, more than ever before, that in some way, perhaps even well before Tobari had arrived in Israel, the explosives had already been carefully concealed throughout the oil field installation in critical, highly vulnerable areas. It occurred to him now that he should have ordered the entire field closed down, all personnel removed from the area until it could be searched by teams of demolition experts properly equipped to handle that type of work.

In order to have the field closed down, that decision must come from the highest authorities, who would, without far more proof than he could offer, deny his request. Even if they should issue the order, where would approximately two thousand people be housed and fed until the danger was over; or until the UPFP set off the explosives and destroyed the field? The thought itself was monstrous, the task of unbelievable magnitude.

Nor would it lessen the need to locate Tobari, who most assuredly would be carrying the ultimate weapon; the instrument necessary to detonate the explosives from some distant point. Whatever the purpose of the UPFP unit now in the Sinai, they were of secondary importance.

When, later, they landed to eat their midday meal in the blistering desert heat and the little shade offered by the helicopter, Saul made some of his thoughts known to Golan and Shaked, the latter agreeing. But Golan was not entirely ready to accept Saul's theory. "If that is the case," he argued, "what need is there for an armed unit moving toward Bashra, cloaked by a Bedouin family, when Tobari himself could do the thing?"

"Other reasons," Shaked proposed. "One, a mop-up operation once the explosives are detonated. Two, to effect the rescue of their people working on the inside there before the explosions take place."

"I don't know what to expect," Saul said. "It is a lot easier to anticipate what an enemy will do in open warfare, even in political maneuverings, than an operation of this kind, dealing with zealots."

"So?" Golan said.

"So we continue to search until we find Tobari and Sadani. And damned soon, else they will blow Bashra into rubble."

They were on the Darb el Haj well north of Tarhad when Tobari said, "It is almost three o'clock, Amon. Find a stopping place and let us see if we can reach them."

"Why now, if it is not to be until tomorrow night?" Sadani asked.

With a show of mild irritation, "Why must you question everything I suggest? This is only a test of our communications equipment, if we can reach Hourani from here, there will be no doubt that we can reach him tomorrow when we will be much closer. Or before, if it becomes necessary."

Again, Sadani felt put down. In Jerusalem, where he exercised full control over his own activities and authority over those at Ein Fara, he may have experienced occasional small doubts, but there had seldom been so total a lack of self-confidence as he felt now. Here in the open desert, playing this game of cat and mouse, he felt uncomfortably ill at ease. He neither understood nor enjoyed this type of activity, nor could he accept Tobari's total enthusiasm for the dangers it implied. "We will have to stop on the open road," he said reluctantly. "If we go off it, the car may sink too deeply in the sand."

"Then stop here, now. There is nothing in sight. This will not take more than a few minutes."

Sadani braked to a halt. Both men got out and looked in all directions, then scanned the empty sky above. Tobari got out the walkie-talkie unit, extended its whiplike antenna to full length while Sadani reached into the car for the thermos of water to slake his thirst.

"Leader One, come in," Tobari called. There was no immediate response and he repeated the call four more times before he picked up a faint reply. "This is Leader One," came Hourani's reply.

"Falcon here. The reception is weak."

"I am between two ridges of rock. Let me—" the voice faded out. A few minutes later it came through again, this time stronger and clearer. "Is this better? I am now out in the open."

"Yes. Much better. What is your location?"

"We are in position at Wadi Talal, six kilometers north of the target zone, well situated."

"Excellent. All else goes well?"

"Our Bedouin friend is restless and complains. He is nervous for the safety of his people."

"Reassure him, but take what measures are necessary, short of shooting, to keep them quiet until you are ready to move out tomorrow night."

"That has been taken care of. Is the hour set?"

"Tomorrow night. After darkness falls, start moving your unit toward the north boundary of the restricted zone. When you are in position to cross the line, rest there and wait until midnight. On the hour, fire your white flare. I will be within sight of it. When I see the flare, the charges will be detonated. When the explosions stop, start moving across those two kilometers. Enter and eliminate everyone who remains alive. Do you have that clear?"

"Yes. Clear. I will contact Masri tomorrow evening at six and warn him. I have promised him six hours in which to move his people out of the camp."

There was only a second of hesitation, then Tobari said, "Negative. Repeat, negative."

"Did I hear 'negative?' " Hourani responded in surprise.

"Correct," Tobari said more firmly. "Forget them. It is too dangerous a risk to contact Masri inside the camp. If he is observed or overheard the whole operation will be in jeopardy."

"But . . . but I have promised him. There are fifty-two—"

"Repeat, *negative*, Leader One," Tobari shouted. Then, "They have served our holy cause. Allah will reward them generously for their deeds. Follow the escape plan outlined for you. That is all. Over and out.''

Tobari heard the word ''*Wait!*'' come through clearly, but cut out and retracted the antenna. With a sardonic smile, he took the thermos from Sadani, rinsed his mouth, spat the warm water out, then drank without relish. Sadani stood silently until Tobari handed the thermos back. As he capped it tightly, Sadani said, ''Hatif, there are fifty-two of our own people in that camp, apart from the hundreds of other Arabs—''

''They are not *our* people, Amon, simply people who were hired by the Jews to work in their oil field—''

''Still, they are Arabs, our brethren who have been promised large rewards for doing a necessary job for us. Without them—''

''Amon, Amon,'' Tobari said, speaking as he would in instructing a child. ''You haven't yet learned that the lives of a few must not be overvalued when the future of millions is at stake, even a nation. Look back into the history of the world, that of our own Egypt, or Turkey, Russia, China, the United States, every great nation on this earth. What has become of countries like Armenia?''

''I understand what you are saying, Hatif, but these fifty-two people in particular are men whom we have paid to do this thing, who could be useful to us again—''

''Amon, was it not you who authorized the assassination of Assaf Hafez when you believed it was necessary?''

''One man, Hatif, who was a danger to all of us.''

''The life of one man who is a danger to a hundred is equal to the lives of fifty-two, or a thousand, when the lives and futures of millions are at stake. Now let us be done with this discussion and move on. Time us very carefully. Find a cave where we can sleep. By tomorrow night we need to be within five kilometers of Bashra.''

From a height of five thousand feet the sun had turned the mountains of the central Sinai into a crazy quilt of red, purple, brown, green and gold. To the west, the desert lay like a vast beige, yellow and dark gray blanket, rippled by occasional wadis and minor outcroppings. The only movement below was the illusion created by shimmering heat waves causing the pilot and observer in the light Air Patrol observation plane to strain their eyes as they tried to pick out a trace of the Bedouin group that had been sighted on the afternoon before.

Hourly, the observer had radioed ''No contact'' to base camp and received the curt order, ''Continue,'' from his communications officer. Later, with dusk approaching, the observer radioed in with the same monotonous message and was instructed to return to base camp.

In helicopter Alef Bayt, similarly, Lieutenant Sartov threw a questioning glance in Saul Lahav's direction. "This close to Bashra, Colonel, they must be resting among the caves by day and traveling by night," Sartov offered.

With the lowering sun causing the mountains to throw long, dark shadows, emphasizing the dunes and rippled, trackless sands below, further search seemed useless. Reluctantly, Saul nodded his head in silent surrender. Sartov turned the helicopter around and headed back to Camp Herzog.

On the ground, Lieutenant Yariv and Sergeant Chesler continued plowing northward according to operational plan.

As night fell and the heat inside the caves became more oppressive, Hourani gave permission to Bedouin and unit members to sleep in the open. The Bedouin at once set up their tents in the area between the two fingers of rock to the north and south, but were again strictly admonished against lighting fires. Smoking would be permitting only inside the caves.

The UPFP men, however, chose not to sleep in tents and spread their blankets on the flat sand. Sentries stationed in the rocks were relieved and, after leaving instructions that he was to be awakened every two hours at the time of the guard changes, Hourani turned in at once.

At the end of each two-hour watch, he was duly awakened. He rose, made the rounds to see that all was in order, the sentries fully alert, then returned to his blanket. It was a moonless night, hot and airless, which made sleep difficult. After thirty minutes of tossing and turning restlessly, he rose and went to a nearby cave and sat just inside its opening and lit a cigarette.

Tomorrow night, he thought with high anticipation. Tomorrow night he would be rid of Twefik and his miserable band of Bedouin and give the order to move on toward Bashra. The ultimate target. This, he contemplated, would be his moment of personal glory and achievement. He knew each well-rehearsed move he would make, each precise order he must give, knowing his men would perform to the letter.

Only one thing continued to give him moments of concern; that he must obey Falcon's express order not to communicate with Zuheir Masri to give him warning. If this caused him to have spasms of acute distress, even some doubts as to the wisdom of sacrificing the lives of fifty-two men, the fate of the other Arabs working at

Bashra gave him none at all. Privately, he considered them to be Israeli Arabs, traitors to Islam and to the cause of all Arabs, and thus, no different from Israelis. Masri's people, although Israeli Arabs themselves, were working for the Holy Cause, which placed them in a far different category.

Still he, Ahmed Hourani, was a soldier, and a soldier obeyed the commands of his leader without question. So be it.

He stubbed out his cigarette in the sand and returned to his blanket. He was asleep within minutes, his conscience clear.

Thus, shrouded in darkness, the camp slept through the night.

When the first streak of dawn appeared in the east, the sentry facing in that direction looked up from his seated position and stared for a moment. At first light, his orders were to quietly awaken the sleepers and order them back into the caves, Bedouin and UPFP members alike. He rose, stretched, then walked a few yards to his right and emptied his bladder onto the sand. He stood there for a few moments in idle contemplation, turned back and looked over the sleeping figures of his comrades, then at the Bedouin tents which were beginning to take recognizable form, envying the men their women, so easily within reach. Soon, with this job behind them, he would be back in Haifa, within reach of . . .

He dismissed the thought of women, which only stirred him uselessly. He turned away now and started back to where he had been sitting, unable to make out the form of his counterpart sentry who was sitting up, facing toward the west. The man on the northern edge was also hidden from his view by the darkness and the rocks that shielded the main body from that side. Somewhere up in the rocks to the south, which faced Bashra, he knew that two men were on the alert. Two, because this was the vulnerable side and one would keep the other awake by his mere presence.

He was hungry and thirsty, but more than anything else, he longed desperately for a cigarette; and although he had several in his fatigue jacket pocket, dared not strike a light, no matter how well hidden. In Hourani's present mood, any breach of his orders could bring swift and savage punishment.

At his guard station, he sat down again, crossed his legs, held his submachine gun on his lap and wrapped the loose ends of his kaffiyeh around his throat. Ten minutes more and he would begin waking the camp.

The sentry facing west now stirred and raised his head. A moment later, he stood up and listened, catching a faint, not unfamiliar sound. For perhaps a full thirty seconds, he remained in that position, right hand cupped to his ear and turned westward to hear better. He turned again and saw that his colleague on the western edge was also standing now, a dark, shadowy figure. Then both turned toward the north at the same moment and saw the sentry who had been stationed there running toward the camp.

When the three men came together, the most recent arrival asked breathlessly, "You heard?"

"Yes," the sentry from the western side said. "A motor. Get everybody up."

Hourani awoke at the first touch, although he had been asleep less than an hour since the last changing of sentries. He listened, then leaped to his feet and strode to the western edge of the camp and listened again. "It grows louder, Ahmed—" the sentry from the north began, but Hourani turned, cutting him off. "Get everybody up and armed," he ordered. "I want a bazooka team at the base of the rocks to the south, another team in those rocks to the north. Assemble the heavy machine gun and place it here, facing west. Everybody else in a line across here with extra ammunition. Quickly!"

Now the Bedouin had come awake, aroused by the commotion and excited voices of the fedayeen. When Twefik and two of his older sons emerged from their tents, Hourani ordered them back inside; but Twefik went directly to him.

"We will not stay here. We are not a part of this thing. I want my money now." He turned and began to wave his arms, shouting toward the tents, "Up! Everybody up! We are leaving!"

Enraged by the old Bedouin's hysterical shouting, Hourani grabbed his arm, but Twefik turned on him with a fierce, angry curse, lashing out with such sudden force that the fedayeen leader was thrown off balance. In the loose sand that had been churned up, he slipped and fell to the ground. Furious, he sprang to his feet and in one move, drew his revolver. Twefik stood his ground, one arm extended, a long, bony finger pointed at Hourani as he shouted his determination to leave with his family. Hourani fired a single shot. The bullet struck Twefik el Nassib's chest and he staggered backwards, sagged to his knees and fell face down in the sand, dead. As his two sons ran toward the old man angry cries of the Bedouin rose over the wailing of frightened women and children, Hourani waved his revolver and shouted, "Back! Get back or you will die, too! All of you!" Signaling to four of his men, he ordered, "See that the rest of them remain in their tents. Shoot anyone who tried to interfere with us or tries to leave."

Tewfik's sons carried the old man's body to his tent. Weaponless, they obeyed the orders of the four armed UPFP men guarding them and remained in their tents, mourning the death of their patriarch and leader.

Now the sky was lightening as the UPFP men moved into the positions assigned to them. Two bazooka men climbed into the rocks to the north, two others to the south. The sentries in both locations returned to the camp and were ordered into the line of men facing the open west, digging shallow trenches in the sand. At the extreme eastern edge of the mountain, where there was a firmer base, the two portable mortars were set up and made ready.

Meanwhile, the sound of the motors came closer, ominously louder, then stopped. The outlines of the one large and one smaller vehicle were barely clear now. For perhaps a full minute there was total silence, then a metallic voice thundered across the open desert into the camp, its echoes ricocheting off the rock walls. "In the camp there! You are blocked and escape is impossible! If you try to make a fight of it, this will only result in useless death! Throw down your weapons and march out with your hands in the air!"

Ahmed Hourani stood facing the west, staring at the shadowy outline of the larger vehicle whose details were becoming more distinguishable. An armored personnel carrier. The smaller vehicle was discernible as a jeep. What abominable luck, to be discovered accidentally by a desert patrol!

The man standing beside him said, "What will we do, Ahmed?"

"There can't be that many men," Hourani replied. "We outnumber them and will fight it out. Let them make the first move. Are the mortars and bazookas in place?"

"Yes."

"Have them aim for the wheels and treads as soon as they can see them clearly. Do not fire until I gave the order and don't waste any shells. Make every one count." When the man ran off, Hourani spoke to the men lying on either side of him, their submachine guns at the ready. "Hold your fire until I fire the first burst. Pass the word along."

In his jeep, Lieutenant Yariv said to the man beside him, "What about Chesler, have you been able to raise him?"

At that moment, the radio squawked. "I have him, Lieutenant."

"Get his location. Give him ours. Tell him to move up at full speed. If we are not attacked first, we will wait for him."

He picked up the bullhorn and spoke into it again. "In the camp! You are in a hopeless position. We are facing you with enough men and equipment to destroy you. Come out now with your hands over your heads—"

Hourani fired his weapon. Submachine guns all along the front line flashed. A bazooka shell plowed the ground ten yards to the left of the personnel carrier. A mortar shell dropped far beyond the jeep. Yariv ordered his men to spread out on the desert floor. A moment later, a third shell struck the left track of the personnel carrier and the Israelis opened fire. The machine gun on the jeep blasted into the front line of the fedayeen while the heavier gun on the personnel carrier swept the rocks on the right, then on the left. A mortar shell was fired from the camp and again overshot its mark by more than thirty yards. The heavy machine gun responded in the direction of the flash, sweeping the base of the mountain.

The advantage was in favor of the Israelis who, out in the open, were able to crawl into a semicircle with ample space between each man. The fedayeen, restricted to the area between the two spines of rock, were only able to root deeper into the sand, from which to return their fire. Unguarded now, the Bedouin had fled from their tents into the rocks to the north, which afforded greater protection, climbing on hands and knees to get to the northern side where their animals were tethered; but the movement was slow, their situation precarious.

The heavy gun on the wounded armored personnel carrier continued to sweep the rocks to the north and south in an effort to silence the bazookas being fired from those positions. Thus far, they were effective, without knowing whether or not the bazooka men had been taken out or were lying back, waiting for an opportunity to fire again. And now, during a brief lull, a shell came winging in from the south. It hit the windshield of the armored car, plowed through it into the empty forward compartment, which began blazing in flames. The machine gun, mounted on the roof of the cab, continued to fire back for a moment, then stopped as the gunner leaped over the side and took a position among his colleagues on the ground.

Yariv ordered the jeep driver to back his vehicle behind the burning armored car and concentrate his machine gun on the south spine from which the bazooka shell had been fired.

Along the line, a heavy concentration of fire was directed toward the front line of fedayeen, then a bazooka shell came winging in from the north position. The jeep swung around and responded. Now the heavy machine gun had been taken out, but the mortar shells continued to overshoot their mark, although coming closer to the burning personnel carrier and endangering the jeep. And now, the light machine gun on the jeep jammed, its operator struggling desperately to clear the breech of the cartridge that was blocking it.

The radio spluttered and Sergeant Chesler's voice came through. The second unit was within a kilometer and coming on at full speed. Yariv took the microphone and gave Chesler directions to pull up to within fifty yards of the burning vehicle, then dismount and join them on foot, leaving the gunners on the jeep and armored car with their weapons.

In the fedayeen camp, four were dead and three lay wounded, out of action. The Israelis had taken two fatalities and three wounded. Yariv held his men in their positions, waiting for the arrival of Chesler and his unit. And now, the Israelis were taking fire from the rocks to the south, machine gun fire of a heavy caliber. Yariv ordered return fire from his ground troops, then the light machine gun on the jeep was clear and turned in that direction. The heavy machine gun in the rocks was silenced for the moment and under intense cover fire, four Israelis streaked across the sand toward the south rocks. Three were able to make it safely, but the fourth man was hit as he tried to climb over a lower ridge and fell into a deep crevice, out of sight.

Lying beside the jeep in order to be within reach of the radio, Sergeant Israel Zeid shouted, "Baruch! Let's move in from two sides and clean the bastards out!"

But Yariv, with his binoculars sweeping the camp, shouted back, "Not yet. Not yet. There are still some Bedouin women and children up in the north rocks. We'll hold here and concentrate on the front line. Chesler will be here any minute. We'll see what the situation is then."

He had hoped it would not be necessary to take this next action, but his casualty count made it imperative. He reached up and took the microphone from Zeid and radioed in to Camp Herzog. When the communicator answered, he said, "Contact Colonel Lahav. Inform him we have made contact with the fedayeen and are taking heavy fire. Some casualties on both sides. There are women and children in our line of fire. Pass the word on to Colonel Pelz. Over and out."

Within four minutes, Saul was on the radio to Yariv. "What is your location, Lieutenant?"

"We are in the Wadi Talal. They are locked inside a cul-de-sac and we are holding them there. The Bedouin are trying to escape toward the north, but some are still in our line of fire."

"Contain them where they are. I will order a gunship to your location. ETA about twenty minutes. Keep them occupied and allow the Bedouin to escape as best they can. Keep me informed when they are clear or if the situation changes."

Yariv surveyed the situation again. The fire from the UPFP was holding steady, and the Bedouin were making progress. All but a few women and children were well up into the rocks, most of them on the downslope and out of harm's way, the fedayeen too preoccupied to pay them any attention. Behind him to the west, Chesler's jeep and personnel carrier had been sighted. On his radio, Yariv contacted Chesler.

"Move your jeep up behind mine, your personnel carrier well to the rear, at a distance of about fifty yards. Have your men spread out and come up low into our position."

Disposition of the arriving vehicles effected, Chesler's unit dismounted and came forward in a crouch, inching their way to the front, firing as they moved in. As the situation was made clearer to Chesler, he dispersed his men to the right and left to keep the UPFP front line pinned down in their shallow ditches. Up in the rocks to the south, three Israelis were continuing the battle with the two UPFP bazooka men, preventing them from firing their heavy weapons, each side trying to pick off the other with rifle fire. Nor were the ground troops on either side able to provide protective fire to their own people in the heights.

Now the last of the Bedouin had crossed the ridge and were on the downslope to the north; and the Israelis were surprised by another bazooka shell which came in from the north ridge and slammed into the front end of Yariv's jeep. Yariv rolled to one side and out of harm, but Sergeant Zeid's right leg was shattered as the jeep exploded into flames. Yariv crawled to Zeid's aid, ripped off his trouser belt and wrapped it around the wounded sergeant's upper thigh while Chesler tore Zeid's shirt into wide strips and tried to stem the flow of blood.

There was a clattering overhead now as Saul Lahav's helicopter came into view. As it approached, the UPFP men began firing in its direction, but Sartov quickly swung off to the left and gained altitude to keep it out of range. On his radio, Saul called in to Yariv on Chesler's jeep radio.

"Back off, Baruch! The gunship will be here in two minutes. Are the Bedouin out of the camp?"

"All out," Yariv replied. "W will move back. Tell the gunship to avoid the rocks to the south. We have some men in there."

"Yes. I will inform them. After the delivery is made, move in. They will make one pass only."

Yariv and Chesler passed the word among the men on the line, then began to move back out of danger of the gunship due to arrive momentarily. With thirty seconds to spare, all eyes were focused on the tiny black dot slanting in from the south. As it grew larger it was suddenly blotted out by a brilliant, blinding white-red-orange flash from its underbelly. The missile landed in the center of the fedayeen camp and exploded with tremendous force that raised a huge geyser of sand with an earsplitting roar.

The battle for Wadi Talal was over.

*   *   *

When the smoke died down and the flaming tents were smothered with sand, the remaining nine fedayeen stood with empty hands cradled over their heads, numb and trembling at their miraculous escape from death. The seven dead and four wounded lay among the smoking debris and churned sand. The Israeli casualty count came to three dead and four wounded, two seriously.

From the north, climbing over the rocks and walking on foot around the western edge of the spine of rocks, the Bedouin began returning, weeping with bitter anger, to scrounge through the rubble for what remained of their possessions; mourning the death of their patriarch, whose body they found and carried into one of the caves; calling upon Allah to witness their anguish.

The helicopter had landed beside the disabled half-track. Saul joined Lieutenant Yariv while Golan and Shaked began assisting the Israelis who were tending to their wounded. Two returned with the body of the man who had fallen into the crevice among the south rocks. The two seriously wounded Israelis were placed in the helicopter for removal to the camp hospital at Bashra. A truck was on its way from the oil field to pick up the lesser wounded and dead.

In the center of the camp, Ahmed Hourani, shaken and distraught, wrists tied behind his back and held apart from the other eight unharmed UPFP men, was being guarded from the outraged Bedouin who stood before him shouting accusations and demanding that Hourani be turned over to them for the cold-blooded murder of Twefik. On the eastern edge of the camp where the seven dead fedayeen lay in a row, a sergeant and two others were searching the bodies for identification under Dov Shaked's supervision. This completed, he reported to Saul and Yariv.

"What is the final count?" Saul asked.

"Theirs—seven dead, four wounded, nine prisoners. Ours— three dead, four wounded, including the two on their way to Bashra. We have completed the body search. None was carrying documents. We found this map on their leader. His name is Ahmed Hourani. He was carrying three thousand Israeli and six thousand Lebanese pounds in a money belt around his waist."

"For what reason?"

"He won't say anything except that his name is Ahmed Hourani."

"Take him in with the rest. I'll talk to him later. Who is the leader of these Bedouin?"

"The old man lying in the cave was the leader. His sons claim that Hourani shot him in cold blood when he tried to move the family out before the shooting began. The elder son has taken over and says the money Hourani is carrying belongs to him, payment for having brought the UPFP here from Syria. Also, that they knew nothing of their purpose in coming here."

"Tell the son to get his family together as soon as they can and be on their way. They will not be rewarded for their part in this affair. If they make any strenuous objections, they will be taken into custody. What about any plastic explosives?"

"Nothing. Only normal ammunition, some bazooka and mortar shells." He held up a walkie-talkie unit and a pair of binoculars taken from Hourani. "If we need anything more to identify them as UPFP—" He pointed to the white E-O markings engraved on each of the items.

Saul nodded and turned to Yariv. "Take over here, Baruch. Let them bury their dead here. Trucks are on the way from Bashra. Take the wounded and prisoners there and hold them for questioning."

"And the Bedouin?"

"Turn them loose. Pawns. They've paid their price."

Saul's helicopter returned from Bashra. Sartov reported their wounded were being cared for in the camp hospital and were prepared to receive prisoners. Trucks for that purpose were on the way and would arrive within a few minutes.

Saul called out to Shaked and Golan, "Let's move out. We still have a black Fiat to find."

Sartov shook his head from side to side. "It's still a hell of a big desert, Colonel," he said with grave doubts.

Once aboard, Saul radioed in to Judah Rosental with a brief account of the engagement, reporting the success of that encounter and noting their failure to find any trace of the plastic explosives at Wadi Talal.

"Then it is obvious," Rosental replied, "that they have already been planted at Bashra."

"I have already ordered another concentrated search by Wolf, Judah."

"But it is such a large area to cover, Saul, and makes it all the more imperative to locate Tobari and Sadani with that damned detonator."

"I know, Judah—"

"Find him, Saul. Until you do—"

By midmorning, sitting in the Fiat parked in a protective wadi, Tobari and Sadani listened to their transistor radio tuned to Radio Israel's news broadcast. When it came to an end and a musical interlude began, Tobari shut the instrument off and placed it on the seat between them. He lit a cigarette and said, "Well, Amon, so far it goes well."

With less confidence, his face bathed in sweat and gloom, deep naso-labial lines running from his nostrils to the corners of his mouth, Sadani said cynically, "What if they are purposely withholding—"

Tobari's smile became a short laugh of derision. "Amon, you have become a true, classic pessimist. If anything had gone wrong, the Jews would leap at the chance to broadcast it quickly, declare it publicly to humiliate Cairo and Damascus and boast of their invincibility to their imperialist friends in America."

Sadani said morosely, "I question that. There have been times when—" His voice drifted off as though weary of jousting at theories and ideas with Tobari. He wiped his neck and face with a sweat-dampened handkerchief and said, "It is this damned heat. I have always despised the desert. Always. It frightens me."

"Look ahead to the bright future, Amon. We are so close to it now. Ah, Amon, when we have gained our goals, all of them, and take this country for ourselves. Look to the day when we will have taken Jordan and incorporate it into the new state of Palestine—"

"Hatif," Sadani said sourly, "I am more interested in today and tomorrow. I need to get out, take Suzi with me. Only God knows how many are out looking for me at this moment."

"And not me?" Tobari said. "Lahav and his people know I am somewhere in Israel after we eluded him on the road to Jerusalem."

"Perhaps, but—"

"Amon, trust me. I have not come this far by being careless. A few errors, minor and beyond control, have been made, admittedly, but in the end, we will emerge in glory, with all the money we need to reach our inevitable goals. Once in power, we will be bold, move swiftly and openly toward our destiny."

"Yes, Hatif, I know. You have always been the bold one, the leader. Always." There was a note of resentment in his statement, as though he should have added, *"And I, the follower."*

"Then trust me now, Amon. Believe in me. By tonight we will make the one move that will put us in touch with our dream."

In the helicopter, in midafternoon, Saul had begun to fight the weariness that comes with frustration. Both Golan and Shaked were showing restlessness as Sartov guided his machine across more endless miles of desert between Wadi Talal and Bashra, seeking any trace of movement along dozens of empty trails.

"Swing back across that small oasis," Saul ordered.

Sartov gained altitude and flew over the designated grove that stood out like a dusty beacon in the otherwise flat desert. It was empty and he swung back to where the spine of rocks rose off the floor like the back of a prehistoric monster. They flew along for a few more minutes until that spine curved downward like the tail of a huge lizard, to where it touched the sand again.

It was Sartov who suddenly raised his right hand and pointed. "There, to the left, Colonel. A narrow road. Or trail." He swung the helicopter around to give Saul a better look at it, which brought Golan, sitting directly behind Saul, to full alert. "I see it," Saul said.

The road ran close to the edge of some rocks, winding and twisting in between small, darkly shadowed formations. Shaked was checking a map, but there was no such road marked upon it in this area. Sartov dropped down lower, barely skimming the tops of the ridges, then began following what seemed to be a trail toward the south. Moments later, they were flying over more masses of rock with deep crevices and wadis interspersed.

Sartov said, "A car could be hidden in any of a thousand such valleys and gullies and we'd never see—"

"Wait, wait," Golan shouted above the noise of the clattering helicopter. "Over there, on my right—"

"What?" Saul shouted back, craning in that direction.

"We passed over it. Circle back, Sartov. Something down there in a wadi. It will be on your left, the one closest to that mountain ridge."

Sartov made the turn and circled back, with Shaked's eyes straining through the sun haze into the crevices below. Golan was arching his back to keep the particular wadi in view. Then Shaked began pointing in the same direction, shouting, "You were right, Yoram! A car parked just off the trail."

Now Saul reached up and over Sartov's head to peer downward into the wadi. "It could be," he said hopefully. "Swing around and put it down on my side. I want a closer look."

On the ground, Sadani and Tobari heard the machinegunlike chatter of the helicopter's blades as it came toward, then over their car. Sadani's body jerked forward as though preparing to get out of the car. Tobari restrained him, grasping his arm. "Wait, Amon. It is likely they can't see us down here."

Then both saw it again as it began to circle and head back toward them. In a sweat of panic, Sadani pulled out of Tobari's grasp. "Hatif! They have seen us!"

"Easy, Amon! All they have seen is a car sitting here, a traveler who has parked off the road to rest. They are up there, we are down here. What can they see from above? And why should they be looking for us? Don't help them by showing yourself—''

But Sadani's panic was overpowering. With one quick motion he had opened the door and lurched out of the car. "Amon! Don't be a fool!" Tobari shouted as he tried to slide across the seat, but only managed to sweep the transistor radio and w-t unit to the floor. "Amon! For the love of Allah!"

Sadani was wild now. He turned, reached in behind the front seat and picked up one of the two submachine guns, rammed a cartridge into the chamber. "They won't take me—" he muttered.

"Put that away, you damned fool! You'll get us both killed!" Tobari shouted.

Eyes wide open, deaf to Tobari's pleas, Sadani moved away from the car, raised his weapon and got off one burst, then a second, and a third.

Tobari was out of the car now and in two giant leaps, tackled the hysterical Sadani and knocked him to the ground, screaming at the top of his voice. Sadani was now totally out of control. Tobari straddled him and angrily slapped him back to some sense of sanity. "Get into the car before I kill you myself!" Tobari shouted into his ear.

In the helicopter, Sartov shot upward and out of range of the bursts from below, then circled overhead and looked to Saul for instructions. "It's them, the lunatics," Saul said. "Keep out of gun range and let's watch their next move. I don't want to go down there and get into an unnecessary firefight."

Sartov hovered. Saul said, "What is our exact distance from Bashra?"

Sartov glanced at his map and made a rapid calculation. "As near as I can make it, between eighteen and twenty kilometers."

Saul sighed in relief. "According to Dr. Levitt, we are far beyond effective range of the remote detonator. We'll have to keep them from getting closer. What is our petrol situation?"

"We're good for another two and a half to three hours."

"And four more hours of light. We're in good shape. If we have to land—"

"They're moving," Shaked called out, unlimbering his submachine gun. "We can take them from behind, Saul."

"No. This time, no corpses, Dov. They've got too much to tell us." He concentrated on the scene below, watching closely as the Fiat began creeping slowly toward the narrow road, up an incline, then onto flat ground. The car turned south and was now picking up speed, throwing a strong wake of dust behind.

"Sartov—" Saul shouted, his mouth close to the pilot's ear; but

Sartov had anticipated the order. He swung the helicopter around in a tight circle and aimed it like a weapon at the car below. Dropping fast, it skimmed over the top of the Fiat, shot ahead for a distance of about six hundred yards, then turned and came back toward it at windshield height. At that moment when the helicopter and car seemed to be approaching collision, Sartov lifted his machine a scant few feet, then made a 180-degree turn and came back to hover directly above it. Sartov was now enjoying himself for the first time since the mission began, eagerly displaying his expertise in a machine that had become a part of himself.

The downdraft was creating considerable difficulties for Tobari, who was forced to grip the wheel of the Fiat tightly to keep it stabilized and on the road. On the seat beside him, a thoroughly chastened Sadani cringed toward the right door, clutching and twisting his hands, blubbering senselessly, emotionally shot.

Coldly, emotionlessly, Tobari assessed their chances of escape as nil. The unpaved road was narrow, rutted, and seemed to lead nowhere. It ran in an almost straight line through open desert with only a few low-lying rock formations that would give them no cover. Eventually, the men in the helicopter would tire of this game and bring their weapons into play. Not, he reasoned, to kill them, but to damage the car, bring it to a halt and take them prisoner. Sadly, Tobari began to see his dream of power and glory coming to an ignoble end. He turned and looked at Sadani with sudden disgust.

In the helicopter, Saul clamped a hand on Sartov's arm. "Put us directly behind them and a few feet above."

Sartov nodded and allowed the Fiat to gain a little distance while dropping lower. Saul lowered the window on his right, bucking the airstream. Leaning out, Uzi aimed at the rear tires of the Fiat, he fired a burst into the wake of sand its rear wheels were churning up. There was little result. His second burst also fell short and the little car speeded up. On the third try, the burst stitched a pattern along the road behind the car and finally reached the rear left fender, piercing it and shredding the tire.

The Fiat swerved erratically toward its left, swung back to the center of the road, limped forward for another few yards and came to a dead stop. Sartov circled it, then landed behind and to its rear, just off the road. Saul, Shaked and Golan leaped out, dropped into a crouch, weapons aimed toward the offending vehicle and advanced on it.

As they reached it, Tobari stepped out into the road from the left side, his hands empty and upraised. Golan and Shaked ran to the right side, opened the door and pulled Sadani out. Shaked patted him down for weapons, found none on his person and cuffed his wrists behind his back. Sartov, meanwhile, had cut his motor, got on the radio to base camp and requested a second helicopter to meet them to bring the prisoners in.

They arrived at Bashra late in the afternoon. Lieutenant Yariv and his men were already on hand, the UPFP prisoners locked in a well-guarded storeroom, awaiting interrogation, their wounded being cared for in a hospital tent. The Israeli wounded had been tended to, their dead awaiting removal to Tel Aviv and Jerusalem for burial. Sadani was examined by the camp medical officer, who found him to be in a highly disturbed state and suggested a strong sedative.

"Not too strong, I hope," Saul said. "It is very important that we talk to him and get some answers that are vital to this operation we have just come through."

"Then we'll start with something mild enough to settle him down without putting him to sleep."

"How long before we can expect to get some intelligent response from him?"

The doctor smiled and shrugged. "In an hour, maybe two, but I can't give you any guarantees as to the degree of the man's ability to respond with clear intelligence."

"Just so he is able to talk and know what he is saying."

Another shrug. "If you will leave us now, Colonel—"

Tobari had been taken to the small room next to Major Wolf's office where he waited under the watchful eyes of Sergeant Chesler, provided with cigarettes and a pot of coffee. For the first few minutes he sat on a hard wooden chair without uttering a sound, hardly moving, his handsome face set in a grim mask. When, later, he stood up and turned toward the window, which looked out on a panorama of activity, Chesler said, "No, Captain. You will remain in that chair until you are sent for. Sit down."

Tobari's face broke into a wintry smile. "Is this the way a sergeant addresses a captain in your army?"

Chesler regarded the Egyptian coldly. "I am not prepared to discuss military protocol with you, nor anything else. My orders are to—"

"Ah, orders."

"Just sit down and keep quiet, Captain. Your turn to talk will come as soon as Colonel Lahav is ready for you."

Tobari reached for the coffee pot on the table next to his chair, poured a cup, then lit a cigarette. He saw no profit in trying to engage the sergeant in further conversation. What would be, would be.

In Major Wolf's office, Saul Lahav finally managed to reach an impatient Judah Rosental, who had been on the phone with Shana Altman to try to learn if she had been in contact with Saul, this between frequent calls from General Bartok's secretary with the same request. What information he had gotten thus far had come from Southern Command's Air Patrol and Colonel Pelz at Camp Herzog, which was hardly enough to satisfy him.

"Saul! What the hell is going on down there?"

"It is ninety-nine percent contained, Judah. We have taken the UPFP unit and I have Tobari and Sadani here at Bashra."

"Thank God. Casualties?"

"Some on both sides. I will fill you in later. The important thing now is to locate the explosives and remove them. Once that is done, I will question Tobari."

"When can I expect you back here? I have some very anxious people on my neck waiting for answers. Also, some enterprising newsmen who happen to own shortwave radios and are clamoring outside my door at this minute."

Saul said, "Let them clamor, Judah. And the sooner I get off this telephone, the sooner I can have the answers you want."

"Then, *Shalom*, Saul. A good job, well done. Let me know when you expect to arrive here. I'll do my best to keep General Bartok and the others pacified."

"*Shalom*."

In the barracks building next to where the UPFP men were being held, one of Wolf's lieutenants sat on a cot in one corner talking to a man who sat on another cot facing him. At the other end of the long room, four armed Israeli troopers held some thirty or forty steel-hatted workers in a group and out of range of the lieutenant and the civilian. When Saul entered with Shaked, the lieutenant rose and came to Saul, pointing to the civilian who had remained seated on the cot, elbows resting on his knees, hands dangling between his thighs, head lowered on his chest.

"That one," the lieutenant said, indicating the man he had been talking to, "is Zuheir Masri, from Haifa. We found him in possession of a single walkie-talkie unit when we searched the workers' quarters. It is possible he is the leader of the others."

"And who are the others?"

"They are men who were recruited from employment agencies during the last sixty to ninety days. Some have already talked."

"Let's get him out of here. Hold him in one of the offices alone and under guard. We will interrogate the others first."

Zuheir Masri was removed from the building and Saul began interrogating the other worker-suspects singly, with Dov at his side to take notes that might be useful later in talking with the one known as Masri. By nightfall, Saul had concluded the interrogation and he and Dov took a light supper, then walked to the administration building where Zuheir Masri was being held, carrying the walkie-talkie unit with him.

"You are Zuheir Masri?"

Masri turned a pair of solemn eyes upward and said disconsolately, "Yes."

"Listen to what I have to say to you very carefully, Masri. Some of your men have already given my people information we need to know about the plastic explosives you and they have planted about this installation. What I want from you is verification and the locations. You will then lead a demolition team to where each has been placed. You have one minute to decide whether or not you will cooperate."

"And if I cooperate?"

"It will be so noted in the charges filed against you. What leniency is possible in your case will then be in the hands of the court."

"And if I do not wish to cooperate?"

"If that is your decision, so be it. That, too, will be taken into consideration at the time of your sentencing. You are not a child, Masri, so I will leave up to you the manner of how pleasant or unpleasant the time you serve will be. You have fifteen seconds left to give me your final answer."

Zuheir Masri looked from Saul to Shaked, using up three seconds of the remaining time. He then turned his eyes downward and said, "I will cooperate."

"'Very well." And to Dov, "Get the information we want, then put a team together to start uncovering the buried explosives. Have it packed to take back to Tel Aviv as evidence, then have Masri's statement taped. Also, those of his people, taken separately."

From there, Saul walked across the open compound to the camp hospital where Sadani was being treated by the doctor in charge while Yoram Golan looked on. He signaled Golan out of the room into the hallway. "What is with him?"

"He is responding, Saul. He is more rational now."

"Excellent. I want you to get a tape recorder and start questioning him. Get as much as you can before he is put to sleep and bring what you have to Major Wolf's office, but give me at least half an hour with Tobari."

Outside, the civilian staff were trying their best to get the workers back on the job, which had been interrupted by the arrival of Yariv's unit, the wounded and dead from Wadi Talal. Major Wolf was busy organizing a security group in the act of setting up a special barbed wire enclosure to contain the prisoners. Saul observed the work for a moment, then called Wolf aside. "Nothing too elaborate, Major," he said. "By tomorrow morning, the prisoners will be on their way to Tel Aviv. Just make sure they are well guarded until then and we'll take them off your hands. If you have no objections, I will make use of your office for the next hour or so."

Wolf smiled happily. "Of course, Colonel. As long as it is required."

Saul went to Wolf's office and dialed the room next door. When Sergeant Chesler answered, he said, "Bring Captain Tobari to Major Wolf's office, Sergeant."

Tobari entered the room and stared at Saul with professional interest. The contrast in the two men spoke volumes; Saul's open-throated shirt and rumpled trousers, his hair unruly, face and hands sweat-streaked; Tobari, militarily erect, his hair recently combed, British-cut safari shirt and matching trousers brushed free of sand and dust, dark brown ankle-high boots wiped clean and glistening as though recently polished. "Colonel," he said in simple acknowledgment.

"Please be seated, Captain," Saul replied, indicating the side chair, then to Chesler, "Leave us, Sergeant. Have someone send in some coffee, please."

Chesler went out and closed the door. Saul took a pack of cigarettes from his shirt pocket and placed it on the desk between them, a lighter beside it; but Tobari made no move to reach for either. "Well, Captain," Saul said, "it seems we have much to talk about."

Tobari regarded him with suave coolness. "I doubt that very much, Colonel. I don't think I can be of material assistance to you in any way."

Saul opened the center desk drawer and picked up the calculator device that had been taken from the Egyptian at the time of his capture. He toyed with it for a moment, then placed it on the desk in front of him. Tobari's reaction was one of total indifference. The door opened then and Chesler appeared with a civilian waiter who carried a tray with a pot of coffee, two enameled mugs, spoons and a small bowl of sugar. He poured the coffee into the two mugs and both men left.

Saul said, "Face it, Captain Tobari. Your days as Falcon—or Ali Fathy," (at which Tobari winced with sudden pain) "are finished. Your UPFP training camp is without leadership or guidance. Your headquarters at Ein Fara is in our hands. Your people there, including Sadani's wife, have been taken into custody. Your grand mission is over."

From across the desk, the Egyptian eyed the Israeli with a look of arrogance which Saul, in Tobari's predicament, could not believe possible. Yet it was unmistakable there; unsmiling lips curved slightly upward in disdain, handsome, clean-featured face showing little or no apprehension, certainly not of fear; a chess master waiting coolly for his opponent's next move. Tobari raised the coffee mug to his lips and took a few sips, then replaced it on the edge of the desk. "There will be others, Colonel, many others. If not the UPFP, there are still the PLO, PFLP, Black September, and more. It will go on—and on—"

"We expect it and will meet those challenges as we have met yours. Arafat's olive branch—"

Tobari smiled at the mention of the name. "And, if your memory serves you, the Freedom Fighter's gun."

"Yes, Captain, that too. We expect that also and are prepared to deal with it when and as it occurs."

Tobari picked up the mug again, then replaced it on the desk. He reached into a pocket and took out one of his own cigarettes and a gold lighter. When it had been lit and puffed alive, he said, "Is it possible, Colonel, that we might reach some—ah—reasonable compromise, you and I?"

"I doubt it very much," Saul replied evenly. "You have nothing to bargain with."

"It is possible that you are wrong, of course."

"In what way?" Saul asked with rising curiosity.

"I can give you names that will involve the highest officials among your enemies, cause them considerable embarrassment among other Arab heads of state, in the United Nations, the United States, the world press—"

Saul was shaking his head negatively. "We don't need that, Tobari. Our friends will know. Our enemies will also know soon enough that another of their efforts has failed."

"Lahav," Tobari said, "you suffer from the same lack in all you Israelis. You have no sense of humor. Or class."

"Hold on to yours, my friend. It may give you some comfort in prison."

"And how long after I am tried and sentenced do you think it will take before others will carry off a number of important hostages, either from Israel or abroad, to bargain for my release?"

Saul studied him for a moment, then said, "For an intelligent man, Captain, with the sense of humor and class you pretend to, you show a decided lack of knowledge in the history of such incidents. For one thing, Israeli policy does not permit bargaining with terrorists or hijackers on the basis you suggest. For another, why should anyone take such an action on your behalf when the UPFP is not part of any recognized official Palestinian organization?''

"Because, Colonel, everything else aside, I am an Egyptian, an Arab, an excuse for my brethren to take such an action. Some may despise, hate, even envy me, but they will not overlook an opportunity to use me."

"Forget it," Saul said. "You will not be martyrized in the world press by us. Consider this, Captain; who really knows the true identity of Falcon, an identity so tenaciously concealed by you? What overtures of friendship or cooperation have you made to organizations similar to yours in the past? No, my friend, you will be tried and sentenced quietly and without publicity.

"Your financial backers in Libya and Iraq? Make no mistake about one thing. We will find a way to inform them, naturally. Ask yourself if they will publicize your failure, thus admitting it was theirs as well, and lose face among other Arab nations. Do you think they will attempt to rescue you from your predicament by the means you have suggested? No, Captain, you have become a liability and they will take their loss quietly and forget you ever existed. As for you, you will have much time, the rest of your life, to ponder over those questions. And many, many more."

Tobari squirmed in his chair, then faced Saul directly. "What," he asked, "do you intend to charge me with, Colonel, and what proof will you present to your court of law?"

"I will cite one charge, Tobari. Fifty-six deaths at Shetula, ordered by you. There w ill be other charges, of course, substantiated by photographs, by the testimony of people in your organization now under arrest who have talked, others who are talking to our people at this moment. Razak, Masri, Hourani—"

There was a knock on the door. Saul called out, "Come," and Yariv opened the door and entered, Yoram Golan behind him. Golan went to the desk and handed Saul a small, flat oblong object. He leaned down and whispered a message and Saul said, "Yes, bring it in." Golan went out and Yariv remained, standing at the door.

Tobari, his face showing considerably more weariness now, said, "Are you finished with me for the present, Colonel? I would like a bath and some rest, if that is permissible."

"Soon," Saul replied. "First, I have something here that I want you to hear. Smoke if you like, Captain."

Tobari did not react to the invitation, but sat toying with his gold cigarette lighter. A moment later, Golan returned with a battery-powered playback machine. Saul inserted the oblong cassette into it. Tobari eyed every move, staring at the machine, examining it warily through narrowed eyes. Saul depressed the PLAY cam. The first voice they heard was that of Yoram Golan.

GOLAN: Your name, please.

(Then Sadani's voice, shakily, yet clear.)

SADANI: My name is Amon Sadani.
GOLAN: Are you known by another name?
SADANI: Yes. Mordecai Aarons.
GOLAN: Which is your true name?
SADANI: Amon Sadani.
GOLAN: You are of Egyptian birth?
SADANI: Yes.
GOLAN: And you have been living in Israel illegally?
SADANI: Yes.
GOLAN: You have stated earlier that you are prepared to give us information about an organization known as the United Palestinian Freedom Party—the UPFP. Is that correct?
SADANI: (hesitating, then) Yes.
GOLAN: Of which one Hatif Tobari, also known by the code name, Falcon, and a former Egyptian Army intelligence officer, is the head?
SADANI: (slowly) Yes.
GOLAN: Of your own free will, without coercion from anyone?
SADANI: Yes.
GOLAN: Continue, please.

Tobari's face became ashen as the tape continued to roll on to its conclusion.

14

At the Jerusalem airport, Saul, accompanied by Dov Shaked and a manacled Hatif Tobari, put down smoothly in Rosental's helicopter. Seconds later, a larger helicopter, borrowed from Southern Air Command, landed a short distance away. In it were Yoram Golan, Zuheir Masri, Ahmed Hourani, and four armed security guards from the Bashra camp. Waiting on the ground were Judah Rosental, Moshe Tal and Asad Hasbani. Behind them stood a sedan and a closed military van to transport the prisoners to SO branch headquarters.

In Rosental's car, Saul brought the general up to date on the final day of the action and subsequent incidents at Bashra. "We got it all, Judah, and Bashra is operating normally, except that they are crying for men to replace those of Masri's who are on their way here in trucks," Saul concluded.

"And Sadani?" Rosental asked.

"He broke down completely after Golan finished with the taping and we left him behind at the camp hospital. The doctors think he will not come out of his state of depression for a long time. It is even possible he may not be able to stand trial."

"So he will be committed to a mental institution out of harm's way. How soon will you be able to give me a full report. Bartok and the prime iminster are eager—"

"I have enough taped statements with me that I can have copied at once for them. I can start dictating my final report as soon as I reach my desk. Then there will be other matters I will need to discuss with you."

"Of course, Saul, but it is important that this story be released to the public as soon as possible."

"You can have copies of the tapes by this afternoon, Judah. The

399

typed report by late tomorrow. I'll have Leah work on it straight through.''

In his office, after greeting Shana and others of his staff briefly, Saul began dictating his report into a recorder, in full detail, closing with the prisoners apprehended and the casualty count.

When, late in the afternoon, it was concluded, he turned the tapes over to Leah Barak, who promised to have the transcript ready by midmorning of the following day. He spoke with Shana for a few moments, then checked with Shaked and Golan, who were recording their individual accounts. The original tapes taken during the Bashra interrogations were in the hands of various secretaries who were transcribing them and would be added as supplementary support to Saul's report.

Below, Tobari was in a solitary cell with a guard team at the door. Relief teams would take over every four hours on a twenty-four hour schedule. The other prisoners were locked in cells and the overflow in the main receiving cell. When Saul was satisfied that everything was secure, he went out to the car park and had Asad drop him at his apartment. There, he undressed, showered, then fell into bed after removing the receivers from his two telephones.

Saul awoke at seven the following morning, hardly refreshed from his ten hours of sleep. He made a pot of coffee, drank two cups, bathed and dressed, then prepared a light breakfast. He moved slowly and without any show of eagerness to get to his office. Later, he sat in a comfortable chair enjoying a cigarette, allowing the events of the past two months to drift leisurely through his mind.

A sudden thought occurred to him and he went to his bedroom and returned with the letter he had received from Miri's lawyer, Sol Rosenthal of Los Angeles. He read its crisp, legal statement of fact, then checked the date and noted that thirty-three days had elapsed since it had been written and mailed in Los Angeles. For three days, he realized, Miri had had her final divorce, legally freed of him. As he was of her.

Without any sense of joy, he stood up and began pacing the apartment. In the bedroom, he replaced the receivers on the two phones, expecting to hear both start ringing at once; but felt no surprise that they remained silent. He went back to the kitchen and reheated the coffee and stood at the counter to drink another cup of it, thinking of Miri in Los Angeles, of his son, Dov, in his grave, feeling anew the impact of his death in 1973 strongly, as it must be with Miri. And thought of the years between their first meeting and today.

In a state of semitorpor, he called up the memory of his mother, saw her playing her violin while he listened with rapt attention and adoration; and the effect of her loss on his father, the doctor who had been unable to save her from death: feeling the full spectrum of emotions; failure, pity, guilt, rejection, anger, pain. So much of him, apart from duty, was made up of empty dreams, false echoes of his life, all patched together into an enormous pattern of meaningless Rorschach pieces.

The phone rang then, restoring him to the day at hand. It was nearing eleven o'clock. He went to the bedroom to answer and heard Leah's voice. "Good morning, Colonel. It is all finished, waiting for your signature."

"Thank you, Leah. I'll be there in thirty minutes." He dropped the receiver into its cradle. Leah, he thought, had worked all through the night again, also a victim of duty. He picked up his jacket and went out.

Leah stood beside him at his desk, while he reread the typescript of his report, meanwhile sorting out various other material containing the more pertinent interrogations taken by Shaked, Golan and himself at Ein Fara and Bashra; from Razak, Suzi Sadani, Tahia Soulad, Zuheir Masri and Ahmed Hourani, plus a final condensed statement that tied them all into a single comprehensive story which included the parts played by Lee Collier as well as the Iraqi and Libyan participants.

Saul initialed each page of the document and signed the last one. "Thank you, Leah," he said finally. "I want you to put these in a large envelope, seal it and mark it CONFIDENTIAL, then return it to me. When that is finished, I want you to go home and stay there until Sunday. You are not to return to work until then." He stood up and stretched.

"You are not leaving, are you, Colonel?"

"There is something else?"

"Only that I reminded you when you came in earlier that General Rosental is on his way from Tel Aviv to pick this up in person."

"He can't do that without me?"

"But he said it was important that he see you."

"Yes. Well . . . I'll wait a little longer."

"Would you like me to bring you some coffee, Colonel?"

"No. Another forty-eight hours of sleep would be much more useful and welcome. Where are Golan and Shaked?"

"Doing what you would like to be doing. At home, sleeping."

"Good for them. They have a more generous superior than I have. Now run along home and do the same thing, Leah. When you return on Sunday, I will dictate a letter to the heads of their services, commendations and recommendations for promotion. For my signature and General Rosental's approval. Also for Navot, Kaspi, Tal and others I will list for you.''

"Yes, sir." She made the notation in her notebook, then said, "Will that mean the end of the Special Operations Branch, Colonel?''

Saul shrugged. "We have accomplished the mission for which we were formed, no?''

"Yes," Leah said with a note of sadness in her voice.

"Don't worry, Leah. If I go back to Tel Aviv, we will still be together.''

"Yes, sir.''

"Ah . . . on your way out, will you ask Shana if she has a few minutes to spare?''

"Yes, sir.''

Within seconds, she was back, ushering in a beaming Judah Rosental. Greetings exchanged, Saul said, "Everything is ready for you, Judah. Transcripts, reports, the original tapes, everything you will need to substantiate the charges, the whole thing. Leah has the envelope on her desk for you to take along.''

"Fine, Saul. General Bartok drove up with me and is with General Goren at this moment. Our appointment with the prime minister is in one hour.''

"Then you have a few minutes?''

"What is it, Saul?''

"This operation is over, Judah. I intend to submit my letter of resignation and ask for retirement.''

In shocked surprise, "Why, Saul? Why now? You are in your prime and there is so much that remains to be done. Your experience is too important, invaluable to go to waste.''

"Judah," Saul said calmly, "we have known each other for so many years. You have been the brother I never had, so it is a little difficult for me to say this to you, but I must. Always, since I returned from school in England, duty has come before everything else in my life. Duty to my country cost me a wife, perhaps even a son who died doing his own share of duty. My whole being has been subordinate to duty and now, I feel I am entitled to a personal life of my own, to live as I please. I want it now, from now on.''

"I can understand that, Saul, but if you are blaming Israel for what happened between you and Miri—''

"I am not blaming Israel, Judah, only myself. I have thought about this—''

"Then think some more, is all I am asking you to do. Don't come to any firm decision you may regret—''

There was a knock on the door. It opened and Shana stood on the threshold, hesitating as she saw Rosental standing in the center of the office, a broken sentence on his lips. As she started to retreat with an apology forming, Saul called out, "Come in, Shana. It is nothing important. We were about to start discussing the dismantling of the Special Operations Branch."

She entered and sat on the sofa. Rosental returned her greeting, then turned back to Saul. "Not so fast, *chaver*. On our way here from Tel Aviv this morning, General Bartok suggested he will request the Special Operations Branch to be declared a permanent establishment. I agreed it would be a very wise move and he will put the matter before the prime minister later today." He paused with a smile, then added, "It's yours if you want it, Saul."

Saul glanced quickly at Shana and saw the glow in her eyes, the broadened smile. "Of course," Rosental continued, "I also reminded Bartok that it would be necessary to raise the head of the SO Branch to the rank of Brigadier in order that he not be subordinate to the heads of its sister services."

Shana burst in with, "Congratulations, Saul!"

"You mean that, Shana? You want it?" Saul asked.

"For you, yes. Very much."

Saul turned back to Rosental, who was watching him with a curious smile on his face. "Thank you, Judah."

"Thank General Bartok, Saul. He agreed to the promotion fully and will include it in his recommendation."

"Then I will leave it in your hands for now. Let me know what happens."

"Of course. I will phone you as soon as the meeting is over."

"I won't be here. When you leave, I intend to go home and try to get another twelve hours of sleep."

"Ah . . . as one further favor, Saul, I'm afraid I will have to ask you to postpone that until sometime later tonight."

"Not another assignment, Judah!"

"No assignment. More along social lines. This evening, there will be a small reception given in your honor by General Bartok. A few members of the press will be present, General Goren, some of your colleagues, perhaps even the prime minister, if he is free. And just in case I am crowded out of the line, let me offer my congratulations to you now, eh?"

"Thank you, Judah." Saul smiled, feeling a new, warm glow. "Let me ask one question, then. As brigadier in full command, I assume I will be permitted to exercise the privilege of managing my own personnel in matters of operations, assignments, promotions, and so forth?"

"Of course, within reason—"

"Then as soon as this goes into effect, I am taking a noncancelable, nonrecallable leave of absence that is long overdue."

Rosental grinned, looking from Saul to Shana. "And I assume your request includes Lieutenant Altman?"

"Naturally, my request will include *Captain* Altman. A leave would be nothing without her."

"Naturally," Rosental conceded.

"For a month," Saul added.

"A full *month*, Saul?"

"Under a new set of circumstances, Judah, a full month. I think you might see that there are no objections from General Bartok."

"I will, Saul, if you will give me a reason for that much time away at a time like this. The general will be sure to ask."

"Then you can tell him, Judah. For three days, I have been legally free from Miri. It will take at least a month to arrange a proper wedding and a honeymoon. Of course, Shana and I will want you and Toba to stand with us as best man and matron of honor."

"Of course," Shana added.

Rosental sighed and smiled simultaneously. "I don't know how you do it, you two, but somehow . . . somehow—"

BERKLEY BESTSELLERS YOU WON'T WANT TO MISS!

MORE BESTSELLERS FROM BERKLEY!

REMEMBER IT DOESN'T GROW ON TREES

**ENERGY CONSERVATION -
IT'S YOUR CHANCE** TO SAVE, AMERICA

Department of Energy, Washington, D.C.

A PUBLIC SERVICE MESSAGE FROM BERKLEY PUBLISHING CO.. INC.